MW01139935

THE CHRONICLES OF THE GUARDIANS

THE ANUNNAKI

MARTIN I HENRY

First published in 2010 by:

Magpie Publishing Company
P.O. Box 180
Boonah, Queensland
Australia, 4310

© **Martin I Henry 2006**

Cover Art by: kipayersillustration.com

National Library of Australia Catalogue in publishing data:

Henry, Martin I

Chronicles of the Guardians – The Anunnaki

ISBN 1456566601

Printed by:

e-book 2010

CreateSpace 2011

CHAPTER 1

"Tim, Come quickly, Aseef has found something." Tim carefully placed the tiny pottery shard back in the tray, with the other small finds that had brought him to the new dig site, deep in Afghanistan. He slid his chair back from the well-worn fold-out table and rose to his feet. As he stepped out of the small tent that was his field office, he followed in the direction of his fast disappearing assistant. He finally caught up with Alan at a narrow pit, that extended several feet into the side of a small hill.

Alan had only beaten him there by twenty seconds, but was already staring quietly at an object just handed to him by the dig foreman. As Tim approached, he noticed keen eyes staring up in anticipation from the trench. Aseef asked eagerly. "What do you think? Funerary?"

Tim looked at the object in silence for a while before extending his hand. Alan passed the small beaded necklace to Tim as carefully as one would a new-born kitten to a child. Tim nodded his thanks and continued to study the object. Finally, much to the delight of the onlookers, he smiled. "Yes... I believe it is funerary. It also seems to date around the same as the pottery fragments. I'd say some time earlier than 2500BC."

There was an audible sigh of relief from all around, but it was Aseef who asked the obvious question. "Do we continue to dig here?" Tim nodded slowly. "Yes, but I think we'll have to widen the trench and get some props, if we're going to go any further into the hill." Tim suddenly cocked his ear as he strained to identify a low frequency hum. "What's that?"Aseef called for silence, as all ears strained to hear the faint beating noise.

Suddenly, one of the diggers smiled nervously and offered his opinion. "I think it is a helicopter." he tentatively offered. Tim frowned. "Way out here? I though this area was free of Mujahideen. And the Russians have never come out here before." Tim noticed the nervous faces that now surrounded him and decided to diffuse the tense atmosphere. "Anyway, the Russian military knows we're here and have promised to keep an eye on us. I'm sure it's only a routine patrol."

The reassurance seemed to work, as the worried faces gave way to nervous smiles. But the noise was getting louder. By now there was no mistaking it for the drone of a large helicopter. Tim scanned the horizon, straining to see the source of the noise. Finally, as the drone became loud enough to inhibit further conversation, Tim spotted the helicopter.

It was indeed Russian. An Mi-8TVK gunship, if he was not mistaken. But something was different. As he watched the approaching helicopter, he recognized the 50 calibre KV-4 nose-mounted heavy machinegun, but it was the modified sides that caught his eye. Instead of being a totally enclosed aircraft, as was the norm, its only visible side was open, with the silhouette of a light machinegun jutting out. It reminded him of the Huey door gunners of the Vietnam War era.

On board the helicopter, the pilot was busy talking with the KGB operative, as the co-pilot and two door gunners scanned the ground below. "We are approaching the dig site where Timothy Fullerton and his team are searching for a lost palace." The KGB man mumbled his response. "Treasure hunters?" he asked, with some scorn in his voice. "No. This man gives his entire find to the government wherever he digs. Seems he is just keen to re-write the history books." The KGB man nodded his approval. "He is a rare breed. I am very much looking forward to meeting him."

Suddenly there was a strange tingling and cracking sound, as dozens of small arms rounds pierced the floor pan of the helicopter and ricocheted around the interior of the cargo deck. The pilot immediately recognised the sound and instinctively threw the helicopter around, so his door gunners could return fire until, as he swept in a tight arc, his nose gun could bear down on the attackers.

The port side gunner saw the area where the gunfire was emanating and immediately returned fire. But before he could neutralize the situation, a tell-tale smoke trail emerged from behind a rock-fall and rose steadily toward the helicopter. The gunner saw it and screamed through the intercom. "Stinger inbound... seven o'clock low."

The pilot threw the helicopter around so hard that the KGB agent was flung against the rear wall panel and knocked unconscious. As he rolled around the pitching and rolling cargo deck, several rounds of small arms fire pierced the floor and smashed though his shoulder. Another fortuitous round found his right ankle. The port door gunner shrieked as several rounds hit him below the protection of his heavy bullet resistant vest, shattering his right femur. The pilot tried in vain to avoid the fast approaching harbinger of death, kindly donated to the Mujahideen by the CIA. It was, after all, the least they could do to ensure the continuance of the cold war.

The pilot was diving steeply towards the ground, frantically releasing anti-SAM flares, when the stinger hit the rear rotor and detonated. The resultant explosion severed the rotor from the air frame and showered the cargo deck with deadly shrapnel. The starboard gunner was hit in the head by a large piece of the rotor that had pierced the un-armoured skin of the cargo bay. It shattered his heavily reinforced visor and penetrated deep into his skull. He was dead before he hit the floor.

Another large shard of white-hot metal somehow made its way through the heavily armoured flight deck bulkhead, piercing the co-pilot's back. He too, died instantly. The pilot yelled for the crew to hang on for a rough landing, as he fought valiantly to control the tightly spinning and fast descending craft. It only took a few seconds for the helicopter to hit the ground.

Meanwhile, Tim and the workers stood open-mouthed as the helicopter suddenly came under a hail of small arms fire. When the stinger hit, Tim was as stunned as the rest of the witnesses. But as they watched the helicopter come in for a rough crash-landing, he quickly summed up the situation and issued orders to his men.

"Looks like the bloody Mujahideen's here. They're not locals, so I'm going to assume they won't be real friendly. Alan, get to the vehicles and see if you can evacuate the diggers. These blokes are usually horsemen, so they'll be relatively easy to out-run. When you get to town, tell the police chief what's happened. Ask him to get in touch with the Russians and tell them it's insurgents, not locals, who are responsible. Otherwise they might launch an unfounded revenge attack." Alan nodded solemnly. "What about you?"

"I'll grab the troopy and see if there are any survivors. I'll meet you back in town as soon as I can." he shouted as he headed towards the nearest vehicle. "OK... but for Christ's sake, be careful."

Tim ran to the Toyota Landcruiser troop-carrier and cranked the motor into life. He slammed it into gear and dropped the clutch. As he quickly closed the two hundred yards between him and the helicopter crash site, Tim noticed several horsemen appear from a small ravine some two thousand yards distant. He smiled as he calculated the precious minutes he would have to rescue any survivors, before they got within accurate firing range.

As Tim arrived at the helicopter he threw the vehicle door open, flicked the gearstick into the neutral position and jumped out, leaving the motor running for a quick get-away. But before he got to the helicopter, he instinctively looked up at the fast approaching foe. To his dismay, the horsemen were now trailing a Toyota Hilux utility. Its tray mounted Browning M1 fifty calibre heavy machine gun already barking viciously in his direction. The rounds were crashing harmlessly fifty or so yards from the helicopter, but he knew the latest development was bad. The gun was inherently inaccurate as the vehicle bounced wildly across the desert, but one lucky round would see him killed.

The sudden surge of adrenalin allowed him to reach the downed helicopter in seconds. As he arrived, the pilot was madly radioing their position to the medivac crew. Tim looked at the carnage inside the cargo deck with dismay, as he yelled to the pilot in fluent Russian. "A vehicle mounted heavy machinegun will be here very soon. How many survivors are there?"

The pilot shook his head. "No idea. The co-pilot's dead ... I'm OK. But as for the others..." Tim checked the crew, as the pilot dragged himself from his seat and passed through the small flight deck door to join him in the cargo bay. When he reached him, Tim gave the shaken pilot his assessment of the situation. "The starboard gunner's dead and the port gunner's shot up pretty bad. The other chap's unconscious and shot up too, but they should make it, if we can get them medivac'd soon. Is anyone on the way?" The pilot nodded unconvincingly. "Yes. A medivac chopper and two gun ships are on their way." But Tim picked up on the uncertainty in his voice. "ETA?"

"Seventeen minutes." Tim's heart sank. Escape in the troopy was now out of the question. The fifty cal would be there in a matter of seconds and meanwhile there were three injured men to extract.

The sound of heavy projectiles tearing through the helicopter bulkhead quickly focused his attention on more urgent matters at hand. The helicopter had hit hard on its belly plate but had remained upright and mostly intact, with the starboard side wedged into a small embankment. The port side faced the open plains, from where the threat was coming. Tim yelled at the pilot. "See if you can get the starboard gun over here. I'll try to take the Toyota out if I can. But even if I do, those horsemen will be here in a couple of minutes. We'll need all the firepower we can muster."

The pilot headed to the back of the cargo deck, helping the gunner as he crawled to the relative safety of the rear of the aircraft. He grimaced with every move, as the pain reminded him of his wounds. Tim noticed they were not heading for the gun. "What are you doing?" The pilot turned to him and gesticulated towards the door gun. "The PK mounts are too strong... we'll never remove it in time. We have a cache of small arms in the locker over there." he explained. "Good, anything that can shoot works for me." Tim yelled back.

Again Tim's attention was drawn back to the fast approaching Toyota, as several rounds smashed through the bulkhead inches from his left hand and tore a chunk off the butt of the starboard door gun. Tim shuffled in behind the port door gun, gritted his teeth and looked out. The Toyota was now only five hundred yards away and rapidly bearing down on the wrecked helicopter, trailing a plume of desert dust that obscured the ensuing horsemen.

Tim held his breath, as rounds from the fifty cal crashed wildly around him. He watched as the vehicle continued to speed towards them, counting on the rough terrain to limit the accuracy of the gunner. He waited for a few more nerve racking seconds, until he was confident he could make the door gun do its job most efficiently.

As the Toyota approached within two hundred yards, he opened up. The 7.62mm rounds were hitting low, kicking up puffs of dust just in front of the vehicle. He leant on the butt to raise the muzzle, as he continued to squeeze the trigger. He walked the rounds up until they crashed through the radiator, danced across the hood and finally shattered the windscreen and began shredding the flesh of the driver. As he died, he released the steering wheel and the vehicle swerved wildly, eventually hitting a small rock that caused it to roll. Tim watched the gunner fly through the air and land heavily against a small rocky outcrop. They were no longer a threat.

Tim looked back at the cargo deck and saw that the gunner had collapsed. But the pilot had managed to open the locker and access the two AKS-74U's, kept there for pilot survival use. Tim rushed over and grabbed one of the rifles and placed it on the floor next to the door gun. "Any more ammo for the PK?"

The look in the pilot's eyes foretold his reply. "Normally yes, but it looks like the storage compartment was torn from the chopper during the landing. I'm afraid what's on the two guns is all we have." Tim shook his head in disbelief. "OK, I'll strip the rounds from the starboard gun and link them up with mine. Meanwhile, make yourself comfortable. We're stuck between a rock and a hard place at the moment. The horsemen will be here in a few minutes."

Tim peered through the dissipating dust, searching for the horsemen. He could hear the advancing hooves thumping against the hard ground. As he listened more closely, he could hear the clinking as the chert pebbles scattered underfoot. Suddenly the first of the horsemen loomed larger than life, less than a hundred yards from the chopper. His AK-74 was raised as he stood high in the stirrups taking aim at Tim. Tim's finger squeezed the trigger and the door gun barked back into life.

The first few rounds hit the horse in the chest killing it instantly. Its lifeless body collapsed to the ground, the rider madly attempting to extricate himself from the stirrups as it did so. But it all happened so fast, that he only managed to sit into the saddle and get his left foot out of the stirrup. As the horse crashed into the ground the rider was trapped by the right leg and crushed under the rolling mount. Whether he was alive or not was not a question Tim had time to ask, as several other horsemen suddenly appeared through the dust.

Tim looked down at the pilot, now lying on the floor next to the door gun, his AKS aimed in the general direction of the approaching horsemen. Several spare magazines were scattered in front of him. Both eyes were wide open as he targeted the nearest of the now charging gaggle of horsemen. The first two horsemen fell from their mounts, as his bullets found their mark.

Tim was also creating havoc as the door gun accounted for eleven riders in the opening minute of the fire-fight. But it seemed that as soon as one rider went down, two more took his place.

Suddenly Tim noticed that the pilot's gun had fallen silent. He looked down and saw him writhing in a pool of blood. A bullet had pierced his left lung and another his right shoulder. "Christ..." he mumbled in disbelief. "Looks like it's down to me!"

Tim continued raking the oncoming horsemen with devastating effect, until the door gun finally ran out of ammunition. The audible *click* of the firing pin striking an empty chamber made Tim shudder. He dropped to his knees and grabbed his AKS. He cocked the weapon and commenced firing at a horseman who had come within twenty yards of the helicopter, killing him with a three shot burst that found the centre of his chest. But, all too soon, his new weapon also ran out of ammunition. He dropped the rifle and grabbed the one abandoned by the pilot.

It only fired seven rounds, before it too was spent. He removed the empty magazine and reached for one of the spares. As he slammed the new magazine home, he felt the searing pain of a bullet piercing his left thigh. As his bone shattered, he dropped to his knees, but managed to maintain his grip on the rifle. He quickly regained his wits and fired a burst into the man responsible for his pain, now only ten yards from the chopper door. The two men following him had also dismounted and were running straight at the helicopter. As they reached their co-attacker's body, they simply stepped over it and continued their rush towards Tim.

Tim swung the muzzle of the rifle across his new target and sprayed the two men with a nine shot burst, killing one instantly and wounding the other. He dropped his weapon and collapsed to the ground, blood streaming from several chest wounds.

The rifle repeatedly ran out of ammunition as Tim struggled to keep the advancing hoard from taking the helicopter. But as he loaded the last spare magazine into the rifle, his thoughts finally turned to his own mortality. What a way to end his career. Killed by tribal militiamen in the middle of a god-forsaken desert. And right as he was about to make the biggest discovery in his career. What a bummer!

He looked around the cargo deck at the dead and wounded men that he had risked his life to rescue. He heaved a sigh and shrugged his shoulders nonchalantly. Resigned to the fact there was no-one left to help him, he still hoped he could hold on until help arrived. Surely the medivac chopper was due any minute.

Driven by a combination of adrenalin, desperation and anger, he switched the selector to *semi* and raised the rifle to his shoulder. "I've still got twenty rounds to go... that's twenty of the bastards." he mumbled to himself. Time seemed to slow down as, one by one, Tim picked off the men advancing on foot.

Bullets continued to smash through the bulkhead, raining debris down on the survivors. Tim was counting his bullets and was down to five, when the incoming fire finally stopped. With a sigh of relief, he lowered his weapon. He had done it. He had survived, albeit with a badly shot-up leg. All he had to do now was wait for help to arrive.

But his world came crashing down as a warrior suddenly appeared at the door, blood streaming from a gut wound and weapon aimed at Tim's chest. Before Tim could raise the muzzle of his rifle a short burst from the surprise attacker found their mark. Two rounds tore through his right shoulder and another through his right arm, shattering his ulna. Tim collapsed to the floor of the helicopter, dropping his weapon as he did so. His fight was over.

The warrior stepped into the cargo bay and stood over Tim, as he lay semi-conscious on the floor. A wry, self-congratulatory smile came to the sun beaten face of the Afghan tribesman, as he placed the muzzle of his rifle over Tim's temple. A single shot rang out.

A puzzled expression came over the face of the Afghani as he dropped his weapon and slumped to his knees. The single shot from a Makarov PM 9mm pistol had shattered his C2 vertebrae. The KGB agent had regained consciousness just in time to save Tim. As he dragged himself to the helicopter door, he looked nervously around for any further attackers. There was no-one to be seen, but the carnage he witnessed took him aback.

There were dead and wounded horses scattered across a thirty degree arc from fifty yards out to over three hundred yards. So too, there were dead and wounded Mujahideen from the helicopter door to more than five hundred yards out. He quickly estimated more that fifty bodies. "Looks like I've missed one hell of a fire-fight..." he muttered in disbelief.

Suddenly he heard the unmistakable sound of rescue. As he peered toward the approaching sound, he saw an Mi-8B medivac helicopter, closely flanked by two Mi-24D gunships. He smiled in relief, as he collapsed to a prone position near what remained of the bulkhead next to the door. His pistol still gripped tightly in his right hand.

Sporadic gunfire could be heard as the gunships circled overhead, mopping up. The vicious howl of the four-barrelled YaKB 50 calibre, nose-mounted Gattling guns was testament to their ruthless efficiency.

Meanwhile, the medivac team efficiently went about their business of stabilizing the wounded, prior to airlifting them to a field hospital. All the survivors were so badly wounded they were airlifted to a military hospital in Russia, as soon as they were stabilized enough to fly.

It was eight days later when Tim slowly opened his eyes. He looked around and recognized where he was. A hospital, for sure. But where? And how did he get here? It was only after he had been conscious for several minutes, that he noticed a broadly smiling face in the bed next to him. Through eyes that refused to focus properly, he thought he recognized him as the KGB agent on the helicopter.

Tim smiled feebly and rolled his head over to see the occupant of the bed to his left. This time he did recognise him. It was the Russian helicopter pilot. He smiled and rolled back towards the man on his right who addressed him. "I must thank you for saving my skin, my friend. Apparently you put up one hell of a fight out there. My name is Alex..."

CHAPTER 2

Some years later...

"Well Mister Johnson? What *was* the common denominator leading to the downfall of history's greatest empires... such as the Persians, Greeks, Romans, and finally the British?" The inattentive student was caught off guard. "Uh... bureaucracy?" he tentatively offered. Tim nodded. "Which lead to...?" The student stammered out a brief response. "Which lead to an uncontrolled increase in the size of the public sector."

Tim motioned for him to continue. "Which lead to?" The student was getting the gist of the questioning, as he offered elaboration. "Which lead to an increased demand for taxes to fund the public sector. Up to the point where the people became burdened beyond their means. Which in turn lead to revolt. Starting in the remotest colonies and gradually working towards the seat of the empirical power until the empire itself was toppled."

"Very good Johnson... very good. And once this rather cancerous astigmatism of civilization was recognised, what did ensuing cultural powers learn from the follies of their predecessors? Austin!" Austin sat forward and peered down at Tim."Well Professor, it appears that they learnt very little. Even today, their fundamental mistake of nurturing large, self perpetuating bureaucracies continues unabated within societies such as ours."

Tim smiled. "Does this mean we risk the same fate as the Babylonians?" The student nodded enthusiastically. "Yes, Sir, I guess." Tim was bemused. "Is that a positive yes or a probable yes?" Austin nodded his head. "I mean, I think we're heading that way.

We too have an expanding and non-culpable public sector. And we have high taxes because of the demands placed on us by the government's often irresponsible social and fiscal policies. It seems like the average person is being bled dry. Or at the very least they're being financially suppressed. I guess one day, someone will say enough's enough."

"And what will happen then?" Tim asked, pushing the student for a conclusion. "Well, I guess there'll be some sort of revolt." he offered. Tim nodded. "And will that work?" Austin shook his head before he answered. "For a while, I guess." But Tim still wanted further elaboration. "Until...?" he pushed. "Until the new power brokers lose sight of their original goals. Then they'll become lost in their own megalomania. I suppose they'll soon get on the gravy train and it'll start all over again."

Tim turned his attention to the entire class. "Very good! So you see, bureaucracy was not invented by modern societies. The desire for leaders to control their subjects, whether by force, religion or laws, has plagued civilization since the advent of tribal leadership. History is full of lessons but we are reticent to learn from past mistakes. I'll leave you to ponder why.

Well, that's it for this year. Now it's up to you to put it all together for the exams. If any of you have specific questions you wish to discuss with me, please book an appointment with Mrs. Woolly. Thank you for your attendance this year, I've enjoyed your participation. Good luck with your finals." he concluded.

Tim leaned on the lectern and heaved a sigh of relief. He stood with an almost trance-like, vacant stare as he watched the students shuffling noisily towards the exits of the lecture theatre. His stare was transfixed until the last student escaped to the outside world and an eerie, shrouding silence settled over the room. Slowly Tim leant over and picked up his briefcase. He looked around the empty theatre as he gathered his notes.

Then, as if somehow compelled to speed his departure, he hastily filed them into his briefcase. This oft repeated task completed, he paused once more and glanced around the lecture theatre.

Not surprisingly, it reminded him of an ancient Greek amphitheatre. The central stage upon which he stood, as the sagacious orator. The tiered rows of seats radiating upwards and outwards from the stage, upon which sat those who sought wisdom and knowledge. Standing alone in the vast theatre, gazing up at the rows of seats, the sanctity of such a respected place of learning was almost palpable. The more things changed, he thought, the more they stayed the same.

He cracked a languid smile as he sighed once more and prepared to leave for the final time. It had been another long year and he was looking forward to the semester break. All he had to do was survive the examination period, mark the papers, grade his students and the next eight weeks were his. At last he could relax, go on a holiday. Perhaps he would go fishing. Or maybe take a trip overseas. Recharge his batteries, ready to repeat it all again next year. Such was the regimented life of a university lecturer.

Suddenly a bellicose voice boomed from a doorway high above the stage. The intrusion wrenched Tim from his thoughts of exotic destinations and brought him crashing back to the present. He snapped his head toward the outburst. There stood the unmistakable silhouette of the faculty Dean. His tall thin frame and frizzy, tonsured hair, betraying his identity.

It was a dramatically staged sight that filled Tim with dread. "So Fullerton, still trying to fill their impressionable young heads with all that antisocial philosophical rubbish of yours? You're supposed to teach them history man, not politics!" The venom in the Dean's voice was obvious as he hurled the odious challenge directly at Tim.

Tim said nothing as he pondered the silhouette of the unwelcome intruder. His pulse quickened as he anticipated the inevitable castigation that was sure to follow. He took a deep breath and braced himself as the Dean continued the tirade. "Should I remind you that your position here is that of Associate Professor of Ancient History? It is not that of curriculum coordinator. Nor indeed, Dean." The last quip he added sarcastically, placing extra emphasis on the word *Dean*.

Although the Dean was a history Professor, petty politics was his forte. The animosity between him and his former student was fuelled by years of bitter rivalry and often erupted into abusive outbursts.

Tim on the one hand was a progressive thinker, dedicated to the full education of his students. He despised the limited knowledge he was obliged to pass on, through the restrictive curriculum. He strongly believed that students should be encouraged to ask questions. Be taught to look for alternatives. And taught to search for the truth. He wanted to instil his enthusiasm into his students in the hope that, one day, they too would be as ardent about history as he was.

The Dean, on the other hand, was a traditionalist. Motivated purely by his own perceived social standing. Feeling little for his subject or his students. It was a classic clash of beliefs. Between them was an unbridgeable schism. On one side stood the uncompromising personified Orthodoxy. On the other, stood the Heretic. Both were now engaged in a battle of wits.

After an awkward and prolonged silence, Tim felt obliged to defend himself with a dignified response. He took another deep breath before challenging the Dean with his reply. "Politics is full of history and history is full of politics. I see the two as inseparable. I was simply explaining the value of history to my students. What good are lessons if nothing is to be learned from them?"

The Dean glared back at Tim with pure hatred in his eyes and almost bellowed as the diatribe continued. "The lessons you should be giving are clearly set out in the course notes! This political rubbish is just filling their silly heads with extraneous nonsense, keeping them away from the facts. It's facts that you should stick to Fullerton... the facts. The indisputable facts! Don't try to elaborate on them. Just present them as they were once presented to you. After all, it's history for goodness sake, and nothing can change our perception of history. Nothing! And don't you forget it!"

Without giving Tim a chance for rebuttal, he shot one final piercing glare at him, before spinning officiously on his heels and disappearing.

Tim breathed a long, slow, rather dejected, sigh as he stood motionless on the stage. He stared blankly in the direction of the departed Dean. As he continued to stare at the empty doorway his shoulders began to droop. He closed his eyes, breathed in deeply and slowly shook his head. As he grabbed his briefcase and headed for the nearest exit, he mumbled angrily to himself. "God I hate that officious, pontificating, sanctimonious bastard!"

"What was that Professor?" The unexpected voice startled him. Tim stopped in his tracks and, quickly gathering his wits, slowly turned around. He felt a little embarrassed that someone may have overheard him cursing the Dean, but was relieved when he saw who it was.

There standing in the doorway was one of his postgraduate students, Cathy. She was older than most of his students. In her early thirties. Blonde, slim, pleasing to the eye and the owner of a wicked sense of humour. She was casually dressed in a pair of tight-fitting faded denim jeans and a well-worn light yellow T-shirt, with the words *Eat More Beef* emblazoned in large black letters across her ample chest.

Her shoulder-length hair was neatly groomed, but remained unfettered, framing her attractive face. She wore white sneakers. Not name brand fashion statements, just practical footwear. Apart from her age, she looked every bit the quintessential university student.

She was doing her thesis for her doctorate and as such, spent much private time with Tim. She saw him as a mentor and someone to aspire to. But she also saw him as someone who was yet to reach his full potential. Tim smiled as he recognized her. "Oh nothing, I was just mumbling to myself. I'm sorry, I didn't hear you enter. What can I do for you, Cathy?"

"Sorry to stalk you like this Professor, but I was wondering if you could help me clarify a few points that I seem to be stuck on." Tim quickly composed himself and nodded warmly. "Sure, what seems to be the problem?" he asked casually.

"Well I'm in a quandary. I can successfully trace the Pharaohs back to the start of the classical first dynasty, as can any other scholar. But I cannot agree with the consensus date for the unification of the kingdoms. Nor do I concur with any of the other dates for that matter.

And I can't go beyond that to ascertain the length of the rule of the pre-dynastic Pharaohs. My main concern is the work of Herodotus. His history books are so contradictory. Almost heretical to conventional thinking, especially with respect to the dating of events." she rued.

"What specifically worries you, Cathy?" Tim asked, probing for the reason for her presence. Cathy looked at Tim quizzically for a moment. "Well I was reading his second book about the priests of Thebes and the three hundred and forty-one statues. According to Herodotus, the priests told him that the high priesthood had passed from father to son, unbroken for eleven thousand, three hundred and forty years.

The priests also told him that before this time the Gods appeared among the people in human form. Yet since the unification, they had not been seen. This seems to be substantiated by Manetho when he suggests that a race of demi-gods ruled Egypt from This, near Abydos, prior to the reign of Menes. Reference to this could also be interpreted from the Turin papyrus. The so-called *sheshu Heru...* the followers of Horus.

Well, ignoring the Gods for the moment, and given that Herodotus was born circa 490 BC, this would imply that the priests had a documented lineage back to around twelve thousand BC. This is some eight and a half thousand years earlier than modern scholars give Egyptian civilization credit for. They seem to favour somewhere around the middle of the fourth millennium. But even the most notable scholars can't agree on the actual date of the unification.

You know yourself that it ranges from 5867BC by Champollion-Figeac to 3623BC by Bunsen. Most scholars seem to take the comfortable date of 4400BC, promulgated by Brugsch. But that was calculated on the purely mathematical proposition that there were three generations to the century. Hardly a scholarly approach one would think. But I guess that's all we can go on, until someone finds a complete king list.

Anyway, the other puzzling thing is that Herodotus also credited the earlier Pharaohs with life spans of Biblical proportions. How can this be vilified and simply dismissed as nonsense by everyone? We're forced on the one hand, through Christian dogma, to accept that Adam and his descendants lived for hundreds of years. Yet, on the other hand, similar life spans of earlier non-Biblical characters are scoffed at and dismissed as mere fantasy. And this is by the very same group of people who believe the Bible verbatim. I just can't understand their logic. Or is there something I'm missing?"

Tim half smiled and stared at Cathy for some time. He was deciding whether or not he should advise her. And if so, what his advice should be. His heart told him to go down the path of questioning and discovery. After all, the quest for knowledge is reputed to be what science is all about. But his own bitter experience in that direction, when he sat for his doctorate, told him that treading the proven path of tradition and academia was the safest route. It was easier to accept the consensus of orthodoxy and not rock the boat too early in one's academic career. At least not until one had one's doctorate.

The protracted silence was finally broken by an audible sigh. He smiled again as he answered. "Well Cathy... for now I can only offer this advice. You're sitting for your doctorate with this paper. Those who mark it will determine your success or failure. You will have to live with this success or failure for the rest of your life. Indeed, your entire career rests on it. Failure can be a very difficult thing to accept. Both for you and those around you.

Unfortunately, the political nature of academia will ensure that most unconventional ideas are shunned and those who do not burst into the field full of praise from their teachers and peers are generally not accepted by the system."

Cathy stood silently as he spoke, occasionally nodding her head to indicate her understanding or agreement. But when he paused, she looked him in the eye and frowned. "What exactly are you saying Professor?" Tim looked around to ensure they were alone. He then spent a few moments carefully choosing his words.

When he finally answered her, it was in a near whisper. "Well, I guess what I'm saying, Cathy, is base your paper on conventional ideas. What the main stream deems to be the facts.

Although I will initially mark your paper, it will have to go before the panel for final grading. If you adhere to tradition, they'll receive it well and mark you accordingly. If you try to rock the boat, I'm afraid it won't be well received and you'll fail."

"So you're saying that I should ignore this information, or treat it as mere fantasy. Even though there's tantalizing evidence to suggest there might be some truth in it?" she asked. Tim shook his head. "Well, I can't really tell you what to do, Cathy. But I would strongly suggest that you follow convention. You don't have to repudiate the work of Herodotus et al.

By all means mention their work as an indication of the extent of your research, but don't dwell on it or use it to postulate. It's in the too-hard basket, I'm afraid. It questions orthodoxy and that's not a wise thing to do at this stage of your career.

If you're still interested in pursuing it after you've received your doctorate, I'd be more than happy to assist you. You can even have access to my personal research data if you like. But for now, I strongly suggest you check your enthusiasm and approach the paper for what it is. Simply your key to a doctorate."

"Is that what you did Professor?" she asked with a wry smile. The question caught Tim off guard and the surprise on his face was evident. Cathy insisted upon an answer. "Well?" She raised her eyebrows to extenuate her sardonic smile. She was proud of the reaction she had provoked, sensing she had Tim on the ropes. He lowered his gaze and slowly shook his head.

He breathed slowly and deeply for several breaths as he gave the question serious thought. His mind returned to dark, almost forgotten, places as he searched for an appropriate answer. It was not long before the uncomfortable silence and Cathy's continuing stare forced him to make a decision. He decided that disclosure might just convince her.

"I was a keen student like you, Cathy. I absolutely loved the subject of history. And I still do! It started with religion actually. I was raised as a Roman Catholic and so was indoctrinated with all the garnered wisdom and dogma of the Church of Rome. But as I grew older I began to question religious orthodoxy. The answers I received were simplistic, throwaway cliché lines designed to maintain faith. No facts, no proof. Nothing!

Remember that fact and faith are mutually exclusive things. If you have facts you have proof, therefore you don't need faith. Conversely, with no facts there is no proof and faith is needed to believe something. But faith is more emotion than logic, so almost anything can be justified. And that's where the Church gets its power. By drawing on the emotions of the ignorant masses.

So, becoming disillusioned with the church, I left the fold. After graduating, I decided to research the history of the Church of Rome, for my doctoral thesis. I dug up all sorts of information... and some hard archaeological facts. Some written documentation of lies, deceit and conspiracy. I could argue beyond reasonable doubt that the tenets of Christianity were based on a perpetuated lie. I even had a friend in Rome. A Monsignor close to the Pope, who was a keen Egyptologist. As I originally specialised in Egyptology, I had become a sort of expert, especially with their unique ancient language. I guess I'm very fortunate that I take to language very well.

Anyway, Monsignor Thomas helped me access the secret archives of the Vatican for a few weeks while the Pope and the majority of his entourage were on a foreign visit. Most of the historical literature they store in the vaults below the Vatican is not of Christian origin. Much of it's Coptic, Pagan or just historical observations by noted authors. Including Manetho by the way. But the Vatican has deemed them too important to be destroyed, even though they're locked away from the rest of the world.

I spent nearly a year in Europe. Searching archives, church documents, registers, acts of parliament, historical records and archaeological sites. I dug up more information on the Church than I could have possibly imagined when I began the thesis. I had information on the council of Nicea, the persecution of the Coptics, the Inquisition, the Conquistadors and a hundred other murderous Church escapades.

Including the Friday the 13th conspiracy in 1307 between Pope Clement V and King Philip IV of France, to destroy the Knights Templar. The Pope wanted to stop their heresy and the ambitious king wanted their wealth. That's where the superstition about Friday the 13th being unlucky comes from. But that's another story.

I had records indicating that millions of people had been slaughtered and hundreds of cultures destroyed over the last two thousand years. All in the name of the Roman Catholic Church and its illusory god.

My thesis was political dynamite. I was so proud of myself. The amount of research I had undertaken was phenomenal. I had logically and sequentially destroyed all the tenets that had become the pillars of Christianity.

The Dean was only Professor David Lethridge, an Associate Professor, in those days. But even so, his adherence to orthodoxy made me nervous about handing in the paper, before I had it reviewed by an independent third party. We had already clashed swords, so to speak, on numerous occasions.

Anyway, I submitted my paper to another Professor for an informal review. I knew old Professor Jameson... Oh! You haven't met him have you? He retired several years ago. He was more liberal-minded than the rest. He had it for a week or more before he called me into his office. He said the work was impeccable, but he had concerns that I would fail. When questioned further, he indicated that Lethridge, who was my professor at the time, was a strict Roman Catholic.

Professor Jameson knew Lethridge wouldn't pass the paper. But I was shocked. I failed to see how one man's personal beliefs could stand in the way of historical evidence and a man's career. But I finally accepted Professor Jameson's advice. I modified the paper and passed." he stated coldly.

"Did you keep the original material?" Cathy asked, with more than a passing interest. "Yes. Or at least I tried to. It disappeared soon after I received my doctorate. My house was broken into and much of my research material was stolen. God knows why someone would steal that sort of stuff and leave my TV alone.

Then I caught rumours that my professor was behind it. On orders from the Vatican it seems. Monsignor Thomas disappeared around the same time. I even went to Rome to try to contact him. The only thing I was told was that he had *gone away*. It was most unusual. No matter where he's been in the past... even in the remote Andes... he's always kept in touch. But I haven't heard from him since. I guess he was murdered for letting me have access to the Vatican archives."

Tim was almost consumed as the memories flooded back. His thoughts had not turned to those dark days for several years. Suddenly Tim realised that his emotions were beginning to surface. He coughed nervously, as if to excuse himself before continuing. "Well things got a bit tricky there for a while, but the important thing is that I passed my doctorate. And I guess the Dean and I have been bitter rivals ever since."

Cathy smiled as she looked into his eyes. The sparkle Tim saw made him feel uneasy. Was this merely a dedicated student, or was there potentially much more to it? The awkward gaze was held for some time. Finally a rather embarrassed Tim decided to defuse the situation. "Well, I really must get going, Cathy. Please consider my advice well. You may only get one chance at this, so don't ruin it because of your pride.

There'll be plenty of time for discovery later." he suggested, with a broad smile. Cathy returned the smile and thanked him for his advice, then turned on her heels and left. Tim felt somehow obliged to watch, as she glided gracefully towards the door through which she had entered the stage. He continued to stare as she exited and disappeared into the shadows of the corridor beyond.

Still feeling a little disturbed by the sudden recollection of the Catholic conspiracy incident, Tim reached down and picked up his briefcase. Again he glanced around the empty room. He gently thumped the lectern with his fist as he mumbled to himself. "God I'm looking forward to the end of the year."

CHAPTER 3

Tim was sitting quietly on his back porch, relaxing, enjoying a single malt whisky. He was thinking of nothing in particular but glad to finally have some quiet time to himself. Suddenly his attention was drawn to a sharp knock at the front door. He sighed at the unwelcome interruption then took a sip of the Islay nectar. It was sixteen year old Lagavulin, his favourite.

He was enjoying the solitude of his own company and hoped that if he ignored them, whoever it was would go away. He waited a few minutes, but the fervent knocking continued. Someone obviously knew he was home, so he accepted his fate. He put down his whisky and ambled off to see who it was.

When he opened the door, he decided he did want company after all. "Charlie. How are you?" he beamed. "Fine thanks. I was just on my way home and thought I'd pop in to see how you were. You're not busy are you?" Tim shook his head. "No. I was just having a quiet drink out the back. Trying to decide what to cook for dinner. Say, do you fancy a barbecue?"

Charlie nodded. "Yeah, that'd be nice. I'll slip home and get Becky if you like. Do you need anything?" Tim thought about it for a moment, then shook his head. "No, unless you'd like to bring some wine for Becky. I've only got beer in the fridge. Unless you fancy a whisky?" Charlie declined his offer. He excused himself and returned to his car. As Tim watched the car back down the driveway, he smiled and waved. Charlie honked his horn as the car sped off and disappeared around the corner. Tim returned to his whisky.

Twenty minutes later, Charlie let himself into Tim's backyard. Bottle of wine in one hand, his wife's hand in the other.

They were met by the unmistakable sounds and smell of a barbecue in full swing. They could hear the steak sizzling in the pool of hot fat that was still oozing from the obligatory sausages, as they spluttered away on the hottest section of the plate.

There is nothing quite like the complex smell of cooking a prime steak and sausages on a barbecue. The meat, onions, spices and marinade all combining with the hot fat. The inviting smell wafting on the afternoon breeze, sometimes carrying for hundreds of yards. Much to the frustration of drooling dogs along the down-wind scent trail. It was enough to fire up the taste buds in any human within smelling range.

As Charlie and Becky turned past the house they could hear the sausages and onions spluttering loudly as they were fed more fat. The unique smell of burning sausages, mixed with the pungent smell of half-cooked onions, grew stronger as they headed toward Tim. Charlie began to salivate. Tim, whisky in one hand, cooking tongs in the other, smiled as he watched them approach. He motioned with his tongs for them to join him at the barbecue. "G'Day Becky. How are you?" Becky smile warmly. "Good, thanks Tim. And you?"

Her voice resounded with the mock air of a worried mother. As she reached him she placed her arms around his waist, gave him a firm hug and then affectionately pecked him on the cheek. "Couldn't be better. Pull up a chair. I'll take that and open it for you if you like. Here Charlie, can you look after the steaks for me? They're just about done. The sausages and onions are done so you can take them off if you like. "

Tim swapped the tongs for the bottle of wine and inspected the label. It was a bottle of Jasper Hill Shiraz, a fine wine indeed. He nodded his approval as he walked off, then paused and turned to his brother. "I guess you'll need a beer?" he suggested. "Yes, thanks!" Charlie turned his attention to flipping the steaks.

That done, he found a steel tray next to the barbeque and began loading it with sausages and onions. Charlie waited for Tim to return. "Well..." Tim began, as he returned with the drinks, "... there you go. Now, what's the meaning of this unexpected but nonetheless pleasant visit?" Charlie shrugged his shoulders. "Oh, nothing really. We just haven't seen you for a while and Becky wanted to make sure she said goodbye before she left. Her and Sue are going back to Scotland to see their parents for a couple of months."

Tim and Charlie's mother was also from Scotland and was best friends with Becky and Sue's mother. That's how Charlie and Becky met. They grew up together and their friendship blossomed into love and finally marriage. Unfortunately, Tim and Charlie's parents had been killed in a road accident six years before. Three years ago, Becky's parents returned to live out their old age in their beloved Scotland. Tim had Becky's father to thank for his taste for expensive Scotch whisky.

"And I thought while they're away it'd be a great opportunity for me to get away from it all for a while. You know... recharge the old batteries. Do something different." Tim nodded his agreement with the thought of getting away for a while, but wondered what he was considering. "Like what?" he probed.

"How about we go up to Queensland and do some fishing or prospecting. I think we could both do with some sun." Tim thought about it for a minute. Suddenly he had an idea. "I've got eight weeks off soon and one of my students comes from a cattle station in Queensland. She tells me they have gold on their property in some of the creeks. She said I'd be welcome to visit anytime. Maybe we could go there and try our luck."

But Charlie was yet to be convinced. "Won't it be hot up there at this time of the year?" Tim nodded, but hurried to reassure him all would be alright.

"Cathy said it might get a bit hot and maybe even wet. But because it's near the coast she assures me that it's almost pleasant up there during the wet season. As long as it doesn't rain too much. Apparently it's best to camp in some of the large caves that dot the property, out of the weather and flies."

"Are the caves that big?" Charlie asked in disbelief. Tim nodded. "Well there's one in particular that's a fair size by the sounds of it. Cathy says that she and her brothers always camped in there when they were kids. They never stayed long though. She said the cave was a bit spooky. It always felt uncomfortable, as if they were intruding or something. But she says the fishing's good from the beach nearby. And if we get tired of fishing we can look for gold in the watercourse that goes by the cave." Charlie turned to his wife with a boy-like smile. "Sounds good to me. What do you reckon Becky?"

Becky placed her glass on the table and looked over at Charlie. She watched him for some time, before breaking into a loving smile. "The poor fellow's been pretty busy this year. It's starting to take its toll. I think a holiday up north would do him the world of good. Besides, I'd rather him be with you so you can look after him while I'm away.

We married young and he never did learn to cook. I'm afraid he wouldn't eat properly if I left him on his own for a couple of months. You on the other hand, being the devout bachelor that you are... you're adequately house-trained. So, if I leave him in your care, I've got nothing to worry about. Well... less to worry about!"

Tim smiled, took a sip of whisky and looked first at Charlie, then at Becky. His eyes shifted back and forth from one to the other for some time as he thought. Finally he walked over to Charlie and slapped him on the back. "Well, as I said, I've got some time up my sleeve.

I was planning to go back to Egypt, as I haven't seen old Mohamed for a while... but what the hell? When can you go?" Charlie did the maths in his head. "Well, I've got about three weeks more work to do on the IBM project I'm working on. But after that, I guess I can leave any time. When's OK for you?"

Tim thought about it for a few moments. "How about the fifteenth. When do you fly out Becky?" he asked. "We fly out on the twelfth." she replied with a smile. Charlie glanced at Becky. She nodded permissively at the agreed date for their trip. "So the fifteenth will be great timing. It'll give us a couple of days to organise things before we leave." Tim nodded. "Sounds good to me. I'll check with Cathy and let you know how it goes."

CHAPTER 4

Two days later, Tim was stopped in the corridor as he headed toward his office. "May I speak with you for a minute please?" Tim's pulse quickened as a quiver of excitement shot up his spine. He knew who it was without turning around. Trying to act as nonchalantly as possible, he slowly turned to face Cathy and answered in a very controlled monotone voice. "Sure, come into my office."

They walked in silence until they reached his office. As they entered, Tim motioned towards a comfortable leather chair positioned opposite his desk. "Please take a seat Cathy. What do you want to see me about?" Cathy smile politely. "Well, I've thought about your advice." she began. "Actually, I've really thought about little else since we spoke. And I just wanted to tell you that I think you're right. It would be foolish of me to jeopardise my doctorate on a notion. Maybe we can get together after I'm finished and come up with something that'll rock the boat."

Tim noticed the sparkle in her eyes and was forced to break into a smile. There was a challenge he knew he would enjoy. "Maybe. But I'm glad you've decided to take the safe road. God knows it can be complicated enough in the scientific world, without piling woes upon yourself at the very beginning of your career. Well done, Cathy. I'm proud of you."

"Thank you, Professor. Well, I'll see you later then?" she suggested. "OK and good luck with your paper, Cathy." he offered. As Cathy rose to leave, Tim remembered his holiday plans and motioned for her to sit down again. He quickly gathered his thoughts and moulded the question he wanted to ask. "There is just one thing I'd like to ask you..." he began hesitantly.

"Would it be alright if my brother and I visited your parent's cattle station over the semester break? I think we both need to get away and recharge our batteries." Cathy smiled warmly. "Of course you can. I'll be there all summer and I'm sure Mum and Dad will be delighted to have you." she beamed. "When were you thinking of coming?"

Tim quickly recalled the agreed date. "We were thinking of leaving around the fifteenth. We'd probably take a few days to get there. We might even stop over to visit some friends on the way up." he suggested. Cathy nodded, then added an invitation. "Well, if you get there in time, we'd be honoured if you'd join us for Christmas dinner."

Tim smiled. "I can't promise anything, but we'll keep it in mind. Thanks very much, Cathy. I know we'll enjoy the break immensely." he admitted. "I'll look forward to your visit." she beamed. "Besides, there's something I'd like to show you. It's..."

Cathy stopped in mid sentence and hesitated for an uncomfortably long time. Tim could see she was wrestling with her thoughts. Finally, his curiosity got the better of him. "It's what?" he cautiously probed. But Cathy just shook her head. "Oh, sorry. I can't say too much. You'll see when you get there." she promised. Now Tim was more curious than ever, but Cathy would say no more. He would have to wait.

CHAPTER 5

The next few weeks were rapidly consumed. Tim had somehow survived the exam period remarkably well and was now in full holiday mode. The packing and planning went like clockwork, the girls were seen off to Scotland and before they knew it, it was time for the intrepid duo to leave for Queensland.

They were in high spirits, as the car slowly crawled its way through the Melbourne traffic. Charlie smiled across at Tim and gave him a wink. As he watched the last set of traffic lights fade in his rear view mirror, Tim gunned the engine and headed north for Queensland.

They took the coastal route from Melbourne, through Sale and up to Bega. As they meandered along the magnificent coastal highway, they were captivated by the spectacular ocean views. So much so, they found themselves stopping to take photographs far too often. If they continued at this rate, they would not meet their tight schedule.

Finally they agreed to put the foot down, in order to get to Sydney. Here they intended to stay with some friends for a few days. They were looking forward to the sights and sounds that are unique to this world-class city. Darling Harbour, the Manly ferry, the opera house and of course the old coat-hanger. So too, the old friends and fine dining.

After their appetite for Sydney's ambiance was sated, they bade farewell to their friends and continued on their northern journey. They struck up the coast until they reached Byron Bay. Here they were determined to spend a couple of days relaxing on the magnificent beaches. They were also looking forward to getting some much-needed fishing practice. Melbourne and work quickly became a distant memory.

Two days of fishing had done the job. Refreshed and eager, they almost reluctantly packed the car and continued their northward push. They drove non-stop, sharing the driving with two hours on, two hours off, until they reached Brisbane. Here they had several relatives, whom they felt obliged to spend some time with. They enjoyed their stay in Brisbane immensely. It was a rare treat to catch up with all their relatives and friends, scattered up and down the east coast.

By Christmas they had worked their way up past Rockhampton, Mackay and, after a small detour and a day of reef fishing off Airlie Beach, they finally made it to Townsville. Here Tim had some friends. One was a lecturer at James Cook University, the other a marine biologist who worked for the Great Barrier Reef Marine Park Authority.

Becky also had an uncle who lived there, so Charlie had promised to drop in to see him. It was there they had Christmas dinner. From Townsville they headed directly to Cairns, only a short five hour drive. Keen to get to the cattle station, they decided to ignore Cairns for the time being and pressed on. They agreed that Cairns would be a fall-back vacation option, should the cattle station somehow prove unsatisfactory.

Even with the stopovers, the trip from Melbourne was longer and more demanding than either of them had expected. They had never driven up the coast, preferring instead the convenience of flying. But they were enjoying each other's company immensely. It had been years since they had spent quality time together.

Two days after Christmas, they finally arrived at the cattle station. Ably guided through the endless dirt tracks by a mud-map Cathy had supplied shortly before she left Melbourne to fly home. They pulled up for a convenience stop, next to an old rusty sign. The hand painted, now almost illegible, faded red writing spelt out the name of the station.

It had been standing there for many years, mutely pointing to the right. A not too obvious fork in the road, in the middle of nowhere. "Well I guess we finally made it." Charlie mused. "Sure looks like it. There's the signpost shown on Cathy's map. We're about five miles onto the property already. Only ten or so to go until we reach the homestead."

They continued for another ten miles along the corrugated and, at times deeply rutted, meandering dirt road. As they came over a small rise, they could see the unmistakeable signs of habitation in the distance.

What greeted them was a typical station layout. A speck of civilization almost hidden in the vast emptiness of the great Australian outback. The building that first caught their eye was a large sandstone homestead complete with a jaded, rusting corrugated iron roof. The streaking rust stains somehow aiding the otherwise anomalous homestead in its effort to blend into the ancient landscape that surrounded it.

The homestead was surrounded on all four sides by a large veranda to help keep it cool during the long hot summers. A small portion of the fenced off yard had obviously seen some concerted watering, as a verdant lawn softened the otherwise dust-reddened homestead. Several large trees, provided much needed shade during the summer, keeping the surrounding ground a couple of degrees cooler.

Also within the homestead yard were several small buildings. The wash house, where the laundry was done. A small butcher's shop where the meat rations were cut up after a kill. A small store where up to twelve month's supply of canned and dried food was stored, in case of isolation during the wet season, when the roads may be impassable for months at a time. Adjoining the store was a walk-in cool room where vegetables and meat were kept in large quantities. And there was the iconic thunder box. The outdoor toilet.

Surrounding the homestead was a large area of diesel-soaked bare dirt. Apart from providing relatively dust free vehicular access around the homestead, this rather unusual feature did have another practical side. In summer the diesel laden dirt heated up more than the surrounding area. This, coupled with the diesel, was a simple way of deterring errant snakes from wandering into the homestead yard. Diesel gives snakes dermatitis which can be fatal. And the snakes in this country are among the deadliest in the world. Taipans, Eastern Browns, Mulga Snakes, Whip Snakes and Death Adders to mention a few.

Opposite the homestead were numerous buildings, some large, others relatively small. Each was purpose built, even if over the years their function had changed. There was the ubiquitous workshop, stocked with innumerable tools, where all nature of machinery had been repaired over the years. Next to that was a large lean-to that once served as a blacksmith's workshop.

At one end, a large London Pattern anvil was still standing, silently perched atop a huge, now grey and split section of what must have been a very impressive tree. A patina of dark rust testimony to the many years since its last use. Several old smithies tools were scattered around the area. Some on a makeshift bench, some half buried in the dirt floor. Still others were hanging on the wall behind the anvil. All were slowly rusting into oblivion.

The forge's steel bed was still covered in a scattering of half-burnt coke and clinker. It was slowly morphing into a flaky red slice of Swiss cheese, as the small rust holes slowly expanded. Small piles of fine dust had escaped from the forge table and were building up like miniature black stalagmites on the red dusty floor. The wood and leather bellows had long since rotted and had fallen forlornly onto the floor where the white ants had reduced it to a fragile exoskeleton.

Now, several four-wheel drive vehicles, battered and bruised though they were, rested in the shade. As much out of the elements as was possible, given the poor state of the structure sheltering them.

Behind the workshop was a large wood-framed, rusting corrugated iron shed that used to be a tack room. A place where all the harness and riding gear was kept in the days of yore, when horsepower had a more literal meaning. Now only a small portion of the wall space had saddlery hanging from it.

Saddles, bridles, blankets and girths for maybe fifteen or twenty horses. A far cry from the numbers that were used a hundred years before. Long gone were the pack saddles, the collars and hames. Gone too were the traces, cruppers, spiders and four-in-hand reins. Gone were the bronco breastplates. Life for the ringer was certainly easier these days. Helicopters and four-wheel drives had taken most of the romance and hard work out of mustering cattle.

One corner of the tack room was still dedicated to the storage of horse shoeing gear, with a scattering of discarded, rusting shoes lying half buried in the dirt floor. A small bench contained a few old and well-worn shoeing tools and several half-opened packets of horseshoe nails. Several hobbles and an old scotch collar hung on the wall, for use on horses that were less than cooperative come time to be shod.

The rest of the shed was now a general storage area. A plethora of improvised steel shelves stored a multitude of things that might come in handy one day. Even if they were never used in the next hundred years.

Next to the tack room was another small rusting corrugated iron shed. Along with the workshop, it had the rare privilege of a concrete floor. This was the generator shed. Here stood the sole source of electricity for the station. Side by side were two generators. The smaller Lister was for light work.

The other was a larger Cat set. This was used to keep the large cool room and worker's quarters going when up to twenty men were employed in the peak season. It was also fired up when large tools in the workshop, like welders and compressors, were needed. Alongside the generator shed was a large diesel tank, mounted on a ten foot high tower. Gravity fed the gluttonous appetite of the generators.

As they approached the homestead, they saw Cathy waving at them enthusiastically, as she rushed out to meet the car. As the vehicle ground to a halt in the diesel-soaked red earth, Tim acknowledged her with a smile. She smiled back broadly, her eyes squinting to exclude the sun's glare and the wind-borne dust now freeing itself from the tyre rims.

She greeted Tim warmly as he stepped from the car. "Hello, Professor Fullerton. Welcome to our place." she beamed. Tim smiled. "Hello, Cathy. Glad to be here. Sorry we couldn't make it for Christmas. We got delayed with friends on the way. So how are you?" he explained apologetically. "I'm fine thanks. So, how was your trip?" Tim raised his eyebrows a little. "It's a long way from Melbourne!"

Cathy smiled. "Sure is. That's why I fly from Melbourne to Cairns, and then someone picks me up and drives me home. Or my uncle picks me up in his chopper. Either way, it certainly beats driving." Then Tim suddenly remembered that Cathy and Charlie had never met. "Oh, by the way Cathy, this is my brother Charlie. He's the computer whiz I told you about."

Cathy reached out to shake his hand. "Glad to meet you Charlie, I've heard so much about you. I didn't know electronic engineers could be so interesting." she teased. Charlie glared mockingly at Tim, then smiled and offered his hand to Cathy. "I don't know what he's told you about me, but I'm sure most of the lies aren't true." he joked.

Cathy laughed as she turned around and acknowledged the two people now standing patiently behind her. The man was tall and lean, about six foot two in his riding boots. His clean-shaven face, half hidden under a battered, sweat-stained Akubra hat, looked leather-tanned by years of exposure to the intense rays of the tropical sun.

He was wearing a faded blue and white striped shirt. Sleeves rolled above the elbow, exposing his deeply sun-tanned, sinuous forearms. His faded denim jeans hung loosely on his long and distinctively bowed legs. They had obviously seen their fair share of horse work. Most evident by the distinct wear marks left by the stirrup straps on the insides of his calves. His heavily scuffed RM Williams Santa Fe riding boots looked like they had never seen polish since the day they left the factory. He was the quintessential Australian outback cattleman. Proud, hard-working, friendly and honest, with no pretence or fuss.

The woman was much shorter, perhaps a little over five feet tall. She wore a plain off-white dress, patterned with the occasional pale red nondescript, almost cliché, flower. Over her dress she wore a white apron, lightly dusted with flour. She had obviously been cooking as they arrived. Her neatly brushed, shoulder-length hair was mostly grey, but still had a healthy sheen as it glistened in the sunlight. On her feet she wore a pair of unfashionable, but obviously comfortable, slippers. Her face was deeply wrinkled from a lifetime of squinting, but her eyes were warm and friendly and she had a welcoming smile on her lips.

Cathy beckoned them over. "I'd like you to meet my parents." she offered. "Dad, Mum... this is Timothy Fullerton, my ancient history Professor and his brother Charlie." The introduction was friendly rather than formal, as is the tradition in the bush. Tim and Charlie thrust out their hands in unison to meet their hosts.

Then, turning back toward her parents, Cathy continued with a broad smile. "... and this is my Mum and Dad." Brett leaned over to shake Tim's hand. "You can call us Brett and Dot, if you like. Glad to meet you." he offered. Smiles and warm handshakes were exchanged between the four, as the introductions gave way to relaxed conversation.

Eventually an offer of dinner and their first night's sleep at the homestead was gratefully accepted. The men were ushered to the shade of the airy veranda, where a gaggle of squatter's chairs had made their home. Cathy disappeared, only to reappear moments later, laden with a large jug of iced water and three tall blue glasses. The ice blocks clinked rhythmically as she walked towards them. "Here, this should wash the dust from your throats." Cathy excused herself and retired to the kitchen, where Dot was preparing the evening meal.

The men spent the remaining time on the veranda in general conversation. It was a good chance to get to know each other. Tim asked about the history of the station, how many cattle they ran, what the markets were doing, how many people worked there. And so built up a picture of Cathy's family business enterprise. It was an interesting conversation that allowed the men to relax and enjoy each other's company.

An hour or so later, they were ushered into the cool and darkened kitchen. As they looked around they noticed the contrasts of station life. The old blending with the new. There was an old wood burning stove sitting forlornly next to a modern gas appliance. There was an old ice chest, now used as a rodent-proof cupboard, sitting next to a modern refrigerator, humming quietly and efficiently in the corner of the room. There were sets of crockery at least a hundred years old, proudly displayed in equally antique cupboards. It was almost like stepping back in time, but the modern appliances stood out as stark anachronisms.

The men were offered seats at the impressive dining table that proudly occupied the centre of the room. It was typical of cattle station dining tables, able to comfortably seat twelve people. Dinner consisted of a well-endowed joint of freshly roasted beef, generously garnished with roasted carrots, pumpkin and potatoes. The accompanying peas and corn were smothered in a layer of rich gravy. This was complimented by a steaming loaf of freshly baked bread, the obvious source of the flour on Dot's apron.

The meal was as large as it was delicious, the likes of which Tim and Charlie had never tasted before. A desert of rich, home-made plum pudding and brandy custard followed. A legacy of Christmas dinner, they were informed.

After dinner their half-hearted offers to help with the dishes were courteously dismissed, so the men retired to the lounge room. Brett offered them a glass of Galway Pipe, which neither declined. Soon the conversation swung back to the history of the station, a subject that had been previously explored but nowhere near exhausted.

Brett told them about his pioneering great-grandfather and how he had settled the property and started raising cattle. He told them of the gold miners who drifted in and out of the area up to the days of his childhood. The two brothers listened intently as Brett finally told them the legend of Chinaman's Gully. It was a small gold mining area on the eastern side of the property, somewhere within the Altanmoui Ranges.

Tim's interest heightened, as Brett detailed the area and its colourful history. Brett finally paused to take another sip of port and let the information sink in. Tim took this as an invitation to ask more questions. "So the riverbed's supposed to be worked out then?" he asked, a little disappointed at the prospect. Brett frowned a little as he answered.

"Well, it's supposed to be, but I've found small specks of gold in one of the rock pools near the big cave." he admitted. Charlie was staring at Brett with a puzzled look in his eyes, as he explained the layout of the stream and the cave. Finally Brett noticed his strange stare. "What's the matter?" Charlie casually shrugged his shoulders. "Oh, I was just wondering how hard it's going to be to find gold without a metal detector. We have pans but... "

Just then, the women arrived, bringing with them a fresh pot of tea and a tray of assorted freshly baked biscuits. The men sat in silence as they were each poured a cup of sweet black tea and offered a biscuit. When they had all settled down, Charlie looked at Brett, signalling his desire to continue the conversation.

Brett laughed as he reached over for another biscuit. He slowly dunked it into his crumb-laden tea, then leant over and quickly sucked the soggy morsel into his mouth, before it could fall back into the cup. He looked at Charlie and smiled as he wiped the corner of his mouth, before picking up the conversation.

"Well it seems the old fellers got really pissed off. You see they were mining through the solid rock bar that runs across the stream right next to the cave, using dynamite. They were following a small vein. But the explosions were getting bigger and bigger as their frustration increased. On one occasion, an explosion caused a section of roof to fall, in the large cave where they were living.

Lost almost everything it seems, because they were living at the back of the cave, far away from the flies. Right under the rock fall. Shortly after that, someone found alluvial gold on the Palmer River, so they all packed up and went chasing it. Rumour has it they left a few bodies under the rubble and bolted. And no-one's been back there since." he recalled. Tim and Charlie listened eagerly as Brett expanded on the legend.

It had been a while since he'd had company on the remote station and he was enjoying the chance to talk with new faces. Tim was intrigued and actively encouraged him to continue. "Well even the blackfellers have got some real bad Dreamtime yarns of the area around the cave." he explained.

"To this day, that whole range of hills there are taboo to the local boys." he added. Tim's ears pricked up at the mention of an ancient taboo, his interest being more than academic. He was a fanatic follower of ancient myths and legends, believing that even the wildest legends were usually based on some facts. He was keen to get as much information as possible. He probed Brett for more. "What's the aboriginal legend then?"

Brett laughed cynically before he answered the question. "Well you know what those blackfellers are like. No written history, just word of mouth passed from one generation to the next. Well it's bound to be stuffed up or exaggerated along the way, isn't it?" he surmised. Tim and Charlie both nodded agreement with the logic, but Tim urged Brett to continue regardless. "Well, it seems that in the Dreamtime, great warriors lived in the mountain. Must have scared the hell out of the locals. They reckon they flew in and out of the mountains on a silver trail." he related.

"How many of them were there?" Tim asked the question enthusiastically, encouraging Brett to elaborate all he could remember. "Well I don't really know. Neither do the local blackfellers. The finer details of the story have been lost over time. But it seems there were quite a few of them. In fact there's some old cave paintings at the edge of the range." he offered.

"The museum people are split. Some reckon they're at least three thousand years old. Others think they're a hoax. Anyway, these paintings show some pretty weird looking characters." Tim was hooked. "In what way?" he asked rather enthusiastically.

"Well, they don't look like your average blackfeller. Their faces don't look human, more like cats really. But that's pretty funny, because there weren't any cats in Australia at that time. So it makes you wonder what made them draw them like that." he said as he frowned.

Tim mused, his brow deeply furrowed with concentration. "That's most peculiar! Some tribes in South and Central America were known as the Cult of the Jaguar. They seemed to think they'd been visited by beings that were half human and half cat. But this is the first time I've heard of such a thing in Australia. This is most interesting." Tim mused.

"Tell me, has anyone ever found large footprints around this area? One's about eighteen inches long, with six toes?" Tim asked in conclusion. Brett looked up at Cathy with a bewildered, almost accusing stare. After he received a puzzled shrug of her shoulders and a slowly shaking head, he turned back to Tim. "How do you know about them?" he asked suspiciously.

"I didn't." Tim reassured him. "But it's a hobby of mine, researching ancient myths and legends. Seems wherever there's a legend of a visit by cat-like hominid creatures, they've found these large six-toed footprints nearby." Brett looked even more puzzled as he leaned towards Tim. "What do you mean... visit?"

Tim smiled and sat back, slowly shaking his head as he thought of a suitable response. "Well, have you heard of Erich Von Daniken and his book *Chariots of the Gods?*" he asked. Brett just shook his head, so Tim continued. "Well, it's a book that speculates about alien visitors coming to earth in our ancient past.

Well from my research, I can't dismiss his theories as pure conjecture. There seems to be too much collaborating evidence. Admittedly, most of it's in the form of myths and legends. But every now and then, I find something tangible that makes me think of extraterrestrial visits to our humble planet.

Do you think you could show us the cave paintings and the footprints while we're here?" he asked. "I'd really love to see them. And of course we won't disclose their location to anyone else' without your express permission." he promised.

Brett looked over to Dot and Cathy. Cathy smiled and nodded at her father and then instinctively looked toward her mother. Dot sat motionless for some time, finally nodding her added approval. "Sure he will."

CHAPTER 6

Early next morning amid the cacophony of countless stirring birds, Tim, Charlie, Cathy and Brett bade farewell to Dot as they piled into an old four-wheel drive sedan. The vehicle looked decidedly the worse for wear. Most of the original panels were dented. One in particular looked like it had narrowly survived an encounter with a T-Rex.

The paint was faded, to say the least. Most of the original duco had long since been worn away by driving thousands of miles through rasping scrub. One headlight was broken and both tail lights were dangling forlornly, now only attached to the car by their electrical wiring. As for the bull-bar; it looked like it had hit a few too many bulls! Brett laughed as the diesel engine fired enthusiastically. "Don't be misled by the looks of the old girl. She may look a little rough but she's in A1 mechanical condition."

Reassured they had a good chance of getting there and back, Tim and Charlie settled into their seats. Brett gunned the engine and clunked the drive train into first gear. As they headed off, Tim looked around. What a magnificent setting. The homestead was built on a slight rise that overlooked a water course. The riverbed was lined with majestic ghost gums that were home to a variety of cackling parrots, screeching cockatoos and warbling magpies.

Beyond the riverbed lay a vast grass-covered flood plain, shimmering with a faint orange-yellow glow under the early morning sun. Tim tried to imagine the huge expanse of water that would lay there following a tropical deluge. Beyond that, to the west, was an infinite stretch of low-set rolling hills, interspersed with savannah plains.

The hills varied in hue from a pale olive green, through various shades of purple and blue. Finally the indigo-blue outline of the most distant peaks melted into the cadence of the shimmering heat waves. Their morphing forms dancing above the horizon in the ever-changing mirage. The countryside was dotted with thickets of scrub, the odd tall tree and the ubiquitous red-orange earthen termite mounds.

All these features seemed to combine mystically to add an order of magnitude to the vastness of the country. The tree-lined riverbed headed east where it meandered off beyond view, presumably towards the base of the purple outline of a far-off range of hills Tim could see dancing in the heat haze. Beyond them, so they were told, was the Pacific Ocean.

The four-wheel drive bounced awkwardly over jagged rocks and innumerable potholes, as they slowly crawled along the rugged track that snaked its way through the rough terrain which separated them from their destination, the distant mountain range. Tim and Cathy sat in the back seat while Charlie sat in the front.

Brett seemed to enjoy the challenge of driving in such unforgiving country. Mile after mile, bump after incorrigible bump, the ground seemed to be constantly challenging the irrepressible suspension. Just when Tim thought they had been over the roughest terrain he'd ever had the misfortune to travel, it happened.

As the car sped into a corner, they encountered a deeply eroded gutter. Brett swerved desperately in a vain attempt to avoid it but to no avail. The vehicle skidded in the soft dirt, struck the gutter almost sideways and lurched wildly. So sever was the jolt that for a moment they thought the car was going to roll. But through sheer driving skill, or was it just plain old good luck, Brett managed to keep the vehicle on its wheels. During the ordeal, Cathy was forcefully flung across the rear seat.

She landed unceremoniously, with her head buried deep into Tim's lap. She apologised as she extracted herself from the embarrassing predicament. "Sorry about that." she apologized.

But there was a hint of impishness in her voice that seemed to negate the apology. Tim reacted to it playfully, for what reason he did not know. It was most unlike him, but understandable given his relaxed mood since he had left Melbourne and the flirtatious attention Cathy had been giving him since his arrival. "That's OK. No damage done." He assured her. "Gee, I hope not..." Cathy added with a sexy smile.

They locked gazes for several seconds, each wanting to take it further, but neither being game to do so. Finally they became embarrassed at their protracted stares and spun their heads to look out of their respective windows. A few miles further along ,Brett informed his bruised and shaken passengers, with a wry laugh, that their ordeal was almost over. "Nearly there... only a couple of miles to go." They all mocked a loud sigh of relief, much to his amusement.

The last mile took forever as the vehicle slowly negotiated dozens of intertwining erosion gullies. But the final five hundred yards of the journey followed a relatively smooth and sandy track along a dry creek bed. Brett finally pulled up and parked the battered car under the shade of a large river gum. Charlie turned to Brett as he alighted from the vehicle and stretched his cramped legs. "That's one hell of a drive. We're going to have fun getting our truck in here. Especially with the trailer. That road's a beauty."

Brett nodded. "It's not exactly on the tourist beat. But you should be right as long as you take it easy." Brett laughed as he brushed past Charlie and Tim and strode off towards a rocky outcrop near the foothills. Cathy sidled up to Tim and grabbed his arm playfully. "Well Professor, what did you think of the ride out here?"

"A bit less comfortable than I'm used to, that's for sure. But I'm certain the bumps and bruises will be worthwhile, if I can get some good photos of this cave art and those footprints. And Cathy..." he hesitated as she looked into his deep blue eyes "...please call me Tim." Cathy smiled. "I'd be glad to... Tim." she purred.

Then remembering that her father was just yards away, she quickly continued in a more serious tone. "I'm sure you'll get some good photos of the art. I've seen it plenty of times before. Sorry I couldn't tell you about it until now, but Dad's a bit protective. You know this is only a leasehold property. He's afraid the Government will take it off us if they think there's something interesting here.

The museum chaps have seen the paintings and are quite happy for them to remain in anonymity. I heard they considered them to be a modern hoax. But no-one outside our family has seen the footprints." Cathy explained. Tim nodded. "I can well understand his concerns. But the secret's safe with us. We'll only disclose the location if your father wishes us to do so. Otherwise it's only of academic interest to me."

Brett interrupted their private conversation as he yelled down from a small rock ledge. They were now lagging well behind. "Come on you two. We're there already." While Tim hurried to join them, Cathy ambled along in her own time. She was in no hurry. She'd seen it all before and it was of no real interest to her anyway. Other things were on her mind!

Tim could not believe his eyes. In front of him was a vast cave. He estimated the arched entrance to be at least sixty feet wide by fifteen feet high at its peak. He could not estimate its depth, as the opening disappeared into the darkness beyond. The floor that he could see was sandy and littered with the debris of centuries of sporadic animal, and perhaps human, habitation.

The walls were a mass of f₍
ochre paintings. He stood th₍
detail and diversity of the
prominent feature of the paiɪ
central figure, towering over all e₍
spectre. The facial features were in₍
the body showed enormous phy
stature. It reminded Tim of the Wo   ₍ar
Wars movies.

The figure was attired as one wɔuld expect an ancient warrior to be. But definitely not what one would expect to find in Australian aboriginal rock art. He was clad in an armoured vest. His breastplate was easily discernible. It reminded Tim of ancient Roman armour, but somehow it seemed more primal than that. He was wearing a duty belt, from which hung several things. One appeared to be a knife, one looked like a pouch and one looked suspiciously like a small two-way radio.

The warrior was holding a weapon in his right hand. It was not a primitive weapon like a boomerang, a sword or a spear. It looked more like a science fiction gun. Or at least an artist's rendition of one. His left hand was raised as if in greeting or salute. On the middle finger of the left hand was a distinctive yellow ochre patch. Perhaps representing a gold ring. As Tim continued to study the detail, he noticed that the warrior appeared to be wearing trousers.

This was interesting indeed. The local aboriginal tribes were thought never to have seen or used trousers until after the Europeans arrived. Then Tim found the most interesting aspect of the warrior figure. He was wearing lace-up boots. They reminded him of modern military style boots. They had flat soles, but no raised heels, and their tops were long, protecting the ankles. And they were definitely laced. The artist who had painted the warrior had a good eye for detail.

r one hell of an imagination! Tim was . He stared open-mouthed at the warrior, shaking his head in disbelief. Eventually his eyes an to wander as he inspected the rest of the artwork.

The traditional, often merely symbolic, paintings that made up the remainder of the mural depicted the local fauna and aboriginal life in general. There were kangaroos, snakes, birds and lizards. There were also water scenes with crocodiles and fish. Aboriginal tribesmen were scattered among the fauna, some standing in awe of the creature, others nonchalantly hunting their chosen prey. Although of the highest quality, the remainder of the painting held little interest for Tim. He was mesmerised by the awesome warrior.

Tim stood back from the wall to get an overall perspective of the drawing. The detail and proportion of the art was perfect. Except for one thing. Everything seemed to be minuscule when compared to the giant sentinel. Tim moved closer to further inspect the drawing. Focussing once more on the warrior.

As his eyes became accustomed to the dim light within the cave, the details of the ancient painting became clearer. Tim stood there shaking his head and muttering to himself. Eventually Brett walked over and patted him on the back. "Well? What do you reckon Professor?"

"I just can't believe it. These paintings are thousands of years old, yet the detail is still perfect. Even allowing for the fading of the ochre. But look at this warrior figure. Why is he so large compared to the native warriors around him? Was he physically larger, or was he just spiritually more significant. You know. More important than the others, therefore just depicted as a larger being?" Tim noticed a second warrior figure among the background drawings. This one was only about half as big again as the aboriginal figures. He wandered closer to inspect it.

The smaller warrior still had a body configuration that indicated massive strength. He too had decidedly feline facial characteristics. But his dress was different. He seemed to be clothed in casual attire, rather than the military style uniform of the larger figure. Tim also noticed something else. "I find it difficult to believe this is the work of local aboriginals. The detail is so precise. Look here. This second warrior has no footwear. See! Now count his toes."

Charlie and Brett approached the painting and inspected the feet of the warrior. It was Charlie who spoke first. "I'll be stuffed. He's got six bloody toes!" Tim nodded as he backed away from the drawing. Then asked no-one in particular. "Do you know what's so funny about that?"

Without waiting for an answer he continued. "There are two things. First, the obvious one. The character has six digits rather than the more normal five. But then we already suspected that from the fossilised footprints that you say are around here somewhere. But the real puzzling thing is that the aboriginals don't normally go into that much detail. Look at the tribal warriors around the central figure.

See... they haven't got any toes at all represented. Just the outline of cliché feet. It's as if the artist who drew this was specifically emphasising the fact that this warrior was truly different. And look at the warrior's hands. Only five fingers... just like everyone else. And look at his modern attire, compared to the loincloths of the natives. How did they know about breastplates, arm guards, belts, trousers and lace-up boots? This is absolutely fascinating.

And there's another thing. Aboriginal artists often drew animal tracks in their art. Over here for example is a set of emu prints. Here's a set of kangaroo tracks. And here's a set of human footprints. But what do you make of this?"

Brett wandered over for a closer look. The marks were distinctive, almost herringbone on shape. "Dunno! But it doesn't look like the tracks of any animal I've come across out here." he conceded. Tim shook his head. "I'm not sure either, but I have a suspicion they're the footprints of the main warrior. I think those lines are the tread patterns on the soles of his boots."

They pondered Tim's theory for a while and came to the conclusion that he might be right. On the other hand, he might be wrong too. Finally Tim looked over to Brett. "Mind if I use the flash when I take the photographs? I don't think there's enough light here for a decent picture otherwise." Brett looked at him and shrugged his shoulders. "Can't see why not. I'd hate you to come all this way and not get some decent pictures. What sort of camera is that anyway?"

Tim offered Brett his camera for inspection. Brett took it from him as one would take a newborn baby from its mother. He held it at arm's length and gave it the once over. With a shrug of his shoulders and raised eyebrows, he handed it back to Tim. "It's a digital camera..." He explained. But when Tim saw the blank expression on Brett's face, he decided to elaborate. "It takes a digital picture and stores it on a small card. I can then plug the camera into my laptop computer and view the pictures.

I can also load the pictures onto a memory stick or disc that can store thousands of images. And I can print the pictures on my colour printer. I have them both in the car. I'll show you how it's done when we get back to the homestead if you like." Brett nodded. "All that computer stuff's a bit much for me. I grew up with box Brownies. Now I use an automatic camera. One they reckon is idiot proof. But I still manage to stuff it up sometimes. I let Dot use it mostly now. But I'd like to see how it works when we get back if you don't mind." he added with a smile.

Tim spent some time alone in the cave while the others waited patiently for him outside. He took care to photograph the entire cave in such a way that he could later lay the prints out and recreate the entire masterpiece in mosaic. For a while he was lost in time as he took photo after photo. Try as he might, he just could not believe that the museum staff had overlooked the significance of the warrior.

According to Brett, the museum guru had casually dismissed the art as non-genuine. He concluded that someone had added the warrior to the original work after the European settlement. But Tim thought this was impossible. The warrior seemed to be the centrepiece of a perfectly composed drawing. Besides, he had looked very closely and the warrior, as far as he could tell, had been painted on fresh rock. It had not been painted over any previous work. Once again it seemed that orthodoxy had chosen to ignore contradictory evidence.

When he finally emerged from the cave, he found the others sitting in the shade of a large ghost gum, sharing a bottle of cold water and chatting. As he reached them they stood up and headed off towards the vehicle. Cathy handed him the bottle. "Drink?" she offered. Tim smiled. "Yes, thanks."

When they reached the vehicle Cathy dragged out a giant picnic basket and an esky. Tim helped her carry them to the shade of the nearest river gum. "Lunch anyone?" They all sat down and eagerly feasted on sandwiches generously filled with home-made pickles and leftover roast meat from the night before. Dot had also packed some biscuits and a large thermos of hot tea. The esky contained some ice, fruit and cold water.

Over lunch they discussed the cave paintings with much debate and enthusiasm. Tim scoffed his lunch like a hungry puppy, eager to look at the footprints. The others finally succumbed, as they watched Tim anxiously pacing up and down.

Brett wiped the tea from the corner of his mouth and placed the cup on the ground. Cathy packed it up with all the others and placed them in the picnic basket. Charlie offered to carry the basket back to the car as Tim and Brett headed off towards the north-east. Tim excitedly approached Brett. "How far is it?"

"Oh, not too far. In fact it's just up here thirty yards or so on your left. I took you to the cave first because I thought you'd like to see the paintings before the footprints." Brett waited for Cathy and Charlie to catch up, then suddenly scrambled up the riverbank and invited everyone to join him.

As the men crawled up the bank, Brett strode off into the bush. "It's just over here." he assured them. As he approached the dry flood plain just upstream of the cave, he stopped and waited for the others to join him. "They're just over there. Beyond that slab of rock."

Quickly and excitedly, they headed towards the rock outcrop, following closely in single file behind Brett. Cathy, still nonplussed by it all, casually wandered along the riverbank, looking for an easier way up. By the time she rejoined the men, they were staring in disbelief at the large hominid footprints that lay frozen in the laminar siltstone rocks before them. Someone, or something, had wandered across a muddy plain a very long time ago. Although exposed to the elements, the prints were in remarkable condition.

They were, as near as could be seen, human. Except of course for the size and the fact they had six toes. The six toes were quite evident in the prints. Tim estimated the footprints to be eighteen inches in length and nine at their widest. They were embedded about an inch into the rock. He eventually asked Charlie to stand next to the clearest of the tracks so that his boot would give some size perspective to the photograph. As a second method of achieving the same, he fished a dollar coin from his pocket and placed it inside the print.

There was a line of sixteen clearly definable prints and Tim set about photographing each of them. The depth of the imprints implied that the pressure on the soles of the feet was even, indicating a walking, rather than a running gait. It looked as if someone had simply strolled from point A to point B.

When he had finished photographing the prints he turned to Brett. "I know you haven't shown these tracks to anyone, but do you have any idea how old they might be?" Brett smiled and looked at Cathy. With a cheeky grin she replied for him. "Of course I couldn't just accept the dating of the museum people based on the paintings. They said the paintings were at least three thousand years old. Which doesn't really account for the paradox of the later addition of the warrior.

But I thought the paintings would have to be much older than that. I believed they had to date back to the Dreamtime. The actual time the warriors were supposed to be here. I thought the drawing and the footprints must be about the same age. And the footprints had to be older than three thousand years. I figured the artist must have surely seen them first-hand. Otherwise it would be impossible for him to include that much detail.

Anyway, up a bit further, in the same layer of siltstone, there are some animal tracks. While I was going to Uni in Brisbane I befriended a geologist. He was interested in dating the animal prints, so I cut one out of the rock. When he took it to his Professor for analysis he had to answer all sorts of questions... but he was sworn to secrecy. Well, to cut a long story short, the sediment was tested and a tentative date of 12,000 to 15,000 years was given."

Tim digested the new information, then turned to Cathy. "Are there any more hominid prints around the area?" Cathy shook her head slowly, then turned to her father. "Not that I know of. How about you, Dad?"

Brett shook his head slowly. "Well, as far as I know, this is it. I've never found any others. Mind you, I haven't really looked all that hard either. But I did ask a couple of the older blackfellers once if they knew of any more. They said there was supposed to be some up in the hills, near a small waterhole. But that area's taboo, so they wouldn't take me there. And I guess I couldn't be bothered looking by myself." he explained. Tim nodded. "Well, these are terrific." he assured him.

Tim wandered off to take more photos. The others milled around for a while, before heading off towards the shade of a convenient tree.

Some time later, Brett approached Tim. "Sorry to spoil your fun Tim. But if we don't get moving soon, we'll be getting home in the dark. This country's a bit unforgiving for that. I try not to drive in the dark unless I really have to." Tim apologized and followed Brett as he headed towards the vehicle. "Sorry for holding you up. It's such a fascinating place. But we can do a bit of looking around at our leisure once we set up camp in the cave, eh?" Brett nodded. "Can't see why not."

CHAPTER 7

Tim and Charlie thanked Dot for a wonderful breakfast and headed out to their vehicle. Brett had long since departed with one of the stockmen to repair a windmill. Cathy tagged along behind Tim, like a faithful puppy afraid to see its master depart. "Now you remember how to get there?" she teased. "Yes. And if we get lost we'll give you a call on the RFD radio." Tim reassured her. "Good. I'm a bit worried about a couple of city slickers venturing out into the bush on your own."

Tim responded defensively but playfully. "I'll have you know that I've travelled through the deserts of the Middle East, Persia and Africa... and the jungles of Asia and South America. And I've managed to survive."

"I was only kidding Tim..." she apologised teasingly, as she leant over and kissed him gently on the cheek. "But still, be careful out there. And especially watch out for snakes in the cave. Oh... wait a minute."

Cathy rushed back to the house. The men looked at each other in bewilderment, shrugged their shoulders and climbed into the car. Cathy returned within a couple of minutes. She was carrying a double-barrel shotgun and a box of shells. It was a beautiful old coach gun with a dark brown patina on the Damascus barrels. It had exposed hammers and a once fine English walnut stock, now lacking any oil and indelibly marked with the ravages of time.

The shells, she explained, were loaded with black powder. They were number seven birdshot. Excellent medicine for errant snakes, she informed them with a knowledgeable smile. And if fired in the confines of a cave, she hinted, the strangely satisfying smell of burnt black powder would linger for days.

"It's not loaded yet." she explained, as she handed the weapon to Tim. Tim thanked her for her thoughtfulness as he accepted the antique weapon through the window. He poked the butt of the shotgun onto the floor next to Charlie's feet and rested the muzzle on the seat next to the gear lever. Cathy smiled. "That's OK. Just remember to look after yourselves and be careful if you do any climbing. If you fall and injure yourself we're a long way from a hospital." Tim nodded. "Thanks. We'll remember that. See you later?"

Cathy smiled with enthusiasm. "You bet. As soon as we've finished the bangtail muster on the northwest boundary, I'll be over to see you. It should only take a couple of days." Tim returned her smile. "We'll look forward to it." Then, to his surprise, Cathy leaned in the window and gave Tim another affectionate peck on the cheek. "I'll see you in a few days..." she whispered.

Tim smiled broadly as he started the engine and threw the vehicle into gear. As the car lurched forward, he leaned out the window. "See you later."

Leaving Cathy veiled in a gently swirling cloud of fine dust, they drove off toward the distant purple hills. They were just visible from the homestead as they shimmered through the mid-morning heat haze. Cathy stood at the homestead gate and watched until the vehicle disappeared from view. With a heavy heart she returned to the house. The next few days couldn't go quickly enough for her.

Tim was concentrating on driving for some time before he sensed that Charlie was staring at him. As casually as his curiosity would allow, he glanced over at Charlie. He was indeed staring at him. He also had a childish, leering grin plastered across his face. "What?" Tim insisted. "Do I detect a chink in the bachelor's armour?" Charlie replied, with more than a hint of mirth. "What?" Tim responded, still protesting his innocence. "I've seen the way Cathy looks at you.

And I've noticed that you pay a bit of attention to her too." But Tim was not giving in that easily. "I don't!" Charlie chuckled. "Don't get all defensive with me, big brother. I think it's a good thing. She's a good looking girl, she's got a great sense of humour and the two of you are history nuts. Perfect for each other, if you ask me." Charlie suggested rather smugly. "But she's at least six or eight years younger than me." Tim protested. Charlie laughed. "So what? She's not one of your teenage, pimple-faced, infatuated undergraduates.

She's a mature woman. From what I've seen of her, there's no reason in the world why you shouldn't chase her. God knows Becky's been trying to marry you off for years." Tim smiled and returned his thoughts to the track. But in the back of his mind he wondered if Charlie was right. Maybe one day he would drum up the courage to take it further.

After an arduous and painfully slow journey, they finally reached their destination. Mostly thanks to the fresh tracks in the softer dirt and small hand-drawn map Brett had given them the night before.

Tim and Charlie stood at the entrance to the imposing cave. They looked hesitantly at each other, then their stares returned to the yawning cavern entrance. It was Tim who finally walked forward. As he approached the shadows beyond the cave mouth he paused to inspect the floor. "Well I hope the floor's solid enough to support the vehicle."

"It should be. According to Brett, it's carved out of solid rock. The sand on the floor near the entrance is only what's blown in over the last couple of thousand years. And by this rough sketch of the cave system that Cathy drew for us, it isn't too far to the camping spot. We just have to go ahead some fifteen yards, then turn left at the intersection, follow that for another twenty yards or so. Then we turn right, and go straight through two intersections.

Then turn left into the cavern at the third intersection. It's less than a hundred yards all up. Seems she knows this cave better than Brett. Mind you, she said she spent a lot of time in here as a kid."

Tim peered nervously into the darkness, as Charlie ratted through their grossly overloaded trailer in search of some torches. After some time, a harried Charlie finally joined him at the cave entrance with some torches. "Here you go. There's your main torch and your spare. Let's go and find this cavern where we can set up camp."

Tim grabbed the torches. He placed the small back-up Maglite in the leg pocket of the khaki cargo pants he was wearing, then went over to the car and picked up the shotgun. He broke it and carefully fished two shells from the cartridge box and inserted them into the gun. He gingerly closed the gun and grabbed a handful of cartridges and shoved them into his left front trouser pocket. He picked up his main torch and turned it on. It was with some trepidation that he nervously led the way into the inky depths of the mountainside.

Comforted by the accuracy of the map, and the fact that Tim and the shotgun were ahead of him, Charlie urged him on. The further they progressed into the cave, the darker it became. Soon the only light that penetrated the heavy blackness was the comforting beams exuding from their torches. As they inched further, the air became cooler. It also became dank.

The smell of bat droppings began to pervade their nostrils. As their ears gradually became attuned to the deathly silence of the inner bowels of the cave, they began to discern the faint squeaking of the resident bats. So too, they began to hear the difference in their footsteps as the sandy floor gave way to solid rock. All the while searching for snakes, they slowly inched their way towards their camping site, by now just a few yards away.

Tim was surprised at the size of the cavern. "See, there it is. Just like Cathy said. Shit it's bloody big. Look at all this wood here. Should be enough to keep us in light and cooking fuel for a while. Mind you, I think it'll be safer if we use the Tilley lamps for light and only use the wood for cooking." Tim mused, more to himself than Charlie. But Charlie agreed nonetheless. "Good idea. How about we get our gear and settle in. The tunnel's pretty clear of debris, so we shouldn't have any trouble getting the vehicle in here. Although I wouldn't leave the car running any longer that necessary. We wouldn't want to gas ourselves, would we?"

Tim smiled at his dry humour. "Yeah. There's no future in dying!" Charlie then looked back over his shoulder. "I'll go get the vehicle. You can have a bit of a look round if you like. But be careful of any snakes... and six toed monsters!" he added with roguish humour.

Tim could hear Charlie chuckling to himself as he headed towards the cave entrance to get the four-wheel drive. He watched Charlie's torch beam dance from side to side as he negotiated his way out of the darkness. Soon the faint light disappeared altogether and only softly echoing footsteps remained. As the footsteps finally faded, Tim was left alone in the enveloping silence to contemplate his surroundings.

Slowly he ran the torch beam around the extremities of the cavern, working his way from the floor to the ceiling. The surprisingly flat floor, the angular walls and the domed ceiling were all rough-hewn rock, as you would expect in any cave, he thought. The floor was littered with small stones and the occasional larger rock. The result no doubt of roof falls.

How such an enormous void was carved out of solid rock intrigued him, as he continued to explore the bounds of the immense chamber. By now Tim was becoming more comfortable with the dense atmosphere that seemed to inhabit the cave at this depth.

So too, his nose was becoming used to the strange combinations of smells. The bats and their droppings, the dank, humid air and the unmistakable smell of stale animal faeces. Probably smaller animals, but perhaps the odd wallaby or dingo had made use of the cave over the years.

The thought of running into a dingo sent a shudder down his spine. His hand squeezed the butt of the shotgun tighter for a few seconds, until the thought passed. The feel of the shotgun was reassuring, so he relaxed, sat down and waited for Charlie. While he sat there probing the depths with his torch, he convinced himself to conduct a thorough search as soon a Charlie returned. Just to make sure they were not sharing their accommodation with anything nasty.

As he sat and waited, Tim sized up the cavern. He figured it to be some seventy yards long by twenty-five yards wide by fifteen to twenty feet high. Large enough he concluded, to allow for a fire without risking carbon monoxide poisoning. Besides, it was not a dead end. From the sketch he had, it seemed that the cavern tapered out on its northern end.

A thin passage emerging from the north-west corner of the cave forked a couple of times and the narrow passages meandered through the rock to eventually join up with the northern branches of all the intersections they had passed on the way to the camp site. They all inevitably led back to the cave entrance. The north-west passage continued on and eventually led to the southern-most entrance to the cave system. This would allow some cross ventilation at least.

The rumbling of the diesel motor and the glow of approaching headlights interrupted his thoughts. He stood staring in the general direction of the noise, until the car finally appeared. Charlie pulled the vehicle into the cavern and shut the motor down. "I'll leave the lights on for a while, so we can unpack.

I don't think we'll flatten the battery in that time. But if we do, I'll switch over to the spare. Shit, it's a big hole isn't it?" he exclaimed. Tim nodded. "Yeah. I was just checking it out and wondering how the hell it was formed. There doesn't seem to be any indication of a watercourse. Although I guess it could be millions of years old. And hundreds of different rivers could have flowed past here in that time."

Further conversation was put on hold while they unpacked the car and trailer. They had sleeping gear, cooking utensils, fishing rods, first aid kit, boxes of food, eskies, cartons of beer, whisky, tarpaulins, Tilley lamps, gas bottles, computers, printers, cameras and stationary. The list was almost endless.

It had been a logistical nightmare packing the car and trailer before the trip. But now all that effort was paying off, as they unloaded everything methodically and efficiently. In no time the trailer was devoid of its load and the campsite was showing some semblance of organization. When all was done, Charlie lined up several Tilley lamps and began to light one. "Now we can have some light when I turn off the headlights."

It was not long before they were fully organised. The camping table and chairs were erected, the eskies lined up against the wall, the small gas refrigerator was purring quietly in the corner near the small passageway, furthest from the old ash laden fireplace.

The tucker boxes were placed next to the table and the bedding laid out in the open space between the vehicle and the fireplace. When they were happy with the camp, they sat down and looked around the cavern. The pale yellow flickering light of the kerosene lanterns made their shadows dance lazily across the walls. Tim sat in silence watching the fleeting phantoms, engrossed in his thoughts. Charlie also sat in silent contemplation for some time before he rose to his feet. "Do you want a drink?" he asked, as he headed toward the esky.

Tim nodded. "Yeah, why not? I think we both deserve a beer after all that." Charlie retrieved two cold beers and handed one to Tim. "Here you go."

They sat and drank the beer in silent introspection. What they had already seen was beyond their wildest imagination just a few short days before. Eventually, once he had finished his beer and generally recovered from the exertion of unloading the trailer, Tim stood to his feet. "Where are you going?" Charlie asked.

"Oh, I thought I'd just go for a wander and have a real good look at the cave paintings. It's getting late in the afternoon, so I don't really want to go looking for footprints. Do you want to come?" Charlie shook his head. "No thanks, I think I'll just sit here and have another beer. I might join you later though."

Tim grabbed a lamp and dropped a box of matches in his pocket. He looked over at Charlie and nodded a farewell, then headed off towards the mouth of the cave. When he arrived at the painting, he doused the lamp and placed it gently on the floor. Facing the painting, he slowly walked backwards, to get a full perspective of the fascinating drawing.

Once again his eyes could not help but focus on the gigantic central figure. With all the time in the world to study it first-hand, he began to look at every square inch of the warrior. The yellow and red ochre that had been combined to draw the facial features were starting to separate, but the artist was so skilled that it was still remarkably detailed, despite the ravages of time.

He noticed the feline facial hair, but could not discern any whiskers. Maybe they didn't have any he thought, as he chuckled to himself. Then he looked at the mouth. It was thin lipped and angular, coming to a point under the nostrils and tapering off at each end, just like that of a cat. The ears were pointed and definitely feline, although they were more on the side of the head than the top, like the ears of Mr. Spock.

Earthy colours of brown, grey and red ochre had been used for the warriors clothing and body armour. This area fascinated Tim the most. He refused to believe that the artist could imagine the dress of this warrior. Even if the museum staff were right and the drawing had been done in the last two hundred years, Europeans had nor worn that type of armour for over a thousand years. Besides, the local tribal elders had sworn to Brett that the painting had been there for many generations. Long before white settlement. As for a hoax. Way out here? Who would bother? And why?

Tim spent the next two hours examining every minute detail of the picture. He was familiar with aboriginal art and concluded that indigenous artists had neither this degree of imagination nor this level of skill. Then he noticed that the brush strokes on the warriors were different from those on the other figures. Again he looked at the detail of the large figure and compared it to the rest of the picture. He exclaimed his conclusions triumphantly to the world. "Of course! That's it."

Charlie had decided to join Tim after all, but his arrival had been unnoticed. As he casually walked up behind him, Tim startled him with his epiphany. "You what?" he asked, in bewilderment. His response startled Tim. "Jesus Charlie! You scared the shit out of me! I didn't hear you sneak up." Charlie chuckled and offered a half-hearted apology. "Sorry." Tim mumbled to himself, then returned his gaze to the wall. "Anyway, I was looking at the pictures more closely and suddenly it dawned on me."

Charlie wandered over for a closer look, but nothing immediately struck him. "What's that?" he asked. Tim pointed to the warrior. "Look carefully at this warrior. Then look at the rest of the painting. The museum staff aren't as stupid as I first thought. The warrior figures were definitely painted by different people." Charlie scrutinised it for some time.

He slowly shook his head from side to side, then shrugged his shoulders. "I can't see it."Tim pointed to a few details. "Look at the style and the brush strokes. The aborigines mainly used sticks and reeds, sometimes pounding the ends to make a rough brush. But the strokes are much finer on the warriors. As if they were done with better quality modern brushes. Even the colours are different. I didn't pick it up at first, but it's obvious now I think about it."

Charlie shook his head. He still could not see anything untoward. "What's obvious?" he finally asked. Tim pointed to a small figure in the background. "The warriors were drawn first, then the rest of the drawing was added around them later. I'll bet one of the chaps was a bit of an artist and drew the giant warrior as a self-portrait. Then sketched his mate in the background. Then, some time later, the local aborigines painted the rest of the picture. But I still think it was very close to the time of the original drawing."

"Makes sense to me, but then again, I'm no expert." Charlie confessed. "Maybe you could take a couple of scrapings of the paint and have it analysed. I saw a TV documentary about that once. Probably the bloody Discovery Channel!" he mused. "Some ancient paints use animal fat or blood to bind them and you can use this to get an approximate age of the painting. So if these paints use any organic binders in them, you could get a likely age of both areas. That'll prove whether you're right or not." Tim was impressed. "Brilliant! I'll do that before we leave." he promised.

But Charlie was less enthusiastic about the painting. "Listen, it's getting dark out here. How about we get back to the cavern and cook some dinner? I could do with an early night." he suggested.

CHAPTER 8

Early the next morning, the alarm on Tim's wristwatch broke the deathly silence of the great cavern, with an irritating high-pitched electronic beep. Unfortunately, deprived of sunlight, it would be impossible to keep track of time without the annoying intrusion. Tim yawned loudly as he crawled out of his bedding. He sat on the edge of the camp stretcher and fumbled in the dark for the torch.

It was next to the shotgun, resting on a small canvas camping chair at the head of his bed. His bleary, squinting, eyes searched the camping area in the dim torchlight. It was not long before he found what he was looking for. A Tilley lantern and a box of matches. He slowly rose from his bed and staggered over to the lantern. Once lit, he found two more lamps and lit them. Satisfied these would give him enough light to prepare their breakfast, he told Charlie it was time to get up.

As the mouth-watering smell of bacon and eggs wafted around the confines of the cave, the men hungrily tucked into their breakfast, washing it down with a mug of hot, sweet, black tea. After the dishes were done and the camp tidied, they sat down for a while and chatted, contemplating their day. Although they were both keen to explore the rest of the cave, it was the footprints that held their immediate interest. It was Tim who made the first move.

He stood up, grabbed a lantern and turned to Charlie. "Well, I think it's time to have another look at those footprints. I couldn't help thinking about them last night. They seem to be in a siltstone layer that's been eroded by running water. Until they were exposed they were probably buried for thousands of years. But I think the original siltstone is still several feet thick.

I wonder what else we can find under there." Charlie frowned. "What do you mean?" Tim explained his reasoning. "Maybe there are other footprints under the cap-stone." he suggested. "Yes, I suppose there could be, but so what?" Charlie asked, not sure where Tim was heading. "Well the exposed prints are eroded. Granted some are in pretty good condition, but most of them are badly worn by the elements." he explained.

"So...?" Charlie began, but Tim cut him off in his enthusiasm. "So... if we could peel back a layer of the cap-stone near the footprints, we might just be lucky enough to find a print in perfect condition. Wouldn't that be a bonus?" They thought about it for a while.

Finally Charlie agreed with Tim's logic, but questioned his ethics. "Do you think it's a good idea? I mean, would Brett approve?" Tim nodded. "I think so. Anyway, if we do find something we could always leave it at the homestead if he doesn't feel comfortable with us taking it away." Charlie agreed with Tim's reasoning, then stood up, grabbed a lantern and motioned towards the cave entrance.

"Well are you coming?" he teased. "Yeah, I guess so. But I was just thinking what we'll need. I noticed the stratum was very laminar, so I think a crowbar, a sledge hammer and a few wedges should do the trick."

They quickly gathered their tools and each grabbed a canteen of water. Tim grabbed a lantern and walked around extinguishing the others. Satisfied they had everything they needed for the time being, they headed off in the sallow lamplight towards the cave entrance.

Once there, Tim extinguished the lamp and sat it on the floor. With a smile and a mutually reassuring nod, they set off towards the mysterious footprints. The going was relatively easy for most of the way, until they came to a small ravine. No wonder Brett chose to detour this. This was not going to be easy to get across. Especially carrying all their tools.

Tim looked at the imposing drop, then at Charlie. "Any ideas?" Suddenly, with a shrug of his shoulders and a cheeky grin, Charlie lobbed the crowbar and bag of steel wedges over the edge into the sandy watercourse below. "How easy is that? A twenty foot drop into sand isn't going to hurt that lot!" Tim smiled in acknowledgment of the clever thought and followed suit with the sledgehammer.

Charlie wandered along the bank some twenty yards, where he found a game trail. Kangaroos were using this steep track to access a waterhole further up the riverbed. Charlie eased himself down the bank and carefully negotiated his way to the sandy watercourse below. Tim watched until he had made it safely to the bottom and quickly followed.

Picking up their tools, they looked around for a few seconds to get their bearings, then headed off towards the riverbed, beyond the end of the ravine. Here a low cliff remained on the cave side, but the terrain flattened out on the other side of the deep sand. They made their way over to the siltstone beds beyond the watercourse, where the footprints lay.

Charlie followed the footprints across the rocky plateau until he came to an abrupt rise, where the footprints stopped. "Jesus Christ, Tim! Whatever made these prints was a big bugger. Look at the length of its stride. Do you thing it might have been the original Yowie?" he surmised.

Tim pondered the legend of the Yowie for a moment. The Australian equivalent of the Nepalese Yeti and the North American Big-Foot. Its existence certainly appeared to be substantiated by the footprints. "Could be." he concluded, with a noncommittal shrug. Charlie bent over one of the clearer prints and inspected it closely. Eventually he got down on one knee, then slowly sank to a sitting position. Finally, after studying the footprint for several minutes, he turned to Tim.

"Do you think it's possible these were actually made by those warriors in the painting? Or do you think that it was just some sort of primeval ape-like creature, left over from the mega-fauna period. Something that obviously frightened the shit out of the local aborigines?" he mused.

Tim walked over and sat down beside him. He too studied the print for some time before looking up. "Well according to South American legends, some giant half cat, half human, creatures did exist. But it's hard to sort fact from fiction. I'd like to think they were some form of intelligent creature, but my gut feeling at the moment is more in line with your Yowie theory. A large, possibly extinct, ape-like creature that lived here long before humans migrated to Australia.

Although that doesn't explain the paradox of the cave painting. I guess I'd still like to cover my bets at this stage. But the painting does show the warriors with six toes. I don't really know. It's all a bit confusing at the moment. I guess the jury's out on this one, until we find some conclusive evidence one way or another."

They sat for a while, silently staring at the footprint, each deep in thought. Each trying to visualise the creature whose only legacy was a trail of footprints etched in stone. Tim eventually stood up and began to survey the immediate area. The print they were looking at was the second last one exposed, so he turned his attention to the last one and beyond. "The siltstone's distinctly layered like I thought." he concluded. "And it's only a couple of feet thick for about ten yards. If we drove some wedges in there we could lift the top layers off and work our way down to this level. I bet we'll find some perfect prints." he conjectured.

Charlie stood up and stripped off to the waist. "Well I guess we better get on with it then." They placed their shirts, camera and canteens under a small ledge to protect them from the intense sun.

Donning their hats, they gathered the sledgehammer and wedges and headed toward the siltstone outcrop. Tim studied the strata for a few minutes before finally pointing to a spot midway into the formation. "I reckon we ought to try about here." Charlie agreed. "Yeah, but it might be easier if we start about five feet to the left, where the rock is the thinnest, and work our way over.

That way, if there are any prints under this ledge, we'll be clearing as we go, perfecting our technique. Rather that belting our way into the middle of the prints and damaging them." Tim agreed with the proposed strategy. "Good idea. Let's give it a burl."

The men began the arduous task of inserting wedges, hammering to failure, then removing the debris. Then repeating the process. They slowly peeled away the layers, in three to four inch slabs. Eventually they reached the layer containing the prints. Then the whole process was repeated for the next couple of feet.

It was a laborious task, but slowly, inexorably, they inched their way towards the area of interest. After about an hour's work they smiled as the wedges began lifting a large slab of siltstone in the bottom layer. They were almost directly behind the last exposed print.

As the slab lifted they backed off the wedges, doubled them up and gently tapped them back in with the sledgehammer. Suddenly there was a loud crack as a slab about eight feet by three feet cracked from the parent rock. They both looked at each other and smiled with pride. Charlie reached for the crowbar. "I'll see if I can get this thing under the edge where it broke off. We may be able to flip it over. If we can do that a couple of times, it should be far enough away to let us start on the next slab." he explained.

Tim nodded as Charlie levered the crowbar into position. When it was as far under the slab as he thought necessary, he motioned to Tim to give him a hand to flip the massive chunk of siltstone.

With a coordinated heave, they managed to lift the slab onto its side. Here it was steadied with the bar while they took a rest. After they had regained their breath, Tim nodded. "One, two, three... go!" With an almighty heave, they flipped the slab of rock onto its back. As it crashed heavily to the ground they pulled the crowbar out and tossed it behind them, almost falling over as they went.

Exhausted and covered in sweat from their exertions, they both lay down to cool off and regain their strength. They lay there for several minutes, side by side, silently staring into the pale blue sky overhead, letting their bodies recover from their efforts. Tim offered some latent advice in jest as he sat up and looked around. "Only mad dogs and Englishmen toil in the midday sun." he laughed.

Still lying on his back, Charlie meekly grunted his agreement with the aphorism. But Tim never heard him. His attention was focussed elsewhere. "Jesus H bloody Christ!" Tim's excited exclamation was in such a tone and volume that Charlie's heart nearly leap from his chest. He sat bolt upright, jerking his body around to face Tim. "What the...?"

But Tim just pointed excitedly at the rock. "Look at that! There are two footprints in this slab. One from the line we were chasing and another at about ninety degrees." Tim explained excitedly, "And there's the indentation of the prints left in the parent rock underneath. I think you'd better come over here and take a closer look at this Charlie." But Charlie was not that enthused. "Why, is it a good one?" Tim nodded vigorously. "A very good one." he replied eagerly.

Charlie crawled over to the up-turned slab and looked at the freshly uncovered prints. "Do you notice anything funny about these?" Tim asked, rather excitedly. As Charlie looked at the prints it dawned on him just why Tim was so excited.

One print was the same as the weathered six-toed prints further along the rock. But the second print was much more incredible than that. "Christ! I see what you mean." Charlie exclaimed loudly. "The other one's not a footprint at all. It's a giant *boot* print. Look, you can even see the stiches and the distinct tread patterns. They're as clear as if you were looking at the boot itself. Shit! You know what this means don't you?" he suggested.

Tim just nodded his head in disbelief, dumbstruck at their incredible discovery. "It means that whoever... or whatever... made these prints, and those over there, wore boots that are, for all intents and purposes, modern. And that must have been thousands of years ago. Footprints don't fossilize in two hundred years.

This puts a whole new spin on things around here. It seems the cave painting might be accurate after all. Maybe the local blackfellers did have a good reason to be scared of this area." he surmised. "I'll have to get some photos, then we'd better cover this up so it doesn't get damaged. I'd like to cut the prints out of the slab so I can take them home with me. This one's almost like having the boot itself. Also, if the boot print in the rock gets destroyed, at least I'll have a negative of it in case there are no more under there."

They worked in silence, wrestling with their confused thoughts, as they began to cut the prints from the large chunk of sandstone. Luckily they were close together at the far end of the slab. One cut and they should have both prints on a smaller, more manageable hunk of rock. They used wedges to mark a scar in the underbelly of the slab. Once the line was finished, the crowbar was used to lift one end of the slab of rock.

When it was high enough, Tim slipped the sledgehammer under it so the crowbar could be re-positioned next to the scar. The hammer was removed and the slab gently lowered to rest on the crowbar. Tim looked over at Charlie.

He needed reassurance that he wasn't about to destroy the priceless specimen. "Well I hope this works." he stated. Charlie smiled and shrugged his shoulders. Not exactly the encouragement Tim was looking for. But, by this point in time, he was pretty much committed.

With a quick upswing of the hammer, Tim brought it crashing down just in front of the crowbar. There was a satisfying cracking sound as the rock snapped along the scored line, leaving the end piece of sandstone some three feet by three feet, separated from the main slab. Charlie looked at the chunk of rock and asked sarcastically. "How the hell are we going to carry this back to the cave?"

Tim shook his head. "I'd like to trim it down further, but I dare not risk cracking through the footprints. I'll use a diamond blade to trim it when I get home. Meanwhile, I guess we'll have to get the car over here and manhandle it into the back. Perhaps we could park the vehicle in the creek bed over there and slide the rock over to it. That way the tailgate would almost be at the same level as the rock and we could simply slide it in.

Why don't you wait here and I'll slip back to the cave and get the car. I'll see you in half an hour or so." Tim suggested. "OK." Charlie agreed. "But could you bring back some more water please." Tim nodded. "Sure."

Charlie watched as Tim started off in the direction of the cave. Then, as Tim receded into the distance, he yelled out after him. "Bring another crowbar back with you." Tim turned and waved, then disappeared.

It was nearly half an hour later when Charlie heard the rumble of the four-wheel drive, labouring its way along the sandy riverbed just around the corner. He had relocated himself away from the heat of the rock ledge and was recumbent in the shade of a majestic old river gum on the edge of the main watercourse. He smiled and muttered to himself as he looked over at the slab.

"That's going to be a bitch to move." he predicted. He was right. It took the brothers nearly an hour of toil and a bucket of sweat to move the slab the fifty or so feet to the waiting vehicle and then load it safely inside.

As they sat in the shade of a tree, drinking cool water and recovering from their exertion, Charlie looked over at Tim and casually asked. "What do you reckon about this footprint? Do you think there's more stuff around here? Maybe some tools or even a graveyard?" Tim stroked his stubble-lined chin as he thought about it. Then he smiled and looked back in the direction of the cave. "Maybe we've overlooked the obvious place."

Charlie frowned. "Where's that?" he asked. Tim smiled. "Well I still can't understand how that cave could have been cut out of solid granite by water. I've seen it before, but in this case there are no obvious signs of water interaction and the walls look too rough. I would have expected them to be a lot smoother if the cave was a result of water erosion. What if our friends deliberately cut out that cave for their dwelling place? That would explain the layout, with all its passages and caverns." he speculated.

Charlie thought about it before answering. "The cave seems a bit rough for a race of people with enough sophistication to have modern boots. I thought they would've dressed the walls a little better. Maybe even left some graffiti or writing. Sort of like the pyramids or the city of Petra." Tim smiled broadly. "I'm impressed! Petra indeed! Maybe you're right. But there's only one way to find out. Let's go and have a real good look at that cave. If you're right, there should be some evidence of the excavation. Tool marks, artefacts or even some written record."

CHAPTER 9

Back at the camp site they prepared for their grand tour of the cave system. Having gathered Tilley lamps, spare torches, geo-picks and canteens, they looked at each other and laughed. They felt like two excited schoolboys preparing for a hike through the jungles of South America. Images of stepped pyramids and Inca gold dominated their thoughts as Tim cautiously led the way towards the back of the cavern. "We might as well start at the back and work our way towards the entrance. What do you reckon?" Charlie nodded casually. "Sounds good to me."

They wandered off toward the rear of the cave, torch beams fighting back the darkness as they probed for obstacles in their path. The debris from the multiple roof falls littered the floor, making their progress slow as they dodged rocks strewn in their path. The further they went, the more rocks they found.

They had not progressed far before they were halted by a wall of debris. "Well this is as far as we can go. Looks like this is where the main cave-in occurred. Let's have a look around and see if we can spot anything interesting. Like some old mining gear."

"Or a kero tin full of nuggets..." Charlie added jovially. Tim looked at the pile of debris. His curiosity getting the better of him, he raised his lamp and inspected the pile of rubble more closely. Suddenly he decided he must climb to the top.

When he reached the summit, he noticed a small gap between the debris and the cave roof. As he raised his lantern, he could see that the roof extended for some distance. He crawled across the rocks for fifteen yards until he came to the rear of the cavern. Here it narrowed appreciably into a passage some ten yards across.

He sat on the rocks, looking intently at the roof and what was exposed of the walls. He shouted back to Charlie. "The passage that heads off here seems too straight to be natural. But I can't see any tooling marks on the walls." he declared. "Wait there! I'll climb up and have a look." Charlie informed him. But Tim was a bit wary of the rock pile. "OK. But be careful. Some of these rocks are a bit loose." he warned.

It took Charlie several minutes to carefully pick his way up the unstable rock slope to the ceiling. Once there he sat down to regain his breath. The stale air made it difficult to breath, forcing him to suck at the air in ravenous gulps. When he regained his breath, he slowly and carefully crawled along the rocks to Tim. "There's a fair gap here between the rock pile and the ceiling, but it tapers out just up there a bit. The rocks go all the way to the ceiling as the roof comes down. But it looks like the passage might go on for a bit behind this cave-in. Do you want to move a few rocks to see if we can go any further?"

Charlie nodded mutely and retrieved his torch from his pocket. He waited for Tim to move off some ten feet before crawling after him. As he caught up with him he tapped him on the ankle and joked. "Get a move on. We've got a dead Chinaman to find." Tim smiled at his brother's droll sense of humour, but deep down he could not get the image of Inca gold from his mind.

It had been a long time since he had felt this excited. The discovery of the boot print had not only ignited his imagination, it had spurred him on to find answers to the enigmatic painting. If only he could somehow prove orthodoxy wrong. He broke into a broad grin as he imagined the infinite pleasure some theory-shattering discovery would bring him. He even let out an audible laugh as he imaged the dumbfounded look on the face of the Dean. Wouldn't he just love to make that pompous bastard eat humble pie!

"What are you laughing at?" Charlie queried. "Oh, nothing really. I'm just excited about what we could find here. I mean that boot print by itself is enough for a whole thesis paper. Who would have thought that civilised man was present in Australia of all places, maybe ten or fifteen thousand years ago?"

Charlie nodded. "Yeah, I see what you mean. But we'll never know if we don't have a look behind here. So I reckon we ought to start moving some of these mongrel rocks." he suggested.

After nearly two hours of careful scratching at the pile of roof-high rocks, Tim could shine his torch through a hole to see the other side of the rock-fall. "Damn! There's about twenty yards of tunnel, then there's another bloody rock-fall. What do you reckon Charlie?" Charlie shrugged his shoulders. "Well we've come this far and I haven't seen any evidence of tools being used to excavate this passage. But then again, it is awfully straight, isn't it?"

But Tim wanted a direct answer. "Should we keep going?" Finally Charlie nodded and smiled broadly. "You bet. In for a penny, in for a pound. I reckon we keep going until we find the back of the cave. If nothing else, once we check it out, we can forget about it and go look elsewhere."

The pair worked for another two hours, clearing a hole large enough for them to crawl across the second rock fall. Tim managed to squeeze through and gingerly made his way down the slope to the floor on the other side. Once he was on firm footing he called to Charlie.

Soon they were standing at the base of the second mound, shining their torches on the third rock pile that confronted them. It too stretched to the roof. "I guess I'd better go up there and have a look..." Tim conceded lethargically. "OK, but be careful." Charlie warned.

Tim was nearly at the top when the rock he was standing on gave way. Then another... and another.

Soon there was a thunderous groan as the rocks slumped savagely. Charlie leapt backwards and crashed to the floor as an avalanche of rocks cascaded towards him. He watched helplessly as a distraught Tim rolled down the slope, riding the flood of rocks like an amateur surfer riding a dumping wave.

As the echo of the racket died, Charlie picked himself up and rushed over to Tim. "You alright?" The tone of his voice betrayed his concern, as he anxiously grabbed hold of Tim's motionless arm. Tim blinked his eyes a few times in a vain effort to clear them of dust. He then shook his head vigorously, looked up and grinned. "Yeah. I think so. Boy that was some rockslide. We'd better be more careful next time."

"We?" Charlie asked mockingly. "Alright. *I'll* be more careful next time." Charlie was astounded. "You mean you're going to climb that again?" Tim nodded. "Why not? It's probably pretty stable now." Tim got to his feet, dusted himself off and hoisted his still burning lamp. Before the dust had settled, he headed up the pile of rocks once more, this time without incident. Safely at the top, he summonsed Charlie to join him, then sat down and waited for him to arrive.

"Gee that's some climb." Tim ignored him. Charlie repeated his statement. "I said... it's a hell of a climb up here." Tim looked around with a glazed expression on his face. "What?" Charlie almost yelled in frustration. "I was just saying it was a hell of a climb up here." Tim shook his head. "Yeah, sorry. I was looking at the wall of this tunnel. Do you see anything odd about it?"

Charlie carefully crawled to where Tim was sitting and held his lamp up to better illuminate the wall. He looked at the section of rock now bathed in light. Then slowly raising his lantern, he traversed the pale yellow patch of light along the wall, closely examining the surface as he went. "Well I'll be buggered! The wall starts out rough, but now it's smooth as a baby's bum.

It almost looks as if it's been painstakingly dressed after the blasting. Or cut by machine. And then glazed or polished. It looks just like highly polished granite. It's unreal. What do you reckon?"

Tim reached over and slowly ran his hand down the scabrous wall. The undressed section of wall was rough indeed. Then he moved over to the polished wall. As he carefully ran his hand along the wall, it felt as smooth as silk. The contrast could not have been more marked. "I have no idea. But it looks like someone went to a lot of trouble to polish the wall. Let's get to the other side of this fall so we can have a good look at it."

After more than an hour of careful excavation, they finally reached the end of the rock-fall. Tim snaked his way through the narrow opening and carefully descended the unstable slope towards the bottom of the pile. He was about two-thirds of the way down when the rocks finally gave way. This time the resultant avalanche was less dramatic and only succeeded in opening the top gap a little wider. This allowed Charlie an easier journey. Tim raised his lamp as high as he could for extra light as Charlie tentatively edged his way down the newly stabilised rill. "It looks like it comes to a dead end about ten yards further along. That's a bit disappointing. I was just starting to think we were onto something here."

"Well let's go have a look at the end of the tunnel now that we're here. There might be some writing or old graffiti or something with any luck." Tim strode off towards the tunnel's end, with Charlie following in his fleeting shadow. Both were now panting audibly. The stale air was still heavily laden with dust from the rockslide, making breathing difficult.

"Well this is it alright. A solid granite wall. But look how square it is. And it's polished like the rest of the tunnel. I wonder..." Tim dropped to his knees and placed his lamp on the ground.

He began to brush dirt meticulously away from the back wall. He continued to sweep with his hands as Charlie sat and watched. After clearing a small path some four inches wide by twelve inches long, Tim bent down and began to blow the remaining dust off the floor. Excitedly he moved his lamp closer and invited Charlie to join him. "Look at this would you?"

"Yeah, the floor's as smooth as the walls. That's amazing isn't it? Not a mark on it." Charlie stood up, expecting Tim to do the same. Instead, Tim remained seated on the dusty floor, staring at the cleared line. Then he cradled his head in his hands. Charlie looked at him worriedly. "What's the matter?" Tim shrugged his shoulders. "Oh, nothing really. I was just had a strange thought." Charlie was puzzled. "What's that?"

Tim pointed to the tunnel walls. "Well, maybe this tunnel was driven by someone chasing gold, but the fine finish makes that unlikely. So what are the alternatives?" Charlie was still not following. Tim looked at Charlie and lowered his voice. "What if this tunnel was driven for some other reason?" he mused.

"Such as?" Charlie quizzed. "I don't know." Tim admitted. "But my gut feeling is we're dealing with something strange here. This tunnel's so perfectly square and smooth compared to the rest of the cave system. Hardly the work of grubby gold miners."

Tim paused for some time, trying to think of a plausible explanation. Finally he rose to his feet and grabbed Charlie on both shoulders. He spun him around until they were staring into each other's eyes. Charlie felt uncomfortable as the stare continued. The anticipation finally became too much for him.

"What the hell are you thinking? You've got that funny look in your eyes, as though you've worked it all out. So tell me. What's your theory?" Tim hesitated for a moment before continuing, a little less than certain of what he was proposing.

"What I'm thinking doesn't make any real sense. But then again, it makes more sense than anything else I can think of. You remember when Brett told us about the aboriginal legend of this area? The locals were convinced that giant warriors lived *inside* this mountain range. Well what if that legend was true." Charlie stood in silence for a moment, digesting Tim's proposition. Then he slowly walked over to the end wall and raised his lamp. With slow strokes he began to caress the surface, using the time to think.

Finally he turned to Tim with a perplexed look in his eyes. "Do you think this tunnel was built by the blokes in the drawing?" he asked tentatively. "It seems a bit farfetched." Tim concluded nervously. "Too bloody right! But then again, why not? I can't think of any other logical explanation for the drawing, the fossilised boot prints and this polished tunnel. On their own they're weird enough. But all three together? Besides, it looks like someone went to a lot of trouble hiding this section of the cave. Why do you reckon that was Tim?"

"I have no idea." Tim confessed. "Maybe this was a service tunnel during the construction of their base. Maybe they filled it in to keep the local natives away once it was finished. The legend says they used to fly out of the mountain. Maybe they had a larger entrance somewhere on the other side of the hills and their craft exited from there. This one seems a little small for that, given the size of the creatures."

Charlie shook his head vigorously as he sat down on the floor. He looked around at the ephemeral shadows on the walls, then withdrew into his mind as he tried to comprehend what his learned brother was postulating. After a long protracted silence, his thoughts were interrupted as Tim rose and walked to the end wall. "Well. What do you think? Man, machine or alien?" Charlie pushed his forehead deeper into the palm of his hand. He then rubbed his hand down his face.

Still slowly shaking his head, he rose to his feet and approached Tim. "It's got to be a machine. But the vitrification begs the question... what sort of machine? If the tunnel's as old as we think, that sort of technology didn't exist." he postulated.

"What technology?" Tim asked. "Well, I'm thinking laser cutting or similar." Charlie explained. "What do you reckon, Tim?" Tim looked around the tunnel in the pale flickering light of the dancing kerosene-fuelled flames. It was all a bit much. He shook his head in disbelief of his own thoughts. "I really don't know. It all seems a bit enigmatic at the moment. Maybe we'll find out more later. Meantime if I'm right, there's an underground dwelling in this mountain somewhere. All we've got to do is find a way in."

Charlie shrugged his shoulders in a non-committal gesture. He too had run out of rational ideas for the moment. He then looked Tim in the eyes and smiled. "Why the hell not. We've got nothing to lose. But where do we start looking for another entrance?" Tim thought about it for a while as he went over to inspect the end wall once more. He ran his hand across its smooth surface as he examined it. Drawing no conclusions, he turned and walked back toward Charlie. As he did so, he casually glanced up at the side wall.

Suddenly he stopped in his tracks and thumped the wall with his fist in jubilation. "That's it!" he proclaimed. "What?" a surprised Charlie asked. "Come and have a look at this." Tim urged. "The side wall and the end wall are both polished mirror smooth. So are the floor and the roof. This is a perfectly square tunnel some ten yards by ten yards. It's been made at great expense. Or at least with some very high-tech equipment. Someone has gone to a lot of trouble to make this tunnel and I reckon they went to a great deal of trouble to hide it. Now look at the colour of the side wall." Charlie wandered over to Tim.

He raised his lamp and inspected the wall. "So?" he finally asked, wishing Tim would get to the point. "Now look at the colour of the opposite wall, the floor and the ceiling." Tim urged. Charlie obediently walked over and inspected the opposite wall. He looked down at the floor. He slipped his torch from his pocket and shone it up at the roof. "Yeah. Dark green granite. It's all dark green granite." he mumbled. "Exactly! Now look at the end wall."

Charlie strode over to the end wall and looked at it carefully. "It's dark green granite." he concluded. Tim nodded. "Yes. But the end wall has a predominantly light green fleck through it. The others have mostly creamy, grey intrusions." Charlie looked at the end wall again, then dropped to his knees and inspected the small strip of floor that Tim had previously cleaned. "You're right. This rock does look slightly different."

Tim took his geologist's pick from its pouch on his belt. He bent over and struck the floor with a sharp blow. A low solid thud reverberated along the tunnel. He repeated this with one side wall, then the other. Finally he approached the end wall. As he wrapped the centre of the wall a strangely higher-toned, hollow-pitched thud resulted. "Just as I thought. This isn't an end wall at all... it's a door. Albeit a very solid door."

Tim dropped to his knees and placed the lamp at the base of the door. He leant down and began blowing at the intersection of the door and the floor. Charlie looked on as Tim took out his pocket knife and ran it along the joint. "I thought so! This is a joint. It's two separate pieces of rock coming together. Not a single piece of rock carved out. Look, the knifepoint disappears a little way under it just here. Looks like we might be onto something. But we won't get through it easily. What's the time anyway?" Charlie looked at his watch. "It's four-thirty. We should go back to camp. We can get a few things ready for an assault on the door tomorrow."

CHAPTER 10

After a restless night's sleep, they set off for the tunnel. This time they were much better prepared. They were armed with two sledgehammers, a collection of masonry chisels, two crowbars, a dozen or more wedges and a bag of assorted bits and pieces. They also took two lamps, two torches, some snacks and plenty of water. It took several trips to ferry the gear into the final section of the tunnel, but at last they were ready to begin their assault on the door.

As Tim prepared to attack the granite door with a sledgehammer, Charlie handed him a pair of safety goggles. "Here, you'd better wear these. That could shatter when you hit it. You don't want to get any splinters in your eyes." Tim nodded and thanked him as he donned the goggles. He then raised the hammer, picked a spot in the middle of the door, and swung with all his might.

Half expecting the door to shatter, he was taken aback as the sledgehammer bounced harmlessly off the door. "This is going to be tougher than I thought." he moaned. Without waiting for a response, he raised the hammer again and proceeded to assault the door. Each blow was aimed at the same spot. Each time it was the same result. Small powdery fragments of granite came away on the face of the hammer as it recoiled viciously, but little else appeared to be happening.

All the while, the dull echoing thuds of the hammer resounded in the chamber beyond. Echoing back an eerie rhythmic drumming, as he repeatedly struck the door. Tim kept this up for nearly four minutes before he paused and inspected his work. Disappointed with the progress, he turned to Charlie and, with a shrug of his shoulders, stated the obvious.

"It doesn't seem to be having any effect. I reckon we have to do this the hard way. I was hoping it was thin enough for us to shatter with the hammer, but I guess not. Looks like we're going to have to use the chisels and wedges." he conceded. Charlie nodded. "Looks like it. Have a break. I'll have a go with the chisels. Where do you think would be the best place to start?" he asked. "Probably in the middle of the door, somewhere near the bottom edge. That way, once we get a start, it'll be easier to expand the hole with the hammers."

The shrill ringing of steel against steel resounded in the tunnel as Charlie pounded the chisel relentlessly with a four pound hammer. It was tiring work. Every six or seven minutes they swapped, giving one time to rest, while the other continued gnawing away at the base of the door. By lunch, they had worn a twelve-inch diameter hole, some eight inches into the granite.

By day's end, the hole had progressed some thirteen inches into the door and had expanded to around eighteen inches in diameter. Content with their progress, but disappointed they had not broken through, they retired to the camp for a much anticipated rest. How they looked forward to a couple of cold beers, some dinner and an early night.

They slept soundly that night, a legacy of a full day's toil, topped off nicely with a couple of cold beers. Neither was fit enough to endure this for long, but they were being driven by irrepressible curiosity.

The next morning, their enthusiasm tempered by the prospect of another arduous day, Charlie stood forlornly at the door and surveyed the scene. Once satisfied that the hole had not miraculously grown overnight, he lazily swung the hammer. As it struck the star chisel he noticed an unexpectedly high-pitched hollow sound. He stopped and cocked his ear for a moment, replaying the sound in his head. "Did you hear that?" he asked.

Tim cocked his head. "What?" Charlie picked up the hammer. "Listen carefully while I hit it again." Tim closed his eyes and concentrated, as Charlie raised the hammer and brought it crashing down onto the head of the chisel. He immediately confirmed Charlie's thoughts. "You're right! That sounded different to yesterday. It sounded less solid or something. Do you think we're nearly there?"

Charlie didn't wait for an answer. He picked up the hammer and savagely belted into the chisel. Again there was a high pitched hollow ring. With one further blow, the chisel finally broke through. As it did so, it slipped from his grasp and rocketed through the small opening in the door. Charlie instinctively put his ear to the hole and listened.

He heard the chisel as it crashed to the floor, then ricocheted several times before coming to a sliding halt some distance away. The resultant echo suggested it had fallen into a large open space. Charlie's elation was obvious. "Shit we've done it! Hand me another chisel will you, Tim?"

Tim watched excitedly as Charlie frantically hammered out the hole to a size where he could peer through it. With this done, he reached over and grabbed his torch. Tim noticed his hesitation. "What's wrong?" Charlie just looked a little sheepish. "Nothing really. I'm just a bit apprehensive about what's on the other side."

With a shrug of his shoulders, he resigned himself to fate. He positioned himself prostrate on the floor, so that both his right eye and the torch could peer through the small hole. Nervously he poked the torch past his flattened cheek and directed the beam of light through the newly chiselled miniature porthole. With the light now probing the darkness beyond the door, he peered into the void. "What's in there?" Tim was impatient, almost pushing him aside in his eagerness to have a look for himself. "Well I can't really see.

It looks like this tunnel just keeps on going. I can't really see much with this torch until we expand the hole." Tim was reaching for the hammer, when he thought he heard something. He stopped and motioned for Charlie to keep quiet. "Shhhh! Listen for a minute." There was silence as they strained to pick up the noise. Eventually Charlie whispered. "What?" Tim shook his head. "I thought I heard something. It sounded like a voice." Charlie listened again, but heard nothing. "What, from in the tunnel?" Tim shook his head. "I don't know. There it is again. It's coming from behind us."

They sat in silence and listened. The sound appeared again, this time clear enough for Tim to recognise it. "Shit! It's Cathy. I forgot she was coming today. You wait here, I'll go see her." Charlie caught Tim's arm as be brushed past. "Are you going to tell her about this?" Tim shrugged. "I don't know. If she's only visiting for a few hours I'll tell her you're out exploring. But if she plans to spend some time with us... I guess I'll have to."

Tim climbed across the rocky obstacle course as quickly and quietly as he could. Once safely on the other side, he paused to dust himself down, before heading towards the camp. Charlie, glad of a chance to rest, sat down and took a swig from his canteen. Then he rolled his shirt into a makeshift pillow, laid down and waited.

"Tim!" Cathy called out, by now nearly in desperation. Tim yelled out to Cathy. "Over here!" Cathy looked over towards his voice and saw the lantern approaching. "Oh, there you are. I've been looking for you for ten minutes. Where have you been?" Tim simply smiled. Then, after a further enquiring look from Cathy, he elaborated. "Just looking around. How are you anyway?" he asked, changing the subject. "Fine. Where's Charlie?" Tim pointed to the back of the cave. "He's out exploring." Cathy smiled wickedly. "Good! Actually, I've missed you..." she purred sexily.

She then wrapped her arms around him and gave him a warm hug. "Well... actually I've missed you too." Tim confessed. Cathy smiled as she reached up and planted a loud kiss on his stubbled cheek. "You look so rugged with that growth. Not the clean-cut shirt and tie Professor I'm used to seeing. Maybe you should grow a beard. I have a thing about men with beards."

Tim looked at her in the flickering lamplight. She looked stunning with her flowing blonde hair, her tight fitting faded blue jeans and her curve hugging white T-shirt. All topped with a broad smile and mischievous sparkling blue eyes. Eyes that were full of life, even in the dim light of the lamp.

Tim's pulse was racing and his heart was pounding almost audibly in his chest. Cathy was still clinging to him, almost as if she were afraid to let go. Tim reciprocated, wrapping his arms around her and pulling her towards him in a tight hug. He leaned down and kissed her gently on the lips.

Just the faintest touch at first, but her response instantly drove him into a full passionate embrace. They stood locked in passion for several minutes, each pouring out years of pent-up emotion. Finally Tim broke free and gasped for air. "Boy. If I'd known you could kiss like that, I'd have chased you years ago." Cathy smiled. "And I would have let you catch me. Besides, you're not a bad kisser yourself."

Smiling at each other, they entwined once more for a long passionate kiss. Although their newfound love was their highest priority for some time, Cathy eventually broke free of his embrace. "Well if you'd like, you can help me unload the car. I've brought out some fresh meat and more ice. It should last us a few days, then I'll slip back home and get some more." she explained. "So you're planning to stay a while? What do your parents think of that?" Tim asked with a sly wink. "Good God Tim... I'm thirty-three! I do what I like.

Besides, Mum likes you. She thinks you'd be a good catch for me. Dad thinks you're all right too. And he's a fussy bastard when it comes to strangers. Anyway, the muster's finished for a couple of weeks, so I'm at a loose end." Tim looked at Cathy and smiled. "I'm glad you're staying for a while, but I've got something to tell you." he began. "What?" Cathy asked excitedly. Tim hesitated. "I think I'd better get Charlie first."

Grabbing Cathy's hand, he gently led her to the rear of the cave. When he got to the first pile of rubble he stopped, raised his hands to surround his mouth, mimicking a miniature megaphone, and yelled out. "Charlie, we've got company." He waited for the muffled confirmation, then turned to head back to the campsite, Cathy still clinging to his hand.

"So he wasn't far away then?" Tim shook his head. "No. Just at the back of the cave." he explained. "Looking for souvenirs from the rock-fall, eh?" Cathy surmised. "Sort of."

When they arrived at the camp, Tim went straight to the esky and grabbed three beers. He placed one beer on the floor next to an empty chair ready for Charlie, twisted the top off the second and handed it to Cathy, then twisted the top off the third. He held his bottle aloft and clinked the neck of Cathy's stubby. "Cheers!"

They had only taken two or three swigs when the faint flickering glow of a kerosene lamp announced Charlie's imminent arrival. "G'Day Cathy. How are you?" Charlie greeted, rather cheerfully. Cathy nodded her greeting to Charlie. "Good thanks Charlie... and yourself?" Charlie slumped into a chair. "A bit knocked up actually. Sitting at a computer all day, I'm not all that fit." he conceded.

They chatted until they finished their beer. In the pregnant pause that followed, Cathy suggested they unpack her car. After the meat, ice and a cold carton of beer were deposited in the eskies, they sat down.

Tim looked at Charlie and nodded almost imperceptibly in Cathy's direction. Charlie understood the unspoken question and nodded an approval for him to confide in her. "Well, I guess we might as well have a couple of beers while we tell you what we've been up to." Tim proposed. Cathy listened intently as Tim told of their footprint discovery. She gasped in awe as he showed her the slab of rock in the back of their car. She squealed with astonishment when he told her about the tunnel behind the rock-fall, and shook her head in disbelief as he described the shiny walls and the door. Finally he told her that they had broken through.

At this point she could no longer contain her excitement. "Well what's on the other side?" she asked. "We don't know yet. The hole's too small for us to get through. All we can see is a corridor disappearing into blackness. Goodness knows how long it is... or what's at the end of it." Cathy was excited and could not wait to see their discovery. "What are we waiting for? Let's get going!" Torn between curiosity and their taste for beer, they reluctantly extinguished the surplus lamps and, grabbing a lamp each and a spare container of kerosene, headed for the mysterious door.

Ten minutes later they were all huddled in the corridor, staring at the door. Cathy put her lamp down and picked up a torch. "Can I have a look?" Tim nodded. "Sure. But you can't see much." he warned. Cathy peered through the hole, straining to see anything other than a polished thirty-foot square tunnel disappearing to the limits of the torch beam.

Finally she conceded there was nothing much to see, except for the errant chisel lying innocuously on the floor, some ten yards away. She retired to sit on a large rock at the edge of the tunnel. From her new perch, she chortled with mocked authority. "Well, I guess you fellows better get on with it then... or we'll never find out what's on the other side."

Tim and Charlie smiled as they took the hint. With a few beers under their belts, this was not going to be pleasant. They were already sweating profusely in the humid confines of the tunnel. They lazily picked up their sledgehammers and walked up to the door. With one either side of the small hole, they took turns hammering at the crumbling granite.

They rhythmically struck blow after blow for nearly twenty minutes, until they were both near exhaustion. As they slumped to the ground dripping with hard-earned sweat, Tim looked over at Cathy and smiled. "I'm not all that fit either. But another session like that and I think the hole will be big enough for us to crawl through. But I think we'll just rest for a while... if it's all the same with you."

Cathy smiled and picked up a torch. She wandered over to the enlarged hole, laid down and poked her head through the opening. As she peered into the distance she groaned softly in disappointment. There was nothing to see, save the mirror-smooth walls of the tunnel disappearing into the blackness beyond the reach of the torch beam. "I still can't see anything. This passage must go into the centre of the mountains. I hope it doesn't just go straight through and come out the other side. That would be most disappointing."

Tim muttered agreement, but remained where he had fallen, in a despondent heap on the floor. Charlie said nothing. He was lying flat on his back, sweating profusely in the stifling confines of the tunnel. He was too exhausted to speak. Cathy smiled and picked up a sledgehammer. She was a country girl, used to pitching in when there was work to be done.

Although not as strong as the men, she attacked the wall with equal enthusiasm. Ten minutes later, Tim rose shakily to his feet and relieved a tiring Cathy of the hammer. "I'll take it for a while. You rest there for another five minutes, Charlie.

It'll be easier on us all if we take it in turns." he suggested. They all took turns hammering at the door for the next hour and a half. With each blow a small piece of granite shattered and dropped to the floor. As they persevered, the pieces seemed to get larger, forcing them to periodically clear the debris from the ever-expanding hole.

Suddenly, after a particularly energetic blow by Tim, a large crack appeared. It started at the top of the ragged hole and travelled across to the left of the door at forty-five degrees. Tim stopped and surveyed the crack. Then, with a mighty blow in the middle of the area, the whole bottom left section of the door moved an eighth on an inch. Tim was encouraged. He tossed the hammer onto the floor and grabbed a crowbar. "Come on you two. Grab that bar and give me a hand. This piece might slide out of the door and fall over. That'll leave a hole big enough for us to fit through."

Charlie grabbed the other crowbar and joined him. Cathy grabbed the end of Tim's crowbar and gave him an impish wink. Together they heaved and groaned as the weighty chunk of granite slowly began to slide across the polished floor. With a final mighty shove, they managed to get it clear of the door. "It's not going to fall over. It's too thick. But I think we can slide it up against the wall, out of the way a bit. Lucky this floor's so smooth and slippery."

Again they pushed the slab of rock with all their might, until it had moved about two feet back from the door. They spun it ninety degrees and slid it up against the wall. "That's got the little bastard out of the way. Now let's see what's on the other side."

CHAPTER 11

At first no-one moved. Each waiting for someone to volunteer to go first. Finally Tim stood up and, with some trepidation, picked up his lantern and headed for the door. "Well I guess it's time to take a look. Are you coming?" Cathy stretched out her hand and Tim helped her to her feet. Charlie rose slowly, almost reluctantly, collected two unlit lanterns and a spare torch and crammed them into his backpack.

He then slung a spare canteen of water over his left shoulder. Cathy grabbed the other lantern and a canteen. Tim waited for them at the door. After a nervous glace around, he crawled through the newly breached portal. The others quickly followed.

When they gathered on the other side, Tim pulled out his torch. "I think I'll use this until we get to the end of the corridor. It seems an awful long way. I also think we should keep an eye out for booby traps... just in case." That was the type of reassurance no-one needed to hear.

Already their hearts were filled with apprehension, as they stood uneasily in the dimly lit corridor. Charlie had broken out in a cold nervous sweat. Cathy had an inexplicable tingling in her fingers and an occasional cold shudder ran up her spine. The air was thick and musty and you could cut the silence with a knife. If the lights were extinguished, it seemed the darkness would instantly swallow them. Wrapping around them like an ethereal funeral shroud.

Tim alone felt at ease. His anticipation of discovery far outstripped his fear. Now he knew exactly how Lord Carnarvon's team felt when they first entered the tomb of Tutankhamen. The adrenaline was surging through Tim's veins as he confidently strode into the unknown.

All the while his torch slashed from side to side, as he checked the floor, ceiling and walls of the corridor. When he reached Charlie's recalcitrant chisel, he casually kicked it against the wall. "I must remember to pick that up on the way back."

The others mumbled in accord as they pressed on. Every now and then Tim would stop, look behind to ensure the others were following, and then shine the torch up at the roof. Never was there a sign of anything untoward on the highly glazed walls. Never did the corridor vary in size. It remained unerringly smooth and straight, a constant ten yards wide by ten yards high.

After walking for some distance, they reached a T-intersection. Tim had been pacing the corridor out as he went. It was as straight as a rifle barrel for just over a hundred yards. He stopped in the middle of the intersection and shone the torch left and right. In both directions the probing beam disappeared into an inky black oblivion.

It appeared that no matter which direction they chose, they were in for another long walk. Tim turned to Cathy and broke the unnerving silence with a low whisper. "Which way?" She stared apprehensively at the vanishing torch beam, as he once again probed the darkness. First down the left corridor and then down the right. Finally she whispered back. "I don't know. Whatever you think."

Tim looked to Charlie for guidance, but he just shrugged his shoulders and smiled nervously. Finally Tim decided to go right. It wasn't a hard choice. He just chose one option over the other, based on nothing more than the fact that he was facing to the right when he determined it was time to move on. Another ten yards or so down the corridor, Tim suddenly stopped and turned around to Charlie. A large smile alerted Charlie to an epiphany. "I think I know what we've found.

I think we've stumbled across an old World War Two command base." he suggested. "What makes you think that?" Cathy asked. "Well it makes sense. A bomb-proof place hidden in the side of a mountain in North Queensland. From here military commanders could issue orders and direct the war in safety. There are lots of them scattered throughout the north of the country they reckon." But Charlie was not convinced. "Yes, but that doesn't explain the old timer's dynamite caving in the roof. It looks as if this tunnel was sealed long before that. Before the First World War even. Besides, it's a bit neat for an air-raid shelter. I mean the polished walls and all."

Tim thought about it for a moment before conceding the point. "Oh yeah. I forgot about that. But I can't see it being anything else. Maybe they blew the roof in again when they were finished here?" he postulated. "Maybe."

Cathy joined the conversation. "Grandpa was here during the war and he never mentioned anything about a command base. In fact he was pretty sure no military people ever came out this way during the war." Tim conceded defeat. As he strolled past Charlie, he gave him a reassuring pat on the back, then strode off into the void. Hesitantly at first, Charlie followed, as Cathy hurried to catch up with Tim.

Tim's effulgent torch beam danced across the floor, up the left wall, over the roof and finally down the right wall, in a continuous helical motion, as he inched his way forward, probing the darkness for any signs of danger. The others behind him swept their lanterns nervously from side to side. The dancing yellow glow added a surreal animated light to the already creepy atmosphere. Still no sign of any booby traps. No sign either of any deviation in the size of the corridor.

Suddenly the corridor gave way to an enormous rounded cavern. Even in the distorting darkness, barely pierced by the minuscule torchlight, it was impressive.

It appeared to be a massive, perfectly circular opening. Tim wandered into the centre of the void and shone his torch upwards. He could just make out the domed roof, high above their heads. As he continued to probe skyward, he saw a balcony, cut into the sheer rock walls. He slowly followed it around with his torch as it ran the full orbit of the chamber. Unexpectedly, he caught a glimpse of shining metal. On closer inspection it looked like stainless steel hand railing, standing about half the height of the opening. There were three rails equally spaced and a post every ten yards or so. He could not help but wonder what lay beyond.

In the limited glow of the lamps, despite the piercing flashes from the torches, the extensive room defied comprehension. With their backs to the corridor that led them to the hallway, they saw a series of five radial corridors, like the spokes of a wagon wheel. They started on their immediate left, then every forty-five degrees another corridor speared into the darkness, culminating in a fifth corridor to their immediate right. As they turned to face the corridor they had entered through, they saw the short corridor, running off to their left at forty-five degrees.

Forty-five degrees to their right was a massive set of doors. They stood and stared, dumbstruck by what lay before them. Charlie was conscious of the small beads of sweat running down the back of his neck and soaking into his collar. His body convulsed, as a cold shiver sped up his spine. Cathy stood frozen to the spot, clinging tightly to Tim's arm. Anxiously darting her eyes back and forth across the vast opening. Finally Tim turned to Charlie. "Look at the size of those doors?"

"I think this blows your military theory. The doors look like they match the size of the monster in the drawing. Looks like this might have been their base. Luckily, by the dust on the floor, they've been gone for a very long time."

Tim quickly flashed his torch down at his feet. He had not noticed it before. But sure enough, there was a fine layer of light coloured dust covering the floor. Their footprints were plainly visible as they cut through the thin powdery blanket and left a shiny trail on the polished floor.

Now that Tim was regaining some confidence, he no longer whispered. "I think you're right about the base. This certainly explains a lot. I also agree that the place is abandoned. No-one's trodden on this floor for yonks. I think we can assume that whoever was here left a long time ago. But I'd still be wary of booby traps."

Cautiously they approached the closed doors. Tim pushed gently on the left door and, to his surprise, it swung open with amazing ease. He looked quizzically at Charlie, who returned his look with a typical nonchalant shrug of his shoulders. Slowly they inched into the room, their lamps hardly turning back the darkness within. Cathy clung relentlessly to Tim's arm. But Charlie had found a new sense of adventure, a new bravado. His confidence fuelled by the logical assumption that the thin veneer of dust on the floor indicated that the place was abandoned. And had been so for a very long time.

The room was enormous and roughly square in shape. Tim estimated it to be at least fifty to sixty yards square. It was laid out with rows of long tables, each lined with very large, but comfortable chairs. The furniture was functional and familiar, yet distinctly different. They slowly wandered about the shadowy room, inspecting it yard by yard in the distorting light of their lanterns.

Around the edges of the room were smaller tables, each with only four chairs. There seemed to be some personal belongings on these smaller tables. There were also shelves along one wall, filled with strange plastic-like cards.

By the wear on the floor near the main entrance, someone had been living here for aeons. But by the amount of equipment lying around, they seemed to have left in a hurry. Or with lightly packed suitcases.

At the rear was a large counter, which ran half the width of the room. Beyond that was another set of doors. Tim cautiously approached the doors. Again he pushed the left door gently. Once again, the door swung silently and effortlessly. Their torch beams were instantly reflected off a multitude of shiny metal surfaces. It too had the look of polished stainless steel.

Tim smiled as he recognised a few items. "I'll be damned! This is a kitchen. Outside must be the mess hall. No wonder the floor near the entrance is worn. This is where everyone came to eat. Would you look at the size of those pots? And look at the cooking utensils. Christ, these spoons are the size of a small skillet. I wonder where the stoves are."

"Over here!" Charlie beckoned. "Look at this. They have pots on them but I don't see any elements or gas jets. I wonder how they work. Maybe by induction I guess. All this metal looks like stainless steel. But they're heavier than I expected. Look, even most of the utensils are made of it. I'll grab one of the forks and take it with us. A mate of mine can tell me what it's made of."

They continued to dart excitedly through the kitchen area for some time, gibbering at each other with each new discovery. It was difficult to come to terms with the immensity of the room. Although it seemed to be fully equipped and ready to go, the undisturbed dust that finely coated everything suggested that it had been idle for quite some time. Tim and Cathy paused and waited for Charlie to join them, as they stood before another door at the rear of the kitchen. Charlie volunteered to push the door open. Again, when the huge door was pushed, it opened effortlessly.

"It looks like a storeroom. Do you want to take a look?" he asked. "Why not? You right, Cathy?" Tim asked, a little concerned that she was being overwhelmed by the eeriness of the place. She nodded hesitantly. "Yes, I guess so. I'm getting used to it now. I must admit, I was a bit nervous at first, but it looks like it's abandoned. I think most of the butterflies have settled down now."

The warehouse was some fifty yards wide by a hundred long. It was divided into aisles by rows of shelving that reached from the floor to the thirty foot ceiling. Tim stood at the entrance, surveying the imposing room with his torch. As the beam flitted to and fro, it suddenly stopped. It was focussed on a large box on the nearest shelf.

Tim muttered in disbelief. "Oh shit! Look at that!"

CHAPTER 12

Cathy and Charlie both gazed at the object illuminated by his torch beam, not quite understanding his excitement. "What?" Charlie finally asked in frustration. Tim pointed at the box excitedly. "That box has some writing on it." The others just nodded nonchalantly. Charlie then added. "Well I guess it would have to. How else would they know what was in their warehouse?"

But they had obviously not looked closely at the writing, so Tim urged them to do so. "Yeah, but look at the writing will you." he pleaded. Charlie wandered toward the box in question. He had only gone a couple of paces when he suddenly stopped. He stared at the box in disbelief as he recognised the writing. Now he understood Tim's amazement. "I'll be stuffed. Is that ancient Egyptian?"

Tim and Cathy joined him. All their lamps and torches now focussed on the box. Tim peered at it for a moment. He turned to Cathy and mused. "It's ancient Egyptian script alright. It says the contents are some sort of beans. This is starting to get a bit weird. Why would this language be used here?"

Cathy studied the ornate hieroglyphs for a few seconds and then looked back at Tim. "Do you think there's a connection between this excavation and ancient Egypt?" Tim slowly shook his head in disbelief, trying in vain to see a logical connection. Finally he admitted defeat. "I can't see it, but there has to be. The language is so unique it can't be a coincidence." he concluded. Tim stood in stunned silence, staring at the box for a few more minutes. He finally shifted his torch beam to the next row. On the shelves were more boxes. Sure enough, they too had Egyptian writing on them.

"It's preserved fruit of some kind." he explained. "I'm familiar with the word, but I don't know exactly what kind of fruit it is." Charlie wandered over and reached for his pocket knife. "The box looks like it's made of plastic. I'll cut it open and see what's inside." Tim and Cathy shone their torches on the box and watched as Charlie cut it open. "This stuff cuts pretty easy, but it's really hard to tear. It's very light too. I wonder what it is. I think I'll take this little bit back with me and have it analysed." He neatly folded the freshly cut piece of material and put it in his shirt pocket, doing up the button to prevent its inadvertent escape.

Then he looked into the newly opened box. After some hesitation, he reached in and extracted a small container. It too was made of a plastic-like material. Embedded within the material was a label, complete with a strange, almost 3-D, picture and description of the contents. "Look at this. It looks like peach slices. What does it say Tim?"

He handed the container to Tim, who studied it carefully for a few minutes. Finally he handed it back. "I still can't work out the fruit from the writing, but it does look like peaches. And it's preserved in... I think it's sugar syrup. According to the label, it should last forever. There's some sort of manufacturer's guarantee of purity and infinite longevity. There's a code along the bottom, but I can't work out what it means. Probably a date of manufacture and a batch number I guess."

Charlie dropped the peaches in his backpack with the fork. "I might grab some more food samples while we're here. It'll be interesting to see exactly what they are... and what they taste like." Cathy and Tim looked at him in a mixture of disbelief and disgust. "You're not going to eat that stuff?" Charlie shrugged his shoulders. "Why not?" Cathy looked at Tim, but when she received only a raised eyebrow and a non-committal shrug, she looked back at Charlie. "OK! You eat... we'll watch."

They wandered in silence up and down the aisles, looking incredulously at the thousands of boxes of food. Tim periodically stopped and read the contents of a box. Charlie cut open several more boxes and took samples. Finally Cathy spoke. "There's enough food here to feed an army. Either there were a lot of people here, or they planned to stay for an awful long time." Charlie and Tim mumbled agreement as they continued to search the warehouse.

Coming to the end of a row, Tim noticed a single door in the left-hand corner of the back wall. He turned to Charlie. "I wonder where that goes." he mused. "Dunno. Maybe it leads to another store. You want to take a look?" Charlie suggested. "Sure, why not?" They walked over to the door and pushed. Nothing happened. As he prepared to give the door an encouraging shove, Charlie noticed the small touch-pad. "Look at this will you? It looks like a keypad. That means this door must be electrically or mechanically operated." He pushed the pad and waited.

Nothing. He tried again. Still nothing. In frustration he shrugged his shoulders and wandered off, turning to Tim to explain his actions. "I guess it must be broken. Either that, or it's electrically operated and the power's switched off. Anyway, I think I've seen enough of the kitchen. Where to now?" Tim quickly looked around. "I want to find out the extent of the accommodation. That'll give us an idea how many lived here at any given time. Whether it's a few dozen or a few thousand."

Charlie nodded. "I'm OK with that." Tim looked around for a few seconds, then pointed to his right. "Let's start with those corridors that run off the large cavern then. That'd be the most logical place for any accommodation." Cathy agreed. "Good idea." As they entered the kitchen, Tim turned left. Cathy followed but Charlie stopped. "Where are you going?

I thought the cavern was over here." he almost pleaded. "It is." Tim assured him. "But I thought while we're here, I'd better just look at the far side of the kitchen. We haven't been over this way before. I thought I saw some bookshelves. I won't be a minute." Charlie hurried to catch up with the others, still feeling uneasy being left on his own.

When they reached the other side of the room, they were confronted by another set of doors. Again they were massive. Each door was at least twelve feet wide and twenty feet tall. Tim pushed the doors open and entered the room. At first glance it appeared to be a control room. There were tables and chairs scattered everywhere. More interestingly, there were strange computer-like keyboards scattered around, each with its incumbent circular screen.

Charlie instinctively rushed toward the nearest keyboard and began to study it with keen interest. "Well I'll be stuffed. Whoever was here was high-tech. Very high-tech indeed. Look at this? The technology here is amazing. The screen looks like some advanced form of LCD... but there's no cabling between it and the keyboard. And the keyboard... it's as pretty as a picture. It looks like a membrane operating system of some sort. But I can't find the CPU. I wonder if it's integral with the keyboard... and what protocol it uses.

I wonder what sort of memory system it's got. I bet it's a fast bastard. Look, there's a stack of cards. They look like sealed floppy discs or something. But I can't see any moving parts... no spindle holes. And I can't see any ports or interface units where these things go.

I wonder how they work. Is this a stand-alone unit or is it networked? Jeez I wish I could turn this thing on and have a play. I could get my doctorate with one of these little puppies." Charlie continued gushing techno-gibberish, as he excitedly climbed into the gigantic chair that stood next to the terminal.

Tim and Cathy looked on with feigned interest, but understood nothing of his conversation. Like a kid with a new toy, his pulse raced fervently. Charlie reached out and touched the keypad, almost as if he expected to get a response. Then, disappointed with the lack of reaction, he slowly, almost intimately, ran his fingers over the screen.

Tim and Cathy watched him for a while, before Tim's curiosity led him away. He turned off his torch to save the batteries and placed it on the table next to Charlie. He reached for Cathy's hand. Hand in hand, they slowly wandered towards the other end of the room, casually glancing at objects as their flickering lamps brought them into focus.

They were almost at the other end of room when Tim stopped in his tracks. His heart began to race wildly. He felt the adrenaline surge as he froze in fear. Somehow he managed to retain enough strength to hold onto his lantern, now shaking violently in his trembling hand. Unwilling to speak he stood there, immobilized at the sight that confronted him.

There, not more than a few yards away, stood ten or more colossal warriors. They were dressed in what appeared to be full battle gear. Their strange dark brown, leather-like uniforms were in stark contrast to the pale skin of their hands. Although their hands were empty, their abundant weapons were plainly visible. They were hanging from their wide leather belts like stage props from a Star Wars movie.

Their gold greaves, shining above their matt black boots, impressive as they were, seemed somehow anachronistic. Their trousers too seemed to be made of a dark leathery material. Their polished gold breastplates were embossed with a large central, almost Celtic, pattern of inter-woven lines. They seemed to be more ceremonial than practical, being tied over their uniforms with heavy gold chain.

As he continued to stare at the warriors, Tim finally became cognisant. He focussed on their faces, taking note of their features. Their hair was fair. Their eyes were a piercing blue. Then he noticed the feline features. The half-man, half-cat creatures from the legends of the South American Jaguar cult. Their faces were covered in a fine layer of hair, with whisker-like tufts protruding above their eyes. Just like those of a cat. Their noses were button-like and triangular. Just like those of a cat. Their ears were pointed and situated high in the side of their heads. Almost like those of a cat.

He was stunned. He could not tell if he was delirious with excitement or nearly fainting with fear. His emotions were running riot as he stood, knees trembling, anchored to the spot.

Illuminated by the quivering flame of his lamp, the warriors stood silently and stared. Their piercing blue eyes focussed on Tim. His adrenaline-flooded mind began asking questions at a million miles an hour. Why were they simply staring at him? Why were they standing in the dark? If they were feline, could they see in the dark? Come to think of it, he had not seen any light fittings anywhere along the ceilings or walls of the corridors or rooms he had inspected. Were they ready to attack? What should he do if they did? Could he communicate with them? Should he try Egyptian?

Tim had all but forgotten about Cathy, standing beside him, clenching his hand with all her might. She too had seen the warriors and was riveted to the floor in fear. She stared vacantly, like a bird hypnotised by a snake. Sweat was trickling down the back of her neck. She was transfixed by the blue staring eyes of the silent gargantuan figures. Her hands were trembling, her heart pounding. She could feel the strength ebbing from her legs as her knees began to quiver. Never had she felt so utterly terrified. Never had she felt so vulnerable and helpless.

Never in her worst nightmares had she imagined creatures so imposing. All the worst-case scenarios were running through Tim's head when Charlie casually wandered up behind them. His approach was not heard. He casually tapped Cathy on the shoulder. The startling gesture was too much for her and she let out an ear-piercing scream. It was not the reaction Charlie was expecting. He recoiled backwards and yelled, more in fright than anger. "What the hell's wrong with you?"

Without turning his head, Tim simply raised his shaking lantern to further illuminate the warriors. They were still standing there. Deathly silent, dead still. Staring intently at the intruders. Charlie, oblivious to their dilemma, kept looking at the back of Tim's head, waiting for him to turn around.

When it became obvious that he was staring at something, Charlie's eyes followed the feeble light as Tim slowly raised his lantern even higher. Charlie saw the warriors and froze. His breath left him and refused to return without a great deal of coaxing. He swallowed hard and gasped for air as he stared in disbelief, his mind trying to comprehend the foreboding size of the warriors. His heart started pounding audibly against his ribs. He felt the surge of adrenaline flood through his body, as his fight-or-flight responses kicked in.

He was thinking flight, but that was not an option. His body had frozen at the intimidating sight. They all stood in stunned silence, pondering their next move. Should they approach the warriors and attempt to communicate with them? Or would this be seen as an act of aggression and invoke a messy response? Should they back away with dignity? Should they turn and run like hell and hope to make it out alive?

They independently decided to wait for the warriors to make the first, hopefully friendly, move. So they waited. And waited. After several agonising minutes, Charlie finally plucked up the courage to whisper.

"What do we do now?" Tim kept staring ahead and slowly shook his head as he whispered his reply. "I don't know, but I wish they would at least smile at us. That stare is going through me like an X-ray."

Charlie muttered something, then, leaning forward, whispered in Tim's ear. "I know what you mean. But if they haven't killed us yet, maybe they don't intend to." Tim nodded. "You're right..." he whispered back, with a nervous laugh. "Look, I'm the one who got us into this mess. I'll approach them and see if we can't apologise for breaking into their camp. You never know, they might be a friendly bunch of chaps."

Charlie was unconvinced, but nodded tentatively anyway. Tim let go of Cathy's hand and cautiously moved a couple of paces toward the warriors. He addressed what appeared to be, by the red outlined pattern on his breastplate, the senior officer. "*Nuk meh... embah aa neb Amentet...*"

He croaked the greeting nervously. It was the best he could do in the ancient Egyptian tongue. Tim hesitated for a moment then slowly approached closer still. "*...mak thenth-k em matkheru...*" He paused, now only some ten feet from the nearest figure. He waited for a response. Still the warriors would not reply. They remained silent. Their fixed stares making Tim even more nervous.

Deciding that a tactical withdrawal might be in order, he moved off to one side. His lantern quaking in tune with his nerve racked body. As Tim moved backwards, he failed to notice one of the small plastic cards on the smooth floor. As he stepped on it, his foot slipped out from under him, sending him tumbling backwards, landing awkwardly on his backside. As he was falling, he instinctively grabbed his lantern handle with both hands, saving it from crashing to the floor. If he survived, the bruise on his backside was going to be impressive come morning.

Trying to retain as much dignity as he could under the circumstances, Tim composed himself while still sitting on the floor. Then he raised his lantern to illuminate the warriors and apologised for his clumsiness. Although their eyes followed him, not one of the warriors had flinched or moved a muscle. It was most unnerving. As he sat there, too frightened to move, he noticed something strange.

The warriors were not standing on the floor. In fact they seemed to be suspended several inches off the ground. It didn't sink in at first. But as he continued to stare, he was struck by a sudden thought. He leapt to his feet and raced over to Charlie. He slapped him vigorously on the back and exclaimed loudly. "What a silly mob of bastards we are!"

Charlie's eyes bulged in disbelief at Tim's sudden outburst of unfettered bravery. "They're not real!" Tim explained, as he raced towards the motionless figures. He prodded the nearest one in the middle of the chest to emphasise his point. "See, it's just a bloody high-tech... scare the shit out of you real... 3D holographic picture. This is just a three dimensional hologram of the former occupants, staring blankly across time. Standing there in all their fierce glory, ready to scare the crap out of any poor bastard who happens to find them."

He motioned for Cathy and Charlie to join him, as he stood touching the almost invisible screen within which the life-size images stood. It looked similar to the computer screens, although it was much larger and rectangular in shape. It appeared to be sitting on the floor, but was obviously also anchored to the wall. Tim finally tried to lighten the mood as he laughed light-heartedly at Charlie. "Well I guess the aboriginal painting was right. That's what they looked like. Rather awesome looking devils aren't they?" Charlie smiled nervously. "I'll say. But that photo's bloody good stuff, however they did it.

It sure as hell looked like they were standing right there in front of us. Look, they even seem to move as I walk around. It's like they're watching me. Shit this place is spooky. I just hope you're right and they've all gone. By the way... exactly what did you say to them?" he asked. Tim smiled modestly. "Oh, I just said I'm sorry. And acknowledged that we were in the presence of the great lords of the underworld. That sort of stuff." Just as he finished speaking, his lantern flickered out. "Christ, I'm glad that didn't happen five minutes ago. I would have bloody near shit myself."

Tim looked over at Cathy and laughed nervously. "Have we been in here that long?" Cathy rushed over to Tim and gave him a rib-crushing hug. The emotional roller coaster was over and she sighed loudly in relief. When she had composed herself, she looked at her watch. "It's ten o'clock already. We've been in here for four hours." Tim looked over at Charlie. "We'd better refuel these lamps and head back to camp. After dinner we can get properly organized. Then tomorrow we can explore this place thoroughly."

As they wandered back past the great hall, Charlie mumbled to himself. "God, this is amazing!" Tim whipped his head around at Charlie and almost snapped at him in his excitement. "What did you say?" Charlie was taken aback. "What?" Tim repeated himself. "I said, what did you just say?" Charlie looked at him for a moment, wondering where the urgency in his voice came from. "I said this is amazing."

"No you didn't. You said... *God, this is amazing.*" Charlie shrugged his shoulders. He was confused with Tim's line of questioning. "So?" Tim was almost grinning by now. "So... that's it. That's how this all ties up." Charlie shook his head in confusion. "What on earth are you on about?" Tim slowed down to explain his thoughts. "The ancient Egyptian script. These blokes weren't copying a text they found on earth.

They brought their text here and the Egyptians copied them. I think we've found the original Gods of Egypt. I think Ptah, Seth, Thoth, et al, were based on real characters. Our warriors perhaps... or those they were protecting."

"What do you mean... protecting?" Charlie asked, still somewhat confused by Tim's hypothesis. Tim smiled. "Well... what do soldiers generally do?" he asked. Charlie shrugged his shoulders. "Fight I guess." It was the only thing he could think of. Tim nodded. "It's rare for a warrior race to exist purely as warriors.

They generally have a purpose, a master. Someone who organizes them and uses them for political or social purposes." he elaborated. "Oh, yeah." Charlie mused.

The remainder of the long walk back to the camp was mostly in silence, as they each mulled over their day's personal experiences. After a few nerve-calming beers and a good feed, they slipped into bed to try to get a good night's sleep. That would not be easy. Tomorrow promised to be an exciting day.

CHAPTER 13

After a restless night, the languid but excited team scoffed down a hastily prepared breakfast. They busied themselves gathering food and equipment for the day's adventure. They took enough food, water and kerosene for twenty-four hours. Just in case they needed it. The men eagerly loaded their backpacks, as Cathy gathered their essential needs.

When all was packed and ready, Tim wandered over to the vehicle and grabbed his camera. "I'll think I'll take this today. I'll need some photos of the complex to study in detail when we get home." Before leaving camp, Tim took a cursory look around, nodding to himself. He was satisfied they had everything they might need. Charlie winked at Tim. "Let's go?"

With anxious smiles all round, they set off for the tunnel. Their mood was jovial, as they headed toward the great cavern. Tim in particular was eager to explore the six corridors that radiated from the main central hall. He knew there was a kitchen and a recreation room. Now he wanted to find the accommodation units.

Although it was a long way to walk, they seemed to get there in no time at all. As they reached the centre of the great domed hallway they stopped. Tim flashed his torch around for a suitable place to begin his search. Eventually he stopped with the piercing beam illuminating the corridor opposite them. "Well, which one do you think we should try first?"

Cathy and Charlie both shrugged their shoulders indifferently. Tim took that as tacit approval for him to make the decision. Looking around, he decided to start with the first one on the right as they entered the hall. Then he decided it would be logical if they methodically checked each corridor in turn.

He advised the others of his plan and they agreed. It was, after all, as good a plan as any. They headed off toward the first corridor, eager to explore. Although excitement ruled their emotions, they were still very nervous. Yesterday's encounter was foremost in their minds as their meagre lights pierced the ominous darkness. There were too many questions that needed answers. Too many things that did not quite add up. And too many things that could potentially go wrong.

When they entered the corridor, they were disappointed. Only fifteen yards long, it terminated in a granite door similar to the one they had smashed through to gain entry into the base. Tim wandered over to the door and ran his hand up and down the highly polished surface. "We didn't bring the sledgehammers, so I don't know how we're going to get in." he moaned.

Then Charlie pointed out the control pad to the others. "Look, there's a control pad like the door at the warehouse. We won't be getting in here unless we can find the power source and get it working." he surmised. Tim reluctantly agreed and then added. "Otherwise, if we have time before we go home, we might see if we can smash our way in. I'd like to explore as much of the base as possible before we leave But I don't really want to break our way into everything."

Disappointed with their lack of success, Tim led the trio to the next corridor. This one was much longer, over a hundred yards as it turned out. Along each side of the corridor, at regular intervals, were more doors. Each with a control pad, similar to that in the first corridor. As they continued to the end, they were met with another door. Tim stood staring at it for some time, disappointed that he had again failed to find anything of significance. "Well what do you make of this?"

Charlie and Cathy stood quietly for some time, trying to formulate some hypothesis that could explain what they had seen. Finally Cathy answered.

"Do you think these are the accommodation units?" she offered as a suitable explanation. Tim shrugged his shoulders. "I guess they could be. It looks like the sort of layout you'd expect to find in a barracks. And it's the logical place for them, right next to the mess. Let's check out the other corridors."

The next corridor was exactly the same. It was about a hundred yards long and ten yards wide by ten yards high. Off each side were five regularly spaced doors, with another door at end of the corridor. Suddenly Tim had a thought. He paced out the width of the corridor while the others watched him. "These corridors are all exactly the same size. Just over ten feet. Given the Egyptian writing we found in the warehouse, I'd say they were an exact measurement wide. Six royal cubits! That's just less than ten feet five inches." he explained.

The others were moderately impressed by Tim's trivial revelation, but said nothing as he wandered off to inspect the remaining corridors. All three were identical to the first. As they stood at the last door, Tim turned to Charlie. "Well I guess we've found the accommodation units. But I'd love to get to the other side of one of these doors.

We still don't know how many men this base could accommodate. I mean, the kitchen is enormous but we've only found fifty or so rooms. Do they accommodate a single person, or are they each a gigantic dormitory that sleeps hundreds? I'm going to have to smash one of those doors before we leave. I really need to know how many men were here at any one time." he insisted.

Charlie and Cathy feigned interest by nodding, but Charlie was not looking forward to another session on the hammer. The first door had nearly killed him. He figured it represented too much hard work. He would let Tim smash down the next door, while he had another look at the computers.

In an effort to change the subject, he motioned towards the small recesses between each corridor. "What do you reckon they are?" he asked. "I don't know. Let's have a look shall we?" Relishing the thought of finding something interesting, they headed off to inspect the nearest recess. "It's a spiral staircase leading up to the balcony." Charlie explained. "Wait here a second. I'll slip up there and have a quick look around if you like. I'll bet it's more accommodation units."

Cathy and Tim stood in the middle of the central cavern, trying to follow Charlie with their torch beams. That proved impractical as he climbed the stairs and eventually disappeared, so they sat down and waited. They could hear Charlie puffing and grunting as he struggled up the giant stairway. When he reached the top, he quickly flashed his torch from side to side.

As expected, to his right and left were radial corridors similar to those below. He wandered over to the one on his right. He shone his torch into the darkness and it disappeared into the inky depths of the corridor. Satisfied that they were more accommodation units, he wandered over to the handrail that rimmed the balcony. He shone his torch around the perimeter of the balcony, then down at the others sitting in the middle of the hall below. "It's the same as down there, just a series of radial corridors." he explained. "But it looks like a door on the opposite side over there. Do you want to come up and have a look?"

Tim thought about it, but concluded it was probably a waste of time. "Not really. As you say, it just looks like more accommodation units. I guess they've all got doors on them like the ones down here. So until we can open the doors, we'll be wasting our time. Anyway, I've been thinking about the layout of the base as we know it so far." he mused. "What about it?" Cathy asked. "I was wondering where the left branch of the intersection leads. The one at the end of the main entrance corridor.

We've always turned right. What if we turned left?" Charlie nodded. "What indeed? Wait there, I'll be down in a second." As Charlie rejoined them, Tim and Cathy stood up. Cathy noticed the fine dust clinging to Tim's jeans and playfully dusted it off. Tim reciprocated. A few moments of quiet anticipation followed as no-one seemed eager to lead the trio. After jostling for position, they finally fell in behind Tim as he headed toward the entrance. Soon they were at the T-intersection.

If they turned left, it would lead them back to their camp. But they pressed straight on. As he walked ahead, Tim leisurely gyrated his torch from side to ceiling to side to floor. He was still wary of booby traps.

About a hundred yards from the intersection, the corridor opened into another expansive cavern. As Tim strode into the opening, something on his left softly reflected the scattered light from his lantern. The unexpected glint caught his eye. He swung his torch around to see what it was.

There in front of them stood an imposing spherical vessel, made of a very shiny or highly polished metal that looked like gold. Tim estimated it to be some seventy-five feet ·in diameter. The unit seemed to be supported by a series of large five foot diameter legs, six in all. They dropped from the underbelly of the sphere and disappeared through the floor below.

On closer inspection, they too were highly polished. Only they were made of a silver metal. Charlie wandered over to the vessel and looked it over. After a cursory inspection, he declared confidently to everyone what he concluded it to be. "Well I'll be stuffed. It looks their power generation plant." he confidently stated.

"What makes you think that?" Tim asked. "Gut feeling!" Charlie admitted. "But look at all this shit. It's sort of familiar, like a nuclear reactor or something. I suppose there's only so many ways you can generate and control power. I wonder what their fuel source was.

That generator looks like it's made of solid gold. If it is, it's got to be worth a fortune in scrap metal alone." he mused. "Let's go have a look see shall we?"

As Tim and Cathy quietly explored the massive golden sphere, Charlie instinctively headed for a control panel along the rear wall of the room. Above the control panel was a series of large Egyptian symbols, carved into the granite. It looked like they had been embossed with gold. Charlie asked Tim to join him, then pointed them out. "Very impressive, but what does that say?"

Tim looked at the writing carefully before answering. "*shefat* ...it means *strength, might, power, energy* ...that sort of thing." Charlie broke into a self-congratulatory smile, then looked down at the panel. "Look, Tim, there's more of these symbols on this panel. What do they say?" Tim looked around. He smiled when he recognised a symbol and frowned when he saw something unfamiliar.

Eventually he pointed a few out to an impatient Charlie. "*mahi* ...*to direct or supervise... ab* ...*to cease or stop... shua* ...*to begin... aten* ...*an opening* of some sort, possibly an air-hole. But I can't decipher them all. They're definitely Egyptian, yet some are totally foreign to me." Charlie looked at the symbols, then looked over at Tim and smiled. He offered him a wild, stab-in-the-dark, explanation. "Well it's obvious these fellows were more high-tech than the Egyptians. Maybe these symbols were never needed in the low science world of the Pharaohs." he speculated.

Tim nodded. "Maybe you're right." he conceded, as he mulled the idea over. Then he pointed to the symbols on the control panels. "So, Mr. Engineer, what do these symbols mean then?" Charlie stared at them for a moment as he thought about their meaning. After some consideration, he decided he had a rough idea of what it was they were dealing with. "Well by the size of the unit, I'd say this was the main power generation room.

And I'd expect those symbols to be labelling the various circuits being fed from here. The entire base is operated from this control panel. See, there are more computers over there." he explained, pointing to his left.

Tim slowly looked around, still trying to comprehend the enormity of their find. It was indeed a bewildering spectacle. Finally he turned to Cathy. "Well, what do you think, Cathy?" Cathy shrugged her shoulders. "I don't know. Charlie's the expert. What do you reckon, Charlie?" Charlie looked over to Cathy and raised his lamp to illuminate her face. "About what?"

Cathy pointed at the sphere. "About how they generated their power. I'm only familiar with diesel generators, and I don't see any fuel tanks around." Charlie shrugged his shoulders. "Well it's probably some sort of nuclear plant. Might even be nuclear fusion." Tim looked at him in surprise. "What makes you so sure?" he asked.

"Well I'm not sure at all." he immediately conceded. "But these people were very high tech. It figures they'd have a very highly advanced power generation system. Besides, there's no plumbing for hydro-power. And there aren't any obvious pipes for gaseous or liquid fuels either. Unless it comes up through those silver legs. But they look a bit too large for fuel lines. So with my limited knowledge of power generation, I'd have to opt for some sort of nuclear power." he concluded.

Tim was sceptical. "Well I can't really comment on that. It's not my cup of tea. But if this is the reactor, then where are all the control rods, cooling systems and so forth you always see on the TV when they show nuclear power stations?" he intimated. Charlie shook his head. "It's got me buggered. I'm an Electronics Engineer... not Electrical. I'm only going on what I vaguely remember from uni. And that isn't a hell of a lot. Maybe it's so high-tech they don't need any of that stuff. Maybe it's something to do with cold fusion.

I guess the gold reactor chamber is the key. Maybe they've perfected cold fusion reactors. You know. Like copying the nuclear reactions that occur naturally in the sun, but without all the heat. The Yanks have been experimenting with that for years. It's perfectly clean. There's no radioactive waste and it runs on hydrogen. It's cheap to run and would power the earth indefinitely if they could perfect it. If only I could reverse engineer this puppy. I'd be rich and famous!" he mused.

"Well don't get too carried away with yourself just yet." Tim warned. Charlie chuckled to himself as he motioned Tim towards the control panel once more. Tim leant over the desk and glanced around, following his dancing torch-beam as it cut a swathe of light through the ever encroaching darkness.

Suddenly something caught his eye. He moved his attention to the shelving above the control panel. As he looked more closely under direct torchlight, he noticed the books. "Have a look at this." he beamed. "It seems to be some sort of library. Maybe it's the maintenance and operation manuals for the plant." he hoped.

"Gee, that'd be handy." Charlie agreed. "If we could read them, maybe we can get this thing running again. If we could get the lights going, it would sure make it easier to explore the rest of this place. Mind you, I haven't actually seen any lights anywhere. Have you?"

Tim was oblivious to the remarks and never heard the question, as he keenly thumbed through one of the manuals. Finally he exclaimed in a voice so loud, it scared the wits out of both Charlie and Cathy.

"Jesus! Look at this, Charlie. It's a drawing of the generator." Charlie almost knocked the book from Tim's hands in his rush to look at it. "Wow! Can you read any of it, Tim?" Tim looked over the drawing for a while, then slowly shrugged his shoulders. "Just like the rest. I can read some symbols and not others. But ignoring the writing for a bit, what do you make of it Charlie?"

Charlie perused the drawing for several minutes before summing up his theory. "Well it's hollow for one thing. And the shell's made up of all sorts of layers inside. In the centre of the sphere's another tiny sphere. What does that say, Tim?" Tim ran his eyes across the text. "It simply says... *se Ra* ...the *son of the sun god Ra*. I wonder what that means." he pondered.

Charlie was convinced he was right. "I'm still guessing it's a fusion reactor. They're copying the reaction in the sun. That little orb in there is the main reaction chamber. Look it's suspended in space. Probably by magnetics or something. I wonder what sort of energy they're extracting from it. We normally only use the heat from the atomic reaction to boil water. Then use the steam to drive turbines. But this drawing doesn't show anything like that. Can you read the name on the innermost layer of the shell?" he asked.

Tim followed Charlie's pointing finger. "It says... *seshen shesp-t*. Which roughly translated means *to make a way through for light rays*." Charlie thought about it for a minute or two. "What's the next layer say?" Tim continued. "It says... *saq shesp-t*. Which basically means *to gather light rays*. Does that make any sense to you?"

Again Charlie thought about it for a while before commenting. "Well, I'm no expert, but it looks like they've duplicated the sun. In miniature. But it looks like they're using photon energy, not heat energy." he explained. "What?" Tim asked incredulously. "Photon energy." Charlie reiterated. "You know... photo-voltaic cells... solar panels." he explained.

Tim nodded his understanding. "Oh, that's interesting. It must be pretty efficient then. I wonder how they handle the heat that's generated." he asked no-one in particular. Charlie shook his head, then looked over to the reactor. "Perhaps that's what the gold's for." he speculated. "It's a great heat conductor. And those silver legs might be supplying coolant."

Tim agreed, but conceded that knowing what it looked like was not going to help them get it operating. He closed the book and began rummaging through the others. Finally he found what he was looking for. "Well bugger me dead! This looks like an operator's manual. I can understand some of it. I think you're right. The high-tech part of the language was obviously never used in the time of the Pharaohs, so I'll have to guess that part. But some of the more general terms are easy to interpret." he admitted with some pride.

Cathy climbed up into one of the large chairs that dotted the control room and sat back. She was in way over her head. She knew nothing at all about such technical matters. So she relaxed while the men quietly discussed their options and continued their quest for illumination.

After some discussion, Charlie sat back and watched as Tim thumbed through the manual. He concentrated for quite some time, before he finally stopped and motioned for Charlie to join him. "It's the basic operating manual for the powerhouse. It looks like a training guide, so it's written in pretty basic language. If you can guess the meaning of the technical symbols from the gist of the text, we might just be able to work this out. Wanna to give it a go?" he asked.

Charlie nodded enthusiastically. "You bet. The worst thing we can do is disappear in a bloody great nuclear explosion." he stated rather chillingly, with a broad smile. Suitably reassured, they slowly worked through the manual, wandering around the plant and looking along the control panel as they did so. It was a strange procession, Tim wandering hither and yon, with Cathy holding a torch over his shoulder, so he could carry the open book and read it at the same time.

Charlie meantime, was trying his hardest to keep out of Tim's way, while at the same time, keeping close enough to look over his other shoulder.

It was painstakingly slow, but eventually they began to match symbols from the manual with labels on switches. Charlie was straining to recall all the work he had ever done on power generation and control. In hind sight it was almost zilch. And that was a long time ago. But gradually it began to come back to him. Suddenly it all made sense. Charlie dragged Tim over to the centre of the control panel where he proudly announced his epiphany. "I think I've worked it out!

See this pattern here? Well that's a mimic diagram of the power station. See... here's the generator. This looks like the main switch-room, below us where all those silver conduits go into the floor. And these are the various circuits that the station feeds.

Look, that one's an accommodation wing. And that one looks like it feeds a workshop or something. See, there are a lot of circuits all concentrated in a long line. Perhaps that's the void on the other side of the reactor on our right as we came in. I didn't have a good look up there, but the cavern looked bigger than the main accommodation area. And I thought I saw something metallic a hundred yards or so up there."

Charlie paused, a slightly concerned look on his face. "It's funny though. I've seen a lot of computer gear out there, but none of it's been plugged into anything. Even the screens are remote from the keyboards as far as I can tell. My guess is that they're either battery powered or they have a power source that transmits through the air, sort of like microwave radiation. Reminiscent of some of the Tesla experiments." he recalled. "That would explain the lack of power points and leads."

Tim shook his head. "What's Tesla?" he asked. "Who?" Charlie corrected him. "Who was Tesla? Nikola Tesla was a man. An ingenious electrical pioneer. Some of the stuff he experimented with was so radical that, when he died, the US government confiscated all his papers. And they haven't been seen since.

Rumour has it that scientists have been covertly working on them for years and things like microwave ovens are the result. Anyway, if I could get this technology patented, we'd never have to work again. This is really exciting stuff we've found here Tim."

Tim shook his head and patted Charlie on the shoulder as he laughed mockingly. "Do you really think you could make people believe you thought all this up all by yourself?" he chided. Charlie feigned a hurt expression. "Of course I could. The hard part would be getting to understand it myself first. That might be the only hurdle between us and easy street. Anyway, let's give this power station a whirl."

Tim judiciously quoted the cautionary notes from the manual, as Charlie hauled himself up into what logically appeared to be the principal controller's seat. He found an adjustment device on the gigantic chair and raised it to a level where he could reach the controls. He was amazed that the chair still worked.

With a mutually reassuring smile and a nod from Charlie, they proceeded to follow the instructions, carefully, nervously... step by step. Tim finished reading out the preliminary instructions as they prepared to start the generator. Charlie contemplated the possible consequences for a moment then turned to Tim with an air of exaggerated histrionics. "Well, this is it old buddy. At least if it goes bang we won't feel a bloody thing. You ready?"

With an approving nod from Tim and a nervous smile from Cathy, Charlie reached over and pressed the large red touch-pad in the centre of the console. They watched eagerly. Nothing. They waited... and waited. Still nothing. Not so much as a whisper.

Finally Tim looked over at Charlie's dejected figure, slumped over the control panel and offered a consoling thought. "Well, I guess it's run out of fuel. It was worth a try anyway."

Charlie sank back into the mammoth chair, feeling very dejected. He watched Cathy climb down from her chair and join Tim as he headed off to explore the rest of the base. Finally, as if afraid to be left behind, he jumped from the chair, picked up his lamp from the console and rushed after them. As he passed around the reactor he turned back for a final look at the now darkened room.

His casual glance turned into a neck-breaking spin, as he noticed a small red light glowing on the panel. His excitement was unbridled as he yelled at Tim. "Tim quick! Come and have a look at this."

Tim and Cathy raced back to the console, curious about the urgency in Charlie's voice. "What is it?" They asked in unison. "It's an indication light on the panel. See? I didn't notice it while my lamp was sitting next to it. But it's definitely glowing red." he explained.

"What does it mean?" Cathy asked. Charlie shook his head. "Well, at an educated guess, I reckon it's telling us that the reactor's working or something. It wasn't on when we got here and I guess it needs some sort of power to light it up. So..."

Tim looked slightly puzzled for a moment, as he stared at the small glowing light. Finally, satisfied that Charlie was probably right, he sat down. He then turned around and shone his torch onto the shiny golden reactor. "Why isn't there any noise?" Charlie thought about it momentarily, as he placed his lantern on the console and leapt back into the chair next to Tim.

"Well, who says it's got to make a noise?" he offered. Tim nodded. "True, we know bugger all about it. Maybe it's supposed to run silently. Who knows!" Charlie agreed, then returned his attention to more important things. He looked at the glowing light and the symbol beneath it. "What's this symbol mean, Tim?" Tim looked at the symbol for a second, then smiled. "*Reshpu*. He was a *Lightning God*.

According to the diagram here, it looks like you're right. It's the same word that's engraved on the power generator. I noticed it when we first entered, but I didn't think too deeply about it. But now I guess it makes sense. Do you want to assume the generator's working and continue with the procedures?" he asked.

Charlie nodded enthusiastically. "Sure. In for a penny, in for a pound. If it's set up like a standard power distribution system, we should be able to activate all the power circuits from this console. All we need to do is identify the circuits and switch them on. So which one do you reckon is the light switch?"

Tim slowly looked at the touch-pads and their corresponding hieroglyphs. He mused over several familiar symbols for a while, wondering which one best represented light. Eventually he settled on one and pointed to it. "That's *stiut*. It means *sunshine, radiance, light-emitter*... that sort of thing. I'd give that one a go."

Charlie edged his finger toward the touch-pad. As he reached it, he hesitated for a moment and looked up at Tim. A reassuring smile compelled him to continue. With no further deliberation, he pressed the small plastic pad. They all audibly gasped as an eerie green radiance began to form in the domed roof high above the reactor. The fog-like luminescent glow slowly expanded like a giant will-o-the-wisp, until its radiance consumed the room. As they watched in awe, the glow became brighter. Within two minutes the intensity appeared to peak.

Cathy was first to ask the obvious question. "Where are the light fittings Charlie?" Charlie's eyes wandered around the room, trying to find the source of the light. After searching unsuccessfully for some time he returned his gaze to Cathy and shrugged his shoulders.

"I don't know. It's almost like the room's filled with some sort of plasma. You know? The sort of thing you see inside a fluorescent tube.

But it's obviously not contained by anything. It's just hanging around near the roof, like a cloud of glowing smoke. What a marvellous concept. I'll have to patent that one too."

They all broke into nervous laughter as they relieved some of the built up tension. Tim was first to get back to matters at hand, returning his attention to the control panel. "Well, do you think we should go for broke?" he asked. "I can't see why not." Charlie agreed. "We ought to hit all the lighting and power circuits we can. That way we can see if we can open those doors of yours. Here goes nothing." he said, as he closed his eyes and pressed the nearest circuit button.

Soon every small indication lamp on the control panel was aglow. All the power circuits had been activated. The computer screen in the centre of the console suddenly lit up, emitting a ghostly light green glow. Charlie looked at it excitedly, as he instinctively reached for the keypad. He looked at the confusing arrangement of keys and touch-pads that made up the interface, but hesitated for a moment. Trepidation was soon replaced with anticipation as he reached out and pressed a random key.

Nothing happened. Disappointed but not beaten, he shrugged his shoulders and pressed another key. Still nothing. He continued pressing keys. Still nothing. He had hoped for a menu, but could not find one. Having run out of keys to press, he conceded temporary defeat. For now, the lights were on and they had a base to explore.

CHAPTER 14

The enormity of the complex suddenly hit home when they stepped from behind the reactor and looked down the gaping void they had passed on their way in. Once ominously dark, now it was bathed in light. A light so strong, it appeared to be full daylight.

The extraordinary glow illuminated the cavernous void as far as the eye could see. The room was over two hundred feet wide with a domed roof some hundred feet high at its peak. As for the length, it was impossible to tell. The room simply disappeared into a vanishing point in the distance.

As their eyes gradually acclimatised to the intense light, they could see the area in its magnificence. The fuzzy details previously seen in the dim, flickering lamplight and the spotlight of the stabbing torch-beams, now leapt out at them, screaming for attention.

They stood there for some time, dumbfounded by the shear magnitude of the excavation. The spectacle far exceeded their initial concepts of grandeur. Here at last, bathed in light, they were able to put the base into perspective.

Tim finally turned his attention to a distant object, shining with a metallic lustre under the intense light. He whispered incredulously. "I don't believe it. Would you look at that?" Charlie peered into the distance. "What the hell is it?" he asked. Tim shook his head as he squinted, trying to define the distant object. "I don't know. It looks like it could be another reactor."

Charlie was still staring open-mouthed at the distant object as Tim headed off towards it. Cathy remained anchored to the spot. She was too astonished to move. Eventually they realized Tim was receding in the distance, so they rushed off to catch up with him.

It was not until he approached within a hundred yards of the massive object that its identity suddenly struck home. Tim muttered to himself in disbelief. "It's a bloody flying saucer!" Then, realizing the enormity of the discovery, he turned excitedly to the others. "I think it's a bloody space ship. My god! The blackfellers were right. These people *were* living inside the mountain. And it looks like they were quite capable of flying out of it too. This room disappears into infinity. I bet this is a runway that goes right through the mountain." Charlie, his senses overloaded, simply grunted.

The craft was circular in shape and looking side-on it was like a rather plump disc. It appeared to be symmetrical, the top half being a mirror image of the bottom. The top and bottom of the craft were flat and where the two halves met, formed a sharp circumferential edge.

It looked to be around a hundred and fifty feet in diameter, with a body about fifty feet deep. There were no obvious external protuberances or openings. No windows or portholes. No antennae. No doors, ladders, footholds. Nothing. Just a very smooth shiny metallic skin. There was not even any writing. No vessel name, no fleet number, no loading information or hatch indications. Nothing. It seemed impervious.

The only thing it did have was legs. Three of them. Long, thin, cylindrical, shiny, metallic legs. They protruded from the ogive section of the underbelly. They seemed to be telescopic, holding the craft about five feet off the floor. At the base of each leg was a fitting, made up of three curved, claw-like, prongs that reminded them of talons. Ideal for gripping they concluded. They also looked like they were telescopic.

Somehow the legs looked disproportionate to the body, as if they could not support its weight. It looked rather awkward, like a duck out of water. Charlie continued to stare at the machine.

He was wondering why it had been left behind. Tim meanwhile had moved over to the craft and was excitedly inspecting it. He began shouting enthusiastically at Cathy and Charlie. "Come and have a look at this!"

Charlie edged forward and looked around the aircraft, cautiously approaching one of the telescopic support legs. He looked up at the connection point of the ship. He could see the sealing surface where the upper side of the telescopic leg joined the body of the craft and formed an airtight seal.

Curiosity forced him to run his fingers down the metal, which to his surprise felt slippery. Almost like it was Teflon coated. He noted the lack of lubricant on his fingers and the absence of oil spills on the floor, implying that the metal was self-lubricating. "Definitely no traces of oil. It must be a type of self lubricating metal." Charlie concluded, more to himself than the others. He looked up to see Tim and Cathy disappearing behind the machine. "Hey Tim! Where are you going?" he yelled.

"I can see two more over here. One looks like its loading ramp's down. You want to have a look?" Tim replied. Charlie needed no encouragement. He hurried to catch up with the others, now some twenty yards in front of him. He only caught up when they stopped to look at the lowered ramp. It was enormous. It projected down from the centre of the vessel. It was a hundred feet long and thirty feet wide.

Tim inspected it closely with Charlie. "It's longer than this half of the ship. It must be telescopic... or it would stick out when they raised it. And you can't even see where the ramp is on the other ship. It must blend in with the rest of the hull perfectly... with a microscopic joint. What brilliant engineering." Tim was amazed at the engineering of the ramp. He looked at every inch of it, trying to understand how it worked.

Finally he looked at Charlie. "It looks like this was the workshop where they serviced and repaired their fleet of aircraft. And I still can't see the end of the tunnel from here." He stared vacantly into the distance for some time. Still trying to come to terms with the enormity of the base. Finally he conceded they had to walk to the end of the tunnel, just to find the end.

Meanwhile he was keen to inspect the spacecraft. "Do you two want to have a look inside?" he asked with a smile. Charlie and Cathy needed no encouragement, as they headed towards the ramp. Tim led the way, but half way up he stopped and looked at Charlie. "I didn't notice any exhaust ports when I looked over the first craft. How do you reckon these things fly?"

"My guess is photon propulsion or electro-gravidic drives. Although I've heard rumours of a faster-than-light inertia-free propulsion unit that works on pulsed energy application. If we find a large central power source and a circumferential toroidal coil system... that might be what it's about. But who knows? These things could be driven by anything."

Tim looked incredulously at Charlie. "Where the hell do you get all this sci-fi stuff from?" Charlie shrugged his shoulders and grinned sheepishly. "I read a bit!" he offered. Tim smiled and shook his head in mock disbelief, then refocussed his attention on the beckoning opening in the ship. "After you!"

Charlie strode confidently up the remainder of the ramp and disappeared into the bowels of the craft, Cathy and Tim hot on his heels. The ramp led into the massive cargo area, which seemed to comprise two thirds of the internal volume of the craft. It was split into two levels. The lower level had a curved contour that followed the shape of the hull. From some of the large containers scattered around the area, it seemed they were shaped to fit into this curve. Somewhat similar to aircraft freight containers.

The upper section had a simple flat deck. More conducive to stacking general cargo. The ramp terminated in the centre of the craft on a circular platform. The upper deck floor had a circular opening, like a balcony. This was the same size as the circular platform. Tim came to the logical conclusion that the platform was in fact a hoist. Used to lift cargo into the upper storage bay.

As they looked around, they saw an arcing ramp at either side of the cargo area that led to the upper section. Tim looked at the ramp on the left, then at the one on the right. He looked at Cathy who just shrugged her shoulders. "Whichever you reckon. It looks like they both lead upstairs anyway." she offered.

Tim headed for the ramp on the left and followed it up toward the top section of the craft. He paused for a cursory look around as they entered the second cargo level. Satisfied there was nothing overly interesting to see, he continued on. Cathy and Charlie followed closely behind.

When they reached the top, they found themselves in a corridor that seemed to circumnavigate the inside of the craft. Charlie looked to Tim for direction. "Which way's the front?" he asked. "I don't know." Tim admitted. "It doesn't look like it has a front. Perhaps it's an omnidirectional machine. Hey do you notice something weird?" Charlie shook his head. "Like what?"

Tim looked at the ceiling of the craft and pointed. "Like the fact that the light plasma, or whatever it is, seems to be inside the craft as well. It's as bright as daylight in here." Charlie looked around then simply shrugged his shoulders. He could not be bothered thinking of a logical reason. His mind was already in overload, so he just accepted it. He stepped forward and turned left. The others turned right.

Charlie figured if the corridor did go around the entire ship, it mattered little which way he went.

Either direction would eventually lead him to the control room. Charlie slowly inched his way along the corridor, still nervous with excitement, but still wary of the craft's owners. The suggestion that the base was abandoned was not always sufficient to fill him with courage. His bravado quickly disappeared when he was alone.

Finally, the relatively narrow walkway opened up into a spacious area, at the centre of which were two large chairs. Each was positioned at the centre of a horseshoe shaped console. As Charlie approached the nearer of the two chairs, he noticed a massive screen that wrapped across the inner shell of the craft.

Drawn as a bee to honey, he ignored the consoles for the moment and changed his course towards the impressive monitor. It was like nothing he had ever seen before. It was vastly different to the screens on the computers they had seen previously. It was a concave surface some three inches thick, which reached from floor to ceiling. A height of some fifteen feet. The surface itself was mirror-like yet opaque, almost translucent. Exposed to the enigmatic green plasma of the base lights, it seemed to glow with a strange opalescence.

He stared at it for a while, before he was compelled to touch it. The coldness of the screen surprised him, as did the small almost imperceptible ridges that ran horizontally across it. He stood there for a few minutes, gently running his fingers across the screen, trying to determine its function and wondering if he could get it working. Finally consigning it to the *to-do* list, he remembered the console.

He turned and walked back to the nearest chair, dragged it over to the control panel and heaved himself up into it. He pondered the computer terminals and small screens that made up the control station for some time. Again everything was labelled in Egyptian.

He was soon lost in the enveloping silence, deep in thought. Completely absorbed by the futuristic technology in front of him. He was oblivious to the world.

Charlie jumped and let out an involuntary gasp as he felt a tap on his shoulder. His head spun around to see who or what had touched him. "Jesus! Don't sneak up on me like that, Cathy! You scared me half to death." Cathy laughed at his reaction. "Sorry Charlie, I didn't mean to scare you. But I guess that's pay-back for the kitchen episode, eh?"

Charlie smiled. "Sorry, I was so engrossed in this control panel, that I didn't hear you coming. Will you have a look at that screen? It looks like it's the window for the pilot. There are no actual holes in the hull for them to look through, but I wonder of the hull can somehow become transparent behind this screen. It's so big! I wouldn't be surprised if it was multi-functional.

You know... not only a visual contact with the outside environment, but a systems flight computer screen as well. Maybe even a general communications screen, you know, like in the *Enterprise*." Although not a Trekky, Tim knew exactly what he was talking about. He concurred with the theory, then disappeared with Cathy to continue exploring the ship.

Charlie watched them go, then returned his interest to the control panel. He was again lost in deep thought when he heard Tim calling from somewhere in the bowels of the ship.

As he approached the room into which Tim and Cathy had obviously disappeared, Charlie called out to them. "What's the problem?" Tim yelled back. "I think I've found the propulsion unit in here." Charlie entered a circular room in the very centre of the craft where Tim and Cathy were waiting for him. When he saw what they had found, his jaw dropped. "I'll be damned! It's a baby gold reactor.

Just like the one at the end of the workshop. But this one's only about ten feet across. And look! It has the same symbol as the main reactor." he observed. "**Reshpu.** The lightning god." Tim reminded him, as he smiled and pointed at the floor. "And look at that. A huge doughnut runs around the outside of this room, embedded in the floor. It looks like it's a bi-metal arrangement. Made of gold and silver I reckon. Or some hybrid alloys that look like them. Is that what you expected to see?"

"Not really expected." Charlie mused. "But it certainly looks interesting. If this is a zero-inertia drive, it means this craft can turn on a sixpence, regardless of what forward speed it's doing. And if you were sitting in it, you wouldn't feel a thing. You almost become part of the machine. There's no inertia felt. I'm guessing that's why it's circular. There's no front or back.

It can fly in any direction and change direction instantly. What's more, it can theoretically exceed the speed of light. Supposedly, once you fire it up, it just keeps accelerating until you want to slow down. I guess accurate navigation's a must or you'd overshoot your mark. Anyway, that means on a long trip you'd just keep accelerating until you reached your design limit.

Christ knows what that would be. Could be hundreds... thousands... even millions of times the speed of light. That would explain how they can get across the vast reaches of space. Unless of course that's all bullshit and they just use wormholes. "

Tim shook his head. "Christ! You never cease to amaze me, Charlie. All that sci-fi crap you hold in that head of yours. But it's a marvellous concept. I guess humans went from hot air balloons to landing on the moon in a couple of hundred years. If these jokers have had millions of years more time to develop their technology I suppose anything's possible. Either way, I'd love to see one of these craft in action."

Charlie laughed. "Jesus! Wouldn't the military be interested in this? Imagine the Australian Air Force with a couple of dozen of these babies. That'd make the Yanks sit up and look." he joked.

Tim was at risk of being overwhelmed with technology. He decided to leave the technical stuff to Charlie and explore the rest of the ship. He grabbed Cathy's hand and wandered off to see what else they could find. Charlie, having seen enough of the propulsion system for now, followed closely behind as they proceeded around the circular corridor.

As it transpired, the engine room was at the centre of the craft, with the control room at the *front* and the crew's quarters at the *rear*, one on either side of a common area. This was decked out with lounge chairs and tables, on most of which sat a small computer.

From the rough dimensions calculated by Tim, the crew's quarters were relatively spacious, but given the apparent size of the pilots, still somewhat cramped if they were confined to quarters on a long journey. It was estimated that, if necessary, the ship could carry around one hundred men and their equipment. Even more in an emergency, if the cargo hold was used for short-term passengers.

After spending over an hour inspecting the ship, they finally concluded their tour, pausing briefly near the bottom of the ramp. It was Cathy who noticed them first. She tugged at Tim's arm. "Look over there. Are they more spaceships?" she asked.

Tim and Charlie followed her pointing finger with their squinting eyes. In the distance they could just make out several shiny shapes. They hurried down the ramp and headed off in that direction.

As they approached the nearest craft, Tim looked at Cathy. "These are much smaller than the other three. They're only about thirty feet across. And look how many there are.

There must be a dozen or more here. Let's see if we can find one that's open." he urged. After visiting five of the smaller craft, they finally found one with its ramp down. Again the ramp seemed to be telescopic, stretching from the centre of the craft to the workshop floor. Eagerly they raced up the ramp.

Again it led directly into the cargo area. Its layout was similar to the larger craft, except the cargo bay was only a single level. Other than that, the craft looked like a scaled down version of the bigger machine. On the far side was a single ramp leading up from the cargo hold. They all headed for it, drawn as if by a magnet. Side by side, they walked into the main body of the craft.

The upper deck was simply a large open area. The ramp opened directly into the control section, which looked similar to that in the other ship. There were two large comfortable chairs in the centre of two horseshoe-shaped control consoles. At the front of the craft was a large monitor screen. Again it looked like a scale model of the screen in the larger ship.

The remainder of the deck space seemed to comprise a lounge, complete with comfortable looking chairs, small tables and the ubiquitous computers. Tim also noticed what looked like an entertainment unit, similar to a DVD he thought. He mused, more to himself than anyone in particular. "This must be the in-flight entertainment."

In the centre of the room was a small dome. While Charlie looked over the controls, Tim and Cathy headed off to inspect the protrusion. Finding a hatch, Tim knelt down and carefully lifted it clear. Inside was a small gold reactor, only this time is was a mere five feet across. Again it was identified as the *Lightning God*. He stood up and looked around. Sure enough, there embedded in the floor was the bi-metal drive coil. "It looks as if they both have the same propulsion system. It's just a scaled down version here.

So I guess, logically enough, that the reactor is proportional to the size of the craft."Charlie just shrugged his shoulders and returned his attention to the control panel. He had seen enough reactors for one day. For now he had other things to look at.

Cathy meanwhile, wandered around casually inspecting the small craft. It did not take long. She soon caught up with Tim and Charlie at the control console. "Well it's quite obviously only a two man crew. Although there's seating for a dozen or so passengers around the ship."

Charlie agreed, then added his own opinion. "Yes, but I think it's only for short hops. Say a few hours or so. There doesn't seem to be a bathroom on board." Tim thought about the last comment as they descended the ramp. Turning to Charlie as they reached the floor he posed a question. "How far do you think they could get in a short flight of say... five or six hours?"

Charlie pondered the question for a moment then, looking up at the magnificent craft, he offered his opinion. "Well, it's hard to say. But I guess if we can go from Sydney to Los Angeles in a very inefficient commercial jet aircraft in around fifteen hours, I would think these blokes should be able to get out of our solar system in six hours. After all, the sun's less than eight light minutes from earth, so even at fifty percent of the speed of light, that distance would only take quarter of an hour or so."

Tim contemplated the relativity of space, time and distance as they moved quietly through the workshop and parking bay complex. Tim had decided that now was as good a time as any to see just how far into the mountain it extended. The others followed.

After walking nearly a mile, they came to a colossal set of doors. Each one enclosed half the entire cross-section of the runway. They were massive beyond belief. Charlie shook his head in awe.

"Would you look at the size of those bastards! It looks like they slide sideways to open and leave this entire runway clear. How far into the mountain do you think we are?" Tim looked back toward the now distant spacecraft. "I don't know. I should imagine we're pretty close to the other side by now. But I'd like to see what's behind these doors." he added. "Probably another rock-slide if the cave entrance is anything to go by. What do you think, Cathy?"

Cathy nodded. "Yeah, I guess we've walked far enough to be at the other side. It's only a mile or so across and I think we've walked nearly that far."

Charlie looked around for a keypad to open the doors, but was disappointed when his search proved fruitless. They stood silently contemplating the impressive doors until Tim became restless. "I noticed a couple of doors back near the larger craft. I reckon we should have a gander. What do you think?" Gaining unanimous nods of approval, he turned around and headed back along the runway.

About six hundred yards from the power reactor, they came across a single door on the northern wall. As they approached it, Charlie noticed the keypad. "It's got a keypad like those accommodation units. Although this one seems to have some sort of key-hole." He pushed the keypad, expecting the door to rise. Nothing happened. The disappointment on his face was obvious. "I guess you need a key to activate this one. I wonder what's behind it. What does this inscription say, Tim?"

Tim looked at the engraved characters for a moment. "*khepesh*" he stated proudly. "Yes, but what does that mean?" Charlie urged. "It means *Weapons.*" Tim explained with a smile. "I think this is the armoury." Charlie's eyes instantly lit up. "That'll be interesting. If we find a key, I guess we'll find out. Boy, I'd love to get hold of some weaponry and see what it could do. I hope they've got training manuals somewhere though.

Otherwise it might be a bit dangerous. Perhaps that sort of stuff's in a computer database somewhere?" Tim mumbled his reservations about ignorantly playing with potentially lethal weapons, as they headed off towards the reactor. Cathy seemed to agree, but Charlie ignored them both. He was a keen competition shooter and had always been interested in guns. He had a good collection of them at home. Tim on the other hand was familiar with weapons, but more in a self-defence, use them if you have to, sense. He had never taken to the gun club scene.

They stopped at the next door they came across, some three hundred yards further on. It was on the south side of the runway, on their left as they approached the generator. It was a large door, some thirty feet across. Tim found a keypad, pushed it and stepped back. The door slid silently and effortlessly to the side, eventually disappearing into the rock wall.

"I'll be buggered!" Tim exclaimed. "It looks like the warehouse behind the kitchen we looked at yesterday. I suppose it makes sense. If you were transporting food into the complex via a ship, you'd have the warehouse right next to the runway. And you'd have it connected to the back of the kitchen. I tell you what though. I never noticed anything that looked like a refrigeration unit anywhere. It looks as if these poor buggers only lived on processed food, not fresh stuff."

They agreed that the warehouse had already been inspected, so as they stepped back into the workshop. Tim pressed the keypad to close the door. They all stood in awed silence, transfixed by the closing door. After it slowly and again effortlessly came to rest with a soft, yet solid thump, they turned and continued on their way.

As they passed the last of the large craft, Cathy noticed another door on the northern side of the workshop. Again it was about thirty feet across.

Charlie reached out and pressed the keypad. They all watched as the door migrated across the floor and disappeared into the wall. They were confronted by an impressive cavern cut into the side of the main excavation.

Once again it was lit as if bathed in sunlight. The omnipresent glowing plasma seemed to have pervaded every inch of the base. They stepped inside and were met by endless rows of shelving, reminiscent of the kitchen warehouse, only much more extensive. Cathy wandered over to the nearest shelf and looked at the strange collection of tools that lay there, silently gathering dust. "What else should I expect in a workshop, but a spare parts and tool store? Would you look at the size of these tools?" she gasped.

Out of curiosity, she touched a very large double-ended spanner. She jumped back as it rocked unexpectedly. Then, more curious than ever, she attempted to lift it. It was amazingly light for its size. She looked over at the others who were keenly observing her actions. "It's as light as a feather, yet it looks as if it's done a lot of heavy work. I wonder what it's made of." she mused.

Tim and Charlie inspected the tool. Neither could determine the metal, but Charlie had his suspicions. He picked up the tool and closely inspected it. "I reckon it's some type of metallic polymer. That would explain its strength and weight. But I wouldn't bet on it. I'll try to find a smaller piece made out of the same material, so I can take it home with me and make a few discrete tests."

Charlie slowly wandered along the shelves until he stopped to look at another strangely familiar tool. As he turned it over, he noticed some markings moulded into one end. He motioned Tim over and pointed them out. "What do you make of these markings, Tim?" Tim looked at the markings and smiled.

"This one's a determinative indicating *to support*. This is a number ... *met tua* ...*fifteen*. I would imagine it was some sort of stand that could hold fifteen units of weight. Probably fifteen talents or about three hundred and forty kilograms."

Charlie placed the tool in his backpack and headed off in search of other suitable test pieces. He soon found several candidates. Once they were safely ensconced in his backpack, he returned to the others. "There seems to be a lot of boxes in here. I guess they're full of spare parts. Maybe we'll come back and open a few later. We might even find a spare generator unit, you know, like the ones in the little spacecraft. With a bit of effort we might be able to take one home with us so I can reverse engineer it." he concluded.

But Tim was ready to move on. "You never know your luck. Well, I've seen enough of the tool store for now. How about you? I think it's about time we returned to camp." No-one argued. Tim had taken all the photos he could and had run out of digital cards. He was keen to download them onto CD-ROM's so he could take more photos on their return. The others simply looked forward to relaxing with a couple of beers.

CHAPTER 15

Cathy and Charlie hurriedly washed down their supper with a couple of beers and immediately retired to their beds. Tim, as tired as he was, unfortunately had other priorities. He spent many arduous hours loading the countless photos onto the computer, editing and cataloguing them. He down-loaded the vast collection of images onto CD's and erased the camera memory cards. Eventually he slumped onto his bed and fell into a deep sleep.

He was awoken abruptly as the pestilent alarm on his wristwatch pierced the silence of the cave. He looked at the time. It was 6 a.m. He moaned quietly as he realized he'd only been in bed three hours. Bloodshot eyes, be-whiskered and yawning incessantly, he was feeling decidedly the worse for wear. Nonetheless his desire to return to the base soon saw him extricate himself from his dishevelled bedding and join the others in a hearty breakfast.

The steak, bacon, eggs, fried tomatoes, baked beans and toast were consumed in silence and washed down with copious quantities of hot, sweet, black tea. With breakfast and ablutions finished, they set about gathering the equipment for another day's exploration. Food, water, backpacks, torches, notepad, pen and camera. Tim picked up two spare lanterns and looked over at Charlie. "Do you think the power will still be on?" he asked tentatively.

"I don't see why not." Charlie reassured him. "The generator probably ran for thousands, of years before we came along." he postulated. "I guess you're right. But I think I'll take these just in case." Tim responded. They picked up their respective loads and set off for the base. Along the way they discussed their options.

Tim, naturally enough, was keen to investigate the history and origins of the race they had seen. Charlie on the other hand was eager to see if he could activate the computers. Cathy cared little either way. As long as she was with Tim, she would be happy. Although her professional interest did favour Tim's preference.

As they crawled along the top of the rock-pile towards the access tunnel they were met with the warm reassuring glow of the pervasive base lights. As they neared the door the ethereal glow intensified. They smiled as they slid down the rear of the final rock-face and crawled through the broken door. In unison they looked up at the resplendent light source. Impressive as it was, it still gave them an uneasy feeling. The strange amorphous glow that seemed to hug the roof like a luminous cloud was a constant reminder they were dealing with the unknown. Something that has never sat well with humanity.

They headed straight for the great hall, off which ran the kitchen and accommodation blocks. Tim strode ahead purposefully, the others struggling to keep pace. When they reached the entrance Tim stopped and looked around. Once Cathy and Charlie had caught up with him, he looked at them and tilted his head in a pointing gesture towards the great opening. "Well what do you reckon?" he asked.

Cathy shrugged her shoulders and Charlie just shook his head. Tim, as always, was happy to assume the leadership role. He suggested a plan of action. "I know you're keen to look at the computers, Charlie. But can I make a suggestion first?" Charlie and Cathy nodded in unison. "Sure." they agreed.

"Why don't we stick together for a while, for safety and peace of mind? We can explore the whole base easily now we have the light, but we still don't know exactly what we're up against. Once we've determined what's here, we can split up if you like.

I brought a notebook so we can draw a map of the complex. But I'm hoping somewhere there's a blueprint that'll show us the layout of the base. You two happy with that?" Cathy looked over at Tim."I'm happy to do whatever you want." she purred. "I'm OK with that..." Charlie added, albeit less enthusiastically. "Well let's see if we can get a rough idea of what the accommodation layout is like." Tim suggested.

By this time, they had walked past the kitchen and were approaching the first of the radial corridors. Tim looked down the corridor on his left, then motioned for the others to follow as he headed for the nearest door. Stopping at the door, he turned to Charlie. "I never noticed that before, but it makes sense I guess." Charlie looked around for something obvious, but found nothing untoward. "What's that?" he finally asked.

"It looks like all the doors are numbered. See the carved symbols above the door? It reads... *pa-aa-n-ursh qebu ua... tcheri-t ua*...which roughly translates as *Guardian Group 1... Room 1*. And the one opposite reads *pa-aa-n-ursh qebu ua... tcheri-t snau... Guardian Group 1... Room 2*." Charlie nodded. He too had missed the engraving. "It looks like they were engraved into the wall with a machine. The symbols are so neatly cut. They're sort of gold plated too, just like the ones at the power station. I guess the contrast between the granite and the gold makes them easy to read."

"Yeah, I guess so." Tim agreed. "It certainly doesn't look like the carved hieroglyphs in Egypt. As neat as they are at Karnak, you can still tell they're hand-carved. But these are perfect. Are you ready?" Charlie and Cathy nodded in unison, so Tim pressed the keypad.

Slowly and silently the massive door began to slide aside. They watched in fascination as it finally disappeared into the wall, still amazed by how it operated so smoothly and quietly.

Tim was the first to look into the room. The area adjacent to the entrance was obviously the recreational area. There was comfortable seating for five or so, placed in a casual semi-circle in front of a large display screen. There were several small tables, one with two fine alabaster cups and a small, shiny, metallic, octagonal plate, still sitting where they had been left. There was a small black box, which looked like a TV remote unit, lying on the floor next to a sheet of what appeared to be paper.

Tim wandered over and picked it up. "Will you look at this? Imitation vellum by the looks of it. It's a menu of some kind... in daily rosters. I bet it's the weekly menu from the mess. Wow! Look at that. A huge computer screen... or maybe it's an entertainment unit like a TV. It looks like the one we saw in the aircraft. I wonder if this thing turns it on."

Tim picked up the black box and began pressing the coloured pads randomly. Nothing. Charlie reached out impatiently. "Here... give me a go." After trying in vain for some time to get a response from the unit, he finally conceded defeat, offering a meek but plausible explanation. "Perhaps it's hooked up to a central unit somewhere and that isn't switched on yet." Tim agreed, then continued to peruse the room.

He noticed the personal belongings scattered around the room. The odd piece of crumpled clothing, some paper, a thin book, some writing implements, two large brown leather belts... a shiny twelve inch double-edged knife, wedged resolutely under the leg of a chair. Tim rescued the knife, inspected it closely for damage and then slipped it into his belt. "A souvenir! It looks like when they left they didn't take much with them. Would you look at this stuff? It's almost as if they left with only the clothes on their backs."

"Maybe they left and expected to return pretty soon... and never made it back." Charlie suggested.

"Or maybe they all died." Cathy added with a wry smile. They both turned to Cathy and frowned. "What makes you say that?" Tim asked. "It would explain why so much personal stuff was left behind." Tim nodded. "I guess that's one explanation. Perhaps they did." They conceded her logic. Given the seemingly abandoned state of the base, it was the most plausible explanation.

They continued to methodically explore the room and its contents. As it transpired, it was a two-man room. Carved out of solid rock, the walls were smooth and vitreous. All with perfectly square edges, just like the rest of the base. A kitchenette and dining area took up the centre of the living quarters. The benches were solid granite, as was a sink unit and the shelving. It was obviously all hewn from solid rock by some sophisticated carving machinery. Lasers or the like, Charlie had postulated. It was a marvel of unrivalled architecture and engineering. It was opulent by design yet simple in function. It was most spectacular.

Either side of the kitchenette, leading to the bedrooms, was an individual work-station. Each had a small reference library, a computer terminal and screen, a chair and a desk. The large wrap-around desk had built-in shelving that housed files and other office paraphernalia. Again all the furnishings, apart from the chair, were carved out of the living rock. Scattered over the desk was a different type of paper, of a porous plastic feel, and some writing implements. Also littered across the desk were copious hand-written notes, files and the omnipresent computer cards.

Each occupant had a separate bedroom, at the far end of the room. It consisted simply of a large bed base, again carved out of the rock, fitted with a relatively firm mattress. This was covered by two saffron yellow linen sheets. A single olive-green woollen blanket was spread over the top sheet. At the head the bed was a single C-shaped pillow covered with saffron yellow cloth.

Cathy prodded a pillow to test its firmness. It was akin to a latex pillow. Firm but comfortable she concluded. Along the outer wall was a clothes storage niche, complete with shelving and suspension rings. Various uniforms, some clearly formal, others casual, one obviously a combat outfit, still hung there neatly. Underneath were several pairs of over-sized polished black boots and leather sandals. Tim noticed the boots and carefully picked one up. After a cursory inspection, he beamed with a large, self-congratulatory smile.

"Look, the tread's identical to the fossilised footprint we found outside the cave. And that was identical to the *tracks* on the cave painting." A shiver shot up Cathy's spine as she looked at the boot. Although it was all starting to fall into place, the implications still did not sit well with her. In the back of her mind was the ever nagging thought of... who were they and where were they now?

The shelves contained mostly personal belongings, as could be expected. Some items were strangely familiar, others were of less definable use or material. But most shelves simply contained apparel such as vests and other ancillary items like belts, thonging, sewing kits and buckles.

Off each bedroom was a private ablution room. The first thing Tim noticed was a gigantic, gold framed, highly polished, chrome-like metal mirror. It was a magnificent sight, still as highly polished as the day it was made. He stopped for a few seconds to gaze at his bedraggled appearance. It had been a while since he had seen himself in a mirror. Scrutinising the tired saturnine creature that was staring blankly back at him, he concluded it was probably for the best if he refrained from looking in mirrors for a while to come.

As he swept his eyes around the room, he noticed the sunken bath, wash basin, shelving and what must have been a toilet.

Again everything was carved from solid granite and again it was most beautifully done. Scattered around on the copious shelves within the bathroom were personal hygiene items, such as hairbrushes, towels, a manicure set and numerous small bottles, that looked like they were made from alabaster.

They were all labelled with small gold hieroglyphs, so Tim picked several up in turn and inspected them closely. They contained such things as perfumes, mouthwash, tooth polish, medicines, essential oils and liquid soaps.

Cathy wandered over to the bath. She looked at the shiny gold spout protruding from the wall and wondered how it worked. She looked around for the taps. There were none. It was then she noticed the small square gold plug near the drain hole. "I wonder where the bath water drained to... and the toilet water for that matter?"

Tim joined her and peered into the large oval sunken bath. "I don't know. But I guess they'd have some sort of plumbing system. See up there? It looks like a ducted air vent. I should imagine they'd have a ventilation system as well. We might find out more about that when we do a thorough search of the base. And no! I have no idea how they got the water in here either!"

Cathy reached up, wrapped her arms around Tim's neck and purred into his ear. "That's a pity. I could do with a bubble bath with someone special to scrub my back."

They met in an intimate embrace. Tim temporarily forgot about the base as their passion flowed through their lips like an electric current. His hands slowly slid from her shoulders, ran down her quivering spine and came to rest as he gently squeezed her shapely buttocks. Cathy's right arm was still wrapped tightly around Tim's neck, but her left hand was free to explore Tim's heaving chest... on its way to more interesting places.

Just as their passion began to peak, they were interrupted by a booming voice emanating from the lounge area. "Hey you two! Look what I've found!" Cathy laughed as she broke away from the embrace and grabbed Tim's hand. "Later big boy..." she teased. She gave him one last quick kiss on the lips and led him back into the recreation area.

As they passed the kitchenette, they saw Charlie staring at some photographs on the wall near the entrance. "Look at these, Tim. There are dozens of them, all 3D like the one's in the rec room. And look they've all got some writing on them. Can you tell me what they say?" Tim peered at the pictures for a minute or two before answering.

"That top bit says... *meti ami-ren-f* ...which infers a *list of occupants*. A sort of hall of fame if you like. Each photograph obviously shows an occupant of this room with a name and some numbers under it. I'm pretty sure it's something to do with length of service and dates, but I can't decipher them. They're just a bunch of numbers. Some very large numbers and something about... *sebi*... which is *an indeterminate period of time*. It's got something to do with the sun. See the sun symbol? But I'm not really sure what it means. Perhaps it's a dating reference system. Hopefully somewhere there's an explanation of it. It'd be useful to determine these dates in respect to our own chronology."

Tim pondered the numbers for a while until Charlie indicated his desire to continue exploring the base. Having photographed and sketched the room, Tim was satisfied for the moment and agreed to move on. Charlie pressed the keypad to close the door as they left. Again they all watched in mesmerized awe as the heavy door slid silently into place, coming to a stop with a faint muffled thud. A small puff of dust indicated that it had completed its first journey in centuries.

They inspected all ten rooms in the corridor and found them to be identical in layout. The only difference being the personal effects. Some rooms were completely empty, save the bed coverings, furniture and kitchen appliances. No clothes, no personal belongings, no books, not even any computer cards. Nothing. They looked as if the occupants had simply packed up and left.

Others were like the first, with personal items scattered about as if the occupants were suddenly snatched away. They also found that every room had its own resident history photo collection. The way that each warrior stood proudly in the photographs suggested that the base had some prestige. It had obviously been an honour to serve here.

Tim photographed each gallery to compile as large a history file as possible. Finally they reached the end of the corridor. Here it was a different matter.

The room they found behind this door was wider and longer than the others. Again the immediate area was the lounge and recreation section. Only this time the semi-circular array of large comfortably padded chairs could accommodate more than twenty. Again there were small tables scattered around the room, with shelving and niches cut into the walls. They held an assortment of books, computer cards and trinkets.

One niche proudly displayed a framed collection of shiny gold medals. Surrounding them were several small photographs. Some were of fascinating, almost surreal, battle scenes. One in particular showed a troop of warriors engaged in fierce hand-to-hand combat with a race that looked very much like extras from a sci-fi movie. Several other photographs were of award ceremonies. Obviously a proud moment for the recipients. But one photograph was more poignant. It looked like an important military funeral procession. Perhaps a friend, relative or a famous commander.

Tim pondered the occasion for a while before he moved on. Against the far wall was a large entertainment screen, with its control box casually lying nearby on the floor. When compared to the other occupied rooms, apart from a single errant cup on the small table nearest the screen, the room looked remarkably tidy. Beyond the lounge to the right was a spacious office, complete with a computer and a large reference library of both books and computer cards. Next to the office was a storeroom. Tim opened the door and nearly fainted with exhilaration as he entered.

He yelled hoarsely to Cathy. "Would you look at this?" Cathy wandered into the room and peered in the direction of Tim's shaking finger. "What is it?" she asked. "It's only the best collection of Egyptian figures I've ever seen. Look at these. There are pottery figures, and bronze... and gold... silver... electrum... granite... faience... limestone... lapis lazuli.... alabaster... and wood... stuccoed, painted and gold leafed. There's even some made entirely out of precious stones. Look there's one made of carnelian... and a tiny one made of sapphire, I think.

This would have to be the best representation of Egyptian deities ever put together in one place. All the ancient gods are here. Ptah... Osiris... Bes... Seb... Maat... Thoth... Amen... Ra... Anpu... Best... Nut... Horus... Hapi... Hathor... Mut... Isis... Chensu and Chnemu... Even the more obscure gods are here. Look there's Anher... Sebek... Heru-chent-chati... and Qebhsennuf. And there's a collection of combination gods and regional gods. There's Amen-Ra... Menthu-Ra... Chensu-pa-chrat and Sefekh-aabu.

This is truly incredible. There are even gods here that I've never seen before. The person who lived here must have collected them like we collect stamps. What I wouldn't give to have this collection at home." he babbled.

Cathy watched his finger as it darted back and forth excitedly along the rows of figures, neatly lined up on the shelves. When he had calmed down, she grabbed his arm and gently squeezed until he turned his head towards her. "Well, why not take this collection home?" she suggested with a smile. "You can tell people you purchased the collection from an old French guy whose great-grandfather collected them in the early eighteen hundreds or something."

Tim shook his head. "It would be a bit presumptuous of me to keep it myself. A collection this valuable should be in a museum." he argued. Cathy cuddled up next to him and whispered into his ear. "Why don't you start your own private museum?" she suggested.

Tim spent the next few minutes staring blankly at the collection, evaluating Cathy's idea. All the possibilities raced through his head. His own museum? It was possible and it was probably ethical, considering the base looked like it had been abandoned for hundreds of years. He liked the sound of it. "You're right. I should start my own private museum. This base has been abandoned for a long time. No-one will mind if we relocate some of the stuff from here. As long as we don't reveal our source, it should be OK."

They continued inspecting the quarters, now almost an anti-climax for Tim, as he mulled over the idea of a private museum. In the centre of the dwelling was a large functional kitchenette, complete with a wonderful collection of the most ornate gold crockery and a beautiful set of what looked like stainless steel cooking implements. It included skillets, various wok-like pans and a plethora of pots.

Next to that was a very impressive dining area, with a large hewn granite table and formal seating for twenty-two. Again, at the far end of the room were the living quarters. In this case just a single bedroom, with an en-suite ablution room and a separate bathroom.

These rooms too were much larger and grander than those in the other quarters. Again everything was majestically carved from solid rock.

When they returned to the dining area, Charlie looked around for some time before walking over to Tim. "Do you think this entire wing was designed to house a single group of soldiers, like a platoon or company or something?" he asked. "What makes you think that?" Tim questioned.

"Well, each of the other rooms obviously housed two men... or whatever. That makes twenty men. Each of their rooms has lounge chairs for six and dining for four. But this room has dining and sofas for twenty odd. Yet it only has a single bedroom, like it belonged to a commander. What does it say on the door?

The last room we were in said *Guardian Group 1... Room 10* didn't it?" Tim slipped outside to read the door sign, then popped back into the room. "You're right. The last room said... ***pa-aa-n-ursh qebu ua ... tcheri-t met*** *...Guardian Group 1 ... Room 10.* This one says... ***pa-aa-n-ursh qebu ua ... utu*** *...Guardian Group 1 ... Commander."* Charlie shot a self-congratulatory smirk at Tim. "I thought so! Maybe the other radial corridors each have a group in them. And I'll bet the upstairs ones are the same. Do you want to check them out?"

Tim and Cathy agreed and headed for the door. As they were about to leave, Cathy pointed out the hall of fame near the exit. Tim peered at the writing. "There aren't so many here. I can't make out the dates, but perhaps the commanders had a longer tour of duty than the other ranks." As they left the commander's quarters, they closed the door behind them. Tim smiled as he grabbed Cathy's hand. "I'll be back for that collection later." he promised.

CHAPTER 16

They continued to wander through the remaining accommodation units on the ground level. Charlie was right. As they went clockwise from corridor to corridor, the set-up was the same. The only thing that changed was the group numbers and the relative state of the rooms. Some were neat and tidy, devoid of any personal belongings. As if they had not been lived in for some time. Others were not so tidy, indicating that the occupants had left in a hurry. Or they had left temporarily but, for some inexplicable reason, had never returned. Each corridor housed an autonomous group - *the Guardians* - from one to five.

When they finally reached the last corridor, Tim reminded Charlie of their location. "This was the short corridor we went down the other day. It's not like the others. Let's see what's down here shall we?" Tim strode boldly down the corridor, stopping when he arrived at the door. He read the inscription above it out loud. "*mer m'shau ur* ...*Commander-in-Chief.* I'd say we've found the base commander's quarters. This should be interesting."

Keen to explore the commander's quarters, he did not wait for permission from the others. Tim quickly pressed the keypad and stood back as the door silently slid aside to reveal another room. Charlie watched the door open, then with a mock bow and a low sweeping motion of his arm, he gestured for Tim to proceed. "After you." he insisted.

Tim hurried in, anxious to see the Commanding Officer's quarters. Cathy and Charlie, somewhat less enthused, followed at a more reserved gait. Again the immediate area was a lounge room, complete with very comfortable surrounds. This was a luxury apartment by any definition.

There were enough comfortable chairs to accommodate at least twenty-five guests. The lounge area was cavernous and the entertainment screen was huge. There was a large, well appointed dining room to the left. It had seating at the magnificent polished granite table for about thirty. The kitchenette was equally as impressive. Its contents were, by far, a cut above anything previously seen.

To the left of the kitchenette was an office. It was set up like those of the Group Commanders, only much more grandiose. It had several niche workstations along one wall, indicating the Commander's use of secretaries, scribes or other assistants.

To the right of the kitchenette was the bedroom. It was similar to those of the other commanders, but much larger. It was also more sumptuously appointed. It had a large comfortable chair nestled in the far corner, pulled up to a relatively small round table. On the table was a beautifully embossed gold pitcher and matching pair of goblets. A large gold plate had a small pile of ashen dust in its centre. The remains of an unfinished meal perhaps. Next to it was a gold spoon and an empty food container, similar to the ones they had seen in the kitchen warehouse. A large colourful hand-woven rug lay on the floor. The repeated angular pattern reminded Tim of an Aztec or Navaho design.

In one corner of the room stood an intricately painted amphora. Its brilliantly contrasting athletes, in gold and ochre red, artistically balanced by the creamy white and jet black background. It stood proudly on a small wooden stool, the top of which was covered in dark brown tanned leather, held in place with large golden rivets.

On the wall hung several large photographs, one framed by an ornate gold surround. It looked like a portrait of the commanding officer as a young man, with his family.

Perhaps it was his graduation or pre-posting ceremony. The pride that exuded from the young officer's face belied the solemnity of the occasion. In contrast, the others in the photo seemed rather sad, as if they were at a farewell. Perhaps it was the last time they saw each other.

Cathy stared teary-eyed at the haunting photo for some time. Her emotions strangely torn between the euphoria of the young officer and the obvious sadness of the others. Whatever the story, she concluded, it must have been a momentous occasion, for the picture was enormous and took pride of place in what was obviously a very private room.

The large bed, which dominated the centre of the room, was neatly made, although, uncharacteristically, a little crumpled. Like someone had been lying on top of it since it was last made. All the other beds they had come across were perfectly made, as one would expect on a military base. It looked as if it was most comfortable. Although now there was a fine white layer of dust gilding the saffron coloured silken pillow and the regal purple woollen blanket. Tim pondered the slightly rumpled blanket for a few seconds. Then relegated the reasons for it being so to the too-hard basket. They continued with the tour.

Off the bedroom was another office. This one was smaller, more in line with the private offices in the Group Commander's quarters. It had a small personal library and a single work-station.

Also running off the bedroom was a walk-in robe, still fully laden with clothes. There were military uniforms, some more formal than others, as well as casual clothing. Again there were boots and sandals neatly arranged under the hanging clothing. Tim's curiosity compelled him to pick up a boot and inspect the tread. It was identical to the footprint they had found in the rocks outside the cave.

A self-congratulatory smile crept across his face. He respectfully replaced the boot, then shuffled off to follow Cathy into the en-suite. It was a magnificently designed and excavated room. The polished floor, the enormous sunken bath, the toilet, the hand basin, the shelving and the sideboards. All sparkling as the effulgent light danced off the ornate gold fixtures. Everything was carved from the beautiful dark green, cream-streaked granite.

On one wall was a large gold surround that housed a full-length elliptical mirror. It had a strange, almost pellucid, metallic lustre. Like that of highly polished chromium or stainless steel. Tim refrained from looking into it. This room too, had personal effects scattered around. It looked very much like it was in use up to the time the base was abandoned. A logical conclusion, given it was the home of the commanding officer.

When they returned to the lounge area, they found a door half way along the left wall. Tim pushed the keypad and watched as it disappeared out of sight. It was another ablution room, obviously intended for the commander's guests. Tim shrugged nonchalantly as he closed the door. Before it had completed its journey, he wandered off towards a door at the far end of the room.

Tim stood back as Cathy pushed the keypad and watched, still hypnotised by the silent movement of the solid granite door. As the door opened, he noticed the colossal solid granite table that dominated the room. Like most of the other fixtures in the base, it was exquisitely carved out of, and still attached to, the living rock. It was surrounded by a multitude of rather uncomfortable looking but obviously functional chairs. Together they took up the majority of the room.

At one end was a large round computer screen, some ten feet in diameter. At the other was a series of shelves, again carved into the granite walls. They contained a reference library of computer cards.

In a niche below the shelf was a computer keyboard. Tim turned to Cathy to state the obvious. "Well I guess this is a conference room. It seems no matter how advanced a race is, they still need to communicate face-to-face every now and then." he opined. Cathy, having seen nothing to hold her interest, casually turned to leave the room. She stopped dead in her tracks and tugged incessantly at Tim's arm until he finally turned around. Although he was mumbling excitedly to himself, what she was pointing at stunned him into silence.

There on the wall behind the door was a large, moderately detailed map of the world. It took up an area of some twenty feet high by thirty-five feet wide. It showed the world from an entirely new perspective, with Australia at its epicentre. Everything else radiating out, like some proud antipodean artist's impression of the world.

As Tim studied the map, Charlie wandered into the room and casually looked over his shoulder. "Strange map of the earth isn't it?" he mused. Tim nodded. "Yeah. I can recognize the continents. But it's sure drawn differently to the Hammer Equal Area projection we're used to." Tim quickly perused the map once more to confirm his initial thoughts.

Satisfied that he was correct, he turned to Charlie. "It's almost like the Piri Reis map. Only the azimuthal equidistant projection is centred right here, over this base. You see? They've used this point as a datum for referencing everything else on the planet. Logical I guess, given the importance of the place. But this map sure will take some getting used to." he admitted.

Tim walked right up to the map for a closer inspection. His finger automatically pointing at the geographic centre of the map. Here a symbol stood in a circle. Next to the circle was a hieroglyph. Protruding from the circle was a large ruby-capped pin.

"This symbol reminds me of something, what do you think?" Charlie came over to the map. He peered at the symbol inside the circle that designated the base. After giving the question some thought, it finally struck him. "Well it looks like a silhouette of one of those spacecraft to me. Maybe that's what it represents, a fighter base or something. Look, there are other bases shown. But they all seem to be drawn much smaller than this one. It's as if this is the main base and these others were ancillary bases. The red pins are smaller too. What do you think?"

Tim looked carefully at the other symbols and at the hieroglyphs adjacent to them. "Well done, Charlie. I think you've hit the nail on the head. I can't read some of the base names, which I'm assuming these hieroglyphs mean. But from the relative size of them, it suggests they're minor bases."

Charlie was pleased that his learned brother had congratulated him on his theory. Riding the wave, he boldly continued. "If we could find one of the other bases, we'd be able to confirm they were less important. Because if they were, they'd have the same maps as here. But if they were equally as important, then their maps would be based on an equidistant projection from their base, not this one. Don't you think?" he offered.

"Now there's a challenge." Tim agreed, "Roam the world in search of other bases. That would definitely prove to the most reticent sceptic that these maps were genuine and that aliens did in fact dwell here for some time." Charlie could feel the excitement building as he contemplated giving up his job to become a full-time archaeologist. Tim could almost read his mind as they stood in silence, fantasizing over the possibilities.

Finally Charlie stepped back from the map to gain a better perspective. He continued thinking about the other bases, as he familiarized himself with the map's unusual projection. After reassuring himself that his interpretation was correct, he offered further insight.

"Well, it looks like there were bases in the Middle East, Tibet, South America, Antarctica, North America, Western Europe and Australia. The map scale's a bit large to be too accurate. But at least it gives us a general idea where they were." he suggested.

"Yes." Tim agreed, answering while he was still deep in thought. "But maybe they have some more explicit smaller scale maps that could give us the exact location of the bases. What about the spacecraft? Shouldn't they have maps in their navigation systems?"

Charlie's brow furrowed as he thought about it for a moment. Then his expression lightened as he concurred. "Of course they would. It should also be in the general computer system. I'll try to find it if you like. If we can ever get those things to talk to us." he cautioned. "Yeah, that would be great." Tim agreed.

Tim ran his eyes across the map and commented on the pins. He re-acknowledged the large ruby capped pin and the six smaller ruby pins dotted across it, corresponding to the bases. There were also other pins with various gemstone caps. Green emerald, blue sapphire and yellow citrine they speculated. They were seemingly scattered at random around the globe.

Tim looked back at the large ruby pin and pondered out loud. "This pin here obviously represents this base and the smaller red pins represent the other bases. I wonder where they had one in Tibet!"

Charlie wandered over to the map and casually offered a suggestion. "The ice cave." he offered. "What?" Tim responded. "The ice cave of Tibet. Haven't you heard of it?" Charlie asked. Tim shook his head. "No. What's that?" Charlie smiled. "There's rumoured to be a cave in Tibet that's full of ice, like a giant iceblock. Apparently it's very ancient. The ice has been there since the last ice age. But through the ice they reckon they can see high tech equipment like computers and stuff.

It's rumoured that's why the Chinese government won't grant Tibet independence. It's scared of losing the technology they think is in the cave. Perhaps they've already defrosted it and found the base." Tim shook his head in disbelief. "Jesus, Charlie! You're a mine of dubious information, aren't you?" Charlie smiled and took it as a compliment.

He then refocussed his attention on the map, as Tim pointed to a small red pin. "Look at this pin. There's a base in South America, somewhere near Nasca. I guess that makes sense of the carvings there. It seems old Von Daniken was right.

Now there's an interesting thing." Tim mused. "What's that?" Charlie asked, looking at Tim's pointing finger. "Although these chaps obviously had a large influence on Egypt, there's no base there. But there is one here. It looks like the Mount Sinai area. That's really interesting." he pondered. But Charlie still could not figure it out. "Why?" he asked, regretting his question the second it left his mouth.

Tim smiled. "Haven't you read the Bible? Mount Sinai was reputed to be the home of El Shaddai... *the Almighty One...* the God of the Israelites. According to the Old Testament, God was enigmatically rumoured to live *in* Mount Sinai. Not as you would expect... as per the Greek gods and Mount Olympus ... *on* Mount Sinai. This does put a new slant on an old story.

Imagine the religious ramifications of this. It would destroy three of the world's greatest religions in one fell swoop. Christ! That's political dynamite. We'd better be very bloody careful if and when we release the information about this place.

There are plenty of powerful people with vested interests out there. Hell, there'll be thousands of radical religious types who are bound to get upset if this information was promulgated. It's scary, knowing how crazy some of those zealous bastards can be.

I think we'd better tread carefully and keep this place a secret. At least for the time being." he suggested. They all fell silent for a time, pondering the prospect of adverse reactions to their discovery. Having no theological barrow to push, they had not stopped to consider the political and religious ramifications before. Eventually they all agreed to keep their discovery a secret. At least until they considered it safe to divulge its existence.

As they began to relax once more, Charlie pondered the location of the other red pins. Then he pointed to the one in Antarctica. "Oh boy! That's interesting." he noted enthusiastically. "What?" Tim asked. Charlie pointed to the pin. "This pin here near Lake Vostok." Tim looked at the map and shrugged his shoulders. "What's significant about that, apart from the fact that Antarctica's been a frozen wasteland for God knows how long?"

Charlie smiled. "Rumour has it the Yanks and Russians are in cahoots, investigating some electro-magnetic anomalies. I've heard whispers they've found an alien base or something, two and a half kilometres under the ice. Perhaps someone out there knows a little more about our history than they're letting on.

I guess like all high-tech stuff, the military want to keep it under wraps until all potential military uses have been exploited. Then they'll covertly release it through sanctioned TNC's for civilian applications." Tim shook his head. "What's a TNC?" he asked, not really sure if he actually wanted to hear the answer. "A Trans-National Corporation. The large businesses committed to globalisation. You know. The New World Order. The one world economy, one world government stuff." Tim shook his head. "Jesus, Charlie! You read way too many conspiracy magazines." he concluded. "I like to keep informed so I can keep my options open, that's all." Charlie stated in his defence.

Tim smiled apologetically. "Well, I guess I'm not really in touch with the political world as much as I thought I was. I always considered politicians were the ones pushing the New World Order agenda. But now you mention it, I guess it's obvious that it's got to be some type of commercial venture if it's to survive."

They continued to discuss the implications of the map and the peripheral bases for some time. They also tried to decipher the meanings of the other coloured pins. Although many were in familiar archaeological sites, there was nothing to suggest exactly what they represented.

Finally Tim conceded there was nothing further they could ascertain from the map except speculation. So they moved on. "Well I hope you can get those computers working. There's bound to be information somewhere that shows us exactly what this map represents." Tim suggested, with a broad smile.

The others agreed, as they followed Tim out of the conference room and back into the lounge area. It was then Tim noticed a door, next to the entertainment screen. He wandered over and casually pushed the keypad. As the door opened, he noticed shelving around the perimeter of the room.

When he stepped in he saw what he thought was a wall in the centre of the room. Soon he realised that it was the end of more shelving, again carved from solid granite. It was when he focussed on the contents of the nearest shelf that he cried out to Charlie. "Charlie, come in here and look at this stuff will you?" Charlie yelled back. "What is it?"

Tim yelled back at Charlie. "It looks like a collection of weapons. From flint knives to Roman armour." Charlie joined him in a heartbeat. Together they wandered around the shelves like two schoolboys in a porn shop. Wide-eyed and drooling. "Look at that chain mail. It's incredibly fine." Tim pointed out.

"I've never seen anything as intricate as this before. And that helmet. Look at the ostrich plumes. And that one with the horsehair crest. It's been dyed a brilliant red. And look at that falcata. That blade is awesome. And look at the detail of the carved hilt. I've only ever seen pictures of this sort of thing. This is incredible. And look at these. They're the stuff of science fiction."Charlie looked at the sci-fi weapons that Tim was pointing at. "Yeah, they look like the weapons the warriors in the recreation room photo were carrying."

They wandered around for some time muttering to themselves. The diversity of weapons was staggering. The collection seemed to cover everything from Neanderthal to Star Wars. Finally Tim turned to Cathy. "You know what this means don't you?" She shook her head. "No, what?" Tim smiled as he proudly announced his theory.

"Look at the gap in weapons." he suggested. "Here are human weapons from the Stone Age. Look at those flint knives and flint-tipped spears. And we have weapons up to the time of the Romans by the look of that scutum there. It's got the golden eagle on it. The emblem of imperial Rome. Then we have super-modern weapons that obviously belonged to our extraterrestrial mates. But there are no conventional weapons as we know them." he observed.

"What, you mean guns?" Cathy offered. "Exactly!" Tim concurred. "There are no guns. Not even early muzzle-loaders. This suggests they left before the development of gunpowder. That Roman stuff is the latest I've seen. I think it's third or early fourth century AD by the wooden pins in the pilum. But I'm no ancient weapons expert. I'll take some photos and get a mate to look at them. He'll be able to give me a better indication of their age." he mused. But Cathy had a better idea.

"Why don't you just take one of the swords? It would be a lot easier for him to identify it then."

Tim looked at Cathy and thought about her suggestion for a moment. "You think I should?" he finally asked, a little bemused by her suggestion. Cathy smiled reassuringly. "Why not? As long as you make up a plausible story about how you obtained it." she suggested.

Tim chose what he considered to be the latest representative gladius, a classical Roman short stabbing sword. It was neatly laid out in its plain brown leather scabbard, at the far end of the collection. It was, unfortunately he thought, without a belt. But it was a thing of beauty. Its grooved iron hilt terminated in a smooth rounded pommel. Both the pommel and the crosspiece were made of bronze.

As he drew the first few inches of the double-edged blade, he noticed it was made of good quality iron. It had a dark brown patina of rust and perhaps grease, betraying its antiquity. The unsophisticated bronze riveted leather scabbard was still supple, in remarkable condition given its age.

Tim looked at it for some time, then with a coy smile, slid the scabbard under his belt so that the sword hung proudly from his waist. Cathy smiled at the sight of the modern warrior standing next to her. Charlie mumbled a back-handed comment about their ancestry, then looking at his watch he yelped. "Jesus! Would you look at the time? We'd better get back to camp if we want any sleep tonight. Besides, I'm dying for a beer."

CHAPTER 17

Standing in the centre of the great hall, ready to begin another day of exploration, Tim turned to Charlie. "Well, I know you're dying to get a look at those computers in the recreation room, but how about we just look at the accommodation units upstairs for a minute. Then we'll come back down here and see if we can decipher anything that might get them working. What do you reckon?" Charlie shrugged his shoulders and nodded. "Sure, why not? We've still got plenty of time left before we have to go back to Melbourne."

They headed off towards the nearest spiral stairway that led to the second accommodation level. It was hard work climbing the over-sized staircase, as it rose some fifty feet to the next level. While they stood panting, trying to regain their breath, Tim surveyed the scene.

They were on a large circular balcony that overlooked the great hall below. There were eight equally spaced, spoke-like corridors radiating off the circular balcony. The one immediately to his right was a long thin corridor with no visible doorways leading from it. The three opposite, across the void of the great hall, were clearly accommodation blocks.

Tim could see several doors leading off the main corridor, similar to the blocks below. The other corridors were at an angle to him, so he could only see their entrances. He decided to do a methodical search, starting with the first corridor on the right and continuing in an anti-clockwise direction. As he wandered off, the others dutifully followed. They were content for the moment to simply go where Tim took them. As they started off down the corridor, Tim looked to the end, some distance away. "Looks like it ends in a large room."

Eventually they reached the end, only to find another small balcony, this time over-looking the workshop area. Cathy, Tim and Charlie stood there for some time. They simply stared at the impressive excavation before them. The massive golden sphere of the power generator dominated the view to the left. Surrounding this was the control panels and ancillary equipment. Opposite them were the doors that led to the warehouse and tool store. About three hundred yards to their right was the armoury door.

Even from this height, they could not see the end of the runway. With its vaulted ceiling still far above them, the runway simply vanished into infinity. Lined up on the workshop floor, as they looked down to their right, they could see the three larger craft and the fourteen smaller ones, dotted along five or six hundred yards of the runway. It was only when viewed from this vantage point, that the larger craft were put into perspective.

It was a phenomenal sight that held them spellbound for several minutes. Finally it was Charlie who made the first move. He was keen to get to the computers. The others reluctantly followed him, as he headed off towards the next corridor.

The second corridor led into another recreation room. Here tables and chairs were almost randomly spread around the room. There was also a gargantuan entertainment screen. And there were the omnipresent computers and comfortable lounge areas, similar to the recreation room directly below. Again there were holographic photographs decorating the walls.

One in particular was very striking. It measured some fifteen feet high by twenty-five feet long and took pride of place in the centre of the right wall. It was an aerial shot of a squadron of the smaller aircraft, four in all, obviously taken from an attendant craft. In the background, far below, they could see the sphinx. Or at least it looked like the sphinx.

This one was also near a great river, although it was not running through a desert like the Nile did in Egypt. It showed fertile lands as far as the eye could see, with groves of majestic trees, their canopies reaching far into the sky. The shimmering, almost dazzling, white sphinx contrasted starkly with the verdant foliage.

The surface appeared to be highly polished as it reflected the sunlight in a vibrant play of glittering rays, that sparkled and jumped from point to point with unnerving animation as they walked past the 3D photo. The other thing they noticed was the absence of the pyramids. Tim commented on the picture to Cathy as they moved on. "It looks like the sphinx alright. But it doesn't look like the one in Egypt. Unless..." he paused as he thought of the possibilities. "Unless what?" Cathy enquired. "Unless they're right." he stated obliquely. But Cathy was not following his train of thought. "Who?" she asked with an almost desperate tone.

"Oh... several people really. There's a theory that the sphinx pre-dates the pyramids by thousands of years. In fact there's a bit of evidence to suggest the Giza pyramids, rather than being the last to be built, were actually the first. Thousands of years earlier than generally accepted.

The others weren't trials in the evolution of pyramid building, they were lesser architects trying to copy the works of the masters. Anyway, looking at the picture, it does seem to indicate..." he paused again as he pondered the picture. "Well theory has it the Egyptian desert is a relatively recent thing. Ten or fifteen thousand years ago it should have looked like this. Theoretically at least. I wonder ..."

He mused to himself over the possibilities as they casually wandered around the area, content with a just a cursory look for the time being. For now they simply wanted to know the extent of the base. They knew a more detailed inspection would follow.

The next corridor was an accommodation wing. Charlie pointed at the hieroglyphs above the first door. "What does that say, Tim?" Tim examined the writing closely before answering. "Let me see. It says... *ami-ariti qebu ua tcheri-t ua*. These must be the pilot's quarters. This says something like *Pilot Group One... Room One*. I guess that makes sense. All those photographs of spacecraft in the rec room. Oh... and the spaceships over there of course.

Did you notice that the uniforms of the blokes in the upstairs rec room were different to those downstairs?" No-one else had. Tim shrugged his shoulders in indifference and wandered off to look at the new accommodation blocks. As they walked through the rooms, they found they were identical to those in the lower accommodation blocks.

The block contained ten two-man rooms branching off from the corridor and a commander's room at the end. All the internal layouts were identical. Again the only differences being the personal effects and the photo collection by the door. The next corridor was the same, except the information on the doors suggested a second group of pilots were quartered there.

The next corridor was directly opposite the stairway they had climbed. Tim stopped and looked across the cavernous void. He was still very much impressed by the size of the base. Cathy noticed that the writing on the first door was different to that of the last two corridors. "What does this say, Tim?"

Tim paused to look at the writing. "It says... *sesh menfit tcheri-t ua*. It seems that this wing accommodated the military secretariat. Probably the secretaries, clerks, computer programmers and other ancillary staff. They've used the term *militia scribe* here. But I think it may have a slightly broader sense in a situation like this." But again the accommodation block was identical to the others.

After a quick look at a few rooms, they moved on to the next block. Tim mumbled to himself as he read the sign. "...*setchemu tcheri-t ua*. This looks like the tradesman's accommodation block. I guess they'd have to have some ancillary trade staff at a base like this. It looks like the warriors below... what were they called again?" Tim asked. "*Guardians*" Cathy offered. "That's right... the Guardians look like they were a purely military force. This upstairs accommodation seems to be for the ancillary staff. Unless the pilots were also combat pilots." he added. "Who does the cooking and cleaning?" Cathy asked. Tim shrugged his shoulders. "I don't know." he admitted. "Perhaps they're in one of the other blocks here."

Tim headed for the second last corridor. As he stood before the first door he read the sign above it. "*baut tcheri-t ua* ...*domestic servants*. Well I was right. I suppose this is the quarters of the cooking and cleaning staff. Do you want to have a look?" Cathy and Charlie declined. They had seen more than enough accommodation units and were keen to revisit other areas of the base. Areas they considered potentially more interesting. Tim respected their wishes and wandered off behind them.

As they headed towards the stairway, Tim noticed a small recess in the wall. On further investigation it turned out to be another staircase, only this time it went up, not down as expected. Tim immediately assumed it lead to a third level of accommodation units. Rather than bore the others, he volunteered to have a quick reconnoitre. "It looks like a stairway to more units. Funny though, there's no balcony above us, just a domed roof. Anyway, I'll just slip up and have a quick look. You two can wait here." he offered. "OK, but we'll only wait here if you hurry..." Cathy teased. Tim forced his tired Lilliputian legs to climb the giant never-ending staircase as quickly as he could.

He was very aware the others were becoming bored. As he reached the top, he found himself at the beginning of a short corridor. Ahead of him he could see a large circular room. Still assuming it was an accommodation wing, he casually wandered off to investigate. But something did not look right. He could see what appeared to be a niched wall in the centre of the room.

As he approached the room his heart began to race, as he recognised what he had stumbled into. Turning back toward the corridor, he cupped his hands around his mouth and shouted to the others. "Come here quickly you guys. I've found a museum." He waited for the muffled affirmative reply and returned his attention to the room.

It was about two hundred feet in diameter, with a domed roof some fifty feet high. Off this radiated sixteen equally spaced corridors, including the small one through which he had entered. Each was the standard ten yards wide by ten yards high. The sides of the corridors were carved into shelves and niches, with a single two-sided half-height wall running down the middle. This too was carved into shelves and niches of various sizes. From where he stood, it seemed that all the corridors, save the short one to the staircase, appeared to be very long. Much longer than the accommodation wings.

A few moments later they all stood open-mouthed, staring at the spectacular room. Again everything had been perfectly carved from the parent rock. The most striking feature was a central octagonal section, about eighty feet in diameter and twenty feet high. It stood proudly in the middle of the circular room, its niches loaded with an impressive array of ancient mementos. Standing atop this central display were two bronze, larger than life-size, figures. One appeared to be an ancient Greek warrior.

The other a barbarian of some description. They were locked in mortal combat. The Greek warrior was down on one knee, eyes staring up wildly at his assailant from deep behind his crested helmet. His helmet had a large crease on the right side. Indicative perhaps of the blow that had brought him to his knee. He was wearing a long cape, now pulled to one side and flowing over the ground around his bent knee, exposing his cuirass and the lower portion of his tunic.

A classic falcata held defiantly with blade point aloft in his powerful right hand was his only weapon. Strapped to his left forearm, his buckler was raised above his head in a desperate effort to fend off the imminent crushing blow.

The enraged barbarian towering over him, held a large battleaxe high above his head. By now the warrior had knelt patiently for millennia in silent anticipation of the inevitable end, but it had not yet come. The barbarian was the epitome of the savage brutality that prevailed in those troubled times. He was magnificently sculptured with rippling muscles and stark Teutonic facial features. He was clothed in animal skins, drawn at the waist with a large belt.

On his feet were thick fur boots, laced to his feet and legs with criss-crossed thongs. He wore no helmet. His wild dishevelled hair was flowing to one side as if being carried by some ethereal breeze. Nor did he carry a shield. His battleaxe, so ominously poised high above his head, was held tightly with both hands. His steely eyes were glaring at the hapless kneeling foe, almost consigned to his fate. It was an exquisitely crafted and very moving sculpture.

Tim stared at the ancient masterpiece for quite a while. Lost for the moment in the spirit of the ancient contest. Suddenly he was jolted back to the present, as Cathy brushed past him. He shook his head as he slowly looked around at the room.

Then he smiled as he realised the enormity of his discovery. From where he stood he could see countless shelves and niches on the periphery of the central room. This section alone must have housed thousands of items. As he began to explore the museum, he noticed some of the niches were minuscule. Only a few inches deep by several inches square. They housed tiny but obviously important items such as jewellery, mineral samples and micro-fauna.

Others were larger, some foot or so deep by several feet square. Some of these had internal shelves, others did not. They housed general items such as pottery, tools, weapons, personal trinkets and countless small round photographs. Some held small collections on their delicately carved granite shelves.

As they progressed along the corridor, they found niches that were quite large. Some measuring twenty or more feet deep and perhaps thirty feet square. One such recess contained an entire great woolly mammoth. It had obviously been expertly preserved. Tim and Cathy stared at its large, yellow ivory tusks, piercing brown eyes and shaggy coat of silver-grey hair. It took pride of place among a collection of impressive fauna that disappeared down the long corridor to their left.

It was an incredible sight that sent Tim off in a garrulous discourse. "Would you look at this stuff here? There are clothes and weapons and tools and animals and... everything. I can't believe it. We've hit the archaeological jackpot here. This is bloody amazing. I just can't believe what I'm seeing. It must have taken them thousands of years to build up this collection."

Cathy and Charlie stood next to Tim as he pointed wildly at the exhibits. He was like the proverbial kid in a candy store. He could not contain his enthusiasm. Whichever way he looked, he found something he wanted. Brain overload had him welded to the spot, his eyes darting back and forth as he babbled to himself.

Charlie was less impressed. The computers still held his interest. He eventually left Tim and Cathy to it and wandered off to determine the full extent of the museum. As he rounded a corner, he yelled for Tim. "Hey, Tim! You'd better get around here. You're not going to believe this." Tim and Cathy raced off to see what Charlie was so excited about. They located him halfway down one of the radial corridors, staring poker-faced at a small display. "What is it Charlie?"

"Look at this will you?" Charlie implored, as he pointed to a photograph. "It's an older looking photograph. It's still round, but not 3D like the others around the base. But it's still miles better than anything I've ever seen. It's definitely only two-dimensional. But look at the colour and clarity. The infinite detail. It's not grainy at all. And look what's in the photo."

Tim peered over at the twelve-inch diameter photograph and nearly choked as he tried to speak. "I'll be stuffed! It looks like a bloody T-Rex. And look, there's some warriors standing around it. It looks like they've shot it and they're posing for a trophy photo.

Christ it doesn't look like the monster from Jurassic Park though. It's pretty close in body shape, but it's so colourful. Bright green and yellow blotches. With darker, almost black, irregular tigerish stripes. Perfect camouflage for a jungle hunter I guess.

And look at the red and blue areas around those piercing green eyes. It's like a baboon's arse. It's a cross between a chameleon and a tiger. It looks as mean as a bucket of cat's piss! I know someone who'd be more than interested in this information. But I guess that'd give the game away too early if I told him about it now. It's a pity really. But look... in the background. There's another one standing at the edge of the clearing. Gee... it looks pissed off! Probably the dead one's mate. And look at the foliage. I've never seen such luxuriant growth before. Those ferns are magnificent.

Look there's a tooth next to the photo. Now there's something no-one else has ever seen. A T-Rex tooth with its original enamel still intact. It's rather impressive isn't it?" he asked no-one in particular. "Look at those serrations. Perfect for tearing flesh and cutting through bone. There's a description of the photo too."

Charlie mumbled impatiently as Tim read the inscription. When finished, he shook his head and read it out loud. Not realising he was still speaking in the Egyptian tongue. Finally Charlie butted in. "Well that was interesting! But what does it say in English?" Tim smiled. "Sorry. It's a little confusing, but it goes something like this..." he offered.

"*This collection is from the original museum of natural history from Satyoloka. It was split up among the colonies and this collection was brought here for safe keeping after the death of the* ... I can't really interpret this bit, but it seems to indicate the end of a planet or solar system or something.

Perhaps Satyoloka was their home planet and it was destroyed somehow. Anyway it goes on... *this picture is of the First Expeditionary Force of Guardians on their second voyage to this* ...solar system I guess. Then it gives a string of reference numbers. Again they mean nothing to me, but I guess they're part of their dating system.

By the photo though, it looks as if they were here a lot earlier than we thought. Look at the next photo. It's a Neanderthal with a Guardian. And look there's an older primate. It could be one of the Australopithecines. Perhaps plesianthropus. Hang on a minute... no. I think it's older than that. Look at the flat forehead. Perhaps it's Kenyaanthropus platyops. I wonder what they're doing with them. Look there's a Guardian with an ape."

"What do the pictures say, Tim?" Cathy asked. Tim stopped babbling and looked at the notes. "Oh yeah, that'll give us a clue. Let's have a look at the flat-headed chap. It says here that... *this is the first generation of* ..."

Tim gasped in disbelief. "Oh my God!" he exclaimed loudly. "What?" Cathy asked, not sure of the reason for Tim's reaction. "It's a little hard to interpret exactly, but I think it says... *this is the first generation of truly functional Anunnaki-ape hybrids.*" Cathy shook her head. "Who are the Anunnaki?" she asked.

"Sumerian Gods!" Tim explained, then continued. "I wonder what they were doing to the apes to hybrid them... and why? This next photo's a bit more specific. It shows a primitive man carrying a load of weaponry." he elaborated. "What does it say?" Cathy almost pleaded.

"It says... *A second generation ape-man being used to transport equipment of the fourth expeditionary group during their* ...sorry I can't read this. But it looks like it's something about preparations for colonisation. "My God! You know what that means?" Cathy shook her head, but took a guess anyway. "Darwin was wrong. We didn't evolve from apes. Rather, it looks like we were genetically engineered from them."

Tim nodded enthusiastically as he continued with his hypothesis. "Hell, this is going to turn science on its head! Look at this one. It's nearly a modern man. But look in the background. There's one of those flat-headed ape-men, looking out from under that tree behind him. This means that we definitely didn't evolve from a single species. This proves that they engineered several species in parallel. I knew there was something in that bloody Genesis story." he mused.

Cathy was intrigued. "What Genesis story?" she asked. Tim smiled. "The Bible..." he began. "In Genesis there are several recondite passages that hint of extraterrestrial encounters and perhaps inter-breeding." Tim explained. Cathy's ears pricked up. She too was raised a Catholic, but had long since wandered from the fold. Her curiosity was aroused. "What does it say?" she finally asked, encouraging Tim to continue.

"Well for example... I think it's Genesis chapter six, that says something like... *And now the Elohim saw how beautiful were these daughters of men, and took them for wives.* Now the word Elohim literally means *the ones from the sky...* implying multiple gods. But it's since been theologically corrected to read the sons of God.

Now why would they use the plural form of gods? Their god was supposed to be a singular omnipotent God. And why would his sons lust after earth women? In fact, who were these sons? According to Christian dogma he had only one son, Jesus.

Anyway, it made little sense to me before, but now I can see some logic in it. I wonder what the Anunnaki looked like. Perhaps they looked similar to us? After all, the Bible says the Elohim made man in their own image. There are references in Genesis to giants too. Again I think it's Chapter six... somewhere shortly after that. It says there were giants on the earth in those days. This is repeated in the book of Deuteronomy. I think around chapter two it even gives them a name. The Zamzam'min or something similar. This is exciting stuff indeed." he confessed.

Tim moved slowly along the collection of old photographs, browsing at them almost mechanically. The information he was seeing was far too much for his mind to process, but now he was on a mission. All of a sudden he stopped and back-tracked. "Look at this will you?" he called to Cathy. "What is it?" she asked, as she sidled up to Tim. "It's a photograph of an award ceremony of some sort. It shows some warriors lined up receiving medals or something. But look at the person presenting them. It's a human. White skin, red hair, red plaited beard and blue eyes. My God, he's a Celt!" Tim exclaimed in amazement.

"What does the inscription say?" Cathy asked, now peering intently at the photograph. Tim studied the writing for a moment before answering.

"It says... *members of the fourth expeditionary force receiving their medals of bravery from his* ...I can't really interpret the next bit. But it seems to be some form of title. Like His Excellency or His Majesty, or something. Anyway, it goes on with a name... *Hesep-ti the fifteenth.* Then it says... *following their rescue of the Crown Prince from the...* The word used is ***An-tiu***. It means *Troglodyte* or some ancient tribe or something similar... *hoards near the swamp of Enkhali.* Then it gives a date."

Cathy inspected the photograph closely. She looked at the elegant linen robe. It was delicately embroidered with red and gold threads. She looked down at the elaborate gold studded sandals and then at the jewellery. Around his neck he wore a small gold pectoral, which appeared to be embossed with a scarab beetle. On his fingers and toes were numerous gold rings, the detail of which was indistinct.

On each forearm he wore a wide gold bracelet. The nearest one also embossed with a scarab. This time its brightly coloured blue wings were spread ready for flight. Then she looked at the fine features of the monarch's face. The piercing blue eyes, the full lips and the shock of red hair cascading from under his regal helmet. This was bright blue in colour, with the golden head of a cobra, the Egyptian uræus, protruding from its peak. It reminded her of the pictures of Ramesses in his war helmet.

Then she looked at the plaited beard. It was only six inches or so long, but was terminated with a small etched gold band, about an inch wide. She smiled and turned to Tim. "I guess Hitler was wrong too! He thought Aryans were the master race. It looks like the Celts have that honour. And the Aryans are a genetic offshoot. I wonder how he'd feel if he knew his *master race* was only a genetic mutation of the real thing."

They laughed at the thought, then Cathy mentioned the jewellery. "Does anything here strike you as odd?"

Tim looked at the picture closely. "Yes... well not really odd. He seems to be wearing a lot of gold, but that ornament around his neck looks familiar. It looks like a fine gold chain, weaved into a circular chord. It's been formed into a circle by tying the ends together. And it's hanging low on his chest..." he almost whispered.

"A shen ring?" Cathy offered. "It certainly looks like it." Tim agreed. Charlie raised his eyebrows, as he leaned over Tim's shoulder to look at the picture. "What's a shen ring?" he asked. Tim pointed to the photograph. "It was a ring that was carried by things like depictions of the sun god, or a deceased person's *ba* or soul. It was a symbol of eternity. It looked like a chord turned into a single loop, with the ends protruding. Sort of like the Greek capital letter Omega. The bottom of the circle was held together with some sort of twine or something. See here. The shen ring is bound by a red chord or something." he explained.

But since the photo asked more questions than it answered, they soon found themselves tiring of it and decided to continue their exploration. They wandered around the museum for some time. Charlie casually browsed around the exhibits while Tim and Cathy took their time. Tim was reading as much as he could, without unduly detaining Charlie. And he was taking photographs like there was no tomorrow.

Suddenly Cathy tugged Tim's arm. "Have a look at this!" she urged. Tim followed her to a large display of jewellery. He glanced past the array of gold rings, earrings, pendants, finger and toe stalls and assorted smaller items. His attention had been drawn to a large pectoral some ten inches in diameter.

It was a black onyx scarab, standing vertically on its hind legs. It had three gold bars protruding from the end of its wing case to a light blue semi-circle below. Above its head was a large red cabochon stone.

It looked like a ruby, set in a gold bezel. Almost joining the blue semi-circle to the red stone on either side of the beetle were two magnificent upswept wings, made of gold and inlaid with precious stones. He recognised the turquoise and lapis lazuli, but the green stone was unfamiliar. It appeared to be a type of jade or chrysoprase. The outer layer of the wings, was encrusted with sapphires. The inner wings were ornately detailed in embossed gold.

"*kheperu neb Ra...*" Tim commented. "That's interesting." he mused. "But not as interesting as this." Cathy offered. Tim looked at the piece Cathy was pointing at. "My God! It's a shen ring. Look at the size of it and it's very worn. It must be very old." Cathy nodded. "What does the caption say?" Tim looked at the inscription, then set about interpreting it. "It says... *The shen ring of the great... king? ...Horus the golden. Saved from the... destruction and kept in... Atur-res ...that's Upper Egypt... until the end of the... Royal Line. Brought to this place for... posterity...* I guess."

"It's magnificent." Cathy noted. "The intricately braided fine gold wire has formed a large gold chord and look. The bottom of the ring is tied with another thin rope." Cathy observed. But Tim disagreed. "That's not rope. It's another woven metal chord, only thinner. But look at the colour. It's bright red. I know of no alloys that colour. Not even pure copper is as red as that. It's the colour of ruby. I wonder what it is?"

CHAPTER 18

Once he'd done a lightning reconnoitre of the museum, Charlie returned to Tim and Cathy. He stood next to them and waited, as Tim finished interpreting a small clay tablet that dated back to the time of Abraham. "I've found a couple of doorways. Wanna take a look? There's plenty of time for you museum geeks to check this stuff out over the next couple of weeks." Sensing Charlie's boredom with the museum, Tim begrudgingly agreed to look. After all, they still had several weeks of holiday left. Now was not the time to be selfish.

"OK. Where are they?" he asked. "There's one just behind you, near where we came in. The other one's at the end of that corridor over there." Tim nodded. "OK. Let's look at this one shall we?" They wandered over to the nearest door. Tim looked at the neatly carved gold-plated hieroglyph above it and frowned. "What's the matter?"

"Nothing really. It's just a bit puzzling." he admitted. "That symbol of a boat is simply the determinative of travel. As it's written, it simply implies *to travel*." Tim observed. "What's the worried look for then?" Cathy asked. "Oh, I don't know. I was just wondering where they were travelling to... and in what?" he mused.

"You mean, like a time machine or something?" she joked. "Well, yes. I guess those old pictures have me wondering whether they've been visiting earth for a hundred and fifty million years, or they only came here relatively recently and time-travelled back to affect these genetic changes." Cathy laughed at the ludicrous suggestion of time travel. "You've been watching too much *Doctor Who!*" she teased. "Yes, I guess you're right. Time travel is a bit far-fetched.

But who knows what technology these chaps have. Anyway, I suppose we should open it up and have a look." Tim reached over and pressed the keypad. He stood back and watched as the door slid sideways with the same unnerving silence as all the other doors they had opened. As it disappeared from view, he stepped forward into a room some thirty feet square. It was completely empty. Charlie and Cathy joined him.

It was Cathy who noticed the look of disappointment on his face. "Cheer up Tim, maybe the *Tardis* is stored somewhere else." Tim acknowledged her wicked sense of humour with a smile, then turned to leave. As he approached the door he noticed something. He stopped and pointed it out to Charlie. "Look at this! There are seven keypads. Each with a label."

"Well what do they say?" Charlie urged. Tim looked at the symbols. "The top one says... *ar n apu* ...some kind of *storehouse for tributes*. The next one says... *ar n tep aui* ...which means a *storehouse of antiquity,* ...something to do with *remoteness of time*... a museum. Hey, this is an elevator! It goes to seven levels. This is level *two*... the museum."

Charlie wandered over to the door and inspected the floor. The difference in the granite was plain to spot. "You're right Tim. Look, there's a small gap between the floor here and the floor beyond the door. It's an elevator alright. What are the other levels?" Again Tim looked at the symbols. "The next one is simply the determinative *to rest* and the number two.

I guess that implies the accommodation wing on the level below us. The next one is also the determinative *to rest*, with the number one. But it also has the travel determinative. I suppose that's referring to the spacecraft. The last three are the same. They read... *shta-t*... Oh my God!" he exclaimed loudly, almost frightening Charlie. "There's a crypt in here. A repository for the deceased. A storeroom of the dead.

God, there are dead aliens on the base. We might be able to see some mummified warriors if we're lucky."

Cathy whimpered softly, as she nervously grabbed Tim's arm and clung to it. "This is getting a bit creepy." she suggested nervously. But Tim was keen to see the crypt. "Game to see if the elevator works?" he asked enthusiastically. "It's a bit of a risk." Charlie warned. "What if it goes to places that are only accessible by lift and we lose the power. How do we get out?"

Tim frowned as he pondered the consequences. "Hell Charlie, I never thought of that. Cathy, do you mind staying in the museum and waiting for us? If we're not out in a couple of days you'd better go get some help." he joked. But Cathy was not amused. "A couple of days!" she exclaimed in horror.

"Sorry honey, I was just kidding. We'll be back in an hour. Two at the most." he assured her. But Cathy was uncomfortable with the whole deal. "I don't like the idea of staying by myself, but I guess you're right. One of us should stay in case the power fails. And I don't fancy the idea of visiting a crypt just yet. I'll have to get used to the idea first. OK, I'll wait for you here. But don't be long!" Cathy reached up and kissed Tim tenderly on the lips, then shuffled backwards out of the elevator. "See you in an hour... and promise you won't be any longer."

"OK, an hour at the most. While we're there we'll see if there's another way into the crypt other than the lift. See you later." Tim smiled at Charlie and gave him a nefarious wink. He'd been in ancient tombs many times before and was not only comfortable with the thought of visiting another; he eagerly looked forward to it.

But he knew that Charlie cringed when he went near a cemetery. He could tell Charlie was absolutely petrified of the idea of going into an underground crypt. Only his desire to save face in front of Cathy forced him to go along. Tim reached over and pushed the fifth keypad.

As soon as the door closed they immediately felt a rapid dropping sensation. Almost as soon as they felt themselves moving, the floor beneath them came to a sudden but very smooth stop. Tim looked over at his decidedly nervous brother and smiled. "Either the crypt isn't very far below the museum, or this is the quickest and quietest elevator I've ever ridden in."

As he spoke, the door opened. Before he stepped out, Tim addressed Charlie, the tone of his voice betraying his seriousness. "Be careful down here, there might be booby traps. We haven't encountered any yet, but they're usually placed around treasuries and tombs. So be careful. It's probably best if you just stick with me for a while until we're sure it's safe to wander about." he warned. "Thanks, that's just what I needed to hear. Dead aliens *and* booby traps!"

Tim cautiously peered out of the elevator. The ever-present glowing plasma had pervaded even this deep into the earth. He was impressed. He looked out from his safe refuge for a few moments until reassured that all was well. He could see nothing that indicated the crypt was booby-trapped. There were no anomalies in the floor, just a solid polished granite surface. So too the walls had no obvious apertures or protrusive sensors.

Without looking at Charlie, he strode confidently forward, eyes darting about as he continually assessed the situation. After he had walked a few yards he stopped. He sensed he was alone, so he turned to look for his missing brother. Charlie was still standing in the middle of the elevator, as nervous as a long-tailed cat in a room full of rocking chairs. "Come on Charlie, it looks OK. Just follow close behind me. You'll be alright. I don't see any booby traps."

The elevator had opened on the edge of a square room, hewn from the solid granite like the rest of the base. Rather than the labyrinthine corridors normally associated with such a place.

Tim was taken aback by the simple linear layout of the crypt. Running off the room were numerous radial corridors. Each the standard ten yards wide by ten yards high and perhaps two hundred yards long. Lining each wall of the corridors were niches housing an impressive display of polished black granite sarcophagi. He noticed how they contrasted with the green and cream local granite and wondered where they came from.

Tim had a quick look around, as a final confirmation that the crypt was not booby-trapped. Confident it was safe to proceed, he strode towards the nearest sarcophagus. As he approached it, he noticed a 3-D photo and a small caption on the side of the coffin. Charlie, who was now standing at his side, looked at the photo then at Tim. "Is that the bloke who's in there?"

"I guess so. It says his name was **Uatch-Neser-t se Api-tchet-f**. That simple means he was Uatch-Neser-t the son of Api-tchet-f. Those names are strangely familiar. I'll take a photo and research them later, but I think the second name is one of the names the Egyptians gave to Osiris.

Anyway, this bloke was a *Guardian of the Second Settlement*... whatever that means. There are two dates... I suppose they're dates... here. I guess one was his birth date. The other was when he died. Or one could be when he came here... the other when he died. Either way, we might find out more if we can access their computer data base."

Charlie nodded and smiled with anticipation. He was keen to have a look at the computers, now the base had power. They offered answers to the overwhelming list of questions that had accumulated in his head. But that would have to wait. For now he was content to support his brother as he mapped the extent of the base.

He wandered mutely behind Tim as he inspected more of the crypt.

As time progressed and the exploration proceeded event free, he began to feel more comfortable. Nonetheless, during the next twenty minutes he was never more than a foot from Tim's elbow. Eventually Tim tried to raise the lid of one sarcophagus, but it was far too heavy. "We'll bring some jacks or something down here one day and have a look inside, eh?" he smirked. "I don't think so, Tim!" Charlie retorted.

"You big girl!" Tim teased. "There's nothing to be scared of. They're all dead! Anyway, there's not much to see in here really unless we can get a lid or two off. So I guess we should be getting back to Cathy. Although I think we'll stop at all the other floors quickly just to see what's there."

Once back inside the elevator, Tim pressed the sixth button and watched as the door silently closed. He still had no idea how the doors worked, but he was impressed with the silent efficiency with which they operated. The elevator took them deeper into the earth until they reached the second level of the crypt. As Tim stepped out, he turned to Charlie. "You can wait here if you like. I'll only be a minute."

He wandered off for a quick reconnoitre. Within five minutes he was back at the elevator and the very much-relieved Charlie. "It's just the same as the other level. Not much to see unless we can get some lids off. One thing though. There's an awful lot of bodies down here. Given the limited number of accommodation units we've found so far, either most of them lived and died elsewhere and were all brought here for burial... or they were here for a long, long time."

He stepped back into the elevator and pressed the seventh keypad. The elevator stopped at the third level of the crypt. Again Tim stepped out by himself for a cursory look around. He returned to the elevated and shrugged his shoulders. "Still the same. I can't see any other entrances though.

It must be part of the security measures they took. Looks like you can only access this area when the power's on. A simple but effective way to keep out grave robbers I guess. That's probably why they set no booby traps. OK! I think I've seen enough for now. How about we head back up to Cathy."

Charlie enthusiastically agreed with the suggestion as Tim stepped back inside the elevator. But instead of pressing the second button as expected, Tim pressed the fourth button. He smiled with an impish grin at Charlie. "I hope you don't mind. I just want to see what this *travelling* thing is about, on the way up."

The elevator stopped and opened into a long corridor. Tim stepped out and looked back at Charlie. "You can wait here if you like. I'll just go and see where this leads. If I find anything interesting, I'll come back and get you."

Charlie did not have to wait long. Tim was back in less than two minutes. Charlie picked up on the look of disappointment written across his face as Tim stepped into the elevator. "Well?" he urged. Tim smiled and shook his head slightly. "I should have guessed. This corridor just goes to a door we passed in the workshop area... to the spacecraft.

It makes perfect sense when you think about it. They had to have access to the spaceships to get the bodies back here I guess... and all that stuff in the museum. Some of those exhibits are impressive, to say the least. I was wondering how they managed to lug them up the stairs. Oh well, one to go, if you're still keen. Although I might just stop at the museum level on the way up. Just to let Cathy know we're OK."

Tim pressed the second button and the elevator rose swiftly and silently. It came to a stop at the museum level. As the door opened, Cathy flung herself at Tim in a gesture of pure relief. After she had near hugged him to death, he gently pushed her away.

"We've seen all the lower floors. There's only the upper one to look at now. But I thought we'd just stop off to let you know we're OK. We'll just slip up to look at the last floor then we'll be back. Ten minutes or so."

Cathy nodded sadly, but then smiled politely as she backed out of the elevator. Tim pressed the top keypad. He could see she was unhappy about them leaving her alone again, but his natural curiosity demanded he carry on. As the door closed, the last thing he saw was the worried look on Cathy's face. He wished he could be with her, but someone needed to remain outside the elevator in case they lost power.

He was still thinking about that forlorn, sad-puppy look when the elevator came to a stop and the door opened. Tim stepped out and flashed a glance around the small room, Charlie following at his elbow. Suddenly it dawned on him what he was looking at. He stopped so abruptly that Charlie ran into his back. "What did you stop for?" Tim did not answer.

He simply raised his hand to point at what stood before them and stammered something meaningless. Charlie looked up and gasped. He shook his head and blinked in disbelief. He was almost convinced his eyes were playing tricks on him. As he realised what he was seeing, his heart began to race with excitement. "Jesus Christ! Is that what I think it is?"

"Yes, it's gold and silver bullion by the looks of it. Stacks of it. And it looks like the pile goes back quite a way too." Then Tim suddenly had a realization. "Of course!" he announced proudly. Charlie looked over at Tim with glazed eyes. "What?" he asked casually.

"The label on the elevator keypad was ... *ar n apu* ...that usually means *storehouse of tributes*. But it can also mean *treasury*... somewhere to store taxes. We've hit the jackpot here old son. This is where they stored their gold and silver. I presume they used it primarily to make their power generators.

Look at the size of those bars. How much do you think each one weighs?" Charlie walked over to the closest pile and eagerly grabbed a bar. He lifted it up and held it in both hands, symbolically weighing it. His face contorting at the unexpected weight. "About forty or fifty pounds I reckon."

"In that case there must be hundreds, if not thousands of tons of gold and silver here. This makes Tutankhamen's tomb look like a pauper's grave! My God! I can't believe it. There's enough here for ten thousand lifetimes. What do you reckon we should do?" Charlie's face erupted into a beaming smile. "I reckon we should take a few bars back with us. Let's put fifty in the elevator now and at least get them to the museum level. If we lose power we'll never get back in here... and that'd be a crying bloody shame."

But Tim was not so sure. "Do you think that's ethical?" Charlie looked sternly at his brother. "What's there to be ethical about? Who else is going to use it? It's probably been sitting here for thousands of years already. Just think of what we could do with a ton of gold. How many millions of dollars is that worth? We can both give up work and do anything we want."

"I guess you're right. We could put it to good use. And there's plenty here. No-one's going to miss a few bars. OK, you've talked me into it! Let's put some of these into the elevator and get back to Cathy."

Tim walked over to the stack of bars and picked one up. He looked at the writing stamped into the polished surface. "It says... *nub en sep khemt* ...that's triple refined gold. This stuff must be very pure. It also says... *kerker ua* ...*one talent*. You were close Charlie. They weigh about twenty-two and half kilos each. That's close enough to fifty pounds."

They selected bars from the nearest stack and lugged them one at a time to the elevator. Fifty bars made a surprisingly small but heavy pile. Just over a ton.

Satisfied with their haul, Charlie was about to press the keypad when Tim realised he had not looked behind the elevator at the other two sections of the Y-shaped room. "I'll be back in a minute. I'll just check over here. It looks like there's some wooden boxes or something behind the elevator."

Charlie waited for Tim to return, but he was quickly summoned. "Charlie... come over here and look at this will you." He rushed over to find Tim bent over a large wooden chest. The lid was bent back and its contents were chinking wildly. "What is it?"

"The gold of the Gods!" he explained with pride. "What?" Charlie asked, not sure of Tim's meaning. "You know how every ancient religion always demanded sacrifices of gold and silver to the gods... amongst other things. Well I think I've just found out where a lot of that ended up." he explained. "Look in here, Charlie." Charlie peered into the open chest and his eyes bulged with disbelief. "What are they?" he asked feebly, already knowing the answer.

"Gold coins. Thousands of them! And look around! There are dozens of these boxes. They look like they're made of cedar. And the bindings look like bronze. I wonder if they're made from the legendary cedars of Lebanon. That's a nice thought."

Tim rushed around madly lifting lids and peering into the boxes, grabbing coins at random and stuffing them in his pockets. Finally he returned to Charlie, still kneeling in front of the original chest. He also dropped to his knees, spreading a selection of coins on the floor in front of him. "This section of the room is full of trunks of coins. One side is all gold coins... the other is all silver coins. There must be millions of them.

There are gold and silver pieces from the Sumerians, Hebrews, Egyptians, Babylonians, Assyrians, Greeks and Romans. In fact almost everyone in the ancient world is represented it seems. Look at these!

Here's a silver *stater* from Syracuse, from the time of Timoleon of Corinth. That's around three hundred and forty BC. And look, here's a silver *tetradrachm* from Athens. From the fifth century BC. And some more silver tetradrachms from Ptolemy XII of Egypt around seventy BC. And here's a gold *solidus* from Julius Nepos at Mediolanum. This means they were here at least up to about four-eighty AD."

Charlie looked at the coins and shrugged his shoulders. He knew nothing of such things, but was inwardly impressed by his brother's seemingly infinite knowledge of all things ancient. He watched Tim regather the coins and place them in his pocket. Then he stood and motioned to the other section of the room. "I'll just have a quick look over there while we're here." Tim nodded then returned his gaze on the trunk of coins. He started sifting through them as Charlie wandered over to the final section of the room.

Charlie sidled up to a large wooden chest, similar to the ones holding the coins, but half as big again. He nonchalantly lifted the lid and stared at the contents. He turned towards Tim and motioned him rather casually. "You might want to come and have a look at this."

Tim dropped the coins he was inspecting and hurried over to Charlie. He gasped as he peered past the raised lid and saw the contents. It was full of solid gold artefacts. Some were jewel encrusted while others were intricately embossed with various themes.

There was a large plate with embossed fruit at its centre. Smaller plates both plain and with embossed patterns around their rims. There were numerous goblets, including one in the shape of a lotus flower. There were ewers and cups and a large jewel encrusted chalice. He noticed several large serving trays, one with riveted handles, others with simple raised rims. There were dozens of assorted candleholders, some for a single candle. Others for multiple candles.

There were also several oil lamps and what appeared to be various religious ceremonial items. Tim rummaged eagerly through the box talking as he went, oblivious to the fact that Charlie had wandered off to look in the other nearby boxes. Eventually he was extricated from the chest when Charlie called out to him again. "I think I've found something that you'll want to take home." Charlie called out.

Tim carefully, almost reverently, replaced the goblet he was inspecting. He then got up from his knees and hurried over to Charlie. There in a large gold-bound highly polished cedar chest was a set of solid gold armour. It was classical Greek. As Tim raised the elongated, bubble-like one-piece helmet it glistened in the effusive base lights.

It had the distinguishing T-shaped opening in the front where the slotted eyeholes extended down to the mouth. The frontal section swept low to protect the wearer's chin and throat. The horsehair crest that ran along the ridge of the helmet from the forehead to the nape of the neck had been stained red. It looked as bright as the finest ruby.

The golden helmet was around an eighth of an inch thick and was finely embossed in a symmetrical pattern, about three quarters of an inch wide, around the slot and the lower edge. The spine, which held the crest in position, was also finely embossed with the same pattern, but this was only half an inch wide. The wolf pelt lining of the helmet was in perfect condition, showing no sign of wear. Tim carefully placed the helmet on the floor, not wanting to scratch its shiny surface.

Packed neatly underneath the helmet was a magnificent breastplate. It was a two-piece affair, front and back, again some eighth of an inch thick. It was sculptured to hug a well-proportioned chest. It was bound together with leather side thongs.

The he noticed it was reinforced with curved shoulder pads, made of gold about three inches wide and three eighths of an inch thick. These were also tied to the main plates with leather thongs. Each over-piece was embossed with a small eagle, front and back. The breastplate itself was embossed with a large eagle, wings spread and talons flexed. Eyes staring wildly to its right.

Below the breastplate hung a finely woven skirt of the purest white linen. It was delicately embroidered around the hem with several fine gold threads. Interlaced with a rich red silken thread, it formed a regal pattern about three inches wide. Overlaying the skirt was a gold armour skirt made up of eighth inch thick overlaying scales of gold. Each smooth scale was about two inches wide and six inches long, terminating in a rounded edge that overlapped the scale below. The scales were fastened together with small gold rings that allowed the skirt to flex and chink softly when touched.

At the end of the box was a pair of stout leather sandals. They had gold greaves attached to their front by a series of sturdy criss-crossed leather thongs. The greaves were about three eighths of an inch thick and were embossed with a prancing horse, reminiscent of the famous Ferrari symbol. Underneath these was a set of thigh protectors, reminding him of medieval armour tassets. These too were about three eighths of an inch thick and embossed with an eagle motif. The leather thongs that held them in place were neatly coiled beneath them.

Tim lifted the breastplate and attached skirts from the box and carefully laid them out on the floor. Lying underneath was a large, round, solid gold buckler, about three feet in diameter. It was almost half an inch thick at its centre and tapered to just over a quarter of an inch at the neatly bevelled rim. The front was embossed with a large prancing horse.

Around the perimeter of the shield was an intricately embossed battle scene, some four inches wide. It featured many one-on-one combat scenarios, showing a diversity of weapons in use against a variety of presumed enemies. The two attaching straps on the rear of the shield were about two inches wide. The leather was thick and supple. Remarkably well preserved with what appeared to be some kind of oil.

The straps were fastened to the shield with large gold rivets, whose heads were rounded and polished smooth. As he strained to lift the heavy shield he saw a magnificent leather belt, some three and a half inches wide, lying at the bottom of the chest. It had gold rivets around its edges and several large gold loops attached to it. It was fastened by a large carved gold buckle.

Lying under the belt and attached to it, was a leather scabbard, a little over two feet in length and about four inches wide. It was tipped with a delicately embossed gold chape, locked into place with gold rivets. The locket was also made of embossed gold and riveted to the scabbard in a similar fashion. Both were emblazoned with small eagles, sitting at rest atop a standard bearing pole.

The remainder of the scabbard had a course gold thread woven in a criss-cross pattern down each side. This pattern was complimented with intermittent gold rivets of varying sizes, creating a simple but effective checkerboard pattern. Riveted in the centre of the outside face of the scabbard was a small, carved gold eagle. Wings spread and looking defiantly to its right. Its one visible eye had been replaced with a small round cabochon emerald.

Protruding from the scabbard was a gold sword hilt. The pommel of which was finely carved into the shape of an eagle's head. It had eyes of faceted emeralds that sparkled mystically as Tim slowly drew the heavy sword from the scabbard.

The blade squealed gently against the mouthpiece as it was withdrawn. The beautiful patina of the oxidized iron blade contrasted magnificently with the gold crosspiece. There was a small red stone inlaid either side of the flattened terminal bulge of each quillon. Tim ran his finger over the edge of the blade. Even though it looked very old and dull, it felt razor sharp. He noticed two Greek letters deeply etched into the ricasso... Ψ Ω.

He wondered what they signified, then concluded they must have been a maker's mark. Maybe Psi was the maker and Omega stood for the place of manufacture. Olympia perhaps? He slid the sword back into the scabbard until it locked home with a crisp *clunk.*

Tim turned to Charlie as he prepared to replace the items. "Look the sandals and greaves don't look like they've ever been worn. Neither does the helmet. The sword blade is amazingly well preserved, there's not a hint of pitting or rust... just a beautiful patina. Whatever oil they used to preserve it in is bloody good stuff.

And look at the hilt. It's pure gold. Inlaid with emeralds and rubies by the look of it. It's totally impractical for combat, so I'm assuming this must have been a ceremonial set. It's bloody beautiful. If I put it all back into the box do you think we can drag it into the lift?" Charlie nodded. "Sure. But we'd better get going though. Cathy will be getting worried by now."

CHAPTER 19

Cathy launched herself at Tim as the door opened. Hugging him tightly, as she wrapped around him like a hungry python. She was so relieved to see him that she was oblivious to Charlie and the other contents of the elevator. When she finally stopped smothering Tim in kisses, she whispered into his ear. "God you had me worried. I didn't think you'd be that long." Tim said nothing. He just smiled and gently prised Cathy's arms from around his neck. He slowly turned her around and proudly pointed at the booty. "Sorry for the delay, but look what we found." he said, pointing to the loot.

"Shit! Is that gold?" Cathy exclaimed in shock. Tim laughed as the expletive slipped from her normally reserved tongue. "Yes, my dear. It certainly is. There's hundreds, if not thousands of tons of it up there." Cathy began to shake uncontrollably with excitement.

She looked from the gold to Tim and back to the gold. He gave her a moment to come to terms with what she was seeing. Then he took some coins from his pocket and placed them in her hand. "And look what else is up there. Gold and silver coins that span several thousand years. Right up to the fifth century AD.

It means they've only been gone for fifteen hundred years or so... maybe less." he postulated. Cathy watched in stunned silence as the men unloaded the bars of gold from the lift and placed them in a neat pile on the floor. As they dragged the large wooden chest out of the lift, she looked quizzically at Tim. "What's in the box?"

Tim smiled knowingly as he slowly opened the lid. Then he stood back and watched with pride as Cathy peered at the contents. "Gold armour!" she exclaimed. "It's absolutely gorgeous. Look at it shine. My god that's the prettiest thing I've ever seen. It looks old.

What period is it from?" she asked. Tim shook his head. "It looks Corinthian from the mid fifth or sixth century BC... at a guess. But the eagles are throwing me off. They look more imperial Roman." he postulated. "I'll have to take your word for that." she smiled.

Tim laughed as he lowered the lid. "Well if we lose power now, at least we've got enough gold to retire. And I've got more than enough material for my own museum. Although some of this stuff's probably better off being left here. I'll just take a few of the more conventional archaeological exhibits. Things like the T-Rex photo might cause too much of a stir right now. It would be awfully difficult to explain where they came from. I don't really want to do that just yet. I've got this nagging feeling that it's not such a good idea."

Charlie looked at his watch and then turned to the others. "We'll have to be getting back to camp soon. I guess we can look at the computers tomorrow. What about it, Tim?" he asked. "What's the time?" Tim enquired. "It's four o'clock already." Charlie informed him. "Jesus time flies when you're having fun! Do you think we've got time to take a quick look at that other door you saw... while we're here?

That'll be this area complete, so we can concentrate on the computers tomorrow." Charlie reluctantly agreed, although he would rather head back to camp for a beer. "You're seriously cutting into my drinking time, but I guess it makes sense to look at it while we're here. I reckon I'd rather start with the base commander's computer tomorrow. If it's all the same with you. I should imagine it'd have more data than any of the other computers we've seen so far. Did you see the size of the card library there?" he reminded them.

Tim nodded. "I certainly did. I think you're right. That computer's more likely to have a complete set of files with it than those in the rec room. Unless they're all connected to a central mainframe or something.

Anyway, it's a good place to start. We'll go straight there tomorrow. Now where's this door?" he asked. Charlie pointed to his right. "It's at the end of this corridor." Charlie led them down one of the museum corridors, past endless exhibits of beautifully adorned pottery, ivory and metal household trinkets.

There were small mosaics, paintings and carved statues, many of which seemed as fresh as the day they were made. Others were decidedly the worse for wear, as if they had been salvaged after a fierce battle or a natural disaster.

Tim paused as he saw a small cuneiform tablet next to a gold chalice. "That's Persian. It's a note from Cyrus saying *this gold cup is a gift to Ishtar*. From the spoils of the Median wars it seems. That dates it around 530 BC. I've got my work cut out for me, just photographing and cataloguing all this stuff." he mused.

The previously unseen museum exhibits fascinated Tim. He had not seen this corridor before. Charlie had to continually stop, return to where Tim had stalled and physically drag him towards the door. Constantly reminding him that he still had several weeks left to inspect and catalogue the contents of the base.

Eventually they reached the end of the corridor and paused in front of a keypad. Tim looked at the writing above the door. " *as-t na shau* " he quoted. A beaming smile suddenly appeared across his face as he recognised the words. "That's a *library* or *record office*. This could be interesting, Charlie. Maybe we won't need the computers after all. Perhaps it's all written down for us in here." he speculated.

Tim pressed the keypad and stood back as the large door slid quietly aside. What greeted them was truly awesome. They all stopped and stared, open-mouthed, for some time. Before them was a long corridor, intricately carved and decorated with hieroglyphs and pictures of varying size and complexity.

On the wall to their right was a giant *ba* bird, deeply engraved into the vitreous green and cream granite wall. Its fine detailed outline was heavily gold leafed. Its wings stretched out to a massive twenty-foot span. The detail of the feathers was astounding.

Each individual feather was brightly coloured in what seemed to be enamel. The colours were turquoise blue, red, green and sapphire blue, with each feather outlined in gold. Its head was that of a fine looking young man. He wore a plaited beard that terminated in a gold hoop. His rufous, shoulder-length, flowing hair and gold uræus headpiece were intricately detailed. His head was turned to his right, staring intently along the highly polished corridor. In each of its outstretched clawed feet, the ba bird held a gold shen ring, bound with a red chord. "Look! Gold and red shen rings, like the one in the museum." Cathy observed.

After digesting the grandeur of the giant ba bird, Tim glanced along the rest of the wall. The corridor seemed to be the standard ten yards wide by ten yards high. Six royal cubits by six royal cubits. It was perhaps a hundred yards long. In the distance it seemed to terminate in a room. Lining both sides of the corridor were columns of neatly engraved hieroglyphs.

They were carved about half an inch into the rock, then gilded with gold leaf to highlight them. Each column was separated by a vertical line, about half an inch wide, again carved about half an inch into the rock. It too was gilded with gold leaf. Each hieroglyph was perfectly carved, again suggesting the work of an engraving machine, rather than the cross-legged, chisel-wielding scribes of ancient Egypt.

The ancient writing lined the wall as far as the eye could see. A blank column occasionally interrupted the body of the text, but the overall effect was stunning. They all stared at the shimmering golden writing. It contrasted beautifully with the dark green granite.

Finally Cathy grabbed Tim's arm and asked him what the writing meant. He scanned the right-hand wall for a moment and then smiled as he translated the first column to himself, confirming his initial suspicions. "It's a king list." he explained. "These are the names of the kings, followed by their city of rule, followed by the... I don't know really. Oh yes! This last bit here is the number of days they ruled for. That's very interesting indeed." he concluded.

"What?" Cathy enquired. Tim pointed to some writing. "Well, for example... this first one says his name was... *neb ta neter-nefer heq-hequ Ausar shera en shera en Heru nub*. Which roughly translates to... *king of the land, beautiful god, ruler of rulers, Osiris, grandson of Horus the golden.* " he read. Cathy's ears pricked up at the name. "Osiris? Isn't that the father of the Egyptian gods? And I though Horus was the son of Osiris." she added.

"Yes." Tim confirmed. "Osiris was the main god. Although according to legends, there were many earlier ones. But their names don't seem to be here. Perhaps they were kings in another place, another time. Perhaps long before this base was started.

It seems that Manetho and Herodotus were quite right. Here it says Osiris ruled for... *heh* plus nine times *hefennu* plus two *t'ab* plus *kha* plus eight times *met* plus *ua* ...that's one million, nine hundred and twenty-one thousand and eighty one days. Hell... that's more than five thousand years!" he explained, before he noticed something.

"Hey Cathy! Look at these cartouches will you?" Cathy followed his pointing finger. "What about them?" she asked, as she continued to stare at them. "I just realised what they are. It's bloody obvious when you think about it. See they're all bound with a red chord... just like the ba bird shen rings." he explained. "So?" Cathy asked. "So, people have wondered what the cartouche has meant, ever since they were discovered.

It's too simple really. The shen ring was obviously a royal emblem. We saw it on the bloke giving out the medals. And we saw Horus' shen ring back there. The shen ring was thought to indicate *eternity*. Perhaps it's because the original god-kings lived for thousands of years that the local people must have thought them to be immortal.

Anyway, the cartouche is nothing more than an extended shen ring surrounding the name of the king. To indicate royalty, immortality, godliness, longevity... that sort of thing." Satisfied they had agreement with his theory, Tim wandered along the corridor for a few yards. Suddenly he stopped. He spoke more to himself than anyone in particular.

As Cathy stood by his side, she was both intrigued and impressed by his mastery of the ancient tongue. She followed his pointing finger and hung on every word, as Tim explained the writing. "Every king here is a direct descendant of the previous king. And his rule is counted in days. That means if we can find a familiar king, whose exact time of reign is known, we can calculate backwards and find out exactly when all these kings ruled. That would give us an accurate chronology of the entire Egyptian period.

Boy, that's something historians have been trying unsuccessfully to do for the last two hundred years. Looks like we might be able to put in a controversial paper at a conference one day after all, Cathy. But we'll have to interpret the lineages carefully. Those gaps in the text show periods of parallel rulers... during times of division. But I've noticed that most of the early cartouches have a red binding at the base. Perhaps these are the related kings or something. In the later ones, the cartouche and the binding are the same colour. I guess we can ponder that later." Tim hurried down the corridor, glancing at the names as he went. Suddenly he stopped and pointed to a name.

"That's... **Suten-net Mena** ...the first traditional king of unified Egypt. But we don't know any real dates for quite a while yet. But at least we're getting closer." He continued to browse among the cartouches as he slowly ambled down the corridor. Occasionally pausing to confirm familiar names and commenting on the plethora of unknown kings between.

Although not arranged in the traditional dynasties, Tim easily picked the dynastic changes by the location of the seat of power and the praenomen used by the different kings.

Eventually he came to a larger than normal gap, some three columns wide. He stopped and stared at the next name for a while. Then read it out aloud. " **Suten net neb taiu neb peh peh Ra se Ra Aahmes** " he quoted. But Cathy knew exactly who he was talking about. "What's so special about Aahmes?" Cathy probed.

"Well, nothing, I thought." Tim offered. "Except for the large gap in the text. But here it mentions that this was the first of the... they use the term **pekhar** . Which can mean... *general or common* ...kings." Cathy though for a moment then offered an opinion. "Wasn't he the first king of the eighteenth dynasty?" Tim nodded agreement, so Cathy continued. "Well didn't Manetho suggest that the line of the god-kings expired at the end of the seventeenth dynasty?" she reminded Tim.

Tim nodded enthusiastically and smiled. "Of course! You're right. This is proof that Manetho's work was accurate, at least in part. Here they're saying the common people took over the pharaonic line after the death of..." He looked back at the previous king. "*suten net Aah mes se pa ari.* I guess this was an Aahmes too, the last in the royal line. From here on there are no more red ties at the bottom. They're all just plain gold like the rest of the cartouche. It somehow seems an ignoble end came to a great tradition right here." Tim sadly concluded.

But he soon got over the saddness and continued along the corridor, scanning the names as he went. Finally he stopped and pointed to a name. "Do you know who this is... *heq taiu qluapeter*?" he asked Cathy.

"No." she confessed. Tim smiled. "It's Cleopatra the seventh, of Marc Antony fame. The last Egyptian to ever hold the title of Pharaoh. But then there's some debate whether she was actually Egyptian or not. She was certainly born there, but consensus suggests she was of Greek descent. From the Ptolemaics. Not Egyptian by blood. But we do know for sure that she began her rule some time in fifty-two BC. I'll research the exact date she started or ended her rule, then we can regress from there. God this is exciting stuff."

Charlie meanwhile was tagging along looking at the hieroglyphs and half listening to Tim, but showing little interest. He was anxious to get at the computers and, being late in the afternoon, a cold beer would not go astray in lieu. Ancient history never held his interest, even at school.

Tim finally noticed his lack of enthusiasm and reassured him that tomorrow would be his day. Charlie smiled at the thought and meekly followed Tim and Cathy as they continued down the corridor. Eventually they came to the last name. " *taksas netkh zeno* ...Zeno!" Tim exclaimed. "He was one of the Byzantine rulers of Egypt. He was around about 475 AD I think.

That means they must have stopped recording the rulers around then." Tim speculated. He paused for a moment, wondering if the last date indicated their final lack of interest or the date of their departure. Deciding it was irrelevant for the moment, he wandered along the corridor to look at the next set of kings. This list started some thirty feet from where the last one finished. As he read the first few names to himself his jaw dropped. Tim stood in stunned silence, slowly shaking his head from side to side.

He stared in disbelief at the new list. Eventually a shrewd smile crept across his now heavily stubbled face. "What's the matter?" Cathy asked, seeing the knowing smile. "Do you realize what this is?" he teased. "Of course not! We can't read Egyptian." Charlie snapped. "Oh, sorry." Tim half-heartedly apologized. "At the start of this next list of names it says this is the second line of kings... the kings of Sumer. Those who. who escaped from the... *persh-t* ...the *destruction*. But it doesn't say what destruction or where they came from, which is a pity really.

But the interesting thing is the names. Look, the first one is... *Adamah*. The second is ... *Sethas*. The third ...*Enas*. Then there's ...*Cainan, Malaleal, Zarad, Henakh*. Don't you see what this is?" he pleaded.

"Not really." Cathy conceded, not understanding the magnitude of Tim's discovery. Tim smiled and nodded. "I'll give you their more familiar names. *Adam ... Seth ... Enos ... Cainan ... Mahalaleal ... Jared ... Enoch!*" Tim explained. Suddenly Cathy clicked. "My God! They're the descendants of Adam and Eve. The Garden of Eden... Biblical creation... the predecessors of the children of Israel!" she announced proudly.

Tim smiled. Cathy was following him and he was pleased she was genuinely interested in what he was reading "Exactly" he confirmed. "But according to this, they're the great Sumerian kings from the beginning of time. The royal descendants from... I don't know really.

But they seem to be a secondary line, originally coming from the same royal line as the Pharaohs before the *destruction*. And look at the lengths of rule. They're in the order of hundreds of years. I wonder if they..." he hesitated. "What?" Cathy pushed, as Tim's silence continued. "I was just speculating, but I guess I shouldn't waste my time. With all this information available to us, I should be able to find out exactly what the history is, instead of trying to pre-empt it."

Tim continued browsing through the names. "Look, here's ...*Abram* to *Zaakob*. Abraham through to Jacob. And the list continues. Look, here ...*Dafid* and *Salomen*. David and Solomon. The list goes through all the Davidic kings."

He continued along the wall reciting Biblical names as he read them. Finally he stopped and stared at a name. Cathy was puzzled by his silence and eventually asked him if there was something wrong.

Tim shook his head."No, not really. It's just this section here starts to get a bit... well... interesting." he explained. "What do you mean... *interesting?*" Cathy insisted. Tim pointed to some names. "Look at these names here ...*Mathan, Zaakob, Zaseph, Zehashua...*" he read verbatim. "Who?" Cathy asked, being unfamiliar with the names. Tim smiled. "As a Catholic girl, you'd know them as Matthan, Jacob, Joseph and Jesus!" Tim explained proudly.

Cathy's eyes lit up as she suddenly realised the enormity of Tim's revelation."You mean Jesus the Christ!" she exclaimed in disbelief. "Exactly!" Tim confirmed. "See, I told you it got interesting here. But that's not the interesting thing." he continued in a teasing tone.

"Christ, if *that's* not interesting, what is?" Cathy blurted out. Tim laughed. "It's the fact that the direct lineage continues after Jesus." Tim explained, as he pointed to some more names. "What? I thought he died on the cross?" Cathy queried. "So the Church would have us believe. Remember I told you about my thesis that got stolen?" Tim asked. Cathy nodded, so he continued.

"Well in that, I had evidence that suggested that Jesus survived the crucifixion and fled to India. There he was purported to have lived out his days trying to convert the masses to his form of sectarian Judaism." he explained. Cathy shook her head in disbelief.

"If he went to India, how did his line continue?" she asked. Tim smiled. "He left his wife, Mary Magdalene, and three children in Judea. But they had to flee the Jewish and early Pauline Christian extremists who wanted to kill them. They eventually found refuge in Herod's estates in Gaul.

But the Catholic Church relentlessly persecuted their descendants there for centuries. Their plight is encoded in the Book of Revelations. I got that directly from the Vatican archives. The Church knows damn well that Jesus was nothing more than a Davidic zealot who tried to reclaim his throne by force. But their entire religion is based on the myth that he was a god.

Now they're obliged to stick with it. No matter how inaccurate, illogical or silly the story is. But the real problem is, that now of course, it's a multi-billion dollar international business. And their political influence is enormous in most *Christian* countries. So you see we're messing with more than simple theology! Pretty scary when you think about it. " he warned.

Charlie had not been listening to the previous conversation, but now he was full of interest. He'd never heard of such a theory. "So does the line continue today?" he probed. Tim nodded. "According to my research it does. It could be traced through the Merovingian line to the Counts of Toulouse and Narbonne. Another branch, from the female line, could be traced to Viviane del Acqs in the sixth century. From there it can be traced to the line of Queens of Avallon. I have a family chart through to modern days at home. I'll show it to you one day if you like." He laughed as he recalled some interesting trivia. "What's so funny?"

"Oh, I just remembered. You know mum's Scottish and her maiden name is Stewart?" he offered. Charlie shrugged his shoulders. "So?" he asked. "So, the house of Stewart is a direct line from Jesus. Why do you think they got such a pizzling for centuries?

Why do you think they never gave the throne of England to a Stewart, when it was decreed they should? They'd rather import the Windsors, from the House of Hanover, from Europe!" he proclaimed venomously.

"You mean we're direct descendants of Adam and Jesus Christ? In the royal sense?" Charlie asked incredulously. Tim nodded. " As far as I can determine." he responded rather casually. "Why haven't you said anything before?" Charlie asked, a little hurt that this startling information had been kept from him. "Would you have believed me?" Tim asked with a wink. Charlie conceded his point. "Probably not."

Tim left Charlie pondering his distinguished pedigree and wandered along until he came to the final name. "*Fergus Mar* . *Fergus Mor,* the forebear of King Alpin of Scots. Ancestor of Walter Fitz Alan, the First High Steward of Scotland, who died in eleven-seventy-seven." he expounded. "When did Fergus live then?" Cathy asked. "He died around 501AD." Tim recalled.

"Oh, I see what you mean." Tim established. "The base must have been operative at the time of Fergus. But abandoned either during his lifetime or shortly after. That means they were here until around 500AD. Plus or minus twenty years or so. I guess we may find some information later that'll tell us exactly when they left. But the most recent coins I found in the treasury seem to validate the timing." Tim expanded.

He then looked down the remaining fifty yards or so of the corridor. The wall was blank. "I guess that's it for the king list." he stated in a tone of disappointment. "But it looks like a room at the end of the corridor. Let's have a look shall we Cathy?" he asked.

Tim looked around and was surprised to see Cathy wandering back along the corridor looking at the opposite wall. He watched her for a while then decided to follow. "We were just going to have a look at the room at the end of the corridor. Do you want to come?"

"Yes, sure." Cathy replied, none too convincingly. "But I was just looking at this wall. We've been so interested in the king lists, we've completely ignored this wall. And I notice it's different. I can't read the writing, but it doesn't look the same to me. It looks more like general writing than a list. What does this say, Tim?" she asked, pointing to some text.

Tim looked at the writing for a moment. Then stood back, smiled wryly and shook his head. Cathy caught the twinkle in his eye. "What's wrong?" she asked, sensing he was about to drop a bombshell.

"Nothing!" Tim reassured her. "On the contrary. But I think we'd better go back to the beginning. This is the Holy Grail, Cathy. It's their history!"

CHAPTER 20

Tim stared silently at the beginning of the text, wrestling with the complexities of the ancient language. The others stood patiently, waiting for him to unravel the primeval message. It was obvious he was finding it difficult to interpret. But eventually he smiled and turned to Cathy. "Well, it's not easy. They use many familiar words in unfamiliar contexts. And they throw in lots of words I've never seen before. So I'll be guessing some of it, but here goes.

It seems that there were two races... the *Anunnaki* and the *Zamzam'min* . I told you the Bible hid many truths. Anyway, these two races lived on separate planets. One called... *Satyoloka* ...the Zamzam'min... and the other where the Anunnaki lived was called... *Brahmaloka*.

I'm not sure where I've heard those names before, but they ring a faint bell from somewhere. Oh well, I'll Google them later if it doesn't come to me." he promised. "Anyway, it appears these two planets each spun around their own axes at the same rate. It says their... *haru* ...*day* ...was divided into twenty... *nenu* ...*hours*. Every eighteen days the planets revolved around each other. This was their... *abt* ... or *month*.

Every twenty months the two planets revolved around their suns. Oh! there were two suns in the centre of their solar system. A large red one and a small blue one. This was their planetary year. Every twenty planetary years or so, their suns revolved around each other. This was their solar year."

Tim paused for a moment and Cathy caught the vacuous, almost distant look on his face. "What's wrong Tim?" she asked, with some concern in her voice. Tim shook his head vigorously.

"Something's bugging me about those numbers. Twenty... eighteen... twenty... twenty. I know they mean something. I just can't put my finger on it." he explained in a rather frustrated tone. "You mean you've seen that sequence before somewhere?" Cathy probed. Tim nodded. "Yes. I just can't... wait a minute! That's it! The Mayan long count." he announced proudly.

Cathy shook her head. "The what?" Tim smiled. "The Mayan calendar... the long count. Their calendar reputedly began around thirty-one hundred and thirteen BC and was only thirteen Bak'tuns long. Which means it's due to expire around two thousand and twelve. The year of the great galactic alignment.

All the dooms-day lot have been saying it's a prophecy of doom. But I always thought the cycle had some astral significance, rather than a prophetic one. I think the pending alignment of our solar system with the galactic centre of the Milky Way was simply seen as the end of an epoch. Their next calendar would simply begin as this one ended and probably last until the next galactic alignment. "

"So, how does their calendar work?" Cathy asked, being totally unfamiliar with Mayan history. "The long count acted like a sort of odometer..." Tim began. "A what?" Cathy interrupted. "A car odometer... speedo. You know, where the mileage ticks over as you drive along. Anyway, they had a month or *Winal* ...of twenty *K'in* ...days. A year or *Tun* of eighteen months. A *K'atun* of twenty years and a *Bak'tun* of twenty K'atun.

So a date would be given by so many Bak'tuns plus so many K'atuns plus so many Tuns plus so many Winals plus so many K'ins. In a string of figures... up to two for each cycle. Hence their calendar was thirteen times one hundred and forty-four thousand days long. Or just over five thousand years. I think the Mayan long count has something to do with these chaps arriving in South America. Remember in the commander's office?

The map showed a base there. I'll bet they landed there around thirty-one thirteen BC and the Mayan calendar began shortly thereafter. The astronomical details required to draft the calendar were probably passed on to the religious chiefs by the *gods*. I think I might have a key to their chronology here."

Cathy looked at Charlie who simply shrugged his shoulders and rolled his eyes. It was of little interest to him and his mind was focussed on the cold beer that awaited him at the camp. She then turned to Tim and confessed her lack of understanding. "You've lost us, but keep going." she insisted.

"Well, apparently their planets were colonised in primordial times from somewhere unknown. This was recorded as day one. Similar to the Mayans, eh? Anyway, their solar system was at the extreme edge of... *agep sba en khau* ...a *cloud star of thousands*. A great star cluster I guess. This was located at the end of one of the two spiral arms of their galaxy.

I presume that's what they're talking about. They refer to it as *sba en khau* ...*star of thousands*. Their star cluster spun relatively quickly. It only took some four thousand three hundred planetary years for half a revolution." Tim mumbled to himself as he quickly did some calculations. "What's that... four thousand three hundred times three hundred and sixty days... that's around one and a half million days."

The others looked on, the blank expressions on their faces accompanied by slowly shaking heads. They were not as keen on the chronology as Tim. All they wanted to do was quickly read the text and go back to the camp for a beer. But Cathy was nonetheless impressed at his mathematical dexterity. "How did you calculate that so quickly?" she asked.

Tim smiled. "Vedic maths! I'll tell you about it some day. Fascinating stuff that should be embraced by the west, but... " Tim noticed their bored demeanour.

He apologized for his mathematical detour before continuing. "Sorry about that, but I find it fascinating. Anyway, this was their *galactic day* ...when their solar system was facing the centre of their galaxy. I suppose they called it that because their night sky would be the brightest when they were facing the centre of the galaxy.

And they had an equal *galactic night* ...when the solar system was facing away from their galaxy. Again, I suppose the night sky would be darkest when they were facing out into space, rather than into the bright centre of their galaxy. How fascinating! I bet it would've been a beautiful sight. The night sky constantly changing like that. Mind you, you'd have to live nearly nine thousand years to witness an entire galactic day.

Well, it seems they had eighteen galactic days. That's eighteen times eight thousand six hundred years. That's a hundred and fifty four thousand eight hundred years per galactic month. Then they had twenty galactic months in one galactic year. That's twenty times one fifty. That's around three million and ninety six thousand years.

Of course! That's it... *sebi*. That's their galactic year!" he announced proudly. But Tim noticed that Cathy and Charlie were still staring blankly at him, so he elaborated. "Sebi... it's mentioned on the museum photos." he explained. "The indeterminate period of time in their dating system that we were wondering about. Well OK. That *I* was wondering about! Well it looks like it's simply their galactic year. About three million odd years. That's the key to their chronology!"

Tim looked at the cursory smiles and slowly shaking heads and burst into laughter, as he apologised for the technical detour. He was excited about finding the key to their chronology, even if they were not. "Sorry about the sidetrack... and the detail. But I guess it was important to them. They wrote it down, not me!"

"That's OK, Tim. Keep going. You've got us sucked in now. We need to hear how this thing ends." Charlie conceded. Tim smiled. He was enjoying himself immensely, even if the others were not. "Well it appears their sun grew larger and threatened their planets." he continued. Then he stopped and looked at Cathy.

"Of course! The red giant went supernova! It finally exploded and destroyed their planets, at the end of the hundredth galactic year. God that's a lot of history! Three hundred million odd years.

Oh, shit! That's why these names and numbers are familiar. The Vedic texts... Krishna et al. Brahma lives for one hundred years on the planet Brahmaloka. Then the universe is destroyed, before it's renewed. Each year is made up of twelve months, which in turn are made up of thirty days. Each day is made up of one day and one night.

Only the texts state that their day is... *eight million six hundred thousand earth years long*. Rather than a galactic day of eight thousand six hundred years. There seems to be a fudge factor in there from somewhere. I also think the Vedic texts have somehow swapped the original calendar for the earth one.

But it makes little difference really. Whether you have twenty months of eighteen days, of twelve months of thirty days, you still have a three hundred and sixty day year. So, that still points to the base in Tibet. It looks like the Vedic texts have encoded the galactic information from their homeland. I'll be buggered. "

"So, what happened then?" Charlie probed, still bored but nonetheless intrigued by Tim's ability to string things together logically. Tim smiled. "Sorry, it seems they were well aware of the impending supernova explosion, so they searched for alternative places to live. They found three solar systems within range which they colonised. One became the new home planet, which they called... **Maten.**

The other two were secondary, embryonic colonies. They use the term... *ha-t kher* ...*in the beginning*. The other planets were called... *Sepet* and *Nibiru*. Well I'll be stuffed!" he finally exclaimed. "What now?" Charlie huffed. Tim smiled "Nibiru! Another Sumerian legend. The mythical planet. The home of their gods, the Anunnaki. Christ! This just keeps getting better.

Anyway, they seem to have simply seeded these two other settlements with small colonies, a secondary royal line and a rotational military force. But here's the thing."

"What, now?" Charlie asked, still rather bored with the whole history thing. Tim ignored his boredom and continued. "They say they colonised the fifth planet from the sun in this solar system. But that's Jupiter.

It's just a giant ball of gas that's totally unsuited to supporting life as we know it. It doesn't make sense. No matter, I'll keep going.

It seems members of the royal family were sent to oversee these new colonies. To continue the line in case of disaster befalling Maten." he speculated. "When did all this happen?" Cathy asked, still a little bored, but somewhat more enthusiastic about the history than Charlie. "I've got no idea, but it must have been a long time ago.

Anyway, some time later, Maten became over-populated, so they sent many people to Nibiru. It was the most suitable planet and there the regnal lineage was well established. They also started two more colonies further out ...*Ka-kam* and *Ka-hebes*."

Tim paused for a moment contemplating something. Charlie noticed his deeply furrowed brow and asked what it was. "Nothing really. I just made sense of the photos in the accommodation blocks. All those warriors and the dates. They were military units who were seconded to the various settlements for a certain length of time. It seems the earlier royals had a very much extended lifespan. In the thousands of years.

I don't know about these blokes though. God this is interesting. I'll go through the fine detail myself later. For now I'll just skip through it until I find something interesting. We've got to be getting back to the camp soon." he reluctantly conceded.

Charlie let out a mock cheer at the thought of an imminent cold beer. Tim pretended to ignore him and slowly wandered off along the corridor. He was scanning the text as he walked, looking for anything that might interest Charlie and Cathy.

Suddenly he stopped and pointed to a section of the text. "That's interesting." he mumbled, more to himself than the others. But Cathy noticed his hesitation. "What?" she probed. "*sba aabti tcha pet* ...the red Horus... Mars. I wonder what this is about."

Tim paused to read the text while the others waited patiently. Suddenly he began to expatiate in the ancient tongue as he read excitedly. His hands pointing at the words as he spoke. After reading the section, he paused and looked at Cathy. "Well I'll be damned!"

"What now?" Cathy almost chortled. "The asteroid belt between Mars and Jupiter. It used to be Nibiru. Nibiru was the fifth planet after all, but it was destroyed some time ago. They give some figures, but I'll have to work out the exact date later. It was hit by a large comet and shattered. Luckily they saw it coming.

Apparently they tried to shift the comet's orbit but... I can't really interpret this. But, it seems they failed and they had to evacuate. Most went to Sepet, some went to Mars and the rest came here. Apparently the Martian settlement was going great guns until relatively recently by the looks of it. One of the asteroids... a chunk of the old planet... was knocked out of orbit by a comet as it passed through our solar system. It glanced off the surface and... *khenp* ...*sucked out the essence*. It seems like the asteroid took most of the Martian atmosphere with it and destroyed life on Mars.

They had too little warning to save everyone but some managed to escape. Including the Guardian contingent and the royal household. They came to earth and... shit!" The tone of Tim's voice betrayed the intensity of his passion. "What?" Cathy asked, almost feeling a compulsion to do so. Tim smiled. "They started the colony in South America! I bet that happened in 3113BC. The start of the long count. Of course! This is all starting to fall into place now."

Tim again wandered off, glancing up and down excitedly as he scanned the text. All the while he was slowly heading towards the room at the end of the corridor. Suddenly he stopped in his tracks. His head spun back to a section of the wall and he yelled excitedly. "Look at this will you!" he pointed excitedly. "What does it say?" Cathy asked, almost reluctantly.

"It says the original settlement on earth was on a large... island I guess. I thought it might be Australia or Antarctica. You know, the bases marked on the map. But it wasn't. Look at the name here... *Atlantis*. You know what that means?" he asked no one in particular.

"Atlantis really existed?" Cathy offered tentatively. "Exactly!" Tim confirmed proudly. "But it goes on to say that a massive earthquake destroyed it. Most of the population was saved, but they were forced to find somewhere else to live.

This is where the Pharaohs come into it. There was already a thriving civilization living in Upper Egypt. In the lower Nile valley. You know, on the delta. This was run by a line of the royal family as seen on the wall behind us. At that stage the upper Nile... or Lower Egypt... was still largely populated by primitive peoples. There was also a primitive culture living in the Euphrates-Tigris valley. They were remnants of their long term breeding program. Their supply of slaves. The forebears of the Asian races by the looks of it." he explained.

Anyway, it looks like the royal family from Atlantis split in two. One going to Lower Egypt to start a new settlement, the other went to Sumer. So that's how it started. I'll be able to use the king lists to find out exactly when this occurred. Edgar Cayce always insisted that Atlantis died ten to twelve thousand years ago. Maybe he was right." he postulated.

Charlie tapped Tim on the shoulder. "Look I know this stuff is fascinating for you two, but it's driving me crazy. Can we just go and have a look at the room at the end of the corridor, then get back to camp. I'm dying for a beer. Tomorrow we can split up and you can read this stuff for as long as you like." he offered.

Tim nodded an apology. "Sorry, Charlie. I'm getting carried away. But, what can I say? I'm a history professor and this is history. OK, let's go take a look at the room then shall we?"

As they headed toward the end of the corridor, Tim noticed a small section of text near the end of the left wall. He stopped and perused the writing. It was another king list. As he began to read it, he suddenly realized what it was. "Jesus Christ! Look at this Cathy. It's a list of their kings."

"Whose kings?" she asked, not really understanding the importance of the list. "Sorry... the Guardians... Celts of whoever. It's a list... no several lists, actually. Look, this section obviously shows the main list of kings. But I'm not sure what these are. Probably other royal lines in colonies or joint rulers or something." Tim looked at the bored faces around him and knew he would need to decipher the new king list at his leisure. The others were keen to get back to camp. "I guess I can come back to this later, eh?" he admitted coyly.

As they entered the large room at the far end of the corridor, they found a vast library cum scriptorium. It was a large palatial, octagonal room. With each of the straight sides being some thirty yards across.

The corridor entered the room in the centre of one flat wall panel, the surface of which was smooth and vertical. The roof was domed like that of the great hall, about twenty-five or thirty feet high. On the walls either side of the entrance hung a collection of maps and star-charts.

The other seven sections of the room were carved into numerous rows of shelves. The lowest shelf was about four feet from the floor, the highest some fifteen feet. These were lined with thousands of seemingly identical books. However, the wall directly in front of them immediately caught their attention. It housed a markedly different collection of books.

Rather than the white-spined, plastic looking books with their stark black writing, these books were leather-bound, with fine, gold-embossed writing. They appeared to be catalogued according to the colour coded stripe across the bottom of the spines. There were dozens of rows of these distinct books, stretching across the shelves. Some grouped together, others sitting forlornly on their own. Some looked relatively new, others, by their faded and well-worn spines, were obviously very old.

As they were surveying the library, Charlie noticed the maps on the wall behind them. He tapped Tim on the shoulder and pointed to a map. "That's the same map we saw in the commander's office isn't it? Except there are no coloured pins. But there seems to be a lot more writing on this one." As the two men stood and stared at the map, Cathy turned towards a map on the other side of the corridor entrance. She stared at it for some time. Tilting her head from side to side, she tried to orient herself with the unusual map projection. It was quite some time before she gave up and turned to Tim. "What do you make of this map?" Tim looked at the map for a moment, puzzled at first by the strange projection.

As he continued to look he noticed some familiar shapes. "It looks like this is a different projection map, almost unrecognisable as we see the earth. For a minute there I thought it might have been their home planet. But look here. Africa and the Americas are pretty much obvious. But Europe, Asia, Antarctica and Australia are a bit strange."

Charlie agreed, as they stood in a tight semi-circle, staring at the strange map. "Do you think this might be a much older map? You know, before full continental drift, when the earth was smaller and younger."

Tim took a few more steps backwards, in an attempt to gain a better perspective of the map. He stared at it for some time. Finally the silence was too much for Charlie. "What's the matter?" he asked.

Tim shook his head. "Well I've come to the conclusion that you're right. This is a map of some antiquity. The continents are different, but Australia's wrong. There's definitely something wrong with this here but I can't quite put my finger on it." Charlie and Cathy both stepped back and stood next to Tim. They all stared resolutely at the map.

Suddenly Tim burst into an excited ramble. "I've got it! I knew there was something wrong. But it's not wrong as such. It's..." he paused as he looked at the map more closely. "What's wrong with it?" Charlie finally asked. "Well, I've decided what's wrong with this map. There's one too many continents.

See, again the map is an azimuthal equidistant projection. But we've assumed it was centred on this base in Australia, like the other map. But, looking at the map more closely, that's Australia over there. The projection for this map is in the middle of this other continent, right here." he pointed. "But that's in the middle of the Pacific Ocean!" Cathy insisted. Charlie moved closer to the map to inspect the errant continent. Tim remained where he was and smiled broadly.

Charlie looked at the map for some time, then turned to see the smug look on Tim's face. "Well, what's there to be so smug about?" he asked. "I think I've solved it." Tim bragged. "See, although I can't decipher some of the writing on this map, it's obvious that it's a predecessor to the map in the commander's office. We can have a look at these other maps in here and cross reference them later. But I'm presuming they'll all show the earth as it's changed dramatically over the millions of years since these people first came here." he postulated.

"Were the changes that dramatic?" Cathy asked. Tim nodded. "Well, there's continental drift for a start. As the earth expanded and the crust cracked, forcing the land masses to migrate. Then there were ice ages, when the polar caps locked up more water, thus exposing more land. That would dramatically change the shape of the continents. And then there's Havi."

Tim paused as he allowed Charlie time to catch up with his train of thought. Finally he received the question he had anticipated. "What's Havi?" Charlie asked, almost afraid that the answer would bore him to death. "Well it's a legend really, more than anything else." Tim explained.

"See the island nations of the Pacific all have a common legend, that there once was a large continent in the middle of the Pacific Ocean, called Havi. It seems that one day it simply sank into the water. The only remnants of it are the volcanic peaks which form the island chains that survive to this day. Places such as Kiribati, Fiji, Hawaii, Tahiti, the Solomon Islands and so on." Charlie shook his head and continuously shifted his gaze from Tim to the map and back.

He then cracked a cynical smile. "You mean this map actually proves the legends are true?" Tim smiled. "Well, as I keep saying, most legends have some element of truth in them. It's generally felt that time only distorts the finer details.

The facts often remain indisputably woven into the legend. But the name, Havi... seems to have been the name of a settlement, rather than the island. See here... it says... **nu-t hafi** ...*the settlement of Hafi*. The name of the continent is here ... **Atlantis**. Just like it says on the wall out there."

Charlie stood back for a while and shook his head slowly from side to side, as he contemplated the map. Finally he turned to Tim. "Well, I guess you two can have the privilege of re-writing the history books then." Tim smiled, nodding his head as his mind raced through the possibilities.

The fame, the controversy and the fortune... the heresy. All had to be addressed before he could respond. "It would be nice, but we'll have to tread very carefully. I think we'll have to gather all the irrefutable proof that we'll need, before one word of this is mentioned to anyone outside. We can't disclose the location of this base, so we'll need to look elsewhere."

"You mean like finding the other bases?" Charlie suggested, with a slightly bewildered tone of voice. "Exactly!" Tim agreed. "Maybe there's another hall of records in Egypt, like Herodotus said. Perhaps it's the same as this corridor. That would allow us to release the information without disclosing anything about this base. Anyway, let's have a look at these other maps shall we?"

CHAPTER 21

They glanced around at the numerous maps hanging either side of the corridor entrance. Cathy finally pointed to one of them. "This one's not much different to the last one." she concluded. "Yeah, but the continents seem to be differently shaped and some are closer together. It's obviously based on the same projection as the last map..." Tim concluded, "...but it looks much older. Probably during an ice age, hence the extra land mass." he speculated.

They looked at the next two maps of the earth. They too seemed to be chronologically regressing, but still based on the projection of the second map. When they looked at the last map Tim stared incredulously. "Well I'll be buggered! This map must be the earth tens... if not hundreds of millions of years ago. Look at how close the continents are together. In fact, Africa, Australia and Antarctica are all joined, just like the Gondwanaland geological theorists have been espousing. But even they got it wrong.

See here, India never was a separate island. It was always joined to Asia. Albeit by a small isthmus and at a funny angle. Seems like it just spun around and collided with the Asian continent. I wonder why there's such a large gap between this map and the others.

Maybe this one was made on their very first visit, before they lived here. And the others were all made during consequent trips and finally when they lived here. See?" he pointed to a section of the nearest map. "There are very few hieroglyphs on this one, and there are no bases marked. Just a circle and the name... *Aati* ...at the epicentre of the map. Somewhere in Antarctica Do you think that's what the Yanks have found, Charlie?" he asked.

Charlie nodded. "Yeah, maybe they had a small base there and someone forgot to turn off the generator before they left." he postulated. While the others were debating the antiquity of the maps, Cathy turned her attention to the star-charts. They made little sense to her so she asked Tim if he could interpret them. "Not really. Many of these names are unfamiliar. I'd only be guessing even how to pronounce them.

But this looks familiar. See this galaxy here? One spiral arm has a star cluster or irregular companion galaxy at the end of it. I know that system. It's the Whirlpool Galaxy, M51 and its companion NGC5195. It's in the constellation of Canes Venatici... between Leo and Virgo. This might be their original home system.

See, there's an arrow pointing at these two stars. This large one and the smaller one next to it, at the edge of that companion system. I guess that's their suns. Look at the names... **Nut** and **Nu**. That's very interesting indeed. They're the names of the two primary creation gods of Egypt. I can't see any planets though. But I guess that's what it is. And look at this! This is very familiar." he mumbled as he pointed at another chart.

"What is it?" Cathy asked. "The southern sky, from here in Australia, centred on Orion. Oh shit! Of course!" Tim exclaimed suddenly. "Orion's sword, that middle star in Orion's sword." he repeated.

"So?" Cathy asked casually. Tim shook his head. "Well, it's not a star at all. It's actually a diffuse nebula. A star nursery. I wonder... yes! Look at this. This arrow points to one of the suns. See the name here. it's **Maten**. Their new home planet must be a part of the solar system of that star. No wonder the Egyptians seemed to be so obsessed with that part of the sky!"

Charlie meanwhile had lost interest and wandered away from the maps. He found himself in the centre of the room looking at a massive horseshoe-shaped desk, behind which was a typically large but well-worn chair.

In front of the chair, at the edge of the desk, one of the leather-bound books lay open. A thin layer of fine powdery white dust covered its text. Behind the book sat a computer keypad, similarly covered with dust. Beyond that, a computer screen. Charlie looked at the faintly glowing light green screen. Although he expected nothing to happen, he could not help himself. He leaned over and pressed a key of the keypad. Nothing. He pressed another and another. Still nothing.

Conceding defeat, he took a cursory look around, finally focussing on the wall to the left of the table. "Look at that will you? A whole wall of computer cards. Shit there must be thousands of them. I think we've hit the jackpot, Tim. It makes the collection in the commander's office look trivial. If we manage to get this thing talking, we'll be able to get some information out of that lot." he suggested.

Tim nodded mutely. His curiosity had automatically drawn him to the open book. He climbed into the chair and, with some effort, dragged himself over to the desk. He leant over and softly blew the dust from the page. As the small white cloud puffed into the air, he focussed on the writing. What he found made him do a double take. He instantly motioned Cathy to join him.

"What's up?" she asked, as she sidled up to Tim. "Look at this. It's written in classic Greek." he explained, as he pointed to the text. "Can you read it?" Cathy asked, assuming he could. "Of course. A lot of history is recorded in Greek. It was the precursor to Latin. Knowledge of both languages is a must for any historian. I'm surprised you never studied them Cathy." he confided. "I tried, but unfortunately I don't think I'm gifted in the language department. Besides, I've never really had the time to put into it either." she explained, almost apologetically. "That's OK. Here, I'll read it to you." he offered. Tim began reading the text to himself. Slowly at first as he wrestled with the language.

But soon it was flowing back to him and the reading became more fluent. Confident in his interpretation, he turned to Charlie. "Do you want to listen too? I think this is going to be interesting."

Charlie wandered over to join the others and shrugged his shoulders. "Sure... why not?" Tim started reading the text verbatim. He had read two sentences when Charlie reminded him that he was speaking Greek and that neither of them could understand a word he was saying. "I'm sorry, I'll translate it for you if you prefer." he smirked. "Thanks... that would make it more interesting." Charlie smiled back.

I am Lord Charan, the last of the Lord Guardians. Our time here is complete. I am waiting now to die. I leave this information in the hope that one day your race will progress beyond barbarism and seek the sciences and the truth. Only then will your true history be known. We have created a being that is too aggressive and its course of self-destruction we can no longer influence. It is my hope that all has not been in vain.

"What does he mean *we have created*?" Charlie interrupted. Tim shook his head. "I think he's referring to genetic manipulation." he offered. "Of course! The museum. Sorry, keep going." Charlie urged.

If you are reading this it is, I trust, in good faith. For what I am about to reveal to you may not sit well. In case you are unfamiliar with the lost tongue of my forefathers, as most were in the final days, I am using the... **sekhai en Haui-nebu** *...that's not Greek! Oh yeah, he says... the tongue of those of Corinth.*

My race is from a distant planet. One of a pair of planets, Satyoloka and Brahmaloka, which revolved around each other as well as our dual suns, Nut and Nu. Still most sadly visible to us from your world, as they were before the destruction.

"How can that be Tim?" Cathy mused. "It means the supernova explosion must have occurred in the last fourteen to thirty seven million years." he offered. "Why's that?" Cathy asked, uncertain of the relevance of Tim's answer. "Well the jury's still out, but consensus has M51 between fourteen and thirty seven million light years from earth, but most seem to think it's thirty one.

Anyway, if it exploded... say ten million years ago... the light from that explosion would still be travelling here. It wouldn't reach earth for another twenty one million years. We see all the stars out there in a sort of time machine. Light that reaches us has mostly left millions of years ago. Even when we look at the sun we can never see it as it actually is. We can only see it as it was eight minutes ago." he explained.

"Gee, that's a bit weird. Does that mean if we could travel away from earth faster than light, we could look back and virtually travel back in time?" Cathy postulated. Tim smiled at the thought. "I guess so. But only as distant observers. God, that's an interesting concept though. I'd like to take that further." he stated excitedly. "But I'd better get on with this, it's getting late." he reminded them.

Many sebi ago our twin planet, Brahmaloka, was colonized by smaller, fair skinned people... the Anunnaki. We knew the planet existed but lacked the technology to go there. The Anunnaki immediately embraced our people, and we lived in harmony as two independent races. However this changed when our royal line was tragically lost. From this time the Anunnaki assumed the role of sole royalty and centralized government. As a gesture of good will, they took the names of our royal line and continued with our traditions. It was from this tragedy that the great co-operation began.

They are the technical ones. It was their technology that allowed us to become what we are. Guardians of the just. We are their military... their guardians and protectors.

Unfortunately we are needed from time to time as there are other beings in the vastness of the universe who are not as compassionate as our races.

The Anunnaki instilled in us the morality of their planet. Their will for a peaceful existence. It is unfortunate that we need to use force to defend ourselves and our principles, but it is a necessity if we are to survive as a race. Sadly, not all the guardians before me were as disciplined as they should have been. Some were consumed by the remoteness of this planet and become barbaric in their own right. But times changed as the inhabitants of earth evolved.

The books you see before you are the Chronicles of the Guardians. In them is every detail of our lives here since we first made a permanent base on this planet. These journals include a chronological account of events on this planet since our scientists first came into contact with it many millions of years ago. This was recorded as being in the six hundred and twenty first year of the reign of Sanakhte the seventh.

During these early visits our scientists accelerated the evolution of humanoid creatures, much like themselves in a primeval way. It was decided to... I suppose it means genetically engineer... *some of these creatures to see if an intelligent being could be produced that could one day be of service to our peoples. Once this had been done, the progress of these beings was monitored spasmodically.*

As they progressed, vegetation and creatures from our own planets were introduced to help feed them. Some clones of the Anunnaki were made by some more radical scientists and let loose on the planet to interact with the other creatures. Eventually it was decided that these creatures had evolved to a state where cross-breeding with our scientists was feasible.

The original chronicles are written in our native language. These are the red volumes you see at the end of the room. The Anunnaki have their own languages, one of which you see here. But we guardians did not prefer them, as they are only secondary languages to us. However, as the civilisation of your planet evolved, the creatures developed the intelligence to use this more technical but less artistic language.

So it was taught to them. As I have sadly observed the decline in understanding of our much-loved language, I have translated the chronicles in the hope of preserving both the chronicle's knowledge and our language. These are the blue volumes you see before you, this being the final volume.

Each Lord Guardian wrote his own books. On his death or retirement, the book was closed and placed on the shelf with his other completed works. The new Lord Guardian would commence his own books. The militia scribes and base troops collated the information and ensured its accuracy and continuity in the event of a Lord Guardian's death before his replacement arrived. The spine of the books gives the guardian's name and the dates of commencement and completion of each journal.

Other than the small frozen bases, Abtu and Aati, this is the only complete base. The others were stripped and their contents either deposited here or returned to Maten. All other bases have however, a hall of records identical to the corridor you passed through to get here. Several temple sites also contain similar records. A detailed map of their locations is to be found in the rear of this book.

Tim stopped reading and looked up at Charlie, who smiled and nodded. He had read Tim's mind and immediately agreed with his thoughts. Tim hurriedly turned to the back of the book and flipped through the map section. "Here it is. Now let's see... aha! That's explains it." he announced proudly. "What?" Charlie asked. "Why no-one has ever found Herodotus' contentious *hall of records* in Egypt. He rightly insisted there was one in Egypt, but they've been looking in all the wrong places. Everyone seems convinced there's hidden rooms in the great pyramid or there's secret tunnels under the sphinx. But it's nowhere near there. It says here it was sealed after the death of the... last king I guess. That must mean *Aah mes se pa ari* ...the last of the demigod kings. That was at the end of the seventeenth dynasty."

"So, where is it?" Charlie insisted. "It's here, at Abydos, under the royal cemetery. I'll be buggered. It's been right under their noses the whole time. According to this, the entrance is concealed under a wall of the tomb of Narmer." But Charlie had no idea who Tim was talking about. "Who?" he asked, in a frustrated tone. "Suten-net Mena... Narmer. He was the first king of the so-called unified Egypt.

According to the notes on this map, he commissioned the hall of records on the advice of a Guardian. It's under the north-east corner of the burial chamber wall. There's an access well under the wall some twenty-five feet deep. It was filled in before they rebuilt the wall. It has a false lined bottom, under which are several rooms. The last one contains a blocking stone... a very large rock. Under that, there's a flight of stairs that lead down to the hall of records." he read.

"That sounds pretty concise. Do you think we could find it?" Charlie asked, now a little more excited about the prospect. Tim nodded. "I've been to the burial complex several times. I even remember Narmer's burial chamber. If this map's right, I should be able to find it with my eyes closed." he bragged. "I guess that's where we head next, eh?" Tim mumbled to himself as he turned back to the text. Then he looked up at Cathy. She smiled and nodded for him to continue.

Our troops were also known as the Aggelos – the Messengers. These were ranked from the Cherubim through the Seraphim, Chasmalim, Aralim, Tarsisim, Ophanim, Ishim and Malachim or Arc Aggelos... to the Elohim... the Lord Guardians. Senior Guardians... the Ishim... were the group commanders. The overall command of each base was the responsibility of the Malachim. I, like those before me, was responsible for the entire earth operation.

The ranks of the general troops were supplemented by ancillary staff and the Cherubim. Made up of cadets and the winged ones, our true messengers.

There were relative few cadets on any base at one time. As part of their military education, many were sent to remote bases like this to do part of their three hundred years of compulsory military service. They were not allowed to participate in battle so were generally assigned servile, sentry or guard duties. They were brought to a base and returned home by service shuttles... three of which remain on the base.

The smaller craft here are the local shuttles, used to wander about this plant. Although they were originally used to shuttle small crews between the three planets of this solar system. When the cadets reach their two hundredth year, the minimum age allowable for active military service, they graduate to the rank of Seraphim.

It is the practice for fresh troops to accompany the Lord Guardian when he takes a new command, although this is somewhat flexible on remote bases such as this. No-one, save the Cherubim, were compelled to leave any base. So many chose to remain on bases where they felt most at home. However, some more adventurous warriors chose to serve on other frontiers. While some returned to their home planet when their tour of duty was completed, others chose to live out their days as warriors on bases like this planet. You will find the burial chambers of the dead below the living quarters. There lie all those who died in this region.

The female of our species were forbidden to come to this planet, as was the custom for any Guardian base. Guardians were celibate and forbidden to choose a mate until they left military service.

To be Lord Guardian is the noblest of all accomplishments for our race. For though we number many throughout the stars, there is only one Lord Guardian per sector. It is an enviable position. The highest rank held and accountable directly to the Royal House. As such, the Royal House chooses replacements for the Lord Guardian. Such an incumbent is a career warrior and is chosen from our best military men. He undergoes intense military and scientific training for one hundred years following his graduation from the military academy.

Then, when he reaches his two hundredth year, he is assigned to apprentice to a retiring Lord Guardian. He must spend at least twenty years in this role before the Lord Guardian can retire. This usually occurs more as a phasing in process than a sudden change of leadership. Some fortuitous Lord Guardians can retire as young as seven or eight hundred years of age, but more normally is it nearer to their nine hundredth year.

In the case of isolated posts such as this one, the retired Lord Guardian may live out his days on the base if he so chooses, often maintaining some influence over their replacements until their death. Or in my case, I was never replaced. This planet was abandoned. Many of us chose to spend the remainder of our years on this planet. We were all old and near our end anyway, with no reason to return to Maten. I am the last survivor, sadly destined to lie in an open sarcophagus, as there is no-one to place the lid. Such is the fate of the last of the Lord Guardians of the Blue Planet.

I wish you well... anthropos.

Tim gently closed the book and looked up at the others. Charlie was looking sombre and Cathy had tears in her eyes. "Well, what do you make of all that?" Tim asked as he looked at Cathy. "It's so sad. The poor old man was all alone. Left to lie in an open coffin until he died. Did you see him when you were down there?" Tim shook his head. "No, he must be in the third level. I had a good look around the first level. But I only stepped out of the lift and had a glance round in the second and third levels. Perhaps we should go back and put the lid on his sarcophagus for him before we leave?"

"It's the least we could do. He sounded like such a nice bloke." Cathy insisted. "OK, it's agreed then? We'll do it before we leave." Tim suggested as he nodded solemnly and slid from the chair. He then headed towards the bookshelf containing the red-spined chronicles.

As he walked away, he turned to Charlie. "Who turned out the lights when he died? It couldn't have been him. He could only access the crypt via the lift... and that needs power to operate." he assumed.

"I don't know. Maybe there's a timing device or something on the shutdown circuit." Charlie offered. Tim concurred, then began perusing the cartouches on the spines. All had a large cartouche at the top, showing the name of the Lord Guardian, and most had a small one near the bottom, followed by numbers.

Some had two such small cartouches, indicating that the tome spanned the reign of two monarchs. "Some names here are familiar." Tim announced. "The pharaohs must have borrowed them from the Guardians." Charlie and Cathy watched on as Tim stopped and re-checked a cartouche.

"What have you found?" Cathy asked. Tim smiled broadly. "An interesting name. We're definitely in for a good read here." he suggested with a wink. "Well, what's the name?" Charlie insisted. Tim looked over at Charlie with a satirical grin.

"... *Yahweh Sabaoth* ..."

CHAPTER 22

The trio was back at the library early the next morning. While Tim and Cathy began browsing through the library, Charlie wandered over to the desk. He struggled as he dragged the gigantic chair up to the computer. He dusted the keyboard off with a few token waves of his hand. This was followed by a rather loud session of puffing, as he blew the remaining film of fine white dust away. Then, with a grunt, he hauled himself onto the chair.

He stared blankly at the screen for some time, pondering his next move. He knew the screen was active by the light green glow that emanated from it. But, frustratingly, that was all he knew about the computer system. While he pondered his plan of attack, he leant over and gently blew the dust from the opaque screen surface. This did not dislodge it all, so he removed the handkerchief from his pocket and carefully wiped off the remaining dust.

Then he methodically folded the handkerchief and replaced it in his hip pocket. He felt like an eager student pilot, sitting in the cockpit for the first time. Impatient to begin, but apprehensive of the plethora of unfamiliar objects that confronted him. For a while he sat in silent contemplation, as he looked around the desk, unsure of where to begin.

Scattered about were dozens of the enigmatic cards, the ones they had termed computer discs, to give them some familiarity. He instinctively grabbed one and looked at it closely. Unable to decipher the writing or determine its function, he placed it back on the table. With a broad sweep of his arm, he gathered several discs into a pile. He picked one up, almost intimately, before inspecting it and returning it to the pile.

Finally, frustrated with himself, he mumbled out loud. "These things have to be something to do with the computers... but how the hell do they work?" Cathy assumed he was talking to her, as Tim was over at the bookshelf. "What was that?" she asked. "Nothing, I was talking to myself." Charlie explained apologetically. "I was just wondering how these bloody cards work.

They must have something to do with the computers. We've only ever seen them near computers. Nowhere else. They all have something written on them. Can you interpret any of these for me, please Tim?" Tim replaced the book he was perusing and walked over to Charlie and Cathy. He picked up a card and looked at the embossed hieroglyphs.

Charlie watched closely as he placed the card on the desk and began shuffling others. Some he placed with the first, others in separate piles. When he had sorted a dozen or so piles, he turned to Charlie and pointed to one of the piles. "These here, I can't really tell what they are." Then he pointed to another pile. "But these I can."

"Well?" Charlie insisted after a short silence. Tim nodded, then picked up a card. "OK. This one for example says... *metcha-t neter* ...*the book of the gods*. This one... *m'tenu* ...*written legends*... *bet* ...*flower or plant*... and this one... *begasu* ...*wild animals*. This one's interesting. It says... *aqet* ...*to pilot*... perhaps it's some flight training or navigational stuff from the space-craft. This one here says... *sehetch* ...*heaven of stars*." he read.

"I wonder if that's a series of star charts." Charlie mused. "I don't know." Tim conceded. "But it's obviously got something to do with the stars." Charlie picked up one of the small cards and inspected it closely. He then stated the obvious. "It's not like a CD or a floppy disc. There's nowhere for a spindle to go. So it's a fair bet it doesn't work like a conventional computer. Not that I really expected that to be the case. These blokes are obviously light years ahead of us.

But how does it work? Where do they interface with this system? Or are all these computers just peripherals of a central mainframe that these things fit into? But if that's the case, why are they here and not with the main frame? No, I think they have to fit in somewhere."

"It's all gobbledegook to me." Tim conceded, as he shrugged his shoulders. "I know nothing of computers, except how to use a word processor and the Internet... just!" They both looked at the keyboard and the cards. Suddenly Tim had a thought. "Look at that area in the centre of the keyboard. Funny, I never noticed it before. It's depressed slightly and it's about the size of those cards. That small writing there says... *ashem* ...that means *to make to go*. Perhaps the cards sit there or something." he offered.

"You mean like a magnetic scanner memory?" Charlie asked a bewildered Tim. "I have no idea what you're talking about. Why don't you see if they fit?" Tim suggested. Charlie grabbed a card labelled *wild animals* and placed it, embossed side up, in the depression. Suddenly the inanimate screen sprung to life with a vibrant burst of colour that made them both pull back in surprise. "Jesus Christ! You're a bloody genius. That was so simple."

"Beginner's luck, eh?" Tim joked. They all looked at the screen, now a vibrant blue shimmering orb about four feet in diameter. The outer circumference was taken up with a series of hieroglyphs, similar to a menu bar. Tim immediately investigated. "Well, what do you reckon?" he asked. "Looks like a menu." Charlie concluded. "Can you interpret it?"

Tim looked at the screen and frowned. "I'll give it my best shot, if you're up to it." he offered. Charlie smiled and wrapped his arm around his brother's shoulder. This was all the encouragement he needed. Charlie quickly scanned the maze of keys that made up the colossal semi-circular console.

His gut instinct led him to an area of symbols on the right hand side of the keyboard. "What do you make of this, Tim?" Tim approached closer and peered at the symbols. He then quickly scanned the remainder of the keyboard. "I don't know too much about computers, but I reckon it's a keyboard." Charlie laughed at the comment, then clarified his question. "I know it's a keyboard, smart-arse. But I think it's arranged into three different areas. A writing area, a function area and a menu area. I just need you to tell me which is which."

"Oh, in that case, let me have another look." Tim offered, as he leaned over the keyboard. This time he studied the individual keys carefully. Finally he offered his opinion. "I'd say that area's definitely the phonetic keyboard area. See there are twenty-four symbols there. That eagle represents the normal length sound of the letter A, as in *aquarium*. That feather symbol means a short sounding A, as in *cat*, and that figure there like a sort of golf club lying down is the long sounding letter A, as in *mate*."

Charlie smiled and encouraged Tim to continue. He had waited for days to get a good look at the computers. Now he could finally interrogate them. "Well, which are the function keys then?" Tim shook his head as he smiled back at his brother's enthusiasm. "Well, I can't really tell at this stage. Most of the hieroglyphs on the keys are unfamiliar. But I'd take a guess at this lot. There are a few familiar words there, although their context is a bit difficult to ascertain. Tell you what. You just get the thing talking to us and I'll try to guide you from there."

Charlie spent a few moments simply staring at the screen and the small housing in which it sat on the desk. Finally he reached over and ran his finger around the peripheral icons. To his amazement, as soon as he touched the screen, it changed. He muttered to himself in surprise.

"What the... Of course! The menu's touch-screen driven." Then he turned sheepishly to Tim and Cathy. "Maybe the third peripheral key area isn't a menu after all. Perhaps it's some sort of filing aid or an auxiliary system driver. Like intercoms, long distance communications and so forth." Tim and Cathy just shrugged their shoulders, so he continued unabated. He looked at the large writing in the centre of the screen and the new circle of menu icons around the perimeter. Tim noticed Charlie hesitate. "What's wrong?"

"Nothing. I'm just a little overwhelmed by it all. How about you looking at these symbols for me to see if there's something that'll give me a hint?" Tim leaned forward to inspect the screen. He was squinting and frowning noticeably as he tried to decipher the symbols. Finally a smile came to his face as he recognized something and announced it proudly. "There's something I recognise... *iam aam* ...*sea beast.* That sounds interesting. Want to have a look?"

Charlie reached over and touched the icon. Immediately the screen changed colour to a bright yellow. In the centre of the screen was a circular picture of a large prehistoric beast. Although only ten-inches in diameter, the quality of the picture was incredible. It looked like a 3D hologram suspended within the plastic of the screen, but the depth of field was beyond Charlie's wildest imagination.

The picture was surrounded by a plethora of menu options, arranged in layers of concentric circular icons that spread out to the edge of the screen. Tim gasped. "That looks like a plesiosaurus! Christ that's a good picture. It's like the actual beast's been captured and placed inside the screen. And look at the menu options. There are hundreds of them. Here try this one." Tim offered. "Why, what does it say?" Charlie asked excitedly. "It says... *iam tchetf-t* ...*sea serpent.*" Tim explained.

Charlie pressed the icon and watched closely as the screen changed. This time there was only a small round blue area, about six inches in diameter, in the centre of the screen, on which sat the black hieroglyphs for *sea serpent*. The rest of the screen was taken up with twenty or more concentric circles of icons. "Which one now?" he asked, feeling a rush of blood. "Just touch any one and we'll see what happens." Charlie reached out and touched an icon at random. Again the screen changed.

This time a ten-inch light orange circle appeared in the centre of the screen. He noticed the same icon he had touched was now in the middle of this circle. The remainder of the screen remained opaque, except for a single circle of icons at the very edge of the screen. Tim leaned over to inspect the screen, then turned to Charlie. "What do you reckon this is about?"

"I'd say we've gone down to a specific file. Perhaps it's about a certain species or something. I'll just..." As he touched the screen it suddenly changed. Again the peripheral zone was taken up with icons, but now there was a full screen colour picture of a large marine dinosaur. It was a magnificent three-dimensional, full-length photograph, plainly showing its long slender grey body, its four fins, its short partially fluted tail and its head. A head with long protruding jaws full of large, menacing yellow-green teeth. It was a semi-profile shot, so only one eye was visible.

Tim gazed at the cold beady little eye. It seemed to stare back. A shiver ran up his spine. "It looks like a mosasaur. Kronosaurus queenslandicus perhaps. A thirty-foot monster whose fossil remains they found in Queensland some time back. I saw part of it at the ANU a couple of years ago. Christ that's a good 3D photo. The clarity is mind-boggling. I wonder how they took it. It looks as if it's been taken right next to the beast... underwater. Look, that icon says... *setchetu* ...*to describe*... press that one, Charlie."

Charlie touched the screen. It immediately generated the same picture in a six-inch inner circle. Surrounding this was a spiral text. Tim leant over to read it. "This is fascinating. It's giving some dating information, but I still haven't worked out their chronology yet. But when I do, it'll tell us exactly when this beast was photographed. Although to be technically correct, in the museum I noticed they called the photos... *ar matu ...captured likeness.*"

"Well what does it say?" Charlie insisted. "Oh, sorry. It's a description of the beast and where they found it. Off the coast of Atlantis apparently... and when it was last seen. It then goes on with something about it being responsible for ..." he paused. "For what?" Charlie almost pleaded. "I don't know. The text ends here."

As he touched the last hieroglyph, the screen flashed. Again the same picture took up the centre, but the text had changed. "Oh... that makes sense. The text just continues on. It appears these things were responsible for many attacks on fishing vessels. Shit! I thought these things were prehistoric... and extinct. They were supposed to have lived in the post-Jurassic period. They were believed to have died out at the end of the Cretaceous period, about 65 million years ago.

But it appears they were still around when Atlantis was inhabited. Shit! I'm sure they didn't settle here that long ago. Now I've really got to sort out the chronology. See here... they say one of the royal nephews was killed when the fishing boat he was sailing in was attacked and destroyed by one of these monsters. Christ there's going to be a shit load of useful and... dare I say... controversial information available in these computers.

But there's too much information to take photographs of. I wonder if we could set up a video and just film the screen. Then we could flick through as much as we can while we're here. We could analyse it later, frame-by-frame. Can you do that?"

Charlie nodded confidently. "Yeah, now that I know how these things operate. I reckon it'd be a piece of piss. But I wouldn't be able to catalogue it that well. I can't read the writing." he conceded. "Just video the front of the card before you sit it in the keypad. That way I'll know what the DVD's about." Tim suggested. "That's a huge task! Remember there are thousands of these things here. And it looks like there's more information on each one of these than on a hundred regular CDs. Where do I start?"

Tim looked at the piles of cards in front of him. "Just start with these ones on the desk. I'll look at the library of them over there. They should be in some sort of order. If not, I'll try to catalogue them for you. Then we can concentrate on the most interesting ones first." he suggested. Charlie nodded. "OK... but we'll have to get the camera and some discs first."

Tim wandered over to the card library and started reading labels. He confirmed they were filed in a logical manner, although exactly what most of them contained was a mystery.

He was just about to leave and head back to camp when he found an interesting section of cards. "I think you may just want to look at one of these Charlie." He said, as he handed Charlie a card. "What is it?" Charlie asked. Tim smiled. "It comes from a section labelled... *thes-t ta kheper* ...which means something like *the thread to make or beget*. It sounds interestingly like DNA, don't you think?"

Charlie grabbed the card and placed it in the keyboard. The screen immediately filled with icons, but the central section remained blank. Instinctively he reached out and touched the blank area. It immediately filled with text. "What does it say?" he almost implored Tim. Tim looked at the writing for some time before he began to mumble to himself. The others waited patiently for enlightenment.

Finally he heaved an audible sigh. "Well?" Cathy probed. "Well, I'll be buggered! I think I know what these chaps are about. This looks like a DNA library. It seems they're so technically advanced, they can custom create DNA. All they need is a suitable surrogate mother and they can create any creature they have ever encountered... or can dream up. It appears this information contains the entire gene string of every living thing... animal and vegetable... they've ever encountered or created.

What's more, they have full data on what each gene is responsible for. This is effectively a digital Noah's ark! God's tool box." The magnitude of this discovery alone was too much for Cathy to absorb. She simply shook her head in disbelief. Charlie was a little quicker to analyse the implications. After he had stared at Tim for a few seconds, he finally asked the obvious question. "Do you suppose our genes are there too?"

"I don't see why not. From the snippets of information we've gleaned so far, it seems we're the product of some cloning or genetic manipulation. Perhaps they took a chimp's genes and manipulated them to grow less hair, stand taller, and develop opposable thumbs. It's not that far-fetched when you really think about it. It makes sense of the Biblical account of creation too." he surmised.

"What's that?" Cathy asked. "Well, as I've said before, in the original Hebrew texts it doesn't say the word God. The term used is Elohim. That's what the Lord Guardian called himself. But in Hebrew it was a generic term, simply translated as *those from the sky.*

Ah... the theanthropic nature of the beast. Anyway, the Bible says that the Elohim made man in his own image. We're hardly like these Guardians are we? It's more likely the Celtic scientists... the Anunnaki... were the ones who actually created life on earth. The Lord Guardian himself said they were the technical ones.

It's possible they had no interaction with some early humans, only the Guardians were seen. Hence the Guardians were worshipped as the gods by some people, rather than the Anunnaki. Maybe that accounts for the mysterious duality of the mythical Hebrew god, as described in the Old Testament."

The others contemplated it for a while before Charlie changed the subject back to DNA. "I'll see if the Thylacine is here. It'd be great to resurrect them." Cathy opined. "A what?" Charlie asked, not sure if Cathy was pulling his leg. "A Thylacine... a Tasmanian tiger."

They continued in silence, each pursuing their own thoughts and interests. Cathy worked her way through the contents of the library. Many of the chronicles had photos embedded in the text, to illustrate the tale being related. Cathy relied on these to keep her interest up. She was careful to replace each book in exactly the same place. It was essential to keep the collection together chronologically so it could be catalogued.

The majority of books were the white-spined, plastic type. Cathy eventually got to these and began thumbing through one. The illustrations indicated it to be a maintenance manual for the power plant from one of the smaller space craft. Another proved to be a recipe book, filled with a collection of the strangest fruit she had ever seen. As she perused books at random, it was apparent the library contained a comprehensive collection of knowledge.

Tim and Charlie meanwhile had busied themselves with the cards. Tim assured Charlie that the task of videoing them, category by category, would be a relatively simple, but time consuming one. Engrossed as they were with the myriad cards, the time flew by at astonishing speed. Before they knew it, Cathy reminded them that it was time to return to camp. While Tim was eager to go, they had to physically extricate Charlie from the chair in front of his treasured computer.

CHAPTER 23

The next three weeks were a blur to Tim, Charlie and Cathy as they spent endless hours exploring the base and cataloguing its contents. Charlie spent the entire time videotaping the computer files. It took up so many DVD's, that it necessitated a trip to town by Cathy to buy hundreds more. Tim too had ran out of memory sticks and CD's for his photographs and had to have his stocks replenished when she went to town. Cathy was gone for three days.

Finally they simply ran out of time. Becky and Sue were due back in five days and the men had to drive to Melbourne to meet them. Reluctantly, they agreed to abandon their camp and the base.

As they were making preparations to shut down the power and seal the entrance, Tim remembered the Lord Guardian. "Charlie, we have a job to do." he reminded him. Charlie racked his brain, but needed more specific details. "We do?" he asked nervously.

"Yes. The crypt, remember?." Charlie's pulse raced as he felt a cold shiver travel down his spine. "Oh shit, that's right. I forgot about that. The Lord Guardian." Charlie's apprehension was blindingly obvious. Tim looked over to Cathy, but before he could say anything, she had pre-empted his concern. "I know. You want me to stay here in case the power goes out and you get stuck down there." she growled.

"Thanks, Cathy. I knew you'd understand. I'd swap you for Charlie in a heartbeat, but the lid will be too heavy for you." Charlie wandered over to Tim with a false air of bravado and wrapped his arm around his shoulder. "Let's go then." They walked to the elevator in silence as they contemplated coming face to face with the Lord Guardian.

What they were about to do filled them with trepidation, but they felt an obligation to seal the coffin. From the sounds of the creature, he deserved that respect at the very least. But at the same time they were curious to see the last of the Lord Guardians. Would he be mummified or would he have simply decomposed to a skeleton? Or simply reduced to a pile of dust?

The elevator came to a halt at the third level of the crypt. As the door opened, Charlie hesitated long enough for Tim to exit first. "We'd better split up and find his sarcophagus then." Tim suggested. "Not bloody likely. I'm sticking with you." Charlie hastily replied. Tim laughed at Charlie's timidity.

Somehow the quick trip in the elevator had stripped him of the brave face he had shown in front of Cathy. But Tim thought nothing more of it. He fully understood Charlie's apprehension. Crypts were a strange place to be at the best of times. Being in an alien crypt was even more disconcerting. "OK. Let's look over here shall we. It seems this corridor isn't full of coffins yet." Tim observed.

Tim wandered off towards the corridor, Charlie following closely behind. As they reached the entrance to the corridor, Tim stopped. In the immediate foreground he could see empty niches hewn from the parent rock. In the distance he thought he could see where the sarcophagi began. He looked around and nodded confidently at Charlie, then strode off.

About half way down the left side of the corridor, they came across the first sarcophagus. It's lid was in place. So too the next, and the next. Tim looked at the right hand side of the corridor. The niches here were still empty. "I guess it's further down." he suspected.

Charlie nodded his concurrence with the assumption and followed Tim as he strode down the corridor. He had gone another fifty yards or so, when he noticed the first sarcophagus on the right hand side.

As he approached it, he saw that the lid was askew. "I guess this is it, Charlie." Charlie's heart began racing. He was not comfortable with this at all. He stopped some ten yards from the open sarcophagus and cringed as Tim approached it.

Tim nonchalantly leaned over to inspect the contents. The supine body had mummified in the dry air of the crypt and was perfectly preserved. He noticed that the Lord Guardian's eyes were shut and his hands were neatly folded across his chest. He even had a slight smile on his feline face. That struck him as odd. He looked posed. "Jesus Charlie, have a look at this will you." he offered enthusiastically.

But Charlie did not share his enthusiasm. "Yeah, right!" he quipped. "Oh, come on, Charlie. It's OK. The poor old bugger's perfectly mummified. You can still see his facial features. And his clothes are in remarkable condition. Boy he looks impressive."

Charlie reluctantly approached and peered into the coffin for a couple of seconds. Satisfied that he had seen enough, he stepped back and looked over at Tim. Tim nodded toward the body. "Don't you think it's odd?" Charlie shook his head. "What?"

"The way he's so perfectly posed." Tim stated casually. But Charlie had not noticed anything untoward. "What do you mean?" he asked. "I mean if you were the last man alive on a base like this and you knew you were dying. What would you do?" Tim asked. "I don't know." Charlie agreed. "Just wait for the inevitable I guess." he suggested.

"Exactly! Logic would say that you deteriorated at a certain rate, but near the end this would accelerate. Logic for me would to be in my quarters, where I would be most comfortable. You know. Food, entertainment, fond memories." Tim postulated. "Well, yes... but?" Charlie muttered. Tim nodded and continued. "Well at some point you'd have to decide that your time was up.

But by that time, you'd probably be too weak to shut down the power and wander off to the crypt. Besides you might lay in the sarcophagus for hours or days before you actually died. Wouldn't it make more sense to just die in your bed?" Tim asked. "Oh, I see the conundrum." Charlie announced proudly. "Exactly!" Tim exclaimed.

Tim was pondering the logistics of the Lord Guardian's last days when he noticed it. There in the sarcophagus, almost hidden by the body, was a small phial. It looked to be made from rose glass. Further searching found a small glass stopper resting under his right thigh. Suddenly he had an epiphany. "That's it! Of course!" he declared proudly.

"What?" Charlie asked. Tim smiled. "Euthanasia." he suggested. "By whom?" Charlie enquired. Tim pointed inside the coffin. "Self administered. See the small phial over there?" Charlie reluctantly approached the coffin, his eyes following Tim's pointing finger. He searched fruitlessly for a while but finally confirmed the existence of the phial.

Tim continued with his hypothesis. "So once he'd had enough, he put his affairs in order, rigged a timer on the generator, came down here, got into his coffin then topped himself." he concluded. "That's about the size of it I guess. Poor lonely bastard!"

Charlie was still feeling uncomfortable and wanted nothing more than to leave the crypt. "OK. So let's put the lid on and get the hell out of here shall we?" he suggested rather loudly.

Tim nodded, but said nothing, as he continued to stare at the mummified remains of the once powerful Lord Guardian. "What an impressive creature. I'll just take a couple of photos before we seal him in." Charlie thought it morbid, but said nothing. To Tim it was a matter of preserving an image of a former great being. No different to taking a photo of an Egyptian mummy.

Once he had taken several photos, Tim stepped back from the coffin. "For some strange reason I feel obliged to say a few words." he admitted. "What, like a eulogy?" Charlie asked, rather awkwardly. "I guess so. After all, no-one was here for his funeral. It must have been such a lonely death for him. I think it's the least he deserves." Tim suggested. "I guess you're right. OK, off you go then." Charlie urged.

Tim looked around for a few moments, trying to work out something appropriate to say. The irony of the situation was not lost on him. A modern historian saying a few words over the body of a highly intelligent alien warrior who died one and a half thousand years before. Nonetheless he finally cleared his throat.

"Well we're here for the final farewell of Lord Charan. Although we know little about him as yet, we're sure that his contributions to his fellow Guardians were substantial. We're unsure where he stood with his relatives, but I'm sure they were very proud of him and his achievements. So I guess it's farewell to a noble being. Sleep in peace Charan, the last Lord Guardian of the blue planet." Tim looked over to Charlie, who simply nodded his approval.

Without a word they reached over and, with great effort, slid the massive lid into place. Charlie then heaved a sigh of relief and headed back to the elevator. Tim followed but paused some ten feet away from the coffin. He turned to look at it once more, then, in a low, almost whispering, voice, said his final farewell. "Farewell my friend."

They walked back to the elevator in silence, each lost in their deepest thoughts and emotions. Their work here was done. It was time to abandon the base.

CHAPTER 24

Cathy was so pleased to see them as they stepped from the elevator. She hugged Tim ferociously and smiled warmly at Charlie. "It's done then?" she asked. Tim nodded. "Yes." She sensed from the terse reply that it had been an emotional farewell, so she probed no further. There would be time enough later for the men to recall their meeting. "Well let's get back to the camp."

They all reluctantly agreed that the time had come, so they collected their things and headed off towards the power station. "Just one thing left to do." Tim declared. "Shut down the generator before we go. I wouldn't want anyone tracing the power source and discovering the base while we're away."

Once again at the control console of the power generation room, the two men browsed through the manuals as Cathy silently watched on. Eventually, confident that he had interpreted the manuals correctly, Tim walked Charlie through the shutdown sequence. For such a highly technical system they were all surprised at the relatively straightforward shutdown procedures. As the generator ceased operation, they noticed the red indicator light fade away.

Almost simultaneously, the light intensity began to attenuate. They continued to watch with some sadness as the diffusive glow that had been their constant companion, slowly waned. The ebbing glow slowly receded to the very top of the cavernous vaulted ceiling, then finally, after giving several convulsions of faintly pulsing light, snuffed out like a dying candle.

They sat silently in the ensuing darkness for some time. Eventually Tim turned his torch on. "Shit, I've got so used to the light, that I forgot just how dark it was in here without it. I suppose we'd better get going.

We still have a bit of work ahead of us before we leave. Re-sealing the entrance for one. We don't want anyone finding this place while we're gone." The others agreed and followed Tim as he headed towards the cave. While Cathy continued on to the camping area to finish packing the cars, the two men began the onerous task of shoring up the entrance.

Nearly three hours later, after piling hundreds of rocks against the broken door and sealing the roof at the top of the last pile of rocks, the two exhausted men dragged themselves back to the camp.

As they approached they could see the ghostly animated glow of the four Tilley lamps gathered around Cathy as she packed the last remaining belongings into the ute. She smiled as they approached. "Would you like a beer for the road?" Without waiting for an answer, she reached into the fridge and grabbed three beers. "Here you go! I've nearly finished packing. We might as well relax for a few minutes before we leave."

They drank their beer in silence. Each quietly recounting their personal thoughts and experiences of the base and its contents. It had been a tumultuous few weeks and all were feeling sad at leaving the base prematurely. They all knew they had hardly scratched the surface. There was so much to catalogue. So much information on the computer system yet to be revealed. That alone could keep them occupied for years. And the contents of the great library had hardly been touched.

It was Cathy who finally broke the silence. "I think we'd better try to erase all our tracks both in here and around the entrance to the cave. If we do accidentally leak some of this information we might attract unwanted visitors. People will put two-and-two together once they see us in cahoots. They may assume the base is somewhere on or near Dad's property. We don't want to make it easy for anyone else to find." The men agreed with her acumen.

They stood up and placed their empty beer cans in the back of Cathy's ute. With all three pitching in, it wasn't long before the camp was cleaned up and all evidence of their stay erased. Cathy left the cave to fetch a stout branch from a nearby tree. When she returned she addressed the men. "Well you two can take the cars to the entrance if you like. I'll just tidy up here then follow you out, removing your tracks as I go. I'll see you in a few minutes."

Cathy began to sweep the floor with quick, wide circular swishes of the branch. There wasn't much dirt where they had camped, but she wanted to remove all recognizable signs of recent human habitat. As the cars drove off, she slowly followed them, erasing any tracks as she went. Once the vehicles left the cavern, Cathy stopped for a few moments and watched as the bright glow from the headlights gradually faded, leaving her alone in the surreal but comforting glow of her remaining Tilley lamp.

She stood transfixed as the sound of motors gradually attenuated to a mute stillness. For a few moments she stood there, consumed by the claustrophobic silence of the cavern. With a quick shake of her head, she returned to the task at hand. Tilley lamp in one hand, swirling branch in the other, she quickly made her way towards the entrance of the cave.

When she got there, she was surprised by the absence of vehicles. She was just wondering where they were, when Tim popped out from behind some bushes. "We took the cars away a bit and cleaned up the tracks as best we could. Thought it might save some time."

Cathy smiled and gave Tim a peck on the cheek. "Thanks, Tim. We're ready to go then?" They caught up with Charlie a few hundred yards from the cave, disposing of the branches they had used to erase their tracks. Cathy threw her branch at the base of a towering river gum and doused her lamp.

Tim then looked at the sad faces that surrounded him. "Ready?" Cathy's smile was unconvincing as she reluctantly, nodded her head. As much as she wanted to stay, she knew it was time for them to go. "Yep! Just follow me. I'll take you down the creek bed for a while. It'll be a bit rough, but the next rain will erase our tracks. Anyone who doesn't know this country won't find the cave unless they use a helicopter."

Tim jumped into the passenger seat of Cathy's ute and yelled across to Charlie. "See you back at the homestead." Charlie followed Cathy and Tim as they threaded their way through the unforgiving terrain back to the homestead. Here they planned to spend their last night before their long drive home.

About halfway back, Cathy stopped near an old watercourse. Jumping out of her car, she ran back to Charlie. "This is the place I told you about. We can leave most of the gold here. There's a little cave behind the trees there. It's got a sandy floor so we can bury it. No-one comes out this way, so it should be safe until we find a way to get rid of it without causing suspicion."

They buried all but one of the bars, keeping it for good luck. Cathy and Tim completed the journey mostly in silence. Reminiscing on what they had seen and contemplating what lay ahead. When they finally arrived at the homestead, it was just on dusk.

As they pulled up they were enthusiastically greeted by Dot. "Hello darling. Hello boys. Good to see you made it back OK. I trust you had a good holiday. Although I can think of a dozen places I'd rather holiday at than a dingy old cave in the scrub."

Everyone smiled and greeted Dot with a hug. Cathy put her arm around her mother as they walked toward the house. "Dad's in town at the bull sale and won't be home until tomorrow afternoon." she explained. "That's OK. We'll probably meet him on our way out." Dot was horrified. "You're leaving already?" she asked sadly.

Cathy nodded slowly. "Yes Mum. Tomorrow morning. I'm going back to Melbourne with Tim and then we're going to Egypt. Isn't that exciting?" Dot nodded less than enthusiastically. "Yes, but I've hardly seen you this summer. Will you be long?" she asked sadly. "I don't know. But we'll visit as soon as we get back. I promise." Dot smiled politely and said nothing. Given choices, she would rather spend more time with her only daughter. But she knew she was an independent spirit and would go when and where she pleased. She also noticed, with an air of quiet satisfaction, the way Cathy was clinging to Tim and her use of the word *we*. She liked Tim and was happy for Cathy. She approved of the union.

Early next morning Tim and Charlie began rearranging the car to accommodate Cathy. They decided to leave the trailer and most of their gear in one of the many sheds at the station. It would make for a quicker and more comfortable return journey.

After their thanks to the host, Tim and Charlie went to the car and climbed in. Cathy stayed back to say her own private farewell to her mother. Dot almost pleaded with Cathy as she kissed her on the cheek. "Now you take care of yourself!" she implored. "Of course I will, Mum. You just take care out here on your own."

Dot nodded. "I'll be alright. Dad's back today and the boys should be back from Spring Hill in a couple of days." Tim smiled at Dot from the driver's seat of his car and reassured her that Cathy was in good hands. Dot knew that to be true, but was nonetheless apprehensive. She viewed any trip overseas as being fraught with danger. She was not the adventurous type that Cathy was. That she concluded, she got from her father.

Although she was happy for Cathy with her new love interest, this also made her sad. It signalled that her youngest was about to leave the nest for good. This meant that years of loneliness awaited her.

Unless, by some miracle, fate found a way to keep Cathy close by. She fought back the tears as she prepared to bid them a final farewell. "I'll take good care of her for you." Tim promised her. "I know you will." Dot replied, with a tear in her eye.

Cathy jumped into the vehicle next to Tim. After checking that Charlie was OK in the back seat, Tim fired up the motor and slipped it into gear. He glanced at Dot and noticed that despite her best efforts to disguise them, the tears were now welling up in her eyes. "Don't worry Dot. We should be back in a few weeks." Dot leant into the open window to give Cathy a final peck on the cheek. "See you soon, honey."

Cathy wiped a tear from her eye as she grabbed her mother's hand. "I promise we'll be back soon, Mum. By the way... just in case we don't get to see Dad. Could you tell him something for me?" Dot nodded. "Of course!" she promised. "Tell him not to let any strangers onto the property until we get back... and be careful."

Dot suddenly frowned. "What do you mean?" she asked, with great concern in her voice. "Dad will understand." Cathy explained. "Bye Mum... I love you." Dot stood with a puzzled and almost pained expression on her face. What had Cathy meant? What was she so worried about? Why would strangers come here?

She mulled the questions over as she watched the car until it tripped over the horizon and disappeared from sight. She stood riveted to the spot, watching until the last vestiges of the dust trail had finally melted into the atmosphere. With a heavy sigh she gave a belated wave goodbye and returned to the solitude of the remote station homestead. A cattle station was a lonely place for a woman. She knew that. It was her lot. That was why she was glad Cathy seemed to have found someone who could offer her more than years of hard work, heartbreak and loneliness. She was happy for them both.

CHAPTER 25

There was a long journey ahead of them as the three weary explorers pointed the car in the general direction of Melbourne. After several hours of driving, they began to fully appreciate their decision to leave the trailer and the majority of the load at the station. Charlie rued that they had not had the chance to use their fishing rods since leaving Byron Bay. With a judicious reminder of the value of the buried gold and the hoard of ancient coins in the car, he was assured there would be plenty of time for that in the future.

Late that afternoon Tim slowed down to allow a passing motor vehicle to have some room on the narrow bush road. As it approached them Cathy recognised it. "Tim, could you flash your lights and pull over, please. I think that's Dad." Tim flashed his headlights at the approaching vehicle and pulled over. The other vehicle came to a stop next to them.

It was indeed Brett. Cathy leapt from the front seat and rushed to the open window of Brett's car and gave him a hug and a kiss on the cheek. "Where are you off to?" Brett inquired. Cathy smiled excitedly. "I'm going back to Melbourne with Tim and Charlie. We have some things to do." she announced.

Brett looked over to the other vehicle and nodded hello to the men. Then he looked back at Cathy. "Well, did you find anything interesting?" he asked, not really expecting a positive answer. "Do you really want to know?" she smiled teasingly. "That good, eh?" he joked.

"Better!" Cathy responded, as she hastily looked over to Tim, wanting reassurance that he trusted Brett with the information. Tim smiled and nodded his approval. After all, it was his property. He had a right to know what they had found on it.

Cathy opened the car door for Brett and led him by the hand to the back of Tim's car. She opened the tailgate and retrieved a small parcel wrapped in an old towel. She suggested he have a look at it. "Jeez it's heavy. What is it?" Brett exclaimed.

"Unwrap it and see." Cathy urged. Brett obediently unwrapped the parcel. What lay in his hands was almost beyond his comprehension. His eyes could not believe what they were seeing, as he stared at the gleaming ingot. Finally he stuttered out a silly question. "Is this what I think it is?"

Cathy laughed. "Yes, it's ancient gold. Thousands of years old. See the Egyptian hieroglyphs on the ingot?" She pointed to the stamped writing in the middle of the bar. Brett was dumbfounded. "How the hell did it get here?" he asked in disbelief. "It's a long story Dad, but I guess I'd better fill you in." Cathy offered.

With some exertion, Cathy took the gold bar and wrapped it carefully in the towel. She walked over to Brett's car and opened the door. She leant in and placed it on the passenger's seat. "I'll give it to you for safe keeping." She told him.

Cathy spent the next fifteen minutes highlighting their discovery as briefly as she could. There was so much to tell that she had difficulty recounting it all. As she divulged their secret, Brett looked both bewildered and excited. Once she had finished, he stood in silence for a while digesting the information. Finally a worried look came over him. "This is serious stuff."

Tim and Charlie could not agree more. Tim decided to give Brett some advice. "Brett, I know you're pretty switched on, but do you mind if I give you some advice?" Brett looked a little taken aback, but nodded his approval anyway. "Well I think you can understand there are vested interests out there. And people willing to do what it takes to protect them. We're talking of billions of dollars invested in the Church for a start.

Not to mention treasure hunters." Tim explained. Brett nodded his understanding and motioned for Tim to continue. "Well, just be real careful Brett. I'd suggest if you had somewhere out of the way Dot could go for a few months, that'd be a good idea. Some relatives perhaps. Until we can verify that the other sites exist, people may come looking for this one. They may want to silence anyone who knows anything about it. By the way we didn't tell Dot anything. We didn't want to worry her." he added.

Brett nodded. "Thanks for that. She doesn't need to know. It would just worry her sick. But are you saying that people would be willing to kill to keep this information quiet?" he asked, with a great deal of concern in his voice. Tim nodded solemnly. "Yes, unfortunately. I've crossed swords with the Church of Rome before. They can be ruthless bastards when they're protecting their theology.

You have to understand that they're running a multi-billion dollar business empire and have, even in recent history, fiercely protected their political and financial interests. As you can appreciate, this has the potential to destroy their power base overnight. And without that power base, their political influence would soon disappear, along with their financial income. I fear the Holy Alliance will find out about this sooner or later. I just hope it's later. After we've verified one or two other sites." Tim said, shuddering at the possibilities.

"Who's the Holy Alliance?" Brett asked. "It's the Vatican's Secret Service." Tim explained. "You're kidding!" Brett exclaimed. Tim shook his head. "No. Although these days it's usually referred to simply as *The Entity*. They also have a counterespionage unit, referred to as the *Sodalitium Pianum*. The Fellowship of Pius. It refers to Pope Pius X, whose decrees against modernism resulted in the formation of the service some time after 1907.

The Vatican can be brutal when it comes to suppressing anything that might throw a disparaging light on their religion. I lost a good friend..." Tim paused as he remembered with great sadness the disappearance of his old friend Monsignor Thomas and the mysterious circumstances surrounding the theft of his research documents. But he quickly banished those thoughts to the back of his mind and carried on with the business at hand. "Anyway, until we have enough evidence to release this information to the public, you need to be vigilant. I have an old adversary who, once he sees me with Cathy, may put two and two together." he warned.

"Meaning?" Brett probed. Tim hesitated before answering him. "Meaning you may get visitors. Not too friendly ones at that. It might even be worth going on a holiday with Dot for a while. That way you'll be safe. The sheer size of the property will make it near impossible for anyone to find the base quickly.

By then we should have worked out our options." Tim anticipated. But Brett shook his head. "No that's out of the question. There's too much to do here. I might be able to convince Dot to visit relatives for a while, but I need to stay. I've got a couple of good stockmen working for me. We should be able to take care of ourselves." he stated.

Tim nodded. "If you stay on the property, just be careful. Carry a gun everywhere you go and don't be frightened to use it. If in doubt, shoot first and ask questions later. Better to be safe than sorry. But don't involve the police. Many of them will have connections to dubious people around the world. Trust no-one. If anyone comes here to cause trouble, it's unlikely they'll be missed, so just bury them in the bush somewhere." Tim suggested, rather strongly. Brett's brow furrowed deeply as he looked long and hard at Tim. He then looked over to Cathy.

She returned his gaze with a sombre stare and slightly raised eyebrows. This was serious advice indeed. Brett's mind was troubled and he was starting to feel decidedly uncomfortable, even a little afraid. Afraid for the safety of his family. Afraid for the future of his cattle station. "Jesus Christ! That's getting bloody serious." he understated.

Again Tim nodded. "Yes, unfortunately. Even without trying to be over dramatic. But that's the reality of the situation I'm afraid, Brett. I can't stress enough how ruthless religious institutions can be. Remember this stuff will affect the Muslims as well. And you've seen how irrational some of those fanatical bastards can be." he stressed.

Brett swallowed hard. He did not like what he was hearing. "How long will you be away?" he finally asked. Cathy looked at Tim, then returned her eyes to her father. "A month or two at most should get us all the verification we need. We intend to use other sites to release the information to the media as soon as possible. That'll take the heat off the main base. I think that's the only way to put a lid on this thing. Your site will remain a secret for now, but I can't guarantee how long that will last." she explained.

Brett nodded his understanding. His immediate concern then shifted to his daughter. "You take good care of her won't you?" he asked, looking straight at Tim. Tim nodded vigorously. "You bet!" he confirmed.

Cathy once again hugged her father and gave him a goodbye peck on the cheek. Then she joined the men in the car as Tim started the engine and bade farewell to Brett. Brett stood next to his car and watched as the four-wheel drive meandered along the dusty track and finally disappeared into the shimmering heat wave in the distance. Slowly he climbed into the car and sat there patting the gold bar for a moment, contemplating what he had been told.

CHAPTER 26

Charlie wandered casually along Swanston Street until he came to the Ian Potter Museum of Art. He hesitated at the university gate for a few seconds, as he reinforced his grip on the black leather briefcase he was carrying. Smiling in self reassurance, he pulled his shoulders back, and confidently strode off.

He turned left into Masson Road and ambled along, still smiling to himself as he passed the old Geology building. But his gait slowed as he approached the Chemistry department. Standing under one of the many gently swaying trees that lined the road, he looked up at the elegant, three-storey, glass-rich building that was the east wing. Again he hesitated. His apprehension suddenly became a self-perpetuating monster, feeding voraciously upon itself. It was un-nerving him as he had never experienced before. What kind of reception he would get from the Professor?

He knew Karl both academically and, to a lesser degree, socially. But now he was unsure of exactly how to approach him. He had mulled the meeting over in his head a thousand times during the countless hours in the car coming home from the station. He thought he had it worked out to a tee. But now it worried him. Now he was unsure.

His early evening arrival had been timed so that Karl had finished work for the day. Although it was still several weeks before university classes began, Karl was employed full time by the university. He not only taught students, he was an integral member of the university's industrial research department.

Charlie had telephoned the day before, to arrange the meeting. Now the time had come for him to lay his cards on the table.

Karl was sitting at this desk churning through mountains of research paperwork as Charlie entered his office. "How are you Karl?" Charlie greeted cheerfully. "Oh! Hi Charles. Didn't hear you sneak up on me. I'm fine... and you?" Karl asked. Charlie smiled warmly. "Couldn't be better. I just got back from a terrific holiday and I'm looking forward to relaxing at home for a bit. By the way, did you get away over the Christmas break?" Karl shook his head. "Not really. I visited my daughter down in Frankston for a couple of days. But that's about it. I guess I spend too much time in here on this damned research project."

Charlie nodded. "So you haven't got much spare time then?" he probed. "Well, not really. I guess I could slow down a bit, if I really wanted to. But I enjoy research and it's a hard task master, I'm afraid." Karl admitted. "Anyway, enough of the small talk. When you called, you said you had something for me to look at. But you were somewhat evasive, promising to explain all when we met. I'm curious, Charles. Exactly what is it you think I can help you with?"

Charlie sighed heavily as he gently placed his briefcase on the table. He carefully positioned it such that, when opened, Karl would not see the contents. He remained silent as he systematically rolled the tumblers to unlock the case. First the left tumbler. Then the right.

Then he simultaneously slid the locks aside with his thumbs. The locks released the catches with an unnervingly loud snap. The noise shattered the silence, startling him and causing his eyes to blink involuntarily. He quickly regathered his wits and opened the briefcase.

Charlie reached in, watching Karl carefully as he did so. As his hand touched one of the small tools he had souvenired from the cave complex, he hesitantly stroked it. He was stalling, albeit subtly.

The thought of what could happen next was making him more nervous by the second. Finally he decided the time for procrastination was over. He grabbed the object of his attention and reached out his hand, offering the tool to Karl. "I found this." he stammered. "What is it?" Karl asked, after a quick visual inspection of the object. "Some kind of tool." Charlie explained. "But what it does is somewhat irrelevant. What's more pertinent is what it's made of. I'm guessing some sort of metallic polymer."

Karl took the tool from Charlie and carefully looked it over. He symbolically weighed it, in an effort to determine its mass. "Seems pretty light. But by the looks of the wear marks on it, I'd say it must be pretty strong. Robust even. Where did you get it from? And why did you bring it to me?" he probed cautiously.

Charlie hesitated for a moment, as he decided how much information to divulge. Finally he determined to give Karl just enough to allow him to reach the obvious conclusion. That the mystery object was worthy of further analysis. "Karl, I know you're not religious. And I know you're an academic who loves research and discovery. So, I presume you have a more open mind that the average person."

Karl smiled at what he perceived as a compliment. "I like to think so." he agreed modestly. "Good. Because what I'm about to tell you is..." Again Charlie hesitated. Again he fought for the right words. He wanted to give Karl enough information to gain his confidence. But he needed to keep details like the location of the base, indeed even the very existence of the base, secret. "Well, what I'm about to tell you is somewhat speculative. It's looking at things outside the box. If you know what I mean." he tried to explain. "Not really." Karl confessed. Charlie shook his head. "Sorry, I guess there's no real subtle way of saying this, so..."

Again Charlie hesitated. "Jesus Charles, it can't be that hard." Karl insisted. But Charlie just smiled feebly at his friend. "I wish it were that simple." he began. "You see, Karl, I have reason to believe this tool is of extraterrestrial origin." Charlie offered tentatively. "You what!" Karl's intonation of incredulity was exactly what Charlie didn't want. Once again he found himself doubting his decision-making abilities.

Had he come to the wrong person? Had he jeopardized the secret? Was he sure he was doing the right thing? For several seconds he fought wildly with his conflicting thoughts and emotions. Finally rationale won. "See, that's exactly what I meant." he calmly stated. "Please hear me out Karl, before you make any kind of judgement." he pleaded.

"Sorry, Charles. It's just that I don't get that sort of hypothesis thrown my way every day. It's way out of left field you know. I'm sorry. Please continue." Charlie smiled. "It's OK, Karl. I'm Sorry. I'm as nervous as a chain smoker in a gunpowder factory at the moment. Not knowing which way to turn and expecting everything to blow up in my face at any moment. Please let me explain."

Karl sat back, almost disappearing into the soft leather of his plush office chair. He motioned for Charlie to sit down in the chair opposite him. Once they were both seated, Karl smiled politely and nodded for Charlie to continue. "I'm all ears." he stated. "Well I hope you appreciate there's limited information I can give you at the moment." Charlie explained. "Like exactly where I found these things. Maybe later I can..." Karl interrupted. "You mean you have more stuff like this?" His voice was now showing genuine interest.

"Sure, but let me explain a few things first. I have reason to believe that aliens, for the want of a better term, have visited this planet for some time. There's anecdotal evidence for it everywhere.

From religion to genetics to the Plains of Nasca. But now, I think we finally have conclusive proof. What we've discovered is political and historical dynamite. It'll re-write the history books, at the very least. Unfortunately, it also has the potential to destroy organized religion per se. So there may be a few misguided souls out there with vested interests, who won't like what we've found. If you know what I mean?" he tried vainly to explain in simple terms.

"Are you that sure? That's a big assertion." Karl insisted. "Positive!" he confirmed. "Look I'll show you something that might..." Charlie stopped for a moment to regain his thoughts. Deciding that he was committed, he reached over to the briefcase and extracted a small sample of fruit he had taken from the kitchen warehouse. "Take a look at this."

Karl leant over and took the small container from Charlie's outstretched hand. As he inspected it, his brow began to furrow. Charlie could almost read the question in his eyes. "What's with the Egyptian hieroglyphs?" he finally asked. Charlie was impressed, but he felt compelled to correct him. "It's not Egyptian. The hieroglyphs are Zamzam'min. The Egyptians borrowed them." he explained. "Who are the Zamzam'min?" Karl asked, now intrigued by it all. "They're a giant race alluded to in the Bible. But that's way too long a story for now. Perhaps later. For now, suffice it to say, I have it on good authority, that this container is thousands of years old."

"Bullshit! It looks like modern plastic. That's impossible." Karl blurted out. "Mayhap. Mayhap not." Charlie stated coldly. "But look at the label. I've never seen anything like that before. Have you?" Charlie calmly asked. Karl shook his head. "No, I must admit it's impressive. But the work of an ancient civilization?" he insisted. Charlie nodded.

"That's why I need you to analyse this material for me. To prove whether it's simply modern plastic or not. That way, I'll know for sure whether it's genuine. Or just an elaborate hoax. What do you reckon, Karl? Game for a go?" he asked with a broad smile. Karl nodded. "What else have you got in there?" Charlie leant over and spun the briefcase around to face Karl. "A few odds and sods I picked up from the... Well a few things I managed to souvenir for you."

Karl spent the next few minutes deep in thought, as he closely inspected the items one by one. Finally he placed them back into the briefcase and looked at Charlie. His furrowed brow betrayed deep thought, but the small upturn on his lips indicated his eager anticipation of the ensuing challenge. "There are a couple of things here that look interesting. I guess it won't hurt if we take a closer look at them. How about we slip over to the lab and have a quick peak at one or two things with the x-ray diffractometer. That might tell us something."

"What's an x-ray diffractometer?" Charlie asked, being unfamiliar with Karl's tools of the trade. "It's an instrument used to determine the atomic structure of material. Particularly useful for determining the form of crystalline structures. Although, it also has limited uses with polymers. If this shows anything untoward, we can look at it with the electron microscope, NMR, mass spectrometer or the x-ray spectrograph. That's about all I can access here at the moment.

Other research centres, both here in Australia and in the US, run more sophisticated instruments. But I guess we can look for options, if we need to, at a later date. Meanwhile, if we don't pick up anything unusual, then what you've got here is good old-fashioned earth technology." he smirked. Karl spoke with a hint of sarcasm, but Charlie shrugged it off. He had expected some cynicism under the circumstances.

"Well let's go then, shall we?" Karl led Charlie to the lab and the x-ray diffractometer. Karl walked around it and looked at it almost as a man looks at his lover. "I've spent hundreds of hours with this thing." he admitted fondly. "Delving into the little explored world of micro-crystalline structures. Nature's building blocks. Nanotechnology is fascinating stuff, Charles. But I digress. Let's have a look at that little tool you first showed me."

Charlie opened the briefcase and extracted the tool. "Here you go. What do we do with it now?" he asked. Karl smiled. "I'll just have to scrape a bit of this material off and get it ready to analyse. Shouldn't take too long."

Charlie watched as Karl prepared a specimen for the test instrument. Getting a thin film of material from the surface of the tool turned out to be more difficult than first anticipated. But eventually he persuaded the metallic mass to give up some of its own for science. He was relatively slow, but very methodical in his approach. Typical of a research academic. He wanted to make sure that everything was done clinically and professionally. He didn't want anomalous results, caused by human error.

Finally, after more than an hour of concerted effort, the specimen was ready. Karl placed it into the instrument, switched in on and stood back with a satisfied smile on his face. "This will take a few minutes. Basically the instrument will bombard the target with x-rays. These will scatter and that pattern will be recorded and analysed by the computer. Eventually we'll get a printout and I can analyse it for any structural anomalies." he explained.

Charlie smiled. He knew very little about crystallography, atomic structure and the like. Karl was the expert. That's why he was relying on him to corroborate his find. He needed irrefutable proof that what he had was of extraterrestrial origin.

He could only get that with independent verification that the artefacts from the base were genuine. Charlie waited patiently as the instrument went through its analytical paces. Finally the printer coughed into life and spat out a single page. Karl eagerly grabbed it. "This is what we need. It's a...." Karl stopped mid-sentence. "That's odd." he mused. Charlie watched intently, as Karl's now deeply furrowed brow began twitching nervously in unison with raising eyebrows.

As he continued to peruse the printout, he began to slowly shake his head. Finally Charlie's curiosity could be contained no longer. "What's odd?" he asked. Karl's frown deepened. "Hard to say just yet. But this doesn't look right. It appears to be an epitaxial microstructure, based on a polymeric macrostructure."

Charlie was instantly lost. "A what?" he enquired. "Sorry, Charles. It seems to be a polymer alright. You know. A natural or synthetic compound that consists of large molecules made of many chemically bonded smaller identical molecules. Like nylon. But it also seems to have a growth of a layer or two of a crystal on top of the polymer layer. Sort of like chocolate coated nylon. The open weaved nylon gives it lightness and the chocolate bonding between the polymers gives it strength."

"Is this common?" Charlie asked innocently. Karl shook his head vigorously. "Hardly. In fact I've never seen it done on this scale before. There's something else." Karl offered. "What' that?" Charlie automatically asked. Karl smiled. "Well if I didn't know better, I'd say what we were looking at was some sort of organo-metallic polymer. Based on Aluminium by the looks of it. But I'll have to confirm the exact make-up of the polymer in due course. Strange thing is that tin is the only metal that's been reported to do this. It forms a snake-like chain of atoms with tin as the backbone.

And it has organic polymers as the ribs, so to speak. They're collectively referred to as polystannanes. But the real weird thing is, that all known organo-metallic polymers are liquid crystals. Not solid like this." he mused. Charlie nodded. He was not following Karl's technical explanations, but he could see that the article had roused his interest.

"So, you think we've got something special here?" Charlie asked enthusiastically. "I don't want to jump to conclusions, but I think it's anomalous enough for me to lose some of my initial scepticism. I think what we have here definitely warrants further investigation." Karl announced proudly. "So, what's the plan?"

Charlie thought about it for a moment. "What would you like it to be?" he asked, almost tongue-in-cheek. I was thinking of thorough analysis, followed by understanding exactly what it was. Then I was thinking we should have a bash at duplicating it, then patenting it." Charlie joked. Karl laughed at the simplistic plan.

But it suited the euphoria of the moment, so he let it slide. "Well I think it best if I do this alone for a couple of days. Security and staff are used to me wandering about and playing with all manner of instruments into the wee hours of the night. You on the other hand, would stick out like a sore thumb. I'm assuming the less people who know about this the better." he queried.

Charlie nodded. "I guess you're right. Tell you what. I'll go now and leave you to it. But please be careful not to mention this to anyone." Karl reached for Charlie's hand and shook it firmly and vigorously. "Sure. Mum's the word. I'll get as many tests done as I can in the next couple of days. I'll call you as soon as I have an idea of what we've got here." he assured him.

CHAPTER 27

Tim was apprehensive as he stood in front of the Dean's office. He was desperately trying to summon the courage to open the door. Finally he decided that the time for hesitation had passed. He knocked curtly and entered. Without waiting for the Dean to ask the obvious question as he burst through the door.

Tim fired the first salvo. "I'd like to take sabbatical leave." he announced boldly. "Who the hell do you think you are, waltzing in here and demanding time off just two weeks before the start of the year? I don't think so, Fullerton." David almost yelled.

"I know it's a bit inconvenient... the timing." Tim offered apologetically. "But something's come up and I need to take a year off to do some research." Tim tried to explain. "Research!" the Dean screamed angrily at Tim. "You're a damned history professor, Fullerton. What's there to research! All the information you'll ever need is in books. All you need to do is read man.

No! You can't have sabbatical leave. Do you have any idea how difficult it would be to replace you at such short notice? Good God, man! The idea's preposterous! As much as the thought of you leaving, albeit temporarily, pleases me. No you cannot take any further leave. Now get out!" he yelled.

Tim spun on his heels and left feeling hollow and disappointed. He wandered off in the direction of his office. He slumped dejectedly into the reassuring comfort of his well-worn chair as soon as he reached it. There he sat in silence for several minutes, pondering his response to the Dean's vitriolic outburst. Given the personal animosity between the two, he had expected some resistance, especially given the timing. But he had not anticipated the venomous tirade that had ensued.

Looking around the familiar surroundings of his office he contemplated his future. He loved teaching, but for now he had more important things to do. Much more important things. The decision was not hard to make. Tim did not bother to knock. He opened the door and strode into the David's office. He marched straight up to him and indignantly threw a piece of paper onto the desk in front of him. "What's this?" David snapped.

"It's what you've wanted for years Lethridge. My resignation." Tim stated coldly. "You can't do this to me! You can't resign two weeks before the start of the year. I won't let you!" he insisted. But Tim's mind was made up. "Sorry old son, but you have no choice. I'm leaving!" Tim ignored David's animated protestations and left the office, shutting the door forcefully behind him, to reinforce the finality of the meeting.

As he stood in the corridor, looking back at the closed door, a smile of relief swept over his face. Although his adrenalin charged body was trembling and his heart was still pounding with excitement, somehow he felt a sense of release. It was like a heavy burden had been suddenly lifted from his shoulders. Wearing a broad smile, he returned to his office to clear out his personal possessions.

David was fuming. He sat at his desk trembling with anger. How dare that arrogant bastard resign. How dare he leave at this time of the year. Suddenly an intrusion snapped him away from his angry thoughts. "Mind if I come in?" a familiar voice enquired. "Of course not Philip. Please take a seat. So, what brings the head of Chemical Engineering to my humble office?"

"I was wondering what Fullerton was up to. I just saw him packing up his office. Has he resigned or something?" Philip asked. David almost snapped at him as he answered. "Yes, unfortunately. As much as I dislike the invidious man, it will be difficult to replace him at such short notice.

The bastard came in looking to take sabbatical leave and when I refused, he resigned. I don't know what he's up to. But I smell a rat." he grumbled, with an obvious hint of hatred in his voice. "It's funny you say that." Philip offered. "I saw his younger brother, do you remember Charles?" David shook his head. "No, I can't say I do." he confessed.

"He's an Electronics Engineer, rather bright lad from memory. Well anyway, I saw him skulking around the campus the other day. He had Karl Rasmussen, my Associate Chemistry Professor, in toe. I tried to find out what they're up to but... Well there seems to be some secrecy surrounding Karl's nocturnal comings and goings. He's spending a disproportionate time in the labs after hours. I know he's part of the industrial research section, but he's spending a lot more time there that normal. You know Bill Reynolds, the Janitor?"

"Oh yes..." David admitted. "That obsequious little grub of a man. Always seemed a bit of a weasel to me." Philip nodded. "Yes, that's him alright. But he's pretty handy when you need to find out what's going on around here. He says Karl's been working late into the night on many occasions. Using the X-Ray spectrograph equipment, among other things. "

David's ears pricked up. "Is that so? I wonder if this has anything to do with the *research* that Fullerton was so keen on." Philip almost sneered as he responded. "Would you like me to find out?" David nodded enthusiastically. "Indeed! What say we do a little snooping, eh?"

The two men were old friends, having known each other since their days together at boarding school. Both were politically motivated members of the old school tie brigade. As such, they were pariahs, universally loathed by students and staff alike. Because of their self-imposed ostracism, they were social friends as well as work colleagues.

They discussed a few theories and expanded on how they could snoop on the pair. Suddenly David terminated the conversation. "Sorry to cut it off there Philip, but I have to attend a board meeting in a few minutes. We have to organize a short-term replacement for Fullerton within the next ten days, so I really must go. How about meeting me at the Regent for lunch tomorrow? Then we can devote some time to ourselves." Philip turned to leave. "That sounds fine. Twelve-thirty, OK?"

CHAPTER 28

Charlie wandered down the dimly lit corridor, heading towards Karl's office. It was eleven thirty at night. Despite the lateness of the hour, he respected Karl's judgement. If he wanted to see him now, it must be important. So here he was.

"Thanks for coming in, Charles." Karl boomed as he saw Charlie approach. "What's the urgency, Karl?" Karl smiled reassuringly. "Nothing urgent, per se. I just couldn't risk talking with you over the phone. Too much eavesdropping. Besides, there are fewer people here this time of night." he explained. "That's OK. What have you found?"

"That fork you had in the briefcase. Is that from the same place?" Charlie nodded. "Yes, why?" Karl grinned. "Nothing really. Except it's a very large fork. And a very expensive one to boot." Charlie was not sure what he meant. "What do you mean... expensive?" Karl laughed out loud and slapped Charlie on the shoulder.

"It's a Platinum-Chromium-Vanadium alloy. About eighty four percent platinum. I wouldn't mind a full set. It would help my superannuation fund immensely." Charlie was impressed. "Really?" Karl just nodded, then continued. "Yes. Platinum's worth over a thousand dollars an ounce you know. And there must be at lease thirty ounces in the fork."

"Christ!" Charlie exclaimed in such a loud voice it startled Karl. "What?" Karl asked instinctively. Charlie looked at Karl and smiled. "Sorry. But I just had a funny thought. All the cooking utensils may be made of this alloy. There must be hundreds, if not thousands of kilograms..." Karl interrupted him with a beaming smile. "Well don't forget your friends when you go back." Charlie smiled and nodded.

"Of course not Karl. Here, keep the fork. Consider it payment for your services." he said with a wink. "Thankyou, Charles. Anyway, I thought you'd like to know that I no longer consider you to be delusional. I'm ninety nine point nine percent convinced that you were right. The polymers you found are of extraterrestrial origin." Charlie was greatly relieved, but curious as to what had changed his mind. "What changed your mind?" he finally asked.

"It's this polymer I've just finished testing." Karl explained. "A sample from that funny shaped block. Well, it's a metallic polymer alright. Similar to the first polymer we tested, yet very different. I confirmed that the first one was indeed based on Aluminium as the backbone. I also confirmed that the ribs were organic polymers. Just a simple Carbon, Sulphur, Hydrogen chain. But this one consists of a Titanium backbone with inorganic polymer ribs.

According to this data, each rib consists of ten Silicon, twenty Boron and twenty Hydrogen atoms. The Boron and Hydrogen atoms form a twin helical linear matrix, similar to a DNA strand. The Silicon atoms are the link between the twin Boron-Hydrogen strands. If you add up the atomic numbers of this chain you get ten times fourteen for the Silicon, plus twenty times five for the Boron, plus twenty times one for the Hydrogen. If you ignore the Titanium backbone, it gives a total atomic number of two hundred and sixty per rib."

Charlie shook his head. "You say it like that number's important." he mumbled. "I'm not sure." Karl confessed. "But let me explain about the polymer first. You see here. The polymer is identical in these sections but every hundredth rib has a sort of node at the end. This comprises a single very heavy metal atom bonded to the twin Boron chains at the end of the rib. It's surrounded by a cloud of ten Chlorine atoms and ten Fluorine atoms.

Now if you add up the total atomic number of this cloud, you get ten times seventeen for the Chlorine and ten times nine for the Fluorine. That adds up to..." Charlie interrupted him mid sentence. "Let me guess. Two hundred and sixty." Karl nodded. "Exactly. But there's one more thing. The heavy metals change in sequence along the polymer. They start at Fermium, the eighth trans-uranium element of the actinide series. Anyway, it has an atomic number of one hundred.

What you have to remember here is the fact that the last named metal in the periodic table is Hahnium, with an atomic number of one hundred and five. There are five further radioactive metals reputed to have been created, but as yet they have neither been confirmed nor named. That takes the last known metal in the series to an atomic number of one hundred and ten.

Well, here's the thing. The next rib contains a metal whose atomic number is one hundred and twenty. I have no idea what this metal is. And the next metal in the sequence has an atomic number of one hundred and forty. Again this is beyond imagination. And the final metal has an atomic number of one hundred and sixty. This is absolutely staggering.

What I don't understand, is how these metals have been stabilized. Fermium isotopes have half lives from one hundred days to thirty minutes. It's logically assumed that the larger the atomic number, the less stable the metal. And this means shorter half lives. But from what you say, these metals have been in this polymer for thousands of years. That's something I can't yet get my head around.

But to get back to the ribs. This sequence is not repeated, as you would expect. Rather, for the next four nodes, the sequence reverses. Going from atomic number one hundred and sixty down to one hundred. Now this alternating sequence is repeated along the entire length of the polymer.

What appears to be happening is these Boron-Fluorine rings at the end of the ribs generate prodigious covalent bonds with each other. See the metal here with the atomic number of one hundred in this polymer string? Well it's bonded to the adjacent string at the metal with an atomic number of one hundred and sixty.

Similarly, the one hundred and twenty is bonded to the one forty and the one forty is bonded to the one twenty. Finally the one sixty is bonded to the one hundred. This is repeated ad infinitum. Now, here's the kicker! All the time, the combined atomic number of the two bonded metals is two hundred and sixty."

"Shit, that number's a bit too coincidental to be dumb luck. " Charlie exclaimed, rather excitedly. "Exactly! And before you ask. Yes I've checked for radioactivity and there is none. Seems the polymer is made up of very stable isotopes of all the elements involved. I haven't defined the exact isotopes yet, but I sure as hell will before I'm done. I'm sure the isotope selection is the key to the whole thing. It's like they've thrown together a whole lot of unstable elements and somehow made them interact to make one very unique and stable mass." he explained.

"How long before you know exactly what's going on?" Charlie probed. "A good couple of weeks with my limited spare time." Karl offered apologetically. "So, what do you need from me?" Charlie offered. "Nothing really. I just thought you'd like the reassurance that I no longer consider you to be losing your mental faculties.

As I said, the evidence seems to be irrefutably pointing to extraterrestrial origins. Who else would waste a rare metal like platinum on common kitchen utensils. It's obviously very abundant where it originated, therefore it has little intrinsic value. It's simply used for its physical and chemical properties. Obviously for kitchen utensils, its key chemical property is inertness.

As for the polymers, they simply beggar the imagination. But I still need to do some tests to determine the chemical and physical properties of the polymers. That may help me understand some of the structure a little better. Even if it doesn't help, we'll need some physical property data for the patent."

"That's got to be a fair way off now doesn't it?" Charlie conceded. "Yes, unfortunately." Karl agreed. "We may be able to duplicate the simple non-metallic polymers, but I still have to work on the metallic ones. I'm finding it difficult to comprehend how they created these super heavy metal isotopes. I've only read about it being done at nuclear research facilities, where they bombard certain isotopes of heavy metals and basically see what anomalies turn up as a result."

Charlie was relieved that the authenticity of the base and its contents had finally been verified by an independent third party. He grabbed Karl's hand and shook it warmly, thanking him for his efforts so far.

He then reiterated the confidential nature of the findings and it's commercial implications. "Well thanks for the heads up, Karl. I guess I'll leave you with it then. But be careful. I don't trust anyone at the moment, present company excepted of course. If there's commercial gain to be made, you never know what perfidious little bastard's going to crawl out from under a rock and try to steal your lunch."

CHAPTER 29

Philip entered the dining room of the Regent Hotel at twelve-thirty on the dot. He stood at the door, squinting as he glanced around the dimly lit room. A waving hand in the far corner grabbed his attention, so he headed in that general direction. "Good to see you're punctual as always." David greeted. Philip smiled as he approached the table. "Old habits die hard, David. How are you?" David nodded. "Fine... and yourself?" Philip reciprocated. "Better now that I know what's going on with the Fullertons." David smiled wickedly. "And what might that be?" he asked excitedly.

"Well, old Bill did some homework for me last night. It seems young Charles was at it again with Karl in the research lab till the wee hours of the morning. Seems they're testing some new polymers. Bill managed to get some discarded read-outs from the X-Ray spectrometer. The fortuitous result of carelessness after long hours in the lab. I must say whatever they're testing is certainly interesting." he commented.

"You said that with some trepidation." David stated starkly. Philip nodded. "Well, the results I saw were confusing. Very confusing. It seems like they're testing at least three distinct polymers. Look here." Philip looked around to reassure himself they were not being watched. Satisfied that their conversation would remain private, he carefully extracted a manila folder from his briefcase and laid it open on the table.

He then took a page of computer-generated images and passed it across to David. "What's this?" he asked. "It's an X-Ray spectrograph of some material." Philip explained. "This superimposed graph here is a standard calibration showing the analysis of PVC. But this trace is of the material they're testing.

Note the peaks there and there. This is no ordinary plastic, David. In fact it shouldn't theoretically exist." he said with a hint of concern in his voice. David was perplexed. "Whatever do you mean?"

Philip shook his head. "I mean, it's completely foreign material. It's like nothing I've ever seen before. I did my doctoral thesis on hybrid polymers and I've headed the research department here for years and I've never seen a trace like this before. It's not theoretically possible. It seems to be a standard organic polymer on the surface. But when you analyse it.

Well without getting too technical, it's just not right." he conceded. "You mean Fullerton Junior has invented something cutting edge that might have commercial applications?" David asked incredulously. Philip shook his head. "He might be a gifted electronic whiz, but when it comes to polymers, I don't think he could invent a waterproof condom." he stated sarcastically.

"No... I don't think so. There's definitely something fishy going on here. Look at this." He pulled another page from the folder. There was a small sealed plastic sleeve stapled to the page. David looked at it and shook his head. "What's this?" he finally asked.

"The piece de resistance." Philip announced proudly. "It's a prepared specimen of another polymer. Only this one's metallic. They were silly enough to leave it in the scanning electron microscope. It's lucky for us, carelessness comes from working long hours. Here, I took this picture of it." he said as he offered David another piece of paper.

But David was still in the dark. "I'm afraid it means nothing to me Philip. What is it?" he begged. "It's mind boggling, that's what it is." Philip espoused. "Look at the crystal structure of the metal. Then compare that with the X-Ray spec here. Again, this is not theoretically possible. It looks like a complex organo-metallic polymer." David began shaking his head vigorously.

"A what?" he almost barked. "A hybrid polymer that uses a metal as a backbone for an organic polymer to build on." Philip tried to explain. "But, as far as I'm aware, they only form liquid crystals. And tin is the only metal that I'm aware of that can form these things." he continued. "So?" David asked, not understanding a word his friend had spoken.

"Well this one's a solid polymer. And it uses Aluminium as the backbone." Philip explained. But David was still confused. "And that's unusual?" Philip smiled broadly. "To say the very least, it's unique.

But the most interesting is this third polymer. This one's the most..." He stopped mid sentence trying to work out how to impress the layman with the enormity of the discovery. David sensed his confusion. "What's the problem?"

Philip looked a little confused, but pressed on regardless. "Well, I'm trying to think of a way to explain these anomalies in such a way that you'll understand what we're dealing with. But it's so technical, I..." he paused as he regathered his thoughts. "Just give it to me as best you can." David offered in a kindly tone.

"Sorry. It's just that this third polymer is so far ahead of current technology, that it beggars explanation. This one's also a metallic polymer, but it's inorganic. It contains no carbon atoms. That's strange enough, but that's not what interests me. See these peaks?" He pointed to the printout.

David smiled awkwardly and shrugged his shoulders. Philip may as well be showing him a Sanskrit text. "Sorry, but it means nothing to me. Tell me in layman's terms what you have there." he almost pleaded. "Well in a nutshell, there are peaks where there are no corresponding elements." Philip explained.

"What?" David almost roared in disbelief. "Yes, I know it sounds funny." Philip insisted. "But the traces indicate that this material has a backbone of titanium.

But, inexplicably, it has various metallic elements in the ribs in the atomic number range of one hundred to one sixty. That's impossible on so many technical levels." he explained, with a hint of exasperation in his voice. "Most of the known trans-uranium elements are man-made. And most of them have half lives measured in the seconds." he explained to a still dumbfounded David. "Sorry Philip, but I still don't see your point."

"David, let me explain something to you." he began in a low, fatherly tone. "The quest for creating elements beyond Uranium on the periodic table has taken nuclear physics to its limits. The resulting metals are very unstable and very short lived. They rapidly decompose into more stable elements, such as lead or strontium.

Even so, no laboratory has managed to create an element with an atomic number greater than one hundred and five. What we're talking about here is a quantum leap in technology. I can't even begin to imagine how to create a metal with an atomic number of one hundred and sixty."

David looked at Philip with a quizzical stare. He knew very little about what was being explained to him, but he did sense the incredulity in his friend's discourse. With subtle encouragement Philip continued. "So what I'm saying is that, either Fullerton has somehow invented something so advanced that our current technology cannot define it. Or more likely..." again he hesitated.

"What?" David insisted after a lengthy period of silence. Philip was decidedly nervous with his response. "Look, David, I know you're a devout Catholic and a bit on the sceptical side, but..." Philip noticed the instantly deepened furrow on David's brow, as he switched into a defensive mode. Hypocritical though he was, religion was his life. Everything else came a poor second. Philip hesitated for an awkward moment, as he grappled for the right words.

Finally, he conceded that there was no sugar coating for what he had postulated, so he simply blurted it out. "Well, I can't help thinking this stuff could be extraterrestrial in origin." David was instantly enraged. It was as though his best friend has just pierced his heart with a dagger. "Don't be absurd man. You can't possibly think that for a minute!" he bellowed.

Philip hurried to calm him down, as other people in the restaurant were now looking at the highly animated David. "Look David, I don't know what to think. There's so much here that defies explanation. But the simple fact is, these polymers can't be defined by what I know about plastics... or metal. And that, my friend, is a great deal."

David soon calmed down, as academic rationale finally overcame his emotions. He apologized to his friend for his unwarranted outburst. "Sorry Philip, the alien theory took me by surprise. But if this is some sort of foreign material, where did it originate? More importantly, where did he get it from?" he asked.

Philip shook his head. "I have no idea, David. It's pretty obvious they didn't manufacture it. That's way too absurd to contemplate. This stuff's far too high tech for any research lab I'm aware of. But Bill did manage to overhear something that might give us a clue." he offered. "And?" David continued to probe.

Philip smiled an evil grin. "And it seems your nemesis, Timothy Fullerton, is planning a little expedition." he teased. "To where?" David almost blurted out in eager anticipation. "To Egypt apparently. Seems the Pharaohs may have something to do with this." he speculated.

"The Pharaohs?" David asked incredulously. "Exactly what I thought!" Philip concurred. "What the hell does an ancient civilization have to do with advanced metallic polymers?" David pondered the thought for a moment. "What indeed! I tell you what.

You keep Reynolds snooping. I'll find out what Fullerton gets up to in Egypt. My brother, Samuel, is an archaeologist. He's been working for the Egyptian government for the last six years. The department of antiquities at the Cairo museum. Not much happens in the circles of Egyptology that he doesn't get to hear about."

Philip smiled. "Excellent! If we can find out what they're up to... Well let's just say these polymers could be of enormous commercial interest. If you know what I mean." David smiled greedily. "Indeed I do! The corporate funding we could get. The media exposure. The patents. But how do we get the credit for it?" he wondered. "Simple!" Philip exclaimed.

"We find out exactly what they're up to and duplicate their findings. We'll then have the polymers and can apply for the patents." he proposed. "But what about the Fullertons?" David asked suspiciously.

"We just accuse them of plagiarism." Philip suggested. "Who would doubt the word of two eminent Professors against two young upstarts? Neither of whom is similarly qualified in the field of research." he brazenly suggested. "Of course. But what about Karl?" David asked, worried that Karl might know too much.

Philip smiled. "Easy! We simply convince him the samples Charles was testing were stolen from my research laboratory. By then we'd have as much fabricated evidence as we need. We should even have some of the material. Besides, we can promise not to compromise him in any legal proceedings if he accepts our version of events." he gloated.

"You're a devious bastard, Philip." David conceded. "I'm just glad I'm on your team. I pity any poor coot who gets on your wrong side." Philip's smile turned into a sneer. "Like the Fullertons, eh?" David laughed cynically. "Especially the Fullertons."

CHAPTER 30

Tim and Cathy exited the customs area of Cairo International Airport and headed towards the taxi ranks. Suddenly a familiar voice boomed across the hall. Tim dropped the suitcases he was carrying and turned to greet his old friend. "Sabah æl-kher sadiqi... wæ kæfæ hælak?" he belted out in perfect Arabic. "Kwæyis æl-hæmdu lillæh... wæ intæ?"

Mohamed responded. "Kwæyis æl-hæmdu lillæh. Oqaddam lik Cathy?" Tim countered. "Tæshærrafna." Then Tim turned to Cathy. "Æsef... hiyæ læ tætækællæm æl-'arabi." Mohamed was apologetic. "Sorry Cathy, I didn't realize you don't speak Arabic. Allow me to introduce myself. I am Mohamed Nasar. Father, archaeologist, bureaucrat, part time tourist guide and good friend of Tim. He and I go back a long way. Don't we Tim?"

"We certainly do. Mohamed works part time for the Egyptian Department of Antiquities. We first met when I was an undergraduate and we've kept in touch ever since. We see each other every couple of years. Either in Egypt or at a conference somewhere in the world." he recalled. Mohamed smiled and nodded his agreement to Cathy, then turned to Tim. "Speaking of which, you were a little evasive on the phone the other day. So what brings you to Egypt at this time of the year my friend? Shouldn't you be preparing for your first semester?"

Tim smiled broadly. "I resigned." Mohamed was stunned. "You what? You live for teaching. What made you do a silly thing like that?" Tim's smile broadened. "I'll tell you when we get to the hotel. It's a bit of a long story. But I promise it'll be worth the wait." Mohamed reluctantly accepted the delayed explanation.

He picked up one of the suitcases. "Well let's get to the hotel then shall we?" As they sat relaxing in the hotel suite sipping ice tea, they engaged in general conversation for some time. Tim was keen to know the status of research in the antiquities department. He was particularly interested in the whereabouts of Samuel Lethridge. Mohamed patiently filled him in but finally his curiosity got the better of him. "Come on Tim... you're up to something. Now what is it?"

Tim enjoyed the moment, teasing Mohamed by deliberately stalling. He slowly reached over and placed his glass on the coffee table, then leaned back into his chair. He looked over at Cathy, who smiled and nodded approval for him to divulge their mission. "How would you like to be the one to discover Herodotus' legendary Hall of Records?"

"What?" Mohamed asked sceptically. "The Hall of Records that Herodotus wrote about." Tim repeated. Mohamed shook his head wildly. "I know that! I was just wondering how you proposed to find something that most people agree doesn't exist." Tim smiled broadly. "But it does my friend... it does." Mohamed was far from convinced. "How can you be so sure?" he asked with a hint of caution. "I have a map, from a reliable source. In fact..." Tim leaned back in his chair and pondered his next move.

He had debated long and hard with himself whether or not to divulge his source of information and had decided to tell Mohamed enough to gain agreement for the search. But not enough to determine exactly where the information was found. Now that the time had come to confide in his friend, he hesitated. Mohamed looked quizzically at Tim, then at Cathy. Finally he asked a direct question. "Well? Are you going to tell me more or not?" he insisted. "Sorry Mohamed, it's just that I can't tell you exactly where I obtained the information. I hope you'll understand. It's not that I don't trust you.

It's... well the information you'll find in the hall of records..." Mohamed interrupted him. "What are you trying to say Tim?" Tim smiled. "Well... I have to keep the other locations secret because..."

Again Mohamed interrupted. "What do you mean *other locations?*" he asked cocking his head slightly as he did so. Tim smiled wryly as he divulged the information. "Well we know of at least six sites where this information is recorded. They are scattered all over the world. We think the Russians and Americans have access to one site and the Chinese have access to another. Although I don't think they know exactly what's in them yet. They haven't gotten into the..." Tim hesitated.

"The what?" Mohamed probed. "The chambers where the records are kept." he offered. "So where are they?" Mohamed asked, hoping for a straight answer at last. But he was to be disappointed. "I can't tell you. Not just yet anyway. There's a lot more at stake than a simple king list. The information in the records is two fold. Firstly it's a king list as per Manetho's reports. And by the way, that's going to be controversial enough. But the real problem is going to be the other information."

"What information?" Mohamed asked, unsure of what ramifications some ancient history might cause. Tim lowered his voice. "Well it's the history of Egypt really and it's going to upset your fellow Muslims, I'm afraid." Mohamed was intrigued. What on earth could be written in ancient times that would upset Islam? "You mean there is information about Allah there?"

"Maybe." Tim offered tentatively. "But I don't want you to pre-empt anything. I'm just warning you that once we open up the hall of records, there may be political ramifications. I need to know whether you still want to go ahead with it, because I can foresee some controversy. Look, I've got some photos on disc. Maybe I should start my laptop up and show you a few.

Then you can decide if the risk is worth it." Tim motioned Mohamed to join him at the dining table as he grabbed his laptop computer and a handful of CD-ROMs. He booted the laptop, then carefully studied the encoded labels of the discs, until he found the one he was looking for. He dropped the disc into the D drive and clicked on the file icon. He browsed down the list and clicked on the appropriate file.

The screen immediately filled with a full colour photograph of the immaculately carved and gold-leafed king list from the base. Mohamed leaned forward for a closer look and groaned audibly in disbelief at what he saw. "This is amazing. You've been here?"

"Yes we have, haven't we dear?" Cathy nodded affirmation from the couch, but declined to join the men. She assumed they would rather be left alone. So she took the opportunity to excuse herself and retire to the bedroom for a nap. "I'll leave you two with it. I'm a bit tired after the flight, so I'd like to have a rest if you don't mind." Tim nodded. "Of course. I'll wake you up for dinner if you like." Cathy gave him a peck on the cheek as she left the room. "Thanks."

Tim quickly returned his attention to Mohamed who was glued to the computer screen. He flicked through a sequence of photographs, allowing his guest time to read the cartouches before moving on. After ten or so photographs he stopped. "Well... what do you think?" he asked. Mohamed shook his head very slowly. "This is fascinating. The thirteenth dynasty. Manetho was right, there were sixty kings. We only have evidence of thirty-two, but here you can see the entire list. This here... is this some form of dating?" He was pointing at hieroglyphs on the screen. "Yes, that's the number of days each king ruled. And this is where they ruled from. And this is some timing from a reference point. You know... like our BC and AD thing. I'm not 100% sure about it yet.

But I don't think it's that important at the moment." he supposed. They spent the next hour looking through the photographs, comparing known kings with unknown ones. Mohamed read eagerly through list after list. Rambling with excitement as the gaps in his extensive knowledge were filled. Tim was careful to stop on Zeno, before he reached the Sumerian king list. This could remain undisclosed for the moment. For now any information divulged would have to be on a *need to know* basis. And at this point in time, Mohamed simply did not need to know anything more.

Tim then produced a file of computer print-outs which showed a complete king list from Osiris to Zeno. It was in accurate chronological order in years BC. Tim had back-dated the reigns from the time of Cleopatra's death. Mohamed was almost speechless, but managed to ask the obvious question. "Do you think this information is duplicated in our hall of records?"

"I'm pretty sure. Look, here..." Tim ejected the disc from the computer and rummaged through the other discs until he found the one he was looking for. He inserted it into the computer and clicked onto the relevant file icon. From there he clicked on a jpeg file, which loaded a photograph of the map from the Guardian's book. "See this map? It's from an ancient book. It details the exact location of the hall of records in Egypt."

"That looks like Greek to me Tim. Is it?" Tim smiled. "Yes, can't you read it?" he enquired politely. Mohamed shook his head. "Unfortunately my Greek is only as good as my Japanese." he confessed. "I didn't know you spoke Japanese." Tim stated in amazement. Mohamed laughed."I don't! I am not gifted with languages, like you, my friend. I have enough trouble with English." Tim laughed and Mohamed joined him. "OK. I'll interpret it for you. See this area here?

Does it look familiar?" Mohamed peered at the screen. "It looks like the royal cemetery at Abydos." Tim nodded. "Exactly! That's why no-one's found it. They've been looking in the wrong place. According to this book, the hall of records was sealed after the death of Narmer. So it won't have any information about later kings like the photos. Although it should have a complete list up to his time. I'm not even sure if it will have any historical information like the other site. The book doesn't say exactly what's there. I guess we'll find out when we get there. See where it is?" he concluded.

"Yes! It's under the corner of Narmer's burial chamber." Mohamed replied confidently. Tim nodded and smiled. "Exactly! We know precisely where to look. Do you think we'll be allowed to dig?" Mohamed thought about it for a moment, then a broad smile crossed his face. "We'll need Zahi's approval. Do you have a copy of the map?"

Tim nodded. "Yes, several. I thought it best if we had a hard copy, so no-one needs to know the full story. I want you to be the only one who knows about the other halls of records. I'm hoping to photograph the Egyptian one, so you and I can compare the lists. If there's anything else there... I guess we'll just have to take things one step at a time. Can we see Zahi tomorrow?"

"We'll see him first thing tomorrow morning if you like. I know he's got an international conference in a couple of weeks, but I don't think he has any other commitments. Except for some early arrivals and perhaps a documentary team or two. But I'm sure he'd love to catch up with you. I'll pick you up at seven if you like." Tim smiled. "Great! I'll take Cathy along too. She's dying to have a look at the museum." Mohamed rose from his chair and headed for the door. "Good. I'll see you at seven."

CHAPTER 31

Tim, Cathy and Mohamed entered the small, cluttered office at seven thirty-seven, to be greeted by the pleasantly surprised Zahi. "Sabah æl-kher!" he almost shouted in excitement. "G'Day Zahi. How are you?" Tim beamed as he offered his hand. "I am well, my friend. And you?" he responded as the two shook hands warmly. "Very well thank you. Oh, Zahi... this is my friend Cathy."

Zahi nodded in Cathy's direction. "Pleased to meet you, Cathy. Now what brings you to Egypt on such short notice Tim? I thought you were not coming to the conference. Did you change your mind?" he asked expectantly. Tim shook his head. "No, I have something important to ask of you. I told Mohamed I was coming, but I didn't tell him why. It was much too important to discuss over the phone." Zahi was intrigued.

"What could be so important for you to be here instead of in your beloved classroom?" he asked. "The Hall of Records!" Tim announced unexpectedly. Zahi sat down behind his desk and motioned for the others to be seated. The perplexed look on his face betrayed his serious reservations.

Once they had settled into their chairs, Zahi leaned towards Tim and looked at him with a suspicious glare. "You are serious, Tim?" he asked in astonishment. Tim nodded and gave him a wink. "I certainly am, Zahi. Look at this." He reached into his coat pocket and extracted a crumpled piece of paper. On it was a photograph of the map from the Guardian's chronicle.

He carefully unfolded it and placed it on the desk in front of Zahi. "I found this in an ancient book. Can you read it?" Zahi nodded confidently. "Yes, it's classical Greek. It's a map of the royal tombs at Abydos.

This one here is Narmer's. Are you suggesting that the legendary Hall of Records is buried under here?" he asked. Tim nodded. "Well, that's what the book says. Would you like to find out?" he teased. But Zahi was still sceptical. "How old is this book of yours?" he enquired tentatively. "I am led to believe it was written in the fifth century AD." Tim assured him.

Zahi tilted his head. "Are you sure? The Greek appears to be much older than that." Zahi questioned. Tim was impressed. "I must congratulate you on your scholarly knowledge Zahi. You're right of course. The Greek is classical. At least a thousand years older than the book. But, I have it on good authority the book was indeed written in the latter half of the fifth century, by an adherent of classical literature. You see, it also contains historical information on the Byzantine Empire." he added.

"And this book, does it include the lost work of Herodotus?" Zahi asked, with a hint of hope in his voice. "I'm not sure." Tim admitted. "It's from a long-lost library that I have yet to fully catalogue. I'm sorry but I'm unable to divulge its location at this time. But the library contains hundreds of volumes. I only had the chance to glance through a few books while I was there, but I hope to return soon to read more." he offered almost apologetically.

"So, you can guarantee the authenticity of this ancient tome?" Zahi asked. Tim nodded. "To the best of my ability. Otherwise I would not have come all this way to ask you for permission for a dig. I know what the authorities are like when it comes to speculative incursions. And I respect your valuable time. So I did not come here to waste it. I also appreciate our friendship and I wouldn't do anything to jeopardise it, nor compromise your position here. I guess what I'm saying, Zahi, is that I have a good feeling about this and I'd like to give it a go.

Under your supervision of course." he added with a smile. Zahi nodded. "Well, with the conference in a couple of weeks, a new discovery of this magnitude would put the icing on the cake. It would be a wonderful venue to release the information. We would get much press. It would be good for the tourism industry... Allah willing.

Sorry to rush you, Tim. But I have a meeting in ten minutes with some rich museum benefactors. You know how it is. We need all the money we can get to keep our research going. I'll have to think about your proposal for a while. But I trust your judgement. May I keep this map? It may help clear it with the Minister." he suggested. Tim nodded. "Yes, sure. I have other copies." he said as he handed over the map. Zahi thanked him. "I'll get back to you later today. Where are you staying?" he asked. "We're staying at the Hilton. Room three-o-four." Tim informed him.

At that point the phone rang. Zahi apologized for the intrusion and picked up the receiver. "Æhlæn... næ'æm... næ'æm... shokran... mæ'æs sælæmæ." He put down the phone and rose from his chair. He stretched out his hand and shook Tim's heartily. "Sorry, I have to go. I'll catch up with you later. Perhaps we could have dinner tonight at your hotel. About eight? I should be able to tell you if we can go ahead with the dig or not by then." he hinted. Tim nodded. "We look forward to it. See you in the lobby at eight."

Mohamed too had other business to attend, so he agreed to meet them for dinner. He excused himself and left Tim and Cathy to spend some time in the museum. They spent the rest of the morning wandering through the museum. Although the exhibits fascinated Cathy, she somehow felt strangely disappointed. Had she not spent time in the base, it would have been much more impressive. But they enjoyed their quality time together regardless.

Once hunger took hold, Tim suggested they go to a suq for lunch. Cathy enjoyed the experience of an afternoon at an Egyptian market place. Her shopping was helped immeasurably by Tim's knowledge of the language and local customs. Particularly the bartering, at which he was somewhat of an expert. She was suitably impressed.

At three minutes to eight, Zahi and his wife joined Tim, Cathy, Mohamed and his wife in the lobby. After the introductions, they headed for the restaurant. Zahi could sense Tim's tension but decided to string him along for a while. A formality of sorts, given his dry sense of humour. While they perused the menus, Tim stared with a mocking evil eye at Zahi, who amused himself by simply ignoring him.

Finally the suspense grew too much for Tim. "Well, Zahi. What's the story?" he almost pleaded. Zahi burst into laughter. "I thought you would never ask, Tim. I spoke to the Minister... Ismael... and we discussed your proposal at great length. The conclusion was as I suggested this morning. If we can find something at Abydos, the timing would be perfect for a major PR scoop at the conference.

He has therefore given us permission to do a limited dig, based on the information in your map. If we find nothing in that exact location however, he insists that we look no further. He wants minimum disturbance of the burial site. It's a tourist attraction that brings in much needed revenue to this country and we can't afford to quarantine it for longer than absolutely necessary. You understand?" he asked.

"Of course." Tim confirmed. "And that's exactly how I feel. If the map is inaccurate, then it's no use trying to dig up half the desert looking for something that may not be there." he conceded. "Exactly." Zahi agreed. "Now when do you wish to start?" Tim thought about it for a moment.

"If the conference is in two weeks, we'd better get digging as soon as possible. How long would it take you to organise the crew?" he asked. Zahi did the sums in his head. "We could do that tomorrow and say... leave for Abydos on Friday. By the time we set up the equipment, we could start the dig perhaps Sunday. What do you think, Tim?" Tim nodded. "Sounds good to me. We'll get our things ready tomorrow and hire a four-wheel drive. We'll meet you at the site first thing Sunday morning."

CHAPTER 32

David Lethridge tapped his fingers nervously as he waited for someone to pick up the phone. What was taking him so long? He should be home from work by now. It was late enough in the evening. Eventually a subdued and obviously inebriated voice answered. "Hello." David was unsure of the voice. "Samuel is that you?" he asked tentatively. "Yeah. Who wants to know?"came the mumble response. "It's David."

"Oh! Hi big brother. How are you?" David was keen to get to the reason for his call and answered him impatiently. "Fine, fine. Look can you talk?" There was a mumbled response that David took for a yes. "Sure. What do you want to talk about?" David was not sure his brother was cognisant enough for an intelligent conversation, but he pressed on regardless.

"Do you remember Timothy Fullerton?" he asked eagerly. "Yeah, why?" His voice was becoming clearer as the conversation continued. "Well I believe he's on his way to Cairo and I know he's up to something. Any chance you can find out what?" There was a short silence on the other end of the phone before he responded. "Sure. Leave it with me. I'll call when I know something."

David hung up the phone, a self-gratifying leer on his face. All he had to do now was wait. But God how he hated waiting. Samuel was every bit the right person for the job. He used all his wile and cunning to ferret out the smallest pieces of information.

He made sure he was at the museum the day that Tim and Cathy met Zahi. After the meeting he covertly followed them back to their hotel. A bribe to the concierge at the right time would gain him access to their room. For now he was content to shadow them.

The phone rang with an implied urgency. David was sitting in his library, reading the Financial Review and supping contentedly on a rare twenty five year old Kellermeister tawny port. Resenting the untimeliness of the intrusion, he reluctantly put down his newspaper and glass and answered the phone. "Hello. David?"

But his interest was immediately aroused. "Yes. Is that you Samuel? The line's a bit noisy." he explained. "Yes it's me. Look I have some news for you, but I still don't know exactly what's going on yet. All I know is that Fullerton and company are going down to Abydos tomorrow." David frowned deeply. "Any idea why?" he asked. "I overheard a conversation between Zahi and Ismael. Zahi was asking permission for a dig down there. I believe it's within the tomb complex.

I heard the name Narmer mentioned. I'm not sure exactly what they're looking for, but I have a man on the dig team who's promised to keep me informed. For a small fee of course." David was thankful for the snippet, but needed to know more. "Samuel, I really need to know what he's up to." he almost pleaded. "Don't worry. I believe he's leaving most of his gear in Cairo. He's payed for the room for four weeks. There's a conference on in a couple of weeks, so I presume he's staying for that." Samuel surmised.

"Good. At least I know where to find him for the next few weeks. Listen, do you think you could..." Samuel interrupted. "Already covered. I've arranged to get access to their room the minute they leave Cairo. If they've been careless they may have left something useful behind." David was pleased. "Like what?" he pondered. "From what I hear they're basing the dig on an ancient map he says he got from a book in a newly discovered old library. But although Zahi has a copy, I can't find anyone else who's seen it. It must be pretty authentic though. Zahi's no fool. He gets requests to dig all the time.

If he gives permission at all, it usually takes several months for the approvals to surface, not hours like this one." he explained. "I knew the bastard was up to something. Any idea where the map came from?" But Samuel was no help. "No, Ismael asked the same question of Zahi. Seems Fullerton was very tight lipped about his source." David pondered the situation for a few moments.

"I know Fullerton hasn't been out of Australia for a couple of years. So he can't have found the map himself. I can't imagine it coming from Australia. That makes no sense whatsoever. So, I guess he must have met someone during the semester break. Someone who's been overseas recently and found the map. Of course!

He went to northern Queensland with his brother Charles. To Cairns I believe. It was supposed to be a fishing trip. But Cairns is an international airport. Someone could have easily flown in to meet him on the quiet. Someone wishing to keep below the radar. Look Samuel, I'll dig around here to see if I can come up with a name. Meanwhile you know what to do."

The light from the hotel lobby shone brightly as it spilt through the glass facade into the street, displacing the early morning darkness. Samuel was watching the lobby entrance from the seclusion of his car, parked eighty yards down the street.

He shivered as the cold night air swept in from the desert and invaded his tired little car. In his hurry to make the rendezvous, he had forgotten his coat. The threadbare jumper he threw over his cotton shirt was hardly up to the job. He knew Tim was heading for Abydos early this morning, but did not know when. Determined not to miss his departure, he had arrived at 4 a.m. As soon as Tim left the hotel he planned to search his room. He was keen to complete his business before he was scheduled to appear at work.

He had been there for nearly three long, uneventful hours. Suddenly he slumped back into the seat, assuming an unnecessarily low profile. The concierge approached the lobby door as a rather dilapidated four wheel drive hire car pulled up in front of the hotel. As the door opened, Tim and Cathy stepped out of the lobby, each carrying a small suitcase. Tim was also carrying a well-travelled brown leather briefcase.

Tim opened the back door and tossed their baggage onto the back seat. Samuel watched furtively as they climbed into the four-wheel drive. He closely monitored the vehicle as it slowly pulled away from the lobby entrance and turned into the street. His heart began to race as the car slowly accelerated into the distance.

He continued watching with perverse satisfaction until it finally disappeared down the road. By now the adrenaline was surging through his body as he anticipated his next covert move. It was time to go.

CHAPTER 33

Tim, Cathy and Mohamed bounced toward the gaggle of workers in their dusty, slightly older than you would normally hire, heavily laden, Toyota Landcruiser. Tim had agreed to give Mohamed a lift to the dig site, along with a substantial portion of the expedition's more fragile equipment. The vehicle came to a premature and very jerky stop. Its front wheel dropped into a large pothole near one of the museum trucks, parked adjacent to the north wall of Narmer's burial chamber.

Zahi saw them approaching and rushed over to meet them. "Sabah æl-kher!" he greeted. "Sabah æl-kher, Zahi. How are you? Looks like your boys had an early start." Tim observed. Zahi nodded. "I am well, my friend. And yes, we have been here since daybreak. I wanted to get the screening tent and barricades in place before the arrival of the first tourist coaches. They usually get here around nine." he explained.

Tim quickly surveyed the scene. "Looks like they've nearly got it set up. Does that mean we can get an early start too?" he asked. Zahi nodded. "Of course. Would you like to come over and inspect the area while they finish erecting the tent?" Tim nodded excitedly. "Sure."

They wandered over to where a gang of fifteen or twenty men were working feverishly, erecting a giant light green and cream striped tent. It looked big enough to hold a circus performance, but was barely large enough to enclose the burial chamber. Tim looked at the tent and smiled at Mohamed. "Lucky it's not under Khasekhemui's burial chamber, that's got to be at least ten times the size of Narmer's." he chuckled. Mohamed laughed as they crawled under the side of the tent. Once under the half erect canvas, they looked around.

Satisfied that it was safe to proceed, they strode over to the northeast corner. Zahi stood at the corner of the burial chamber and took Tim's map out of his pocket. He carefully unfolded it and studied it for a while, finally twisting it to orientate it to the boundary walls. Satisfied with his terms of reference, he called over to Tim. "According to this map, we are standing on top of the access well. It is supposed to be some ten feet or so square. Perhaps we can dig here and avoid damaging the chamber wall." he suggested.

Tim nodded. "Well I guess there's only one way to find out. I wonder how far under the floor the well wall is. Originally it was supposed to be twenty-five feet, but with the movement of sand over time it's anyone's guess." he speculated.

Zahi agreed, then suggested a plan of attack. "We will get the crew to commence digging as soon as the tent is secured. The floor is lined with limestone pavers, so we will have to take those out first. We must catalogue them as we go, so we can put them back in the exact location we found them when we finish. If we find nothing." he explained apologetically.

They left the tent as they had entered, then stood back and watched as the working party finished erecting the gently flapping shroud. They were a seasoned crew and knew their job well. In no time the tent was complete, the barriers were in place and the crew ready to begin work.

Two men were posted as guards to ensure no snooping tourists interfered with their work. The rest gathered in a semi-circle, awaiting further instructions. The foreman approached Zahi and asked what he wanted them to do next. After a few brief words he returned to the crew and drew them into a huddle, from which he issued his instructions.

While four men began removing the floor stones, the foreman held a clipboard and began calling numbers.

One of the crew scribbled a number on the underside of each slab as it was lifted. The slabs were removed and stacked in a neat pile at the far end of the tent.

After about forty minutes of steady work, the bare sandy floor was ready for inspection. Zahi and Tim walked around looking for any signs of a wall, but there was nothing. Tim turned to Zahi. "Well I guess it's buried under here somewhere. Can we get them to take off a few feet of sand in this area here?" Zahi nodded.

They stood back and watched as several men grabbed picks and shovels and began to loosen the compacted sand. Working quickly, they soon had an excavation some ten feet square and three feet deep. As yet they saw nothing but sand. Zahi urged them on. Three feet... four feet.... five feet. Still nothing!

Tim was beginning to feel a little anxious. He felt sure that the well would have reinforced walls just under the surface, but they were not there. He consulted Zahi and they decided to press on.

When the hole was just over seven feet deep, one of the workers swore as his shovel struck something solid and jarred his hand. The others stopped digging and moved to the other side of the excavation. Silently they stood and watched as one man carefully began scraping the sand away from a single square piece of stone.

It soon became apparent that it was a brick, hewn from solid limestone. He removed the brick and scraped around the area, but found nothing more. Feeling disappointed, he thrust his shovel deep in the sand in frustration, only to receive a second jarring. This time, as he scraped the sand away, he revealed the unmistakable top of an ancient brick wall.

"Looks like you were right, Tim. This looks like the well. Ahmed! Get them to follow the wall along and see if it changes direction." Half an hour later the men had exposed a wall which ran for seven feet then turned ninety degrees for five feet.

Tim looked at the sandy excavation, then at the crumbling chamber wall. "Sorry, Zahi, but it looks like we're going to have to pull that wall down after all. At least to the edge of the well. Otherwise sand will just keep rilling into the well and undermining the wall until it collapses." he explained.

Zahi nodded. "I was thinking the same thing myself. Unfortunately this will take some time. Again we must catalogue each stone that we remove, so we can rebuild it when we are finished here." Zahi summoned the foreman and they spent some time discussing the task. Ahmed called his men together and quickly relayed the information. The discussion was accompanied by mass nodding and obvious consensus agreement with the plan. Zahi returned to Tim, Cathy and Mohamed.

"We might as well go for a walk. It will take them many hours to remove that wall and dig out the entire outline of the well. Once this is done we can better assess the task before us. Allah willing, we should know the exact size of the well by lunchtime." he speculated.

Tim and Cathy spent the next three hours mingling with the tourist throngs on their daily invasion of the burial site. The Abydos site covered an area some four hundred yards by three hundred yards and contained the chambers of at least thirteen kings and queens.

Some chambers, like that of Khasekhemui were huge, while others, like that of Narmer and Djet were relatively small. Being her first visit to Egypt, Cathy was fascinated by the antiquity of it all. Although she had always loved history and archaeology, she finally realised why Tim had such a deep passion for it.

Meanwhile, Mohamed and Zahi sat at the edge of the tent and watched the crew painstakingly dismantle the wall, brick by brick. Mohamed eventually caught up with Tim and Cathy in the burial chamber of Queen Merneith and suggested they join Zahi in the tent. Greeting them on their arrival was a gaping hole.

It was rilling from about six feet beyond the now exposed upper portion of the well. The well itself proved to be a rectangular structure, about ten feet by twelve feet. They had already exposed the top five feet of the wall. From now on, the going would be much slower. The men needed to install ladders and extract the remaining sand using a windlass. They decided to break for lunch.

By late afternoon they had excavated twenty feet into the well. Zahi was pleased with their efforts and rewarded them with an early end to their shift. As Tim left the tent he was shocked to see a squad of armed soldiers heading in his direction. Zahi, following behind him, saw them too, but was quick to reassure Tim that all was well.

"It's OK, Tim. We do this all the time these days. Whenever we do a dig we get the military to guard it. They could not make it here until this afternoon. But I did not expect to find anything so soon. So I began without them." he explained. "Well that makes me feel a bit more secure. Fancy a feed?" Tim offered. Zahi nodded. "Sure let's go."

Next morning they returned to the site at sunrise. The excavation crew were there, with several of the men already down the well. Zahi met Tim, Cathy and Mohamed with his usual enthusiasm. "We will see how far we get today, Tim. What do you think?" Tim looked around. "Well, according to the map, the chamber is around twenty-five feet deep. I guess that means we're nearly there." he suggested.

Again there was nothing much they could do, except watch the painstakingly slow procedure of filling the windlass bucket with sand, manually winching the bucket to the surface, removing the bucket, taking it to the back of the tent and emptying it, replacing the bucket, lowering the bucket and starting the cycle over.

Because of the relatively small size of the well, they were restricted to three men operating with two windlasses. One filled each bucket while the third acted as a relief shoveler and pseudo-rigger. Hooking the bucket to the windlass claw, calling the surface crew when to raise the bucket and warning the shovelers when a bucket was being lowered. The men were split into two crews, which rotated every twenty minutes.

Tim watched on wearily as they painstakingly inched their way towards the bottom of the well. The continual clacking of the windlass ratchet and the endless babble among the workers was nearly driving him insane.

It was so boring that eventually Tim and Cathy lay down and rested their eyes. In the balmy, tranquil atmosphere created inside the tent by the warming rays of the early Autumn sun, radiating through a clear desert morning sky, Tim soon nodded off. Cathy too was soon dozing contentedly in his arms, her head resting on his chest. Mohamed and Zahi sat down next to them and let them rest.

Tim was awoken by the cacophonous sound of excited yelling and grating shovel blades, scraping across a rocky surface. The noise was emanating from the well. He sat bolt upright, struggling at first to understand what the excitement was about. "What's up?" he asked Mohamed.

"It appears the men in the well have reached the bottom. They're cleaning out the last of the sand at the moment." he explained. "Hopefully we can go down and have a look in a few minutes. Perhaps we should have a bite to eat now. If we find anything down there, I don't know when we'll get the chance to eat again."

Everyone agreed that it was a good time to eat, so they left the tent and headed for the vehicle, where Cathy had a large esky packed with food, ice and cool drinks. They sat next to the vehicle and ate their lunch.

Lunch was accompanied by the gratifying chatter and scraping, as the men cleaned out the bottom of the well. Nobody spoke as they hurriedly disposed of their meal. Everyone was keen to return to the well. Cathy noticed that Zahi was not his normal loquacious self. He simply ate his food quickly, all the while anxiously glancing in the direction of the tent.

The other men too, were abnormally quiet. Although she could not feel it, for whatever reason, she understood their apparent anxiety. She offered to clean up, saying she would join them shortly. The offer was gratefully accepted and the men stood as one and rushed over to the well.

Zahi leaned over and asked the excavation crew how they were going. They suggested it would be cleared out in a few minutes. He walked over to the foreman and congratulated him on the speed of their work, then informed Tim of their progress.

They gathered at the edge of the excavation and watched excitedly as the last bucket of sand was removed and the windlasses broken down and taken out of the tent. "After you, Tim." Zahi offered, as he motioned towards the long, and somewhat precarious, aluminium ladder that led to the bottom of the pit.

Tim cautiously worked his way over to the ladder, trying to disturb as little sand as possible. As he swung onto the most easily accessible rung, he instinctively looked down. He watched as a small trickle of sand slid down the rill from his footprint and cascaded over the exposed well wall into the void below.

One of the men at the bottom of the well grabbed the ladder to steady it, as Tim cautiously descended towards the limestone-tiled floor. Once he reached the bottom, he stepped off the ladder, thanked the assistant for his help and called to the surface for Zahi and Mohamed to join him. Once all three were at the bottom of the well, Tim looked at Zahi.

"Well? What does the map say now?" Zahi took the map from his pocket and read it again. "It says there is a false floor, under it, a stairway to a corridor." he read. Tim looked at the floor. It was made up of large slabs of limestone, about five feet square, that stretched across its entire width. The joints were so precise that he could not fit the blade of his pocket knife between them. "What do you think?" he asked Mohamed. "Looks like they have to be lifted up, but I don't see how we can get anything between them to lift them."

Mohamed sent the workers up the ladder and called for Ahmed and a broom. They searched the floor inch by inch, as they swept the remaining sand to one side. Suddenly Zahi gave an excited yelp and pointed to a small stone embedded in the floor. "Look, Tim. A small keystone. There's another one at the other end of this slab. I think we should remove these and see if they reveal a means to lift the rock." he eagerly suggested.

They looked down at the freshly revealed joint where an eight inch square stone had been inserted into the main slab. Ahmed called for some tools to be thrown down. He then went about trying to remove the nearest keystone. It took some time to work out, but eventually he managed to lever it up a short way, but that was as far as it was willing to go.

Eventually, probably more in frustration than science, he twisted it clockwise. With a gasp of surprise he fell backwards, as the small stone suddenly loosed from the slab. Smiling with great satisfaction, Ahmed stood up, dusted himself off then returned to inspect the resultant hole.

There at the bottom of the hole was a solid bronze pin, about an inch and a half in diameter projecting up some four inches. Threaded through the end of the pin was a half-inch thick bronze ring about five inches in diameter. It was obviously a lifting lug. Ahmed quickly removed the second keystone.

This exposed another large bronze ring attached to a pin. He called for the A-frame and pulleys from one of his trucks. They attached the end of a rope to each of the rings and watched nervously, as the men above them swung a large A-frame over the well and began threading the other end of the ropes through two large pulleys. When this was done, Tim and Ahmed looked around the circumference of the slab. After some discussion, they concluded the best thing to do was raise it a few feet, then swing it over to one side and drop it on the adjacent slab. Once there, they could safely inspect underneath. If the slab had to be moved further, it could be easily done. Otherwise it could remain there, safely out of the way.

They all watched anxiously as the men on the surface began to take the strain on the ropes. As they took the full weight of the slab, the planks supporting the feet of the A-frame began to dig into the sand, sending small rivulets cascading over the well wall, showering those below. They retreated from the falling sand to the far wall and watched as the ropes began vibrating, as they bore the full strain. The slab remained stubbornly in situ, as the tension on the ropes steadily increased. Soon they were so taut, they could be used to play a tune.

Suddenly the slab issued a moribund groan and one end popped out of the ground with a jerk. So unexpected was the movement, that the rope pullers reeled back, losing their grip. As the rope slackened, the slab crashed back into position with a resounding thud, sending a small cloud of fine dust billowing into the air.

Castigated for their lack of concentration, but encouraged by their initial success, the men again pulled on the rope. Now that the slab had been loosened, both ends rose steadily as the chants of the men resonated down the well. When the slab was about four feet from the floor, they moved over to it and began pushing it aside.

As it swung over the adjacent slab, Ahmed yelled to the workers above and the slab dropped sharply onto the floor with a solid thump, that almost deafened those in the well. Ahmed began cursing the incompetence of the crew who were meant to lower it gently, but stopped suddenly when he realised the others were staring into the opening below the slab.

He sidled up to them and looked at the small flight of stairs, carved from the parent rock, that disappeared into a dark void. Zahi was impressed. "Congratulations, Tim. Your map was indeed correct. Now we must get some lights and see what it is we have uncovered. Some fresh air in there may also be prudent." he suggested.

Ahmed called out to the workers for torches, and ventilation equipment, then sat back and waited. Tim called out to Cathy who was by now standing at the top of the well peering down at him. "Would you like to join us?" he invited. She nodded, but was not all that keen. "Is it safe?" she enquired. "Who knows?" he answered in a flippant, almost jocular manner, before adding a caution.

"Watch that sand when you get on the ladder, it tends to slide away from under your feet pretty fast. I'll hold onto the ladder for you as you climb down." Cathy nervously edged her way to the ladder and tentatively placed first one foot, then the other, on the starting rung. Rung by rung, slowly and painstakingly, she made her way down the flexing ladder to Tim.

Her relief at reaching the bottom was obvious, as she hugged Tim profusely. The depth of her ordeal betrayed by her rapid pulse and profuse sweating. She admitted to Tim that she was not good at heights. Tim gave her a reassuring kiss, gently wiped her brow with his handkerchief then led her to the void. "See... the book was right. Here's the stairway leading to the underground chamber. Say, Zahi... that map showed several false rooms.

That means we'll probably have to break through a few walls. Could I get the boys to throw down a couple of sledgehammers?" he asked. Zahi nodded. "Sure, but we can't enter the chamber until we finish ventilating it. Then we must look at what is in the first room. Perhaps they left some treasure or something in there to convince thieves there was no other chamber beyond."

Tim nodded. "OK. Look out! Here comes a bag of torches." he warned. Tim untied the bag from the dangling rope, grabbed a large torch and handed it to Zahi. "Let's see what's down there, shall we?" Tim turned on his torch and shone it down the stairway.

He could see nothing. Disappointed, he sat down in the rear of the well and watched as the crew set up the ventilation gear. It was an agonizing forty minutes later when Tim got the approving nod from Zahi. He turned on his torch and carefully descended the stairs. At the bottom, he found himself in a large room, some twenty-five feet square.

As he flashed the torch around, he noticed several large vases and what looked like dissembled furniture. Piled in one corner was a collection of personal items, some of which shone with the unmistakable lustre of gold, as the effulgent torch beam danced off them. Against the far wall was a modest black granite sarcophagus. Its lid was still intact. He instinctively walked over to it. As he glanced around, he noticed the walls were resplendent in brightly painted hieroglyphs.

He paused to read a cartouche. It was Narmer's mother. Zahi's entrance startled him back to the present time. "Well, look at this. I thought the cunning old devil would have a bit of a collection here to try to deter grave robbers from looking any further." he skited. "My goodness! A sarcophagus! I wonder whose it is." he mused. Tim pointed at the cartouche almost hidden amongst the delicately carved hieroglyphs on the lid. Zahi read it out loud.

"It's someone by the name of... *Thuaa* ...a royal mother, it seems. This is a great find indeed, Tim. We will need to catalogue everything in here and remove it to a secure warehouse before we move on I'm afraid." he explained apologetically. But this stuff alone will be interesting enough for the conference.

Do you want to photograph the walls, Tim. So we can interpret them at our leisure? Also could you photograph the chamber as it was found? Before we disturb anything. That way we can recreate it in a museum exhibit sometime in the future." he explained. Tim nodded. "Sure, we've got a couple of weeks yet. What will you do with the sarcophagus?"

"We'll have to remove it for safe keeping. Unfortunately, once these things are discovered, thieves are relentless in their determination to rob them of their jewels. As you know, the trade in black market antiquities is still a very robust one. Despite international legislation to the contrary and our best efforts to prevent it. We have most sadly lost much of our heritage that way.

That is why we have a small group of trusted workers. They are well paid and loyal. Discoveries like this are rare and valuable, so we do not announce them until all relics have been exhumed and are in a place of safe keeping." he explained. "We will relocate these artefacts to the surface, then bring a truck inside the tent to keep the discovery away from prying eyes." he explained.

Tim began photographing the chamber, as Cathy watched on. Zahi, Ahmed and Mohamed set about organising the important task of cataloguing and removing the contents of the tomb. It would be several days before they could continue their quest.

CHAPTER 34

A small package was slipped to the concierge and a key found its way into Samuel's hand. Without saying a word, he quickly glanced at the room number on the disproportionately large white plastic tag - 304.

As he entered the room, he quickly glanced around. Although he was confident it was empty, he needed to make sure. Satisfied he was alone, he quietly closed the door and strolled into the living area. After a thorough but fruitless search, he muttered an obscenity to himself and stormed off to the bedroom.

Again it was devoid of anything that looked out of place. The unmade bed was the sole indication that someone was using the room. Suddenly he had a thought. The closet. Of course! He slid back the mirrored door of the closet and peered inside. To his relief there were two large suitcases stashed high on a shelf. Several sets of clothes, some male, others obviously female, hung neatly on the rack. He went straight for suitcases. His best bet, he thought.

He grabbed one and flung it unceremoniously onto the bed. Once opened, he carefully felt his way through its contents. It was to no avail. The suitcase only contained female clothes. He replaced the suitcase and grabbed the other one. It too was rudely flopped onto the bed. Again its contents were roughly handled, but carefully scrutinized. Although the contents were obviously Tim's, again it was to no avail. After finding nothing, Samuel was feeling dejected.

It was then he noticed the jacket. It was hanging in the closest, almost hidden between two long summer dresses. He recognised it as the one Tim had been wearing when he met with Zahi a few days before. he took it down and hurriedly searched the pockets.

Samuel smiled as he felt something in the left inside pocket. It was a small piece of paper. Pulling it out, he carefully unfolded the crumpled A4 sheet. What he saw made his spine tingle with excitement.

It was a computer printout of a photograph. A photograph of a very old book. And on the open page of that very old book, was a very old map. Samuel sat down and studied it for some time. "I'll be damned!" he muttered in disbelief. He grabbed the mobile phone from his pocket and dialled a number stored on the SIM card. He nervously tapped his fingers on the coffee table as he waited for the call to be answered.

"Hello, David. I've got it!" he boasted. "Got what?" David asked. "The map Fullerton used to get permission for the dig." Samuel announced rather proudly. "What does it show?" David asked impatiently. Samuel paused for a moment as he looked at the map. "It's Narmer's tomb alright. The map shows a hidden chamber under Narmer's tomb. And you'll never guess what's in the chamber." he teased.

"What?" David asked, rather pointedly. He was not in the mood for games. "According to this it's the Hall of Records!" Samuel crowed. David was astounded. "You're kidding me! Do you mean that ignominious bastard's going to get all the glory of finding the Hall of Records." he fumed.

"Looks like he got lucky." Samuel said matter-of-factly, but David was furious. "Damn it!" he cursed. "But wait, there's got to be more to it than that." he protested. Samuel was curious. "What do you mean?" David hesitated for a moment, as he pondered his response. For now, he decided, he would keep the quest for the origins of the curious polymers a secret. "Can't say over the phone. Suffice it to say, I need to know exactly what they find there. It's very important. I'll explain later."

CHAPTER 35

Ahmed stood with the sledgehammer raised, aiming carefully at the mark Tim had drawn on the wall. He let fly with an almighty blow, that saw the hammer viciously recoil from the rock surface at a frightening speed. Tim and Zahi anxiously inspected the section of wall that had worn the full brunt of the impact. It showed no sign of damage. Tim looked thoughtfully around the now empty chamber.

His gut feeling told him the opening had to be on this wall. He finally turned to Zahi. "This is the wall alright. But the false panel is obviously not in the centre. In fact the whole wall seemed solid when we sounded it out. You seem to have a knack for understanding the thinking of the pharaohs. Where would you put the false wall?" he asked.

"If it were me, I'd put it where it was least likely to be found." Zahi professed. Tim looked around. "Like where?" he asked. Zahi smiled. "Like up there!" he said as he pointed to a place high on the wall, where a separate text of hieroglyphs talked about entering the great heavens. Suddenly it made sense to Tim. "Of course! An entrance high up would be tricky to detect. Let's get a ladder down here and I'll sound out the wall up there." Ahmed organised for a twenty foot ladder to be lowered into the well.

When it finally arrived, Tim grabbed it and rushed it down the stairway to the burial chamber. He wasted no time in placing the ladder against the wall and grabbing the small geologist's pick he always carried with him on such expeditions. He scrambled up the ladder as far as he dared, while Mohamed steadied it for him. He tapped against the wall, methodically progressing from left to right. Listening for any change in the pitch of the ringing hammer, indicating a thinner section of wall.

All the while, his tapping softly resonated in the chamber beyond. The others watched in fascination as he expertly tapped his way across the wall. Suddenly he stopped and looked at Zahi. "Did you hear that?" he asked. Zahi shook his head. "No, have you found it?"

"I think so." Tim stated tentatively. "Listen to this." Everyone strained to pick up the near imperceptible note change of the ringing hammer, as Tim traversed a section of the wall. As he continued, the change in pitch was increasing. Finally he stopped and tapped several times. Then he tapped a section of wall some four feet away. This time the difference was plain to hear.

There was definitely something different about that section of wall. Tim continued tapping for some time as he delineated the different zones, marking the extremities with a pencil. Finally he looked down at Zahi. "Well the opening isn't real big. It only goes from here to here. And from up here to over there."

Everyone watched, as he pencilled in a few final marks that defined the extent of the opening. Once completed, he climbed down the ladder and addressed everyone. "Well, what do you think? I've taken photographs of the wall and I printed some hard copies the other night. I knew we'd have to destroy some of the wall to get to the chambers behind. What do you think Zahi? Can we continue even if it means destroying some of the artwork in here?" he asked.

Zahi nodded. "I think we have no choice. The map has been right so far. I think the discovery of the hall of records is so important, that it justifies the destruction of this small section of text. Besides, as you said, we have photographs of it. If the worst comes to the worst, we can repair any damage and repaint the text. We have a few experts in this field, who touch up tomb paintings from time to time. It will be difficult for anyone to tell the difference." Tim handed the sledgehammer to Ahmed and motioned toward the ladder.

Ahmed smiled nervously as he climbed, trailing the heavy hammer behind him. When he reached a comfortable height, he studied the small pencil marks carefully. He then swung the hammer. He took as big a swing as he dared, given his precarious position. The hammer struck the wall with a resounding thud, but once again, it bounced off the wall without inflicting any visible damage. The only consolation was the difference in the sound of the blow, which egged Ahmed on with new enthusiasm.

As he withdrew the hammer, small particles of paint-covered plaster fell away from the wall. But there was no other damage evident. So too, the second blow had no real effect on the wall. Not to be discouraged, he swung the hammer again and again. Each time a little more plaster fell. But again, closer inspection revealed no real damage. After ten blows, the frustration began to show, as he enthusiastically cursed the lice-infested slave who hid the entrance.

Showing the first visible signs of anger, Ahmed swung the hammer at the wall with the ferocity of a charging bull. It struck the wall with the sound of an explosive charge. The force with which it struck was so great, that the impact tore the ricocheting hammer from his grip. It went flying backwards, crashing to the floor below, as the startled onlookers dived for cover.

Ahmed meekly apologised and clambered down the ladder to retrieve the errant hammer. While he was apologising to Zahi for his indiscretion, Tim climbed up the ladder to inspect the wall. "I'll be buggered! You've done it Ahmed." he stated. "No wonder it didn't sound too different. It looks as if they actually installed a massive stone plug in the wall, rather than plastering up the hole like most chambers. Look! This end has been pushed back half an inch." he gleefully noted. Ahmed smiled with satisfaction at his work. Then frowned and muttered to himself "læ æhibb hæzæ!"

Tim smiled. He did not like the looks of it either. He considered the options for a while, then discussed a method of dislodging the blocking stone. It offered minimum fuss and limited risk of damaging anything on the other side. His suggestion was relatively simple.

Get a car jack and a substantial length of timber, place the jack on the opposite wall and simply use it to slowly push the block back through the wall with the timber pole. They discussed the finer points of the proposal, until all present agreed that this was the easiest and least risky solution. Ahmed returned to the surface to organise the materials.

It took more than an hour to assemble the right equipment and set up the jacking system, but finally they were ready to move the block. Everyone watched in silence as Mohamed began to slowly work the handle of the hydraulic jack. At first nothing happened as the timber pole took up the strain. But eventually, the block yielded to the jack and began its slow, but inexorable, migration. Inch by inch they watched as Mohamed relentlessly pumped the jack handle.

Suddenly the block toppled backwards and disappeared into the adjacent chamber, with a thunderous echoing thud. The plan had worked perfectly... up to now. In their eagerness to dislodge the block, no-one had anticipated the ensuing chaos.

As soon as the weight of the stone block had been released, the beam and the jack were no longer supported and they came crashing down to the floor with a deafening thud. A choking cloud of fine white dust rose rapidly from the crash site and began to fill the room. At the same time, the muffled sound of the limestone rock could be heard, as it thumped heavily onto the floor of the adjacent chamber. It raised a small cloud of malodorous dust that quickly flowed through the newly opened portal, offending the noses of all.

The jack bounced dangerously close to Cathy's foot, while the beam slid out of the opening, skidded into the opposite wall and ricocheted straight back at Zahi. Whether it was anticipation, instinct or just plain luck, he somehow managed to avoid the timber missile.

Tim quickly checked that Cathy was OK. He then proceeded to shake his head vigorously, in a vain attempt to quell his ringing ears. It was Zahi who regained his wits the fastest and raced up the ladder with torch blazing. He was muttering something about no time to stand around waiting for the dust to settle. As he peered through the three foot by four foot hole, he enthusiastically slashed his torch from side to side.

At first he saw little through the light diffusing haze of fine dust that remained suspended in the chamber. But as he flashed his torch beam around, he gradually began to make out the walls. Soon he was beaming, as the atmosphere cleared, allowing him to view the room with some clarity. He was impressed as he glanced at the walls and described them in detail to Tim, standing below him, steadying the ladder.

"My goodness, Tim. You should see what's in here. It's a beautifully painted chamber. There's a large portrait of Osiris that must be twelve feet high. And there's a funerary scene with Tehuti and Heru. This is wonderful. This is the best preserved work from the first dynasty we have ever found. This is truly exciting. It too is a large room like this one. But unfortunately it's empty, save one small stone box. How disappointing. But the smell is awful. I think we had better get the ventilation gear here to pump some fresh air into the chamber before we enter it." he suggested.

Zahi climbed down and arranged for the chamber to be ventilated. After this was done, he asked for another ladder. When it arrived, Ahmed carefully balanced it on his shoulder as he climbed the first ladder. When he reached the aperture, the fun began.

They all watched in amusement as Ahmed somehow managed to extricate himself from the ladder he was carrying and slide it through the small opening. Looking very sheepish, he asked Mohamed to climb the ladder and help him through the opening. It was a tight squeeze, not without considerable risk to both parties.

They were precariously balanced some fifteen feet above the unforgiving limestone floor below. But eventually he managed to make it through the small breach and climb down the second ladder. Once someone was holding each ladder it was a simpler, and decidedly safer, task to gain access to the other room.

Tim and Zahi joined Ahmed while Cathy and Mohamed remained in the first chamber. Zahi headed over to the small granite box and inspected it closely. He was mystified by the lack of inscriptions. He was just about to slide the lid off when Tim joined him. "I wonder what's in the box." he mused.

Zahi shook his head."I have no idea, there is no writing on it. But whatever it is, it must have been the source of the stench." he offered. Tim leaned over as Zahi slid the granite lid aside to reveal several mummified cats. The poor state of the bandages betrayed the haste with which they were prepared. They had obviously been done by an inexperienced person, or done on the cheap.

The partial mummification process had long since given way to putrefaction. Zahi arranged for its extraction as Tim searched for the false wall shown on the map. Cathy listened intently at the tap, tap, tap of Tim's geo-pick. She was trying to discern the different tone, as he made his way around the wall. Finally, low in the left corner of the right-hand wall, he found what he was looking for. There was a tiny, but still recognisable, change in the tone of the ringing hammer. Tim smiled as he beckoned Zahi to the spot. "I think I've found it. This one's a little bigger.

It's about five feet wide by four feet high." he explained. Ahmed did not need to be told. He climbed the ladder and asked Mohamed to pass the hammer. The location of this secreted entrance was much more conducive to swinging a sledgehammer and Ahmed made the most of it. This time it only took three blows before the sealing stone began to slide backwards.

Encouraged by his early success, Ahmed dropped the hammer and raced up the ladder. He almost pleaded with Mohamed to pass the jack and timber as quickly as possible. Once again it took longer to set the jacking system up, than it did to push the stone through the wall. Only this time, there was no catastrophic failure of the system.

As the stone finally left the confines of the wall, the log simply dropped a foot to the floor. The jack did likewise, resulting in little noise or dust. Much to the delight of those in the confined space, who were already labouring to breathe in the dry, dusty and noticeably stale atmosphere.

This time, it was Tim who leapt to the fore. He cleared away the jacking timber, then lay on the floor to peer through the newly opened portal. As his torch probed the darkness of the next chamber, he was surprised to see bare walls. The only thing he saw was a large rock in the middle of the room. He turned to Zahi to break the bad news. "Sorry mate, there's nothing in this room except a bloody big rock. No wall paintings, no artefacts. Nothing!" he stated disappointedly.

Zahi arranged for the ventilation gear to be set up. Once again Tim was forced to patiently wait, while the stale air in the chamber was replaced with fresh air. After an agonizingly long half hour, the ventilation gear was finally switched off and they were given to go-ahead to enter the room. Tim quickly crawled through the opening, followed closely by Ahmed, Zahi and Cathy.

As they swept their torches around the room, Tim's initial assessment was confirmed. The chamber was completely void of any carvings, paintings or hieroglyphs. It was completely empty, except for a large slab of stone some four feet high by five feet wide by ten feet long, standing mutely in the centre of the room. Zahi followed Tim over to the rock. They stood in pregnant silence, staring at the rock, pondering its purpose. Tim smiled.

"I'll be damned, Zahi. It looks an unfinished sarcophagus. How clever! This would have fooled anyone who managed to get this far without knowing what we know. Now, according to the map, the entrance to the hall of records is right underneath it.

What a brilliant piece of thinking. The outer chamber may have been looted, but the next chamber would have been of little interest. If grave robbers had made it this far, they would have assumed the sarcophagus was never completed and therefore this room was never used for a burial chamber. Ipso facto... no treasure. No-one would ever think of looking *under* such a large slab of rock. Even if they did, I doubt whether simple grave robbers would have the means to move it."

Zahi nodded slowly, as he agreed with Tim's assessment of the situation. Whoever designed the entrance had been rather clever.

Once the euphoria of the discovery of the final room had dissipated, Tim turned to Ahmed and asked how he intended to move the great rock aside, to expose the much-anticipated stairway to the hall of records. They discussed various options for a while, before Zahi reminded them of the time. It was late in the afternoon. Whatever was needed, could be discussed over dinner and seconded in the morning.

CHAPTER 36

Tim was at the dig site at sunrise, keen to get the false stone sarcophagus moved aside as quickly as possible. He was casually chatting with Cathy and Mohamed, when Zahi arrived with several workers. Their black smoke belching, world war two vintage, truck shuddered as it came to an unexpectedly hasty stop. Its front left-hand wheel had found Tim's pothole.

Tim watched excitedly as the truck disgorged its human cargo. Once dismounted, they quickly set about relieving the truck of its burden. A large hydraulic press, many steel beams, a bag of bolts and nuts. "I see you managed to get everything Zahi." he commented.

Zahi smiled. "Yes, although the one hundred ton hydraulic press was a late acquisition from my cousin's engineering works early this morning. The use of which will unfortunately result in me being obliged to entertain my cousin and his family at the next state antiquities banquet. And the man has the table manners of a goat!" he groaned. Tim laughed as he slapped Zahi on the shoulder. "It'll be worth it, if all goes well today my friend." Zahi nodded. "Yes, Allah willing, I trust it will be so."

It took the crew nearly an hour to transport all the necessary heavy duty jacking equipment into the final chamber and set it up ready to move the blocking stone. This time timber was considered too dangerous, in case the enormous compressive load imparted on the wood by the jack caused it to fail. In which case, there was the real risk of everyone in the vicinity being sprayed with splinters from the exploding timber. A most unpleasant prospect.

The steel beams to be used to jack the rock had been hastily cut and welded during the night.

Each had a flange plate, with three boltholes, welded to each end. They were made to be almost identical in length to the stroke of the hydraulic press. So that, as the rock moved, the jack could be retracted and another steel beam inserted into the system. It was anticipated that this method, although somewhat slow, would nonetheless be the safest and most efficient method of moving the gargantuan rock.

Tim could only observe, as Ahmed expertly orchestrated the proceedings. He watched attentively as they bolted the two larger steel beams together. These were to be the initial push rods. As they began pumping the hydraulic press for the first time, he instinctively held his breath and squinted his eyes. God knows why, it offered no physical protection, but it's just what you tend to do in these circumstances.

The hydraulic press moved freely at first, as it took up the small gap between the push rod and the rock. But as the system took up the strain. Tim noticed the man operating the manual jacking lever slowing down, showing the first visible signs of exertion. Soon he was demonstratively labouring against the hydraulic pressure of the press. It had reached its physical limit and it declined to cooperate any further. It was a stalemate. The rock refused to move and the press refused to extend any further. "What do we do now Tim?" Ahmed exclaimed in exasperation.

Tim shook his head. "I guess we'll just have to...." Tim was interrupted by a large cracking sound, that startled everyone, as it echoed loudly around the chamber. "What was that?" Zahi gasped. They all looked at the rock. "I guess it was the rock finally giving in to the press." Tim suggested. "It looks like it's moved about a quarter of an inch. Try the lever again Ahmed."

Frantic instructions were given and the press began to cooperate once more. This time, they could see the massive rock slowly sliding across the floor.

Within minutes the press had reached the end of its first stroke. Tim approached the rock and inspected the newly exposed floor. It had indeed moved. But how far did it need to go to expose the passageway? If there was a passageway.

Meanwhile the crew frantically retracted the jack and installed the first small beam. "It looks like we have to move it a fair way, Zahi." Tim conceded. "It's gone nearly a foot now and there's still nothing but floor. I hope there's a passageway under here, or all this will have been in vain." he added ruefully.

"I too hope there is something here. I have called in many favours to get permission for this dig. To find nothing would be disappointing. However, our finds to date are exceptional by any standards and will bring renewed interest to the conference. They alone have justified our faith in your map.

Besides, it has been accurate so far. We should have no reason to doubt it now." he offered. Tim smiled at the reassurance and stood back, placing his arm around Cathy's waist. "Here goes nothing..." he mused, more to himself than anyone in particular.

They watched intently as the, now heavily sweating, labourer once again coerced the press into action. Inch by inch the massive block of stone crept away from the jack. Tim and Zahi both involuntarily held their collective breath, as they searched for the first signs of the fabled passageway. It was Tim who spotted it first.

"There! There it is. A small crack just opened up." Tim shouted excitedly, as he pointed to the small crack in front of the rock. Zahi rushed to Tim's side and looked at the small crack in the floor that was now opening wider with every thrust of the jacking lever.

Soon it was nearly a foot wide, but again the work was delayed as the press was retracted and another beam installed. The discovery of the crack in the floor had driven the crew to fever pitch enthusiasm.

They wildly bolted the next section into the pushrod and began furiously cycling the hydraulic pump lever. Again the gigantic rock groaned as it slowly and reluctantly migrated across the floor at a near glacial pace. By the time the next beam was being inserted, the crack had opened up to over two feet. Large enough for Tim to cautiously poke his head in.

But not yet large enough for him to feel comfortable about entering the void. He grabbed a torch and lay on the floor next to the opening. He turned on the torch and extended his arm through the hole. He was in an awkward position as he nuzzled his head into the opening. But he was desperate to see what lay beyond. "It's a stairway alright. But I can't see much really. I guess we'll have to move it a bit more so we can get in here more easily." he announced dejectedly.

Two more extend and retract cycles saw the stairway open up sufficiently for them to gain comfortable access to the stairwell. Unable to contain his enthusiasm, Zahi instructed the crew to get the ventilation gear set up. Forty-five minutes later, satisfied that enough fresh air had been circulated into the passageway, Tim motioned to Zahi for the ventilation equipment to be removed. "Ready?" he asked with a smile. With an affirmative nod from Zahi, Tim placed a foot on the top step and looked down at the steep descending staircase. He grabbed a torch and, with a reassuring smile from Cathy, slipped into the black oblivion beneath the floor.

For several minutes those above remained silent, waiting for the reassuring sound of Tim's voice. Finally they heard an excited yelp. "Hey Zahi! You'd better come look at this!" Zahi needed no further encouragement. He quickly grabbed his torch and climbed down the staircase, bending backwards as he manoeuvred under the sarcophagus. As he disappeared Cathy looked at Mohamed. He smiled and shrugged his shoulders. "Why not?"

Cathy returned his smile and scampered down the stairway, torch beam slashing hither and yon, vainly searching for Tim. Mohamed followed quickly on her heals. The other men were ordered to remain in the room.

When they reached the bottom of the stairs, they found themselves at the entrance of a large corridor, into which Tim and Zahi had obviously disappeared. Cathy noticed that both sides of the passage were covered in hieroglyphs, masterfully carved in the living rock and painted by the skilled hands of ancient artisans. They were not of the same quality as the perfectly engraved, gold embossed script at the base. But they were, nonetheless, spectacular.

She joined Tim as he and Zahi were progressing along the right-hand wall. "The legendary king list. Just like the book described." Tim explained, with a heavy sigh betraying his relief. Zahi was transfixed to the wall, excitedly reading through the list of names. He only managed a muffled grunt in reply.

Tim decided to leave him and explore the rest of the passageway. As he turned to move off, he noticed Cathy and Mohamed standing behind him. "Look Cathy, the king list appears to be the same as the..." he pulled himself up before disclosing too much information, then finished his sentence "...book!" Cathy gently grabbed Tim's arm and steered him toward the end of the corridor, leaving Mohamed with Zahi.

"I wonder if there's another room at the end." she whispered. "Want to find out?" Tim nodded and strode off, hand-in-hand, his torch piercing the darkness as he illuminated the floor, searching for trip hazards. He was surprised when the end wall suddenly appeared. The corridor was not as long as he expected. It was less than fifty yards long. And, disappointingly, there was nothing at the other end. Just a blank wall. Tim instinctively grabbed his geo-pick from his belt.

He began methodically tapping the wall. He moved from side to side, starting at the bottom and working his way as high as he could reach. Every hammer blow sounded exactly the same, a dull reverberating thud. Tim turned his head toward Cathy with an obviously disenchanted look in his eyes. She smiled and shrugged her shoulders, leant towards Tim and whispered. "It's OK. They had no use for a library here. Remember the book said they collected all the Malachim records and took them back to the base for safe keeping."

Tim nodded. "Of course! Well that makes me feel a bit better." Tim then lowered his voice. "I know the king list is on the right hand side of the corridor. I made sure I pointed Zahi to it first, to keep him occupied. Now we need to find the history." Tim spun around and shone his torch on the opposite wall. Nothing! He was stunned. "Shit!" he exclaimed. "What?" Cathy asked, a little concerned about Tim's tone.

Tim whispered into Cathy's ear. "There's nothing here!" he said in near panic. Cathy smiled and flashed her torch towards the entrance. "I think it's back this way. I saw some hieroglyphs on this side of the passage about halfway along." she reassured him.

Tim smiled. "Of course. At the base, the history took up a lot less room than the king list. Let's slip back and have a look." As they walked back toward the centre of the passage, they heard muffled voices as Zahi and Mohamed excitedly continued through the king list.

Tim kept his torch beam in the middle of the opposite wall, looking for anything that may have been carved there. Without warning he suddenly stopped, causing Cathy to run into him. "What is it?" she asked.

Tim looked over at Zahi, then whispered so only Cathy could hear. "Look here. It's the end of the historical information. You were right. The writing's smaller here too, so it takes up very little room. It only takes up twenty feet or so, in the middle of the wall.

So Zahi won't reach it for a while. It'll give me a chance to read it first." he explained. Cathy stood back and watched with fascination as Tim began to read the information painstakingly carved into the rock millennia before. She admired the way he could stand back and read the hieroglyphs with great speed, almost without hesitation.

She watched his progress with awe as his torch beam rapidly ran down each column of writing, before flicking to the top of next. Tim was only skipping through the text, looking for key passages to confirm that the information was the same as the base. Finally he came to the end where he whispered proudly. "Well that's it! It's pretty much the same as the base."

Zahi was progressing steadily through the king list and was approaching the beginning of the historical data. Tim, not wishing him to see it just yet, pointed his torch beam toward the floor and waited for him to acknowledge his presence. "Well, what do you think, Zahi?" Zahi drew a deep breath and exhaled loudly. The noise echoed softly along the corridor. He then shook his head slowly from side to side.

Eventually a small smile appeared on his weather-beaten face. As Tim watched, the smiled broadened until, finally, Zahi was standing there wearing a beaming grin. He approached Tim with arms outstretched and gave him a manly hug. "My friend you have brought me to the greatest ever archaeological discovery in Egypt. This discovery will be the focal point of the conference and you will be the greatest name in archaeology this century." he promised.

Tim smiled and hung his head in embarrassment. "I don't need any credit Zahi. It is you who have tirelessly fought to define your country's vast history and preserve it for prosperity. It is you who allowed us to dig here. Perhaps it should be you who takes the credit." Zahi was touched by Tim's magnanimity.

"Perhaps we can both take a little of the lime-light." he suggested. "I trust you will be staying for the conference now?" he added with a broad smile. Tim nodded. "I guess so. I'll take some photos then get back to Cairo." Zahi nodded as Tim reached into his pocket and extracted his digital camera. "And now you have a conference paper to write, as my special guest speaker." Zahi added playfully.

"Thanks Zahi, I'd like that. I'll put something together about this king list." It only took Tim a few minutes to photograph both walls in their entirety. Finally he wandered over to Zahi, still concentrating on the king list. "I have to go Zahi. I'll meet up with you in Cairo." Zahi turned from the colourful cartouche-bound hieroglyphs, grabbed Tim's hand and shook it vigorously. "See you in a couple of days, my friend. Allah willing."

CHAPTER 37

Zahi watched as Tim and Cathy left the hall of records. Once they had disappeared, he raised his torch and returned to the hieroglyphs. He continued reading in silence. It was the most exciting thing he had been involved with in all the years he had dedicated to the discovery and preservation of Egyptian history.

Slowly he worked his way along the wall. Smiling to himself as he recognized familiar names. Stopping to ponder unknown rulers from long lost dynasties. As his reading took him back in time, he drifted off into a state of serenity. This was how Egyptology was meant to be. A tranquil voyage of discovery. Unhurried. Uncomplicated. Almost mesmerizing.

Eventually he reached a gap in the list. The wall was empty. Quickly he moved to his left, his probing torch beam searching the rough hewn walls for any continuation. He seemed disappointed, even though the list had gone back further than he had thought possible.

Suddenly in the distance, he saw some writing. With his heart now pounding with anticipation, he rushed to join the torch beam as it danced invitingly on the newly found hieroglyphs. But once he began reading the new list, he hesitated and cried out aloud. "Oh no! It can't be." His verbalised self-doubt alerted Mohamed. "What's wrong my friend?"

Zahi's voice was trembling. "This king list. is wrong. Look at what it says. Look at the names. This cannot be true. It contravenes all that the prophet has told us." Mohamed quickly perused the new list and came to the same conclusion. "This means Abraham's ancestors were kings of Sumer?" he asked tentatively. "Yes and by logical deduction, so too Abram himself. No, this cannot be so. Abram was a simple man of God."

Zahi swung around in disbelief and brushed past Mohamed, as he stormed off toward the exit stairway. Mohamed stood anchored to the spot, watching Zahi's torch beam slashing at the darkness as he strode off indignantly. Suddenly he stopped. His torch beam had found something on the opposite wall. The spot of light carved across the darkened wall, searching for the beginning of the newly discovered text. Here the searching torch beam and Zahi's probing eyes met.

Mohamed wandered over to see what he had discovered. Silently the two of them began reading the ancient text. As they progressed along the panel, Zahi began shaking his head. The shaking became more vigorous and was soon accompanied by deep guttural groaning. Mohamed stood silently by his side. He too was reading information that was tearing his very soul apart. "Can this be true Zahi?" he whispered.

"I pray to Allah no. But this writing has been here for a very long time. At least three and a half thousand years before the prophet Muhammad wrote the Koran. I am confused. Frightened and confused."

Both men could not break themselves away from the wall until they had reached the end of the heretical writing. By this time, Zahi was a shattered man. Mohamed was mortified. "Mohamed you must promise not to tell anyone about this. Not your family, nor friends, nor any colleagues. No-one. Do you understand?" Mohamed nodded sadly. "Yes, but we must let the authorities know, surely."

After a short pause, Zahi nodded sternly. "I will inform the Minister of Antiquities. He will probably want to look at this himself. Come Mohamed. We must put a guard on this place and ensure that no-one else comes down here." Mohamed and Zahi left the corridor and made their way to the surface. While Mohamed set the security arrangements in motion, Zahi went to his vehicle and retrieved a satellite phone

He dialled a number and waited. "Ismael? This is Zahi. Sir, I'm afraid I have some bad news." he confessed. "What is it?" Ismael enquired, in a rather officious tone. Zahi was reticent to elaborate further. "I'm sorry Ismael, but I cannot discuss this over the phone. But I feel this is so important that you should come here immediately."

There was silence on the other end of the line for a moment. "That important you say?" Zahi nodded sadly before answering him. "Yes." he confirmed. Ismael grunted. "It's late in the afternoon. I cannot see any way of getting there tonight. I have an important engagement with the President this evening. I will see if I can arrange a helicopter for first thing in the morning. Is that soon enough for you, Zahi?" he asked rather condescendingly. "Sorry Ismael, I am a little confused at the moment. Certainly it can wait until the morning."

CHAPTER 38

Zahi paced back and forth, as he waited impatiently for the imminent arrival of the Minister. As the first amber hues of the pre-dawn sun began to pierce the dark cloudless sky, he turned to look at the gently billowing tent that shrouded the now controversial excavation. His frustration with waiting was evident to those who watched nervously from a safe distance.

Zahi had not been his normal eloquent self since he had emerged from the final chamber late the previous evening. He had the demeanour of a very worried man. It was as though he had suddenly borne the weight of the world on his shoulders. His sense of humour had deserted him and the puffy bags under his eyes betrayed his anxiety and lack of sleep.

During the long and restless night, he had determined what to say to the Minister, when he finally arrived. He had decided it best to lead him into the controversy gently. He would start with the king list. But only the Egyptian information. The rest was too inflammatory. He hoped he could still use this at the conference, along with the treasures they had collected from the antechamber. New discoveries always made headlines and inevitably renewed interest in Egyptology worldwide. This, he knew, would be good for tourism. And tourism was essential for Egypt's economy.

But what about the rest of the information? He was still unsure of the extent of its ramifications. It not only affected Islam and its states, many of which were held together solely by the tenets of the Koran. It also threatened Christianity. The Church of Rome. The ghost of the Roman Empire. This ancient political and financial colossus was now under threat.

What's worse, it threatened the very existence of the state of Israel. His mind boggled at the implications. What a dilemma.

The sound of a fast approaching helicopter interrupted his sombre thoughts. The Minister had arrived. He watched as several security men disgorged from the chopper immediately after it landed, some two hundred yards from the tent. As he recognised Ismael, he strode towards him, squinting to keep the desert sand, kicked up by the rotors, from his eyes. As he reached him, he instinctively thrust out his hand in welcome. "Sorry to drag you away from Cairo, Ismael. But I really think you need to see this." Ismael squinted in the bright sunlight. "It's really that important then?"

"Yes, unfortunately." Zahi assured him, as he hurriedly lead the Minister to the tent covering the dig site. As he entered, he brushed past the four security guards. Their provocative black uniforms and matt black 9mm MP3 sub-machine guns mutely emphasizing the gravity of the situation. The tent was deserted. Only the two of them were to go into the chamber. Zahi picked up two torches, turned them both on and handed one to Ismael. "This way Ismael. If you'll follow me. But be careful. Some of the ladders are a bit tricky."

Zahi patiently assisted the Minister on the arduous descent to the hall of records. He was a bureaucrat and therefore not that familiar with the physical intricacies of archaeology. He was also overweight and unfit. It was going to be a long journey.

Zahi paused to allow Ismael time to regain his breath and took the opportunity to show him the beautiful burial chamber from which they had extracted their booty. Treasures that were now safely ensconced in the bowels of the Cairo museum warehouse. Zahi informally asked permission to use them as the keynote for the upcoming conference.

"Of course. It is perfect timing as you suggested. It will be good for the tourism industry." Somewhat relieved, Zahi motioned for them to move on. Eventually they reached the final chamber. Standing in front of the massive unfinished sarcophagus, Zahi motioned toward the stairway descending from the middle of the room. "The hall of records is at the bottom of these stairs. Just watch your head as you go under the slab of rock. I will go first to light up the stairs with my torch for you."

Ismael nodded and watched as Zahi disappeared into the inky depths of the subterranean chamber. "OK Ismael. I'm at the bottom. You can come down now." The minister quickly joined him at the base of the stairs. Zahi led him to the chamber and shone his torch on the right hand wall as they entered. Ismael followed suite.

Although he knew the Minister could not read the ancient Egyptian texts, Zahi was careful to make sure that the first thing he saw was the king list. They stopped as they reached the first of the hieroglyphs. "Here is the great king list. It appears Manetho was indeed correct when he postulated some of the lesser known periods. I have taken photographs of the beginning of the list to use as a teaser at the conference. With your permission of course."

"I cannot see why not. But what is it you deem so important, that you drag me all the way down here to see?" Zahi took a deep breath and exhaled loudly before answering. "There is a section of the king list that I did not dare photograph." he explained, quietly and rather understatedly. "Well, let us look at it then." Ismael insisted.

Zahi led the Minister along the corridor until he reached the gap in the hieroglyphs. "Up to this point everything is as it should be. Albeit the dating is going to cause some controversy. The kings go back long before we previously thought possible.

But from here it is…" he hesitated for some time. Ismael picked up on his concern. "Is what?" he pushed. "Disturbing!" Zahi blurted out. Ismael was confused. What could possibly be that disturbing in some ancient text? "In what way?" he enquired. "Well, they are not kings of Egypt. They are kings of Sumer." Zahi began. "Why are Sumerian kings listed in an Egyptian tomb?" Ismael cut in. "Perhaps to give some historical perspective to this region?" Zahi suggested before continuing. "But regardless of the reasons for the list being here, there is a problem." Again he hesitated and again Ismael urged him to continue."And what is the problem?"

"Can I suggest you see for yourself?" Zahi suggested. Ismael shook his head. "You know I can't read this stuff." he explained almost angrily. "Yes, I know. But I will interpret it for you." Zahi looked at the Sumerian king list and hesitated. But he quickly shone the torch up to the start of the list as he sensed Ismael's impatience. He began to read the list verbatim. He had only read a few names when Ismael interrupted him. "Are you saying what I think you are saying?"

Zahi slowly nodded."I'm afraid so Ismael. This is reputedly a list of the Sumerian kings. But it starts with Adam and ends with Enoch." Ismael shook his head in disbelief. "You mean to tell me that the ancestors of Abraham were all Sumerian kings?" Again Zahi nodded. "Yes, and if some historians are to be believed, their line descends right down past Jesus, the prophet of the Christians. According to legend the line is still continuing in France and Scotland to this day."

Ismael was still confused as to the reason for his presence. "I see this as interesting, but hardly earth-shattering. Did you bring me here for a history lesson?" Zahi sighed once more, before changing direction. Then he confessed his staged performance to Ismael. "I showed you the less controversial information first.

To ensure that you would appreciate the implications of this find gradually." he explained feebly. Zahi shone his torch to the opposite wall and headed off down the corridor, to the historical section. When he reached the beginning of the writing he paused and waited for the Minister to catch up. "This is what I am very much concerned about." He pointed to a new section of text. Ismael looked at the text briefly, then returned his gaze to Zahi. "What is it?"

Zahi frowned deeply as he continued. "A written history of this planet. It spans millions of years, up to the time this chamber was buried. It was written thousands of years ago. Long before the prophet wrote the Koran. In fact it was written over a thousand years before Abraham left the city of Ur." The Minister now showed signs of unease as he stood silently, open mouthed, waiting for Zahi to continue. Zahi sensed his hesitance but probed for permission to continue. "Shall I read it to you?"

"Please." Ismael insisted. Zahi translated the story as best he could. Ismael stood silently listening to him. He wanted so much to interrupt several times, but forced himself to listen to its entirety before he commented. Finally Zahi came to the end of the text. He nervously looked up at Ismael, waiting for his opinion. It was swift in coming. "What we have here is a blasphemy!" Zahi was taken aback by the malice in Ismael's voice. But he remained silent, allowing the Minister to vent his frustration.

"It makes a mockery out of everything we know, understand and believe in. This information must not be allowed to escape. Who knows about this?" Zahi hesitated. The ramifications from this point on could be deadly. He had thought of the political consequences before he called the Minister. Only now were they emerging in stark clarity from the shadows of doubt. "Only five people have seen this room.

Yourself, me of course and my assistant Mohamed. The other two were Timothy Fullerton and his girlfriend Cathy." "Where are they now?" he enquired, with a sense of urgency in his voice. "Mohamed is still on the site. He supervises the workers. He is a trusted member of my staff. He is already under oath not to talk of this place." Ismael nodded. "And the others?" he asked with equal fervour. "They are in Cairo. Tim is preparing a presentation for the conference. He too is a trusted friend. I am sure he will not divulge information against my will."

"We will see." The Minister stated almost angrily. He then slashed his torch beam around the chamber as he took one final look at the controversial writings. He used this short time to decide the fate of the discovery. His decision was as brief as it was final. "This information must not be revealed. Seal it up!"

Zahi nodded in mute agreement and turned to follow the Minister out of the chamber. He knew it would mean the king list would be lost. But not forever, as he had first feared. Even controversial history is history nonetheless and it would be a crime to destroy it. Simply sealing up the hall of records would suffice for now.

CHAPTER 39

Once back in Cairo, Tim and Cathy began cataloguing their photographs. Tim was acutely aware that he would be asked to limit his talk at the conference to the less controversial kings on the list. As for the history, he was certain this would be taboo. Anticipating Zahi's likely request for restraint, Tim spent the next day putting together a suitable power-point presentation. He assumed Zahi would need to approve its contents, so he forced himself to refrain from the slightest controversy.

Satisfied that his presentation was historically significant, yet politically correct, Tim ran through the slide show for the final time. When he reached the end, he called Cathy over to appraise it. "Cathy could you look at this for me please?" Cathy nodded and wandered over to the table. "Sure. What am I looking for?" she asked.

"Well I've assumed Zahi needs to approve my presentation, so I've made it as politically correct as I can. I think I've left out all of the contentious stuff. But I'd like you to run through it to double check, if you wouldn't mind. The power-point is in note mode, so you can see the notes that go along with each slide. I guess I'll have to promise Zahi that I'll stick to the notes verbatim. I don't think it's a good idea to ad lib through this one." he wisely suggested.

Cathy smiled and nodded as she approached the table. "Sure. Let's have a look at it shall we?" Cathy and Tim went through the presentation slide by slide. Cathy had a few valid comments that prompted Tim to change the notes accordingly. But on the whole, she was pleased with his efforts. "Looks OK to me. I don't think there's anything too controversial here.

But I guess if anyone looks at the king list closely they may concur with your hypothesis regarding the timing of the Exodus by the Hebrews." she noted. Tim smiled. "Yeah. I thought of that. But I've mentioned it in lectures many times. I think this list just adds weight to the notion that Joseph was made vizier in the north of the country at the time of the Hyksos kings.

The list proves that Egypt was divided into many smaller kingdoms on many occasions, including the Hyksos period. Manetho was right all the time. Anyone looking at the story logically would have to conclude that this was the only time in Egyptian history, when a foreign shepherd could plausibly be accepted into such a high ranking position.

Generally the Egyptians held shepherds in low regard. After all, the Hyksos were known as the *Shepherd Kings*." he explained. "But how does that differ from the Church's supposition that the Hebrew exodus was under Ramesses the Second?" Cathy enquired. "Simple really. Timing and Biblical genealogy." Tim explained. "Of course!" Cathy smiled.

Tim flicked open a worn notebook. "Here's the genealogy of the Jacob clan in a nutshell. 1650BC was the start of the 17th dynasty and Joseph was born circa 1644BC. He was sold as a slave around 1627BC and rose to power around 1614BC. Eight years later Jacob and his clan moved to Egypt. Then Jacob died at 130 years old, around 1585BC. Now 1567BC was the start of the 18th dynasty. This was Aahmes, the king who started the reunification campaign.

According to the Bible, this is the time that *a new king arose who new nothing of Joseph.* Now Moses was born circa 1562BC. Amen-hetep the First comes to power around 1546BC and Joseph dies around 1534BC. In about 1526BC Tehuti-mes the First came to power and around 1522BC Moses fled Egypt because he'd been a naughty boy.

But in 1512BC Tehuti-mes the Second, the son of Tehuti-mes the First, rises to power. Then in 1504BC his sister, Hat-shep-set takes over for a while, and did a bloody good job too. Anyway, she was killed off by the rightful heir Tehuti-mes the Third, the son of Tehuti-mes the Second, in about 1482BC.

This is when Moses returned to Egypt. In the Bible it says that Moses was away from Egypt and *after a long while, the king of Egypt died.* Well I guess 40 years is a long while, but in actual fact there had been three kings in the meantime. But the Bible alludes to this by saying that Moses returned to Egypt *when all who threatened his life were dead.* This again coincides with the death of the king, his son and his daughter. Tehuti-mes the Third was only a child, if he was born at all, when Moses fled Egypt, so he logically wouldn't know him."

"It all ties in perfectly with the new king list." Cathy concurred. "Of course." Tim agreed. "The genealogy of the Jacob clan reinforces the timing. See, Moses was the grandson of Jacob and it's doubtful whether he was born before the family moved to Egypt. Even so, his exact birth date only puts the time out a few years either way. My research indicates that Jacob went into Egypt about 1602 BC.

The Hyksos ruled there from about 1818 to 1567BC. So this timing is logical. Moses left Egypt at 80 years of age. That puts it around 1482BC. But now we can get the exact dates from the king list. Perhaps I should do that for this lecture." Cathy shook her head vigorously. "Not a good idea, given the circumstances. Can I suggest you do it later and use the information in a future lecture? Or maybe a book? It might be advisable to keep this one controversy free." she advised.

Tim nodded. I guess you're right. I just have a passion for Biblical history. I find it offensive the way it's been distorted by the Church for political gain. But I also find it amusing.

Millions of people believe these promulgated myths verbatim. To the defiance of logic, mathematics, archaeology and even what's written in other parts of the Bible. Unbelievable lack of common sense! Oh well, I guess I just lack faith." he confessed. "Anyway, we've got plenty of time to re-write history when we get back to the station. Meanwhile you're right. I shouldn't rock the boat." he agreed.

Suddenly a shiver went up Tim's spine and his smiled turned into a look of concern. "What's wrong Tim?" Cathy asked. Tim shook his head despondently. "I just had a terrible thought."Zahi must have found the history by now and he won't like what it says.

It won't damage the Egyptian tourist industry. On the contrary, it will probably increase it substantially. But it's a slap in the face for Islam. And Egypt is basically an Islamic country. Admittedly more moderate than most, but nonetheless Islamic." he explained. "What do you think he'll do?" Cathy asked, a worried tone evident in her voice. Tim thought for a moment. "Follow his academic heart I hope."

CHAPTER 40

David Lethridge waited nervously, as he stood in line at the customs hall. Samuel had called. He had something to tell him. Something important. Too important to discuss over the phone. Something he needed to hear in person. So David had dropped everything and caught the next flight to Cairo.

Soon enough he was through customs and walking into the arrival hall. He scanned the crowd looking for Samuel. "Over here!" Samuel shouted, as he saw his brother emerge from the customs hall. David turned to his right, to see Samuel striding in his direction. "Let me get one of those cases." Samuel offered.

"Thank you. Now, what's so important that you dragged me half way across the world to discuss?" David demanded indignantly. Samuel quickly swept his eyes around the airport before answering. "Not here! Wait until we get in the car. Too many ears!"

They quickly scurried off to the car park, where Samuel had left his old, battered and sun-faded, yellow 1979 Citroen. The two small suitcases and a black leather briefcase were quickly crammed into the boot. Samuel unlocked the car and they both climbed in.

As soon as they turned onto the main road, David demanded an explanation. "So what is it that you so urgently needed to tell me?" he demanded. "Well they found the Hall of Records alright. It had a king list that went back thousands of years earlier than we thought possible." Samuel began.

"And..." David pushed impatiently. "Well it seems the king list was somewhat controversial." he continued. "In what way?" David queried. Samuel shrugged his shoulders. "Well it appears that it also contained a king list from the early Sumerian period."

David was so far unimpressed with the information he was receiving. "So?" he snapped impatiently. Samuel smiled at David with an evil grin. "Well the names on the Sumerian list are exactly the same as the descendants of Abraham. Right back to Adam. The last one was Enoch. Apparently he must have been the king at the time the chamber was sealed.

Strange that. I seem to remember the Bible saying that Enoch was special. All of Adam's descendants were specifically said to have died. But Enoch was different, he didn't die. He was said to be God's friend and one day he left with God and was never seen again. Remarkable coincidence, eh?"

"Indeed!" David conceded with a huff. Samuel nodded and continued. "Anyway, the spelling's obviously not quite the same for the king list, but it's very obvious who they are. Without exception. Speculation is that Abraham was actually the last of the Sumerian kings. Logical extrapolation I guess.

He obviously fled when the Elamites sacked Ur. Forced out, rather than deciding to leave under the guidance of God, as we've been led to believe. "

David pondered the ramifications and concluded that they were not that serious. He then thought of the polymers. "Did they find any relics? Anything unusual?" he asked as casually as his excitement would allow. "Well there was a burial chamber full of relics. Some nice stuff, plenty of gold... typical funerary. But nothing unusual." Samuel offered.

David was not impressed. What was he doing here? Why had Samuel thought that a Sumerian king list warranted him travelling half way around the world at a minute's notice? He felt the anger welling up until he could contain himself no longer. "You mean you dragged me to this God-forsaken, fly-infested, heathen-filled country just to tell me that Fullerton found a list of Sumerian kings?"

Samuel smiled a malevolent smile. "Well not really." he teased. "What do you mean?" David demanded. "The list is only the beginning. Apparently there's another panel in the Hall of Records that is..." Samuel hesitated as he chose his words carefully. "What?" David demanded angrily. "... historical." Samuel conceded.

"What's that supposed to mean?" David retorted furiously. Samuel shook his head. "Well apparently when Fullerton left, Zahi stayed down in the chamber for some time. When he appeared at the surface, he was ashen faced and would not elaborate on what he had found. He gave explicit orders that no-one was to enter the chamber. He even bought in extra armed guards. Anyway, he immediately called the Minister of Antiquities, who flew down by chopper the next morning. That's why I got you on the next flight over."

David was still none the wiser. "What did he find that was so important?" he probed, now feeling that Samuel was finally getting to the point. "My source managed to slip into the chamber in the middle of the night, after Zahi and Ismael had returned to Cairo. Next morning they were ordered to seal it up." he explained.

"Yes, yes. So, what did he see?" David demanded impatiently. Again Samuel smiled before he continued. He was enjoying his brother's frustration. "Well that's what all the fuss is about. Apparently the history written on the wall says this planet was visited a long time ago by a warrior race and some scientists. The way the text describes the history of earth puts a new slant on the Biblical account of creation."

David frowned. "I don't like where you're going with this." he warned Samuel. "Neither did Ismael." Samuel retorted cheekily. "Apparently the creation story in Genesis is a carbon copy of the historical data, describing the work of these scientists. But the timing concerned him most. The history predates the Hebrews and therefore invalidates the Bible."

David slumped back into the car seat to come to grips with what he had just been told. Finally he asked a rhetorical question, to which he already knew the answer. "So this evidence of aliens has the potential to destroy Christianity?" David asked, his voice nearly breaking with horror. "Exactly!" Samuel confirmed. "And Islam. Not to mention Judaism. The political ramifications are also far reaching."

"Who else knows of this?" David snapped. Samuel did the adding up in his head before he responded. "Apart from Fullerton and his girlfriend, there are only a handful of people. Zahi, Ismael and Mohamed, the dig team supervisor. Oh, and my man too." David wanted confirmation of the exact number of people who had seen it. "That's it?" he questioned rather bluntly.

Samuel nodded. "I think so. Mohamed didn't permit any of the diggers to enter the chamber and Ismael was the only outsider allowed in." David nodded impatiently. "Has Ismael informed anyone else of the potential threat?" Samuel shook his head. "Not to my knowledge. But I assume someone higher up will need to know why he sealed the chamber so quickly. Perhaps the President himself?"

David's mind was whirring as many contradictory thoughts ran through his head. "It's imperative that we get to Fullerton, to see how much he knows. And more importantly, who he's told about it. I also need to know where he got his original information. We need to get all his photos from him, before he starts spreading them around." Samuel shook his head. "That won't be easy. Knowing him, he's probably sent copies hell west and crooked already." he surmised.

David was in a tizzy. "Take me back to the airport." he demanded. "I need to get to Rome immediately. The Pope will know what to do. He has the resources we need to stop this from escalating. Can you imagine what damage this sort of thing can do to the Church?

This is blasphemous and scandalous. We need to do something about it." he fumed. Samuel obediently turned the car around and headed back toward the airport. With any luck, David could catch a flight to Rome that evening.

As he dropped David off, Samuel handed him a small dossier. "Read this before you get there. It's a summary of what's written in the chamber. There are a few photographs too. But be careful. Make sure you give it to the Pope and no-one else. If you're caught with it, it could be a death sentence."

David swallowed hard as he alighted from the car. This was already getting way too complicated. Samuel helped extract his luggage and gave him a reassuring embrace. "You'll be OK, David. Good luck in Rome."

CHAPTER 41

David sat nervously fiddling with his tie, as he waited for His Holiness. As anticipated, he did not have to wait long. "Welcome, my child. Bishop Renaldo informs me that you have some disturbing news." the pontiff began. David immediately rose from his chair and bowed deeply. "Disturbing indeed, Your Eminence. I have come from Egypt where a certain person has uncovered things that will not sit well with the followers of the Church of Rome.

Or indeed the followers of Islam and Judaism." he added. The Pope nodded. "Please go on." he invited. "Well, Your Eminence, it appears this person has found evidence that directly contradicts the Bible. A written history of this planet, from time immemorial, until around 3000BC. It literally spans millions of years. In it, there are details and proofs that, until modern times, would not have been understood." he explained. A concerned look crept across the Pope's face as he fought to maintain his composure. "How is this?"

"It talks explicitly of the DNA mutation of primates by the visitors, to develop a race of workers. Their descendants are the African negroes and Asian races of today. These scientists were so advanced, they cloned themselves to create mankind as we know it. It goes on to tell how they introduced plant and animal species from their home planet.

They even planted a garden and named it Eden. They also mated with the sons and daughters of the cloned beings. But, most disturbing of all, it names the giant warriors who protected these people." he explained. "Well?" the Pope insisted. "They are as in Deuteronomy, called the Zamzam'min." he explained in a shaky voice.

The normally unemotional papal face began to turn pallid, as the ramifications of what he was hearing struck home. These were names and deeds straight from the Pentateuch. The cornerstone of three of the world's great religions. This indeed, had the potential to ruin his empire.

Try as he might to maintain decorum, the fear in his voice was disturbingly evident to David. "I see where this is leading. The parallels with the myth of creation are all too obvious. Indeed, it seems to correspond to the Book of Genesis a little too closely for comfort. Tell me, my faithful friend. What else does this furtive history tell us?" he asked, now in a calm, calculated voice.

David shook his head, as if to negate what he was about to say. "Well it says the chamber was sealed by the Guardians, as they called themselves. They were leaving Egypt to live at another place. It seems Mt. Sinai is mentioned. But it does not elaborate. But I fear the person who discovered this chamber already has information on this other place." he suggested.

The Pope leaned forward and almost whispered. "What makes you so sure?" David swallowed hard. "He convinced the Egyptian authorities to allow him to dig, based on a map he had photographed from an old book. No-one knows where the book came from. I suspect he has an accomplice. Possibly in Australia. My concern, Your Eminence, is that, if there is another site and we don't stop him,..."

The Pope interrupted him. "Yes, I see your concern. Of course we must not allow this information to see the light of day. It has the potential to destroy the Church and everything we have worked so hard to gain." he stated rather coldly. David shrugged his shoulders. "What can we do?" he asked, genuine concern evident in his voice. "What is the fate of the chamber in Egypt you talk of?" the Pope asked.

David smiled. "The Egyptian authorities have sealed it up. They fear for Islam. There were only a handful of people who saw it. They have been… Well I am assured they are not the problem. The problem is this Australian. He has seen and photographed the writing in the chamber. It is he who represents the greatest threat." he postulated.

The pontiff nodded. "Indeed. I need to know all that you can tell me of this person. I may be able to influence some people to detain him. I do not wish him harmed at this point. It is too important that I speak with him face to face, to find out exactly what he knows." he explained.

David filled in all the gaps he could. He purposely began with information on the doctoral thesis, in a calculated bid to portray Tim as a vindictive, iconoclastic person. Someone on a personal vendetta against the Church of Rome. Although the Pope was new to the position, he was aware of the manuscript affair, as it was known within Vatican circles. In fact, he had even browsed through the document himself in order to satisfy his curiosity. David continued to paint a sinister picture of his nemesis, theatrically culminating in the activities of his brother, Charles, in the research laboratories.

As David spoke, the papal scribe, the only other witness to the discussion, could not believe what he was writing. He nevertheless obediently transcribed the conversation verbatim. The Pope was going to need as much detail as he could muster, if he was going to convince the Brotherhood to collude with him. Finally David had run out of facts and half truths to regurgitate. Seeing the worried look on the now colourless face of the Pope, he sat back in his seat. It was not until that moment, as the excitement of meeting the Pope waned in the solemnity of the situation, that he remembered the dossier.

He clumsily opened his briefcase and fumbled for the package his brother had entrusted him with. He grabbed the manila folder and handed it to the Pope. "I have this, Your Eminence." The Pope accepted the dossier. "What's this?" he asked, as he opened the folder. "Photographs of the chamber and a synopsis of the interpretation." David explained.

"Excellent. Thank you very much." David stood for a moment, then looked fearfully at the Pope. "Is there anything more I can do?" he asked. The pontiff smiled and shook his head. "No, thank you. You have already done enough. You have been most helpful. Thank you for bringing this to my attention in such a timely manner. The Entity will take it from here." he assured him with a sardonic smile.

"Thank you, Your Eminence. I am pleased to be the Lord's humble servant." David blurted out. The Pope smiled as David kissed his ring. "If we can contain this problem, all will be well. Your rewards will be great, for your judicious assistance. You have obviously worked hard and risked much to get this information to me."

David smiled greedily to himself. Ruining Fullerton would be reward enough, but any gratuity the Vatican threw his way would be a bonus.

CHAPTER 42

After completing the review of the slide presentation, Tim and Cathy decided to celebrate their success. "I know this great little Italian restaurant. Do you fancy a nice dinner this evening?" Cathy nodded. "That would be wonderful. It's been a while since we sat down to a cosy meal together. You know, just the two of us."

They jumped into a grubby taxi, they found parked opposite the hotel lobby. The heavily stubbled and unpleasantly redolent driver, took them for a short white-knuckle ride. After five near misses in just over a mile, Tim was relieved when they finally stopped outside a small restaurant.

It was tucked away in an alley, not far from the suq they had visited a few days before. As they alighted from the taxi, Tim looked up at the restaurant facia. In proud Arabic it stated *Anton's Italian Restaurant*. Underneath it added boastfully *The Best Italian Food in Egypt*. It was an unpretentious building, with a typical glass-fronted design.

Hanging in the windows were slightly faded, half-length, red and white chequered curtains. Tim watched as they swayed gently, pushed by the subtle currents of air generated by the ceiling fans. Several of the tables were occupied by customers, mostly tourists. They were busily involved with their food, their wine and each other. He smiled and strode confidently inside, Cathy clinging to his hand.

"Untavolo per due, per favore." Tim asked the waiter. A loud voice boomed from the rear of the restaurant. "Tim!" Tim looked around for the source of the voice. "Buongiorno Anton... come stai?" he asked with a smile. "Bene! Bene, grazie Tim..."

Tim noticed that Anton's eyes were wandering in Cathy's direction. "Sorry Anton. This is my girlfriend Cathy." Cathy's face erupted into a joyful smile as she stretched out her hand to meet Anton's. It was the second time she had been introduced as Tim's girlfriend. She felt tingly, even giddy with excitement and responded enthusiastically to the introduction. "Pleased to meet you Anton." she beamed.

"So, Tim, what brings you to Cairo? I haven't seen you for a couple of years now. They been working you too hard?" Tim shook his head. "No, I just came over to catch up with some old friends. And do a bit of research. How's the restaurant going?" Anton shook his head. "Cosi, cosi." Tim laughed and slapped him on the back. "Always cosi, cosi!"

They laughed, arms across each other's shoulders, as Anton led them to a private table, in a secluded corner near the kitchen. Tim and Anton continued quietly talking in Italian for some time. Cathy, feeling a little excluded, but forgiving the old friends nonetheless, perused the menu. To her dismay it was written in Italian and Arabic but not English. Tim noticed the frustrated look in her eyes as she put the menu down, so he turned to Anton. "Cosa mi consiglia?"

Anton smiled. "Prosciutto e melone... zuppa pavese... tacchino con sugo di melagrana!" Tim smiled back. "Sounds terrific. We'll have that for two thanks Anton." Cathy watched as Anton strode off toward the kitchen. Once he was out of earshot she turned to Tim. "I didn't know you spoke Italian." Tim just shrugged his shoulders. "I picked it up during my period of research in Italy. It's a pretty easy language to follow, particularly if you're familiar with Latin."

Cathy squeezed his hand. "You'll never cease to amaze me, Timothy Fullerton. By the way... thanks." Tim looked confused. "For what?" Cathy smiled broadly. "For introducing me as your girlfriend.

It's the second time you've done that. Does this mean...?" Tim smiled as he interrupted her. "I guess so, Cathy. Although I'm not much good with this sort of thing, as you know. But I do love you. And I'm not afraid of anyone knowing it. I think we've got to know each other well enough for our relationship to go to the next level." he suggested.

Cathy laughed. "What next level? We're already living together!" she opined sarcastically. Tim smiled and stared lovingly into her eyes. "By the way..." she continued, "...what did you order?" Tim hesitated as he recalled the menu. "Starters, soup and main. Trust me... you'll love it." and she did.

The meal was sensational. Melon with cured ham, followed by Pavian chicken broth, then turkey with pomegranate sauce for mains. This was complimented with a bottle of fine red Italian wine and finished off with cannoli and Turkish coffee. It was a taste sensation for Cathy. She was used to the bland tastes of traditional Australian bush cuisine. Meat and three veg!

They were sipping their coffee and talking quietly, deciding whether to go back to the motel or go for a walk, when Anton emerged from the kitchen and approached the table. Cathy watched as he came up behind Tim and bent over. He whispered something inaudible in his ear. Tim looked puzzled and motioned for Cathy to join him, as he stood up and headed for the kitchen door.

As they entered the kitchen a large, well-dressed and neatly manicured man confronted them. "Dobriy vyechyeer, Tim." he greeted in Russian. "Preevyet Alex... kak deela?" Tim responded, almost fluently. "Spaseeba khasasho a kak vi? he continued. "O ke" Alex responded, before acknowledging Cathy's presence with a polite smile and a nod. He then motioned Tim to come closer. He too whispered in his ear. Cathy could just hear parts of the ensuing conversation.

But being conducted in Russian, she was unable to understand. She did however, get an uneasy feeling as she watched the expressions changing on Tim's face. They seemed to change as the conversation continued. From interest to concern to... something. Was that worry or just concentration?

Without an explanation to Cathy, Alex turned on his heels. Tim turned to Anton and apologised for his early departure. He gave him money for the meal, including a generous tip, said goodbye and quickly followed in the direction of Alex. As he went, he turned to Cathy and motioned with the flick of his head for her to follow. Not knowing why, but trusting Tim implicitly, she obeyed.

The trio wound their way past the hot and smoking ovens and gas stove-tops, with their wildly bubbling concoctions. They then threaded their way through the racks of well worn pots and pans. As they headed for the rear door, they hurriedly weaved their way through the confused cooks and waiters that filled the relatively small kitchen.

Cathy soon found herself in the alley behind the restaurant, confronted by a small van. As she approached the van, the side door slid open and a second man's smiling face greeted her from the dark interior. A gold filling sparkled as it caught the light from a lamp over the rear door of the restaurant. Suddenly overcome with a sense of dread, she looked at Tim. "It's OK." he reassured her. "I'll explain on the way. Please get in." he urged. "We have to leave."

The second man beckoned Tim to climb in, which he immediately did. Cathy hesitated for a moment. Then seeing Tim's outstretched hand motioning the urgency of his request to follow, she grabbed it and climbed in. Alex slid the door shut, walked around the vehicle and climbed into the driver's seat. He looked over the seat at Tim with an uncomfortable smile and nodded.

He quickly started the engine and drove off. "Where are we going?" Cathy asked nervously. "Nairobi!" Tim mumbled hurriedly. "What! In this! That's got to be a couple of thousand miles from here. And what about our stuff back at the hotel?" Cathy asked in confusion.

"More like three thousand miles..." Alex cut into the conversation, in an effort to reassure Cathy that things were OK. "Sorry about this Cathy. I didn't have time for introductions, but Tim told me who you were. I am... well let's just say that I used to work for the KGB, but now I work for... well the Russian foreign diplomatic service. I have already taken the liberty of collecting your things from the hotel. Discretely of course."

Cathy was starting to get a little concerned. "Why?" she asked, almost afraid of the answer he might give. Alex smiled reassuringly at Cathy. "Well it seems you two have caused some concerns here. The information you discovered is inflammatory, I am told. It is such that... how can I put it?

There are vested interests, particularly the Church of Rome and the Supreme Islamic Council, who do not wish this information to be divulged. As a result, your king list has been photographed for release at the conference but the more... how do you say... controversial... kings have been ignored.

The other historical information is also to be ignored. The dig site you were at is being concealed as we speak. It has not been destroyed, just re-buried. As far as I can determine, only five people have seen it. You two, Mohamed, the Minister of Antiquities and Zahi."

"How do you know this?" Cathy enquired nervously. Again Alex broke into a broad smile. "Zahi is an old friend, as is Tim. He fears for your lives, since you have an ancient map showing the location of this site. And he knows that you have photographs of the entire wall. He suggests you go to ground for some time and do not inflame the current panic by publishing the photos.

There are many spies of the Holy Alliance throughout the world." he explained. "So, why are we going to Nairobi?" Cathy insisted, still unable to grasp the implications of what Alex was telling her. "To get you out of Egypt and back to Australia." he explained. "It will be safer over there, but you will still need to be careful. Do you have any weapons, Tim?"

Tim shook his head. "Not here. In Australia I do. Do you think it's that bad?"he asked, a surprised tone evident in his voice. Alex nodded with great animation. "Mohamed was found dead in his tent at the dig site this morning. A heart attack they say. But we both know he was as healthy as a mule. Ricin is my guess." Alex pronounced coldly. Tim was stunned. "Shit! How are we going to get back to Australia?" he asked.

"US Air Force direct to Pine Gap. Here, take these for the trip home. There's no customs in Pine Gap, so you can keep them." Alex reached for a battered khaki duffel bag, sitting on the floor in front of the vacant passenger's seat. As he grabbed it, he swung it over the top of the seat to Tim.

Tim carefully opened it and rummaged through its contents, in the pulsing orange half-light of the passing sodium vapour street lamps. Cathy watched on. Her curiosity peeked as Tim began to extract items from the bag and place them on his lap.

Although not knowledgeable on weapons per se, Cathy had seen enough TV to recognise the shoulder holster with the menacing butt of a pistol protruding from it. She also noted the spare magazines on the opposite side of the webbing. "What's that?" she asked, already knowing the answer. "It looks like a H&K USP in .45 ACP." Tim informed her casually. "Yes, I can see it's a gun. But what's it for?" Cathy insisted. "Just in case!" Tim answered nonchalantly. Cathy was now getting more concerned. "In case of what!"

"I warned you things could get nasty if the Vatican learned of our discovery prematurely. By the way, Alex. How did they find out?" Alex cleared his throat before answering. "It seems the Minister of Antiquities was informed of the discovery by Zahi. It is his duty. He flew to Abydos today by helicopter to inspect the find.

It was he who directed Zahi to close it up again. I am thinking he reported it to the Supreme Islamic Council, who would have reported it to the Holy Alliance. However, I did hear the name Samuel Lethridge mentioned. He works at the museum. Do you know him Tim?" he asked.

Tim scowled. "Yes... I know the slimy little bastard!" he muttered under his breath. "Who is he?" Cathy asked. "David Lethridge's brother. He's the one I suspect was behind the theft of my research notes. David's a religious fanatic... as Catholic as they come. Somewhat of a hypocrite in my books. But Samuel is a morigerous, evil little bastard. I think David's the older and smarter of the two. I've got a feeling he makes the bullets and gets Samuel to fire them, if you know what I mean." Tim explained.

Alex shook his head. "Well you'd better be careful when you get to Australia my friend. It seems you've stirred up quite a hornet's nest."

Cathy watched with morose fascination as Tim removed his light jacket and manoeuvred himself into the shoulder holster. Once on, he stood up from his seat as high as the mini-van roof would allow, and removed his belt. She watched as he replaced his belt, expertly threading the holster loops as he went.

With the calm practiced way he adjusted the rig to make it comfortable, she knew he had done this before. "You often wear a gun?" she asked, as casually as the circumstances would allow. "Only when it's necessary... or I need to look cool!" Tim responded playfully. She laughed.

He did look rather mysterious, rugged, and independent. A modern Indiana Jones, perchance with a slight James Bond mystique. Cathy watched Tim as he donned his jacket and sat down, but was startled when he drew the pistol. "Is it loaded Alex?" he asked, as he casually pointed the pistol at the floor.

"The magazine is full, but the breech is empty." Alex informed him. Tim pulled back the slide. Over the monotonous drone of the engine and the noise of the tyres rhythmically bouncing along the rough road, Cathy could still hear the unmistakable metallic click, as he released the slide and it picked up a round from the magazine and slammed it into the breech.

Tim then hit the de-cocking lever which released the hammer with a disconcerting thud. He then returned the pistol to the holster and reached into the bag to retrieve a second rig. "You ever used one of these things?" he asked with a wry smile. Cathy shook her head. "No, but I've shot rifles at home. We get a lot of wild pigs, so my brothers and I used to go shooting quite a bit when we were kids." she explained.

Tim was impressed. "What did you use?" he asked. Cathy hesitated as she recalled her father's arsenal. "We had a Remington .270 bolt action and several .308's. Dad's favourite was the SLR." she recalled. Tim smiled. "That's a mighty fine rifle, I've used them myself. On pigs... and other vermin."

The way he emphasized the last few words made Cathy feel uneasy. She got the distinct impression he was no longer talking of killing wild animals, he was referring to human vermin. The thought of Tim having killed other men filled her with a strange combination of shock and interminable fascination.

She was immediately torn between inquisitiveness and repulsion. But Tim was a good man. She knew that. No matter what he had done in the past, it would have been for a very good reason.

But how many men had he killed... where... when... and why? Despite her curiosity, she decided it best not to probe for details. Perhaps there would be a more suitable time to explore Tim's incongruous past. Reluctantly she let it go and sat in silence as Tim continued.

"This pistol's similar to the SLR. It's a semi-automatic. You pull the trigger and it shoots a round then re-loads itself. I always keep a round up the spout so you only need one hand to operate it. With this one you don't need to worry about a safety. All you have to do is load it and hit the de-cocking lever. This effectively makes it safe.

The pistol is double action for the first shot, single for the rest. Otherwise, if you carry it unloaded, you have to use both hands to cock it when you need it. And that could be the difference between winning a gunfight and coming second. And there's no prize for coming second!" he added with a chuckle.

Cathy cringed at first as he handed her the shoulder holster, but quickly analysed the situation. She decided that self-preservation was paramount. Tim helped her don the rig and make it as comfortable as he could. He then un-holstered the pistol and removed the magazine. With Cathy watching on curiously, he opened the breech to check it was empty. "Here, I'll show you how it works. You can play with it for a bit, while it's empty.

That way, you can get comfortable with it before I load it for you. This is the magazine release. It lets you drop the magazine when you need to change it. The spares are on the other side of the rig. The magazine comes out like this... and goes back in like this. But make sure you have it facing the right way and push it all the way up until you hear it click.

Otherwise the ammo won't load properly and it'll probably jam. This is the slide release. When the magazine's empty the pistol will stay open.

After you've changed magazines you need to hit this button to close it up again. This is the safety. On this model it's pretty much optional, so I'll leave yours off." he suggested. Cathy was not so sure. "Isn't that dangerous?" she asked. Tim shook his head. "Not really. See this? It's a de-cocking lever. It releases the main spring and hammer so the firing mechanism isn't under strain, while it's waiting for someone to pull the trigger. This is a double action pistol. Which means you need to pull the hammer back before it can drop forward and fire. But it's all done by just pulling on the trigger.

See when I de-cock it, the hammer drops forward. It then takes a bit of pressure when you pull the trigger to bring the hammer back ready to fire... like this. Once you've fired the pistol it reverts to a single action. The hammer stays cocked ready to fire until you hit the de-cocking lever. Once cocked, the second shot goes off a lot easier than the first because the hammer's already pulled back for you. You just need to release it.

When the pistol's de-cocked in a holster, it's almost impossible for it to go off accidentally. Apart from that, there's another good reason not to use the safety. A problem with novice shooters is stage fright.

When you're first confronted with a situation where you need to use your gun, you're usually under immense mental and even physical pressure. You're sort of in a state of shock. You generally find that your fine motor skills are diminished. Which means you can still pull out the gun and shoot it. But you're likely to forget to release the safety.

It takes a great deal of training to master the auto pistol. But in a bind, I think you'll get the hang of it soon enough. Perhaps we can stop somewhere on the way and give you a few practice shots. Looks like we've got plenty of spare ammo." he noticed. But the thought of sneaking out the back door of Egypt carrying a gun made Cathy feel decidedly uncomfortable.

She looked nervously over at Tim and wondered how he could sit there so calmly under the circumstances. Eventually she accepted that it may just be Tim's imperturbable nature and assumed past experience that would save the day.

They sat in silence, contemplating the future, as the van steadily bumped along the inadequately maintained road. After about half an hour had passed, Alex turned off the main road and drove up to a poorly lit building on the southern outskirts of the city. As the car came to a halt, the silent and mysterious second passenger slid the door open and climbed out. He looked back at Tim and Cathy and nodded, then turned his head towards Alex. "Poka..."

Alex nodded as the door slammed shut, then turned the car back towards the main road. Cathy was still mulling over the need for the gun and it was starting to worry her. Finally her concerns drove her to ask the obvious question. "The Church of Rome basically represents Christianity, so why would the Supreme Islamic Council speak with them? I thought they hated each other vehemently." she wondered.

"They do." Tim confirmed. "But when it all boils down to it, they share the same god! As do the Jews. Well actually the Christians effectively stole the Jewish god, then usurped him with his "son". But that's a long story. Anyway, with evidence to refute the existence of their common god, their respective world-wide empires would disappear. Along with their immense wealth and political influence.

This is something they simply can't allow to happen. And I have absolutely no doubt whatsoever, that they'll go to great lengths to stop anyone upsetting the status quo. Historically the Christians have been quite ruthless in the suppression of adverse knowledge. Remember the Spanish Inquisition, the Knights Templar, the Conquistadors... and my friend Monsignor Thomas?

And now Islam seems to be on the defence with Mohamed turning up dead." he moaned. Tim then mumbled something unintelligible, as his mind raced back to the baffling disappearance of his friend in Rome. This momentary relapse quickly reinforced the serious nature of their current predicament. Now he had to contend with the mysterious death of another friend, as well as the wrath of three religions. The ramifications would be far reaching. He began to worry for the safety of Charlie and Cathy's family back in Australia.

Finally Alex broke his chain of thought as he chipped in. "This is why you must fear for your lives. Two lives... two thousand lives... two million lives. It is nothing, to retain the influence, wealth and power of these religions. You must be very careful my friends." he advised them.

Cathy slumped back deeply into the car seat, placed her head in her hands and stared at her knees. What had they got themselves into? How would they avoid the eyes and ears of the vast network of zealots and spies that would inevitably be sent to hunt them down?

Alex was silent for a while, as he thought ahead. Planning a suitable strategy for his friend. Eventually Tim leaned over the front seat to talk with Alex. As he did so, he noticed a faint glow emanating from the passenger's seat. He turned to see a laptop computer sitting on the seat with its screen facing Alex. "What's this?" he casually enquired. Alex smiled broadly. "I have called in some favours. I thought we could use all the help we can get. It's a long way to Nairobi with many route options available to us.

This is a live feed hook-up to a Russian spy satellite in geo-synchronous orbit over Ethiopia. You cannot see much at night, even though I am using the thermal imaging cameras. See the light green dot in the middle of the screen?"

"Yes!" Tim nodded. "Well that's us." Alex explained. "The satellite is set to track this vehicle's beacon. We will always be in the middle of the screen, unless I choose otherwise. I have it set at the moment to look at a ten-mile radius from us. We can narrow it down if we want to have a closer look at something." he explained. "How close can you zoom in?" Tim asked out of curiosity more than for any real reason.

Alex shook his head and smiled. "That I cannot tell you... it's a military secret. What I will tell you though, is if we need to look at some people on the ground, I can tell you whether they are smoking or not." Tim was impressed. "You use this stuff all the time then?"

"Oh no!" Alex assured him. "In fact if it was not for you, I would not have it at all. Luckily there are those in Russia who would greatly like to see the demise of Islam. You know all that Islamic separatist stuff in Chechnya? Well to put it simply, the government sees this as an opportunity to redress the terrorist problems.

I simply explained to them that our best chance to defeat Islamic extremism, was to help the Americans get you out of here as quickly as possible. To do that effectively, I needed the satellite. They eventually agreed. It was also suggested that the sooner you release this information the safer you'll be." he added.

"Does the Australian Government know anything yet?" Tim asked. Alex shook his head. "No, your government's too... how you say... slow to react. They must debate everything like foolish children. There is no time for such nonsense when things like this happen.

You need instant responses and someone needs to take unchallengeable control. I guess the Americans will tell them eventually. But I presume it will be after the dust has settled. Now my friend, may I suggest you try to get some sleep. We will not be stopping except for fuel, food and the call of nature. We will need to share the driving if we are to keep our schedule."

Tim nodded. "Which way are we headed?" Alex thought about it for a while before answering. "I am thinking it is safe to follow the Nile south for the moment. Perhaps as far as Asyut. Then we will head east to the coast... to Al Ghaidaqah. From there, we will follow the coast road to the Sudan border... all going well. Once we get to Sudan we will again follow the coast. Except we might detour around Port Sudan.

We will continue along the coast until we get to the Eritrean border. We will follow along the western boundary inside Sudan. I do not want to go into Eritrea, unless we have to. It is still very unstable there. Warlords everywhere at the moment.

Somewhere along the Sudanese border we should be able to cross into Ethiopia. Exactly where, I am unsure, until we get there and have a look. So relax, my friend. We have a long drive ahead of us. At least two or three days, if we make good time." he stated rather jovially.

Tim sank back into the seat. Cathy was already snoozing, resting her head against the side window, using her jacket as a pillow. Tim eventually nodded off, sleeping shallow and oft interrupted for several hours.

CHAPTER 43

The phone rang, almost unnoticed in the hubbub of the busy office. A tall, lean and well groomed man, instinctively reached out to answer it. His shortly cropped dark hair was military in style. He wore neatly creased, black dress pants and a matching suite jacket. Under the jacket was a newly starched white cotton shirt. An almost indiscernible bulge in the left side of the jacket betrayed his concealed pistol. It was a Colt .45 ACP. An old but reliable design, first patented in 1911, but still a favourite with ex military types. Simple, powerful and effective. His black polished shoes completed the conservative outfit.

His strong southern US accent was obvious as he answered the phone. "Bob here." he snapped. "Bob it's Peter. Can you meet for coffee in five minutes?" he asked rather curtly. "Sure." Bob casually hung up the phone and ritualistically shuffled some paperwork on his desk. He shot a casual glance around the office, to see if anyone was paying undue attention to him. In the covert world of the CIA, it was often difficult to tell friend from foe. Satisfied that things were normal, Bob slowly rose from his chair. He straightened his jacket as he walked past the pool secretary. "Just going for a coffee Cindy." he informed her casually.

Once outside the building, he instinctively looked up and down the footpath. First right, then left. Nothing untoward. He shrugged his shoulders and strode purposefully in the direction of the local coffee shop. As he stepped inside, a loud voice greeted him. "Bob!" Bob looked around until he found the source of the greeting. "Hi Peter, what's up?" he asked. "How about we go for a walk?" Peter politely suggested. "OK." Bob agreed, knowing better that to ask questions in a busy place.

He followed Peter out of the coffee shop and across the road. He assumed his boss had his reasons for the secrecy. His curiosity would have to wait. They walked in silence until they reached a small park, where a solitary green wooden bench beckoned them. They sat down it the shade of a leafy oak tree and instinctively surveyed the immediate surrounds. There were several people wandering hither and yon, the closest of whom was walking a large shaggy white dog, some thirty yards to their right.

Satisfied that their conversation would not be overheard, Bob probed for an explanation. "What's this about then?" he whispered. Peter looked around, then lowered his voice. "I intercepted some traffic that I thought you'd be interested in." he winked as he spoke. "Where's it originating?" Bob probed. Peter smiled. "Rome." He knew that would confuse Bob. Europe was not within his portfolio. "Rome?" Bob questioned. "That's right. It seems the Holy Alliance is in an awful tizz. They're looking for an Australian Egyptologist. They want him real bad. Seems they've taken the highly unusual step of seeking the aid of the Brotherhood."

"You mean the Brotherhood of Islam?" Bob exclaimed in surprise. "Yes." Peter confirmed. "They've been in contact with the Supreme Islamic Council." Bob shook his head in disbelief. "Jesus Christ! What's this joker done to piss them off?" Peter laughed. "Not much really. It seems he's discovered the Hall of Records or something. I've been checking it out with our mythology boys. Seems this particular chamber was supposed to be nothing more than a legend. But our Aussie friend got a map from somewhere that led him straight to it."

Bob shook his head. "So what's the big deal?" he asked. Peter smiled. "Quite a lot apparently. Seems the information contained in the Hall of Records is extremely controversial.

I'm not sure of the details, but they're saying it has the potential to destroy organized religion. The Pope's going ape-shit. And why not? He's got a multi-billion dollar business empire to protect. And this guy's about to bring it crashing down around his holy ears.

That's why the Catholics are cooperating with the Brotherhood. A most unholy alliance, but I guess Islam has a lot to lose too. More political than financial in their case though. Christ knows what the Israelis are doing at the moment. I haven't heard them mentioned, but I guess they'll want a piece of this Aussie as well. Look I'm telling you this because, quite frankly, you're about the only one I can trust at the moment."

"Why do you say that?" Bob asked, still unsure of his potential involvement. Peter laughed. "You're the only one around here who hates religion as much as I do." Bob laughed and slapped him on the back. "That serious, eh?" Peter's face suddenly lost all trace of humour. "You bet! A few men on the thirteenth floor are thick as thieves with the Holy Alliance. I'm afraid they've taken to this rather personally. They've put an APB on this Aussie. Some of our operatives in Egypt are looking for him as we speak. They're using Interpol to keep an eye on transport and immigration world-wide. The poor bastard hasn't got a snowflake's hope in hell on his own."

"What's his name?" Bob asked, now sensing that he was getting roped into something controversial. Peter hesitated as he recalled the name. "Timothy Fullerton. But there are two of them. He's travelling with a woman." Bob shook his head. "Jesus! That's not good. If those ruthless bastards get hold of them, they'll torture her first. Guaranteed to get him talking real quick. What then? Do you think they'll kill them?"

Peter shrugged his shoulders. "I don't know, but I assume so. Once they've told them what they need to know, they'll be of no further use.

Besides, it sounds like this is an all out search and destroy campaign. Christ knows how many they'll have to kill to contain this information. But I'm sure they're willing to kill thousands."

"So where do we go from here?" Bob probed, sensing Peter was still holding back vital information. "I've already talked with the Russians in Cairo. Alex owes me a favour. Besides, the Russians are just as pissed off with Islamic extremism as we are. They're keen to get on board anything that may help quieten the radicals down a bit. With any luck, he should have been extracted by now.

But I need someone to go to Nairobi to collect him and take him back to Australia." Bob shook his head. "Why Australia. Wouldn't it be safer to bring him here?" Peter shook his head with great animation. "No. I can't trust anyone here at the moment. This thing's too political. Besides there are other reasons why it's better to get him back to Australia." he hinted.

"Like?" Bob asked, getting more curious by the second. "Well Fullerton's a history professor at the Melbourne University. He has a passion for Egyptology. Apparently he just got back from a trip to north Queensland and resigned his position. No reasons given, except that he wanted to do some research. His Dean is interesting. You remember that Catholic conspiracy a few years back. A couple of our goons got involved with the Church of Rome over a god-damned doctoral thesis. Five people died over that." Bob nodded. "I remember."

"Well, this Aussie is the same one who wrote that thesis. And his Dean is David Lethridge." The penny suddenly dropped. "Oh, I seem to remember his brother was involved somehow too wasn't he?" Peter nodded. "He stole the thesis and took it to Rome." Bob sat back on the park bench as he contemplated what he had heard so far.

"Jesus! If they killed five people over a few controversial notes, imagine how many they'd kill to keep this hidden." Peter nodded. "Exactly!"

Bob was still sure there was more information to be had. "What else did you find out?" he asked as casually as he could. Peter shook his head, as if he did not believe what he was about to say. "Apparently this information he stumbled across concerns a race known as the Guardians." Bob was astounded. "Shit! I thought no-one knew anything about them except us." Peter smiled wearily. "Well it looks like they do now.

According to our archives, there was a cave painting of some large feline warriors found in Queensland some time ago. Under our guidance, the Australian museum people dismissed them as a hoax. But our boys weren't so sure. And then I found a coincidence that's just too wild to ignore. The paintings are in a cave located on a property in far north Queensland, owned by the Paxton Land and Cattle Company."

Bob shrugged his shoulders. "So?" he asked. "So..." Peter explained. "The woman this Aussie's running with is Cathy Paxton!" Bob immediately saw the connection. "Shit! Do you think they've found a base?"

"Exactly what I was thinking. The coincidence is intriguing. We know from the sketchy information from Tibet, there are supposed to be several bases scattered around the globe. We have a few clues, but don't have any real evidence yet. The god-damned Chinese are trying to beat us to the punch, so they can get any technology that may be there. But as far as I'm aware, no-one's actually found one of these bases yet. The only thing we know for sure is the localized legends of giant feline warriors. Seems these creatures are somehow linked to the bases. Perhaps they're the fabled Guardians. But this time apparently, there's hard evidence." "What sort of evidence?" Bob probed, now fully aware of the wider-reaching implications.

Peter smiled as he recalled the events leading up to this conversation. "Well Tim Fullerton has a brother, Charles. He went to Queensland with him, but stayed in Australia when the others went to Egypt. But it appears Charles brought something back with him." he offered. Bob raised his eyebrows. "What?"

"Seems he wanted to test some high tech polymers or something. That's what brought him undone. He was using the research labs with a researcher at Melbourne Uni. But they left some printouts and a sample in the lab late one night. Lethridge grabbed it and smelt a rat. He was convinced that the Fullertons had discovered something of extraterrestrial origin.

But he's a fanatical Mick, so we have him to thank for the Papal involvement. Anyway, our techno expert in Australia has information on the polymer. He borrowed it from Lethridge. Seems Lethridge wanted to steal it from the brothers and patent it."

"What's so special about this stuff?" Bob asked, still unsure of the polymer's significance. Again Peter simply smiled before elaborating. "Our contact says that it's definitely extraterrestrial in origin. Is has stable isotopes of heavy metals that are unheard of here. Hell, it's all too technical for me.

My main concern is the base. If they have found a base, Christ only knows what else could be there. The possibilities are endless. Fuel, electronics, transport, weapons and power sources. The list goes on. But it's critical we get to this technology before anyone else. The Holy Alliance obviously knows nothing of the base yet. But if they get hold of Fullerton, it would only be a matter of time. That's why I've acted covertly on this. It's too important an opportunity to squander."

"So where do you think the base is?" Bob probed, suspecting that he already knew the answer. "On or near the Paxton ranch in Australia.

Nothing else makes sense." Peter concluded. Bob nodded his concurrence. "I see. So, what do you want me to do?" Bob asked, already suspecting the answer. "I've got a man on the ground in Egypt. He's keeping tabs on Samuel Lethridge. David Lethridge is due back in Australia in a couple of days. I've got someone ready to grab him and get him out of circulation. He has a co-conspirator at the university, one Philip Hamilton-Smythe. He's already in custody, so there are no loose ends in Australia, apart from the brother, Charles.

But don't worry about him. I've organized to get him to the ranch, where we can look after him. I have a feeling that the brotherhood will be after him too, once they put two and two together. I've already sent a SEAL team to the ranch to secure the area. We swung a defence deal with the Aussie government. Said we wanted to do some covert anti-terrorism training in the outback. Away from prying eyes. There's a no-fly zone for a two hundred mile radius of the ranch for the next thirty days.

What you need to do is go home and pack a bag and get over to Andrews Air Force Base as soon as you can. I've seconded a transport to get you to Nairobi. It should be arriving any minute now. It'll leave as soon as you get to the base. Not even the flight crew know what's going on. Their purported mission is to covertly extract a couple of American citizens.

So once you've got Fullerton and the woman, you'll fly directly into Pine Gap. From there we've got a small jet that'll fly you to the ranch. By the way, you'll have another passenger too." Peter informed him.

Bob tilted his head. "Who?" he asked suspiciously. "We need to get this information into the public domain as quickly as possible. Otherwise these bastards will never leave it alone. So I've seconded a respected science reporter to accompany you. If they have found a base it'll make compelling TV.

He gets a scoop, Fullerton gets his information out to the world and we get our technology. But we need to keep a low profile on this one, Bob." Bob looked around nervously. "Who else knows?" he asked. "No-one!" Peter reassured him. "Not even the Director. We've got to keep this under wraps if we can. It's imperative we play this one close to our chest. There's too much at stake, either way this thing goes.

The transport crew haven't even logged a flight plan. It's totally covert. I picked the crew from a few buddies I use for extractions now and then. If we fail and the bad guys get Fullerton, we need to back out quietly. But if we get Fullerton, we need to keep it quiet. We also need to get a look see at that base. We need to have first dibs on the technology. Particularly if it has military potential."

"I guess I'd better be on my way then." Bob concluded. Peter nodded and reached into his coat pocket. He pulled out a small satellite phone and handed it to Bob. "This is a secure line, Alex has the number. Call me as soon as you have Fullerton. Meanwhile I'll keep you posted if anything comes up. Good luck Bob." Bob smiled as he rose to his feet. "Thanks, Peter. But I have a feeling Fullerton needs it more than me."

CHAPTER 44

Tim had lost count of the hours since they fled Cairo. On the first night they had followed the Nile then turned towards the coast. They had taken the coastal road to Sudan, then followed the Sudanese border south, past Kassala, before they crossed into Ethiopia.

Most of his waking time had been spent either driving or navigating. All the while, the roads ahead were checked for any suspicious activity. Several times they saw unidentifiable people milling around and vehicles parked in odd places. Some were armed, others perhaps not. Their intent unknown, they had managed to find alternate routes that bi-passed these potential trouble spots.

Some were short detours, others took them hundreds of miles away from their planned route. Alex had taught Tim the rudiments of the computer satellite tracking system, which he passed onto Cathy, so each could rotate. Drive, sleep then watch the computer... drive, sleep, then watch the computer. All the time keeping one ear on the short wave radio receiver.

Cathy marvelled as they skirted the outer reaches of the legendary city of Addis Ababa, sprawling across the Ethiopian plains. They were travelling south, following the famous Great Rift Valley, aiming to cross the Kenyan border near Dawfi. Cathy was driving in the country around Lake Oromiya Kilil in southern Ethiopia, while Tim slept across the back seat. Alex was intently studying the satellite image.

Suddenly Alex asked Cathy to pull over. "There's something ahead that I don't like the look of. But just up the road it looks like there's a possible detour. I would like a few minutes to check it out before I decide which road to take." he explained.

Cathy nodded her understanding and obediently pulled to the side of the road. She left the engine idling, as she watched Alex interrogate the computer. His brow was deeply furrowed in concentration as he stared at the screen. "Look at this..." he offered.

Cathy leaned over and followed Alex's finger, as it moved about the screen. "There's no radio traffic, but there are twenty or more armed men there. Manning an extensive roadblock by the looks of it. The worrying thing is that the majority of them look like civilians. I don't know for sure, but there seem to be a few Ethiopian troops among them.

Yes look at this man... definitely either militia or a regular. Yes... he's a regular. See, there is a military vehicle... and another. This does not look good at all. I don't know if they're looking for us or not, but I've got an uneasy feeling about this. There are too many civilians for a simple military roadblock. The involvement of civilians is most disconcerting, it reinforces my suspicion they are looking for us. Either way, with all that fire-power, I'm not willing to take the chance. What do you think?"

Cathy nodded her agreement. She too was keen to avoid any confrontation. "I'm with you. It looks too suspicious for me. Where to then?" she asked. Alex zoomed the screen out, then in, then out again. He continued in silence for several minutes, looking for the best way around the roadblock. He checked the alternate routes for buildings, road blocks, people, parked vehicles or anything else that might hinder their progress. Gradually he fine tuned the route, until he was satisfied that it offered their best chance of success.

When he was content with his preferred option, he began to issue the instructions to Cathy. "There's a turn to the right just up here a mile or so. It goes to a small village on the lake. It doesn't look like anyone's around, but I think we'll detour around the village just the same.

There's a small track that takes us right past the lake... down to here." he pointed. "It then follows the shoreline along here for several miles, then intersects another track coming in from the main road... over here." Again he pointed to a spot on the screen. "This should bring us out about ten miles south of the roadblock. It looks like the road's clear for the next twenty miles at least." he sighed with relief.

Cathy slipped the van into gear and turned back onto the road. A little while later, Alex pointed out the turn-off and Cathy followed it. He expertly navigated her through the various bumpy twists and turns, intersections and detours. Cathy felt at home on the rough dirt tracks. They reminded her of the cattle station roads she learnt to drive on.

Eventually they returned to the main road, and headed south. Relieved that the roadblock was behind them, Cathy soon settled back into her rhythm as they continued on their way. Cathy drove for another hour or so, then woke Tim to take over the driving. Alex was keen to continue monitoring the computer screen, as he considered this area to be the most dangerous. So Cathy grabbed a blanket and curled up on the back seat. She was asleep in minutes.

Tim had been driving for several hours when they reached a small town where fuel was available. He pulled alongside the antiquated, manually operated fuel bowser, standing forlornly outside the general store. He got out to stretch his cramped legs. Almost instantly, a tall, grey-haired, wiry man, wearing nothing but an old pair of threadbare khaki shorts, approached the vehicle and asked if he needed fuel. Tim nodded and pointed to the diesel tank cap. The man obliged, fuel was added, cash was exchanged and no questions were asked.

With a tank full of fuel, Tim resumed driving. Alex remained in the passenger's seat, carefully balancing the laptop on his knees.

After several miles, Alex became uncharacteristically quiet. Tim gave him several sideways glances, trying to see what information he was gleaning from the screen. "What are you looking at, Alex?" he finally asked. Alex frowned. "Nothing in particular. But this is potentially the most dangerous part of the journey. This is the last border crossing and we've been driving for nearly forty-eight hours. I feel you two will be missed in Cairo by now and many people will be looking for you.

Once they check that you have not left by air, they will assume you are trying to escape overland. As there are very few vehicles in this part of the country, I am having a close look at any I see ahead of us. That goes too for any vehicles I see coming up behind us. I am particularly looking to see if there are any more roadblocks, unusual traffic movements, groups of people standing near roads and that type of thing.

You were asleep when we bi-passed the last roadblock. There were about twenty men, both civilians and Ethiopian troops. I don't know whether they were looking for us or not. But we decided to err on the safe side. That Cathy of yours is some driver. I'm amazed you didn't wake up with some of the rough country we went through. Although this is a four-wheel drive van, I'm afraid it has limited off-road capabilities. And Cathy seemed to test it to its limits.

That little town back there was the last major settlement before we get to Kenya. The border is only a hundred miles or so from here. If there is anyone after us, I'm thinking they'll make their move along this stretch of road. It's very isolated out here." Tim was impressed by Alex's professionalism and considered himself lucky to have him on side. Cathy meanwhile was nestled into the rear seat trying to make up for the lack of sleep the night before. They had only travelled a few more miles when Alex asked Tim to pull over. "What's the problem, Alex?" Tim asked worriedly.

Alex pointed to the screen. "There is a vehicle parked up ahead. It may be nothing, but I would like some time to check it out before we travel too much further." Tim obediently pulled over and Alex invited him to come to the passenger's door, so they could both view the laptop screen. As he peered in through the window, Tim saw the screen zooming in on an off-white, rather battered looking, Toyota Landcruiser Troop Carrier.

Alex stated the obvious. "That's an unusual vehicle for these parts. It's mostly oil companies and the military that use them. Most of the locals use utilities if they can afford a vehicle. They're a lot more versatile."

As the screen zoomed even closer, Tim could make out three men standing around the vehicle. Alex moved the cursor over one of the men and pressed the F3 key on the laptop keypad. The screen began to zoom in on the man in question. Finally they could see him as is if he were only fifty feet below them.

Alex stared at the screen for a while then pointed at the man's back. "See this? Looks like a rifle sling." They both stared at the screen for several frustrating minutes until the man eventually turned around. "I knew it!" Alex announced proudly. "That looks like an AKM. This does not look good, my friend. I think we had best look at the other men, to see if they are armed as well."

Tim watched as the screen zoomed out, until all three men were visible. Alex placed the cursor on the second man and hit the F3 key once more. Immediately the screen zoomed in on the second man. Both Tim and Alex analysed the picture for a few seconds. Tim concluded that he too was armed. Another shift confirmed that the third man was also armed.

Alex looked at Tim. "What do you think?" he asked. "Can we go around them?" Tim asked. Alex shook his head. "Unfortunately no. Look..." He hit the F2 key and the screen zoomed out into a wider shot of the area. The road was clearly visible, as was the riverbed.

So too the long waterhole and the lone bridge crossing it. When Tim spotted the bridge, Alex's answer sunk in. "I'm guessing that bridge is the only crossing in this area." Alex nodded. "It's the only one for a hundred miles. Although the river is not flowing, its banks are very steep and impossible for this vehicle to negotiate. So what do you think? Do you want to risk the time in going back, or should we take our chances and try to cross here?"

Tim thought about it, while he stared intensely at the computer screen. They were stuck between a rock and a hard place. Finally he offered a suggestion. "What are the chances they'll shoot us on sight?" Alex shrugged his shoulders. "Not high. It's more likely they'll just stop us to verify our identity. But after that... I don't know. They may just want to take you somewhere for interrogation. They will probably be keen to know the source of your information. They will definitely want to know if you have told anyone else about it.

But us two?" Alex added in a decidedly melancholy tone. Tim heaved an audible sigh, as he pondered the dilemma. He tried to quickly think of all the possible scenarios and determine a workable solution to each of them. "Well, we can't really afford the time to go back." Tim surmised. "If these people way out here are looking for us, just imagine what's going on behind us. They could be linked to the mob at the last roadblock. That means there's an active, coordinated search going on.

No, I don't think we can risk going back. It's much safer inside Kenya. They don't seem to be so radical there. Besides, I don't think they'd be expecting us to be this far south yet. I think we should approach these blokes with caution and see what happens. After all, we have the advantage of surprise. We know they're there and they don't know that we know! Perhaps we could...?"

Alex and Tim spent some time discussing the pros and cons of each thought as it came to light. Desperately trying to cash in on their advantage of being pre-warned. Tim commented that the low afternoon sun and fading light might just work to their advantage.

While they were discussing the finer points of their favoured plan, Cathy awoke and staggered out of the van to join Tim. She walked up behind him and wrapped her arms around his waist. "What's going on?" Tim squeezed her hand affectionately and tried to down-play the seriousness of the situation. "We may have a bit of a problem up ahead. There are three armed men waiting by the side of the road. This is the only practical way into Kenya from here, so I'm afraid we're being forced to run the gauntlet."

Cathy's heart sank, as she comprehended the situation. Tim smiled reassuringly and ushered her into the van. "Look you're best lying down across the back seat and pretending you're asleep. Short of them coming inside and jabbing you with a rifle butt, you shouldn't move. OK?" he urged.

Cathy nodded. "OK. But are you sure?" she almost pleaded. "Nothing's for certain, honey, but it's our best chance. I'll sit in the seat here, opposite the sliding door. Now remember... you must play possum!"

As Tim climbed into the back of the van, Alex folded the screen down and slid the computer under the front seat, out of view. He sidled over to the driver's seat and started the engine. He clunked the vehicle into gear and slowly pulled back onto the goat track that sufficed as a road in these parts. Alex accelerated up to cruising speed and leant back towards Tim. "All OK back there?"

"As ready as we'll ever be." Tim reassured him. Tim wandered back to Cathy and sat down next to her. He reached under her jacket and retrieved the pistol from its holster. He checked that the safety was off and it was loaded.

"Just remember, for the first shot the trigger will be fairly stiff, but after that it'll be a lot easier to shoot. Look, if the shit hits the fan, I don't want you joining the fire-fight unless it's absolutely necessary. But if the worst comes to the worst..." Tim hesitated, as his mind went through the worst case options. "Well the border's only sixty or so miles from here."

"Oh, no... please don't even think like that Tim." Cathy pleaded. Tim smiled in reassurance. "Sorry, Cathy. Look, I'm sure we'll be OK. Just keep your wits about you." Tim went back to his seat and motioned for Cathy to lie down. She obediently did so, staring up at Tim with a nervous smile and frightened seal puppy eyes. He smiled back at her and motioned for her to roll over, so she was facing the back. "Now keep that pistol close to your chest, but for God's sake don't point it at anyone unless you intend to shoot them. And keep your finger next to the trigger... not on it!"

Tim then turned his attention to Alex. "How far now?" he asked, a little concern evident in his voice. "A couple of miles. Just over that small rise ahead." Alex informed him.

As they crested the rise, they saw a man, some two hundred yards ahead, walk out into the middle of the road as he saw the approaching vehicle. Alex backed off the accelerator and slowed the vehicle down. As they approached, the two other men left the, now very elongated, shadow of their vehicle and stepped up to the edge of the road. Their rifles, hanging by their slings off their shoulders, were tucked into their sides and balanced by one hand, muzzles pointing at forty-five degrees to the ground.

The man in the middle of the road was frantically waving one hand in the air, signalling his desire for the vehicle to stop. The other hand held his rifle at waste height, pointing menacingly in the general direction of the van.

As the vehicle came to a stop, the man on the road casually strolled over to the driver's side window, which Alex had wound down in preparation for the meeting. All the while his rifle was held at waist height, intimidating the driver. Alex had his elbow casually resting on the window sill, his other hand crossed in front of his chest. The airy sleeves of his off-white cotton shirt concealed the pistol resting on the sill under his elbow. He smiled as the man approached and Alex addressed him in fluent Arabic. "What can I do for you, my friend?" he asked casually.

"We are looking for Professor Tim. And I see we have found him." he smirked, through a set of yellow stained teeth. Alex smiled. "I think you are mistaken, my friend." he said sternly, in an effort to confuse the man. But the man smiled and reached into the top pocket of his shirt.

He retrieved a folded sheet of paper, which he carefully unfolded with his free hand. "I think not. We have a photograph of the Professor... see. There are people in Cairo who desire strongly to talk with you, Professor. Now if you don't mind, I will ask you to get out and join us in our vehicle."

During the conversation Cathy pretended to sleep. The man had either not seen her, or was not interested. Meanwhile, the other two men had approached the side door. One stood back a few yards, the other reached for the handle. He unlocked it and forcefully slid the door open, so that it crashed against the end stop with a loud thump.

He met Tim's cold stare with a yellow, toothy grin. He raised the rifle so the muzzle pointed in Tim's direction. Tim looked at the intimidating muzzle. He squeezed tighter on the grip of the forty-five that sat on his lap, hidden under a magazine. He noticed that the man held his finger along the trigger guard, rather than on the trigger.

Good paramilitary training he concluded. Either that or he'd watched way too many war movies. Tim's gaze switched rapidly from the muzzle of his protagonist's rifle to the muzzle pointed at Alex. He kept flicking his eyes from one to the other as the man at Alex's window talked. Soon he noticed that the weight of the rifle was taking its toll on the man at his door.

Somehow his heart did not seem to be in his work, or perhaps it was just the end of a long and tiring day. He watched intently as the muzzle lowered. Ever so slightly at first but sure enough, inch by inch, gravity was taking its toll. It was slowly but inexorably lowering. He watched until the muzzle was pointing at forty-five degrees, now threatening the floor of the van instead of Tim's butterfly infested gut.

He quickly stole a glimpse past the yellow-toothed door opener at the muzzle of the other man's rifle. He was still standing several paces from the door, looking rather torpid. He was casually gazing around the general area, paying little attention to the proceedings. Tim noticed that his rifle muzzle was still pointing at the ground. He too had his finger resting on the outside of the trigger guard.

Tim quickly flicked his eyes over to the rifle levelled on Alex. The man was just asking him to get out of the car. To emphasise the authority of his request, he motioned with a wide sweep of the rifle muzzle towards the front of the van. This was the moment Tim had been waiting for.

In an instant he brushed the magazine aside and raised his pistol. In a heartbeat two thunderous explosions rent the air, sending two rounds smashing into the chest of the nearest man. His knees instantly buckled and a horrified look crossed his face. He dropped his weapon as he hit the ground and rolled onto his back. Convulsing wildly as the two hundred and forty grain hollow point bullets did their work.

The unmistakable stain of fresh blood discoloured his threadbare khaki T-shirt, as it escaped the entry wounds and spread across his chest. The massive exit wounds in his back leaked blood prodigiously. By the time he had stopped moving, he was lying in a massive pool of blood. His lifeless body lay spread-eagled in the hot dust, his wide eyes staring mutely at the yellowing evening sky.

As soon as the first two rounds had found their mark, Tim swung the muzzle toward the second man, standing some six feet behind the first and three feet to his left. Within milliseconds, he double-tapped the pistol. Two more ear-piercing explosions reverberated inside the van. The heavy bullets found their mark with two sickening thuds.

Again the bullets had found the centre of his chest. He slumped as his body spun ninety degrees, then came crashing down, face-first into the dust. His AKM disappearing awkwardly under his pelvis as he violently flopped around. The H&K was efficient. His death throes were over in seconds. Tim maintained his bead on him as he watched the khaki singlet turn red. Blood continued oozing from the gaping exit wounds in his back for some time.

As soon as Tim's first shot rang out, Alex raised his elbow from the sill and squeezed the trigger. A series of loud explosions followed in quick succession, as he emptied five rounds into the man at his window. The brass cartridges chinked wildly, as they were ejected from the pistol and bounced around the van. The first three bullets landed in the centre of his chest, brutally tearing through his heart and lungs. As they travelled through his body, the hollow point projectiles expanded rapidly to create a vicious wound track. Only one made it all the way through his body, to exit his back and disappear into the scrub. As his knees buckled, his body slumped, the fourth shot caught him in the throat.

It clipped the spine as it tore through the jugular vein, spraying blood along the side of the van. The now deformed projectile made a mournful whining sound as is sped off into the distance. As he continued to fall, the fifth round penetrated his face, just below his right eye. It went crashing through his cheek bone, shattering into shrapnel. The hundreds of tiny fragments tore savagely through his brain, one larger piece managing to exit through a small hole in the rear of his skull.

As he slumped to the ground, his contracting finger engaged the trigger of the AKM. It loosed off a burst of five or six rounds, before it hit the ground and fell from his grasp. The bullets smashed into the ground just in front of the van, kicking up small puffs of dust, before ricocheting harmlessly in the direction of the startled birds roosting along the riverbed. The unfortunate man lay in an ignominious heap next to the van, blood slowly draining from his body, through the numerous wounds inflicted by Alex's forty-five.

Cathy let out an involuntary scream as the shooting began, but in the few seconds it took her to roll over and sit up, nervously clutching her pistol, it was all over. Tim was quick to reassure her that the situation was in hand. He walked over to her, holstering his pistol as he went. When he reached her, he quickly turned her pistol toward the side of the van, then gently prised it from her trembling hands and replaced it in her holster. "You don't need this now, Dear." he reassured her, in a low comforting tone. "I'll just put it back in here for safe keeping. Do you want to stay here while we clean up?" he asked.

Cathy looked dazed. "What? I can't hear you properly. My ears are ringing like mad. Jesus, that was louder than I expected it to be."

Tim smiled and repeated his question. Cathy shook her head. "No, thanks. I think I'll get some fresh air, if that's OK with you." she responded.

As they stood together outside the van, Tim tightly held Cathy close to him for several minutes, until she stopped shaking and both their pulses returned to something near normal. He was careful to face her away from the bodies, so she did not have to witness the unpleasant sight.

Meanwhile, Alex had alighted from the van and was surveying the carnage. "I'm impressed Tim. Two double-taps and it's all over." Tim smiled wickedly. "Well that's the way I train... when I get the chance." he explained calmly. "What'll we do with the bodies?"

Alex looked around for a few seconds. "I suggest we put them in their car and push them into the river. Out here it's unlikely that anyone heard the shots. So hopefully they won't get found until the waterhole dries up. Either way, it should buy us enough time to get to Nairobi." Tim agreed.

Alex and Tim dragged the three bodies to the Troop Carrier. Alex instinctively stripped them of their weapons and searched them for any ID. Finding nothing, they tossed them unceremoniously into the back of the Toyota and slammed the door. Tim then inspected the front of the vehicle.

In the glove compartment he found three passports. They were Egyptian. Underneath was a small, rather grubby, goatskin leather satchel. He opened it to find a large wad of cash. He proudly showed his find to Alex. "What do you think?" Alex spat on the ground. "Brotherhood of Islam!" he growled in disgust. "Look at the travelling they have done. Syria, Iran, Iraq, Pakistan, Afghanistan, Somalia, Sudan. These men have travelled extensively in the world of terrorists. And it seems they are not short of cash. Possibly bounty hunters or assassins?" Alex grunted as he stuffed the passports and wads of cash into his shirt pocket. "This may come in handy." he smirked.

Tim jumped into the driver's seat of the Toyota, wound down the window and started the engine. He drove the car two hundred yards upstream where he found a small clearing at the edge of a large algae-stained waterhole. He straightened the car up, facing it directly at the riverbank. He moved the transfer case into low range four-wheel drive and engaged first gear. As it crept towards the waterhole, he opened the door and pulled the hand throttle out. The engine revved just a little over idle speed and maintained a brisk walking pace.

About twenty yards from the river, Tim casually stepped out of the car and closed the door behind him. He walked alongside, reaching through the open window to grab the steering wheel. He steered the vehicle to within ten feet of the steep embankment that defined the rim of the waterhole. At this point, he pulled his arm out of the window and stepped back from the car. He stood mesmerised as the vehicle slowly crept toward the edge of the waterhole. It all seemed to be happening in slow motion.

As the front wheels approached the crumbling bank, it gave way. The rear wheels continued to push the vehicle over the precipice and into the water, some fifteen feet below. It seemed to float awkwardly, nose down, for some time, as water slowly leaked into the car through worn door seals. Eventually it sank to the level of the open window, then the water gushed in. Ten seconds later it had disappeared altogether.

Tim stood transfixed on the last bubbles of escaping air as they bobbed momentarily on the surface, before disappearing with an inaudible pop. Once the resultant waves had attenuated to almost imperceptible ripples, Tim smiled in satisfaction of a job well done. The car had disappeared. All that remained was a small oil slick on the clear patch of dirty yellowish water that was now void of algae.

Within a few minutes the algae redistributed across the waterhole's surface and all evidence of the vehicle disappeared. Tim broke a small branch off a nearby tree and began to clean up the tracks as best he could. He did not know why. The chance of anyone finding the car or even the tracks was so remote, the odds were almost incalculable. But old habits die hard.

Once satisfied that the tracks were at least not so obvious, he walked back to the van. Alex was cleaning the last of the blood from the side of the vehicle, while Cathy was kicking clean dirt over the bloodstained earth where the three men had died. Finally satisfied that all traces of their encounter had been erased, Tim looked at Alex with a resolute smile. "Well I guess that's that! We'd better get going, eh?" he suggested.

CHAPTER 45

There was persistent loud knocking at the door. Its ferocity and volume proclaiming the importance of the visit. Charlie rolled over and looked at the faint red numbers of the digital alarm clock through bleary eyes. It was two thirteen a.m. He mumbled to himself as he slid out of bed, his feet probing for the floor. He stood up and donned his bath robe. A monogrammed souvenir from a stay in a Hyatt Hotel on one of his early trips to the USA. As he turned the light on to find his slippers, Becky awoke and asked what he was doing.

The continuous pounding on the front door answered her question. "Who could that be at this hour?" she asked. Charlie shook his head. "No idea, but it sounds like they want us to answer the door." Suddenly Becky had a chilling thought. "Oh hell! I hope it's not the police." Charlie frowned at the thought. "Why would it be the police?"

"What if something's happened to Tim?" she suggested. Becky new nothing of the discovery. She only knew that Tim and Cathy had gone to Egypt. And with the rise of Islamic militancy, the Middle East was no longer a safe place. Charlie, on the other hand, knew the risk Tim was taking was greater than Becky could possibly imagine. The thought of something untoward happening to Tim made Charlie shiver involuntarily.

But he soon dismissed the likelihood as being improbable. Tim was smart. He was also a careful man, well capable of looking after himself. He had, after all, been to the Middle East on many previous occasions. Still, the knocking was loud and persistent. Just like the cops to wake someone in the middle of the night with bad news. He staggered off in the direction of the door, determined to put an end to the noisy intrusion.

As he opened the door, two tall, well dressed men greeted him. The American accent was all too obvious. "Are you Charles Fullerton?" one asked. Charlie nodded. "May we come in? We need to talk."

Charlie was confused. Letting two strangers into your home in the wee hours of the morning was not the normal thing to do. But after quickly considering the possibilities, he ultimately agreed to their request.

He nodded and opened the door sufficiently to allow them access and directed them to the lounge room. "Take a seat. What's this all about? Is it about Tim?" he probed. The tall man retained an emotionless face. "You need to pack a suitcase and come with us. Your wife too. You are in danger if you stay here. We need to get you to a safe place. Somewhere we can protect you."

"This is about Tim isn't it?" he insisted. The shorter man nodded. "Yes. It seems Mr. Lethridge has stirred up a hornet's nest with the Catholic Church. Tim's on their wanted list at the moment." Charlie shook his head in disbelief. "Shit! Where is he?" he asked with a great deal of concern evident in his voice.

"We don't know exactly. He was extracted from Cairo yesterday, but we haven't heard anything since. He's travelling overland to avoid the authorities. Every man and his dog's looking for him by now. We've got a plane ready to fly him to Australia. We're hoping to have him back here in a couple of days." he explained.

"Where are you taking us?" Charlie asked. "To the Paxton ranch in Queensland. That's where they'll bring Tim. But no phone calls. No-one must know where you are." he warned.

His monotone voice and cold unemotional stare gave Charlie the distinct impression that the Americans feared for their safety as well as Tim's. "What about Cathy? Is she OK?" he almost pleaded. "As far as we know. But we're not doing the extraction. The Russians are returning a favour."

Becky had slipped into the room unnoticed. Her sudden question startled Charlie. "What's going on?" she asked, looking suspiciously at the strangers. Charlie turned casually to his wife and smiled. "Becky, be a love and go pack a couple of bags." he asked."We need to leave with these gentlemen as soon as we can." he quietly explained. Becky was bewildered. "Where are we going?" she asked, shaking her head in confusion. Charlie smiled. "To Cathy's place."

CHAPTER 46

For the next sixty miles Alex drove, with Tim glued to the computer screen, searching for further trouble. But it was not to be. He zoomed into the senselessly small security hut on the border and stared at it intently. "Looks like there's only one guard there... and no vehicles. Although I did notice a single military vehicle about twenty miles south, heading for town." Alex just grunted. As he rounded the corner, he could see the lonely sentry post in the distance. He said nothing as he approached. Tim too remained silent. Cathy again played possum as she lay on the back seat, her female form covered by an old army blanket.

As Alex pulled up to the rather flimsy, whitewashed wooden boom gate, he retrieved the three Egyptian passports from his pocket and placed the equivalent of one hundred US dollars inside the cover of the top passport. The guard lazily approached the van. He looked it up and down with a cursory glance of routine nonchalance that made Tim relax a little. It was obvious he was not expecting anyone in particular.

Alex handed the guard the passports and watched his reaction carefully, his hand reassuringly stroking his concealed pistol in its holster. A smile broached the corner of the guard's mouth as he noticed the money protruding from the ends of the passport. He slowly and officiously opened the top passport and retrieved the wad of cash, counting it as he did so. Obviously used to such things and more than satisfied with the generous bribe, he folded the wad and placed it in his top pocket. He then closed the passport and handed all three back to Alex. To him, the van, its occupants and its reason for visiting Kenya were now irrelevant.

He smiled broadly as he bade him farewell. "Naharak sæ'id." Alex smiled as he accepted the passports. The guard raised the boom and motioned for them to proceed. Alex politely thanked him and drove off. "Shokran." As they left the checkpoint, Cathy quizzed Tim. It all seemed way too easy, considering what they had been through to get this far. "What did the guard say about the bribe?" she asked innocently. Alex laughed. "Nothing. He simply said *have a nice day!*

He even spoke Arabic. Guess he thought we were Egyptians from the passports. Though he obviously didn't bother to look at the photos too closely. We're not even the same skin colour! But once he saw the money, he lost all interest in us. Cash still works wonders out here." he laughed. Cathy chuckled at the naive simplicity of it all. She leaned over and gave Tim a peck on the back of the neck.

After all the excitement of the last twelve hours, they all found it hard to sleep, as they ground away at the hundreds of miles remaining between them and Nairobi. Tim and Alex now took turns to drive. Cathy manned the computer. It helped them avoid several meandering herds of goats, one wayward giraffe and a traffic accident being attended to by the local constabulary.

Just near Kilinyaga it saved them the embarrassment of running into the tail end of a small, slow-moving military convoy. But, by and large, the remainder of the trip through Kenya was uneventful.

At long last they reached the northern outskirts of Nairobi. Never before had Cathy been so pleased to see a city. She was a little surprised though, when Alex pulled over to the side of the road and parked the car, leaving the engine idling. He reached past Cathy and retrieved a satellite phone from the glove compartment. He pressed a pre-programmed number and waited.

Tim meanwhile had awoken from a shallow sleep and was wondering why they had stopped. It took him a few seconds to come to grips with what was going on. When he noticed the phone, he relaxed and slumped back into his seat. The call was answered and Alex spoke a few muffled words. The only one of which Tim caught was *OK*. Once the call was completed he returned the phone to the glove compartment and drove off. He turned around to Tim and gave him a sly wink. "Our man is ready!"

The mini-van pulled into a dark alley near the centre of the city, only a few miles from where the telephone call was made. Alex drove slowly towards a shiny black Mercedes Benz. It was parked in the shadow of a dilapidated wooden building that, judging by the faded signage, once served as a warehouse.

About twenty yards from the car he pulled up and signalled with three flashes of his headlights. Two were returned. "OK! Tim, Cathy... this is as far as I can take you. The gentleman in the car is CIA... his name is Bob. He will take you to the US aircraft for your trip home."

"Thanks, Alex. I..." Tim began, but Alex cut him off. "It's OK, my friend. You have done the same for me in the past, remember? I will do my best to protect you from this end. I have the advantage of being covertly involved. I am relatively safe. You do not have that luxury. Perhaps when this is over, we can meet again. Meanwhile you must be careful my friend."

Tim smiled as his mind raced back all those years to when he had first met Alex. It was Afghanistan, during the Russian occupation. He remembered the Mujahideen... the fire-fight... the medivac extraction. Well he did not actually remember the extraction, he was unconscious at the time, but Alex had told him all about it. But he did remember, with some fondness, the weeks in hospital lying next to Alex that followed. He smiled to himself as the memories flooded back.

"We've had some fun alright Alex! And yes... I'll look after myself and Cathy. And we'll meet up with you when it's all over. That's a promise." he said solemnly. "Tim..." A frown began to appear on Alex's brow, as he continued in an unusually serious tone of voice. "...be sure to talk with no-one. Bob is OK, but many CIA operatives have close ties with the Church of Rome. Not even the aircrew will know who you are. No-one must know that you are back in Australia. It will be safer that way. Avoid your home and familiar places. Take refuge in the outback. Take care my friend."

Tim and Alex embraced, then Cathy gave Alex a hug and a peck on the cheek. "Thanks, Alex. It's been really nice meeting you. And if he can't look after me, then I'll just have to look after him!" she offered spryly.

They grabbed their luggage and headed towards the Mercedes. As they approached, a man alighted and swiftly walked to meet them. He was tall, lean and well groomed. His shortly cropped dark hair was military in style. He carried himself well, striding with almost arrogant confidence. He wore neatly creased black dress pants and a newly starched white cotton shirt. His black polished shoes stood out as a stark rarity in Africa, where scuffed footwear and bare feet were the norm.

His strong southern US accent was obvious as he greeted them. "Hi... I'm Bob!" he said warmly. "Tim... and Cathy..." Tim offered, as they shook hands. "Let's get this kit stowed and get the hell out of here. The locals are a bit on edge at the moment. But I don't think they're looking for you here just yet. I trust you're carrying." Tim nodded. "Yeah."

"Both of you?" Bob asked, feeling out the new couple. Tim nodded. "Good! We've intercepted a lot of comms traffic about you two. The Supreme Islamic Council has seconded the services of the Brotherhood of Islam. They're a ruthless bunch of bastards.

And they've got contacts everywhere. Their network is so complex, even we don't know the half of it." he rued. "Funny you say that!" Tim added. "We've got a couple of AKM's and some spare mags in our luggage too. A gift from a couple of the Brothers." Tim explained. "Where did you run in to them?" Bob asked, with a hint of urgency in his voice. "Just north of Dawfi.

Three of them had a roadblock set up at the only river crossing for hundreds of miles, so we decided to chance it. Alex had a spy satellite hook-up to a laptop in the van, so we knew they were there. That helped!" Bob was impressed. "Did you talk with them?" he asked, trying to extract as much Intel as he could while he had the chance. Tim nodded. "Yes. Well, at least Alex did before we shot them. Seems they didn't want us dead. At least not yet. They said they were going to take us back to Cairo. From there who knows?"

"From the intercepts we've made, the Brotherhood is fully aware of the situation and are obviously willing to do anything to stop you. However, unless your roadblock team reported to anyone when they found you..." Tim shook his head. "No they didn't get the chance. We smoked them almost as soon as they recognised us. And we didn't find a radio or satellite phone in their vehicle. " he explained.

"What did you do with the bodies?" Bob asked casually. "Put them back in their car and dumped it into a waterhole. Hopefully they won't be discovered for quite a while." Tim explained.

"Good job. That means they still don't know you've left Egypt yet. You're extremely lucky Alex extracted you when he did. A few more hours and you wouldn't have made it out. Intel suggests that every border crossing from here to Egypt is now sealed tighter than a fish's arse at fifty fathoms. I don't think a stray dog could get through at the moment." Tim and Cathy looked at each other in relief as they followed Bob.

They climbed into the car and settled into the comfortable leather of the rear bench seat. Both sighed audibly as the car started and the cool air-conditioned air hit their hot and dusty faces. It was such a luxury after the drive in the Spartan mini-van. Bob reversed out of the lane and meandered through the narrow streets, as he headed towards the airport.

A few minutes later he struck up a conversation. "Do you know a David Lethridge?" he asked. Tim nodded. "Yes, he's the History Dean at Melbourne Uni. Why?" But Bob did not answer. Instead he continued with another question. "And a Philip Hamilton-Smythe?" Again Tim nodded. "Yes, he also works at the university. He's the Chemistry Dean there. Why do you ask?"

Tim suspected the worst and Bob confirmed it for him. "Well... they're the ones you've got to thank for all this. Apparently your brother stirred their greedy interest with some polymer research. Lethridge is connected to the Church of Rome. He's the one who informed the Holy Alliance of your doctoral thesis. His brother stole your work and sent it to the Vatican. But I guess you knew that already. Anyway, you've been on their official watch list ever since. So one thing led to another and he got a couple of CD's from your house. Interesting shit so I hear."

"Damn, I was looking at a couple of the discs with photos of the gallery and I forgot to put them in the vault before I left." he stated apologetically. "You have a vault?" Bob asked. "Yeah, but it's not at my house, it's on a mate's farm. It's a secret stash I organized after my house was burgled. I wanted somewhere safe to keep stuff." Bob was impressed. "Smart move. It may just save your skin if they think others know about this too.

It appears as though your house has been ransacked. They've been looking for the rest of your information. But if they failed to find it, you might be lucky.

They may think you've given it to other people. Once too many people are involved, they know they can't keep it quiet. Speaking of which. What's your strategy?" Bob asked as casually as he could. "What do you mean?" Tim asked. "What are you going to do when you get home?" Bob elaborated. "Go bush!" Tim offered almost jokingly. Bob nodded. "Then what? You can't stay hidden for long. Someone will find you sooner or later. Meanwhile your families and friends will be at risk." Tim conceded his point. "I guess so. What's your suggestion?" he asked, assuming his new minder had a plan.

"Get it out in the open as quickly as you can. Once it becomes general knowledge they can't stop it. It's too late." Bob proposed. Tim shrugged his shoulders. "How do we do that without risking the ransacking of the information and relics?" Tim asked. "Be discrete with your informing source. Use someone of influence... like a well-known and respected science journalist. Take them to your source. Blindfold them if necessary to keep the location secret.

Let them take photos. Give them physical evidence... lots of it. Let them inform the world. Then... and only then... will you be safe. It may take several years for the ramifications to filter through. But after that you'll be seen as a hero figure. By some at least. Others may still want to see you punished."

Tim was a little taken aback. "Punished? For what?" Bob laughed. "For heresy, blasphemy or whatever. Religion is an unforgiving institution, full of blind zealots. But as long as the Government's on your side you should be OK." Tim shook his head. "Thanks for the cheery outlook!" Bob laughed once more. "That's OK. Just preparing you for what's ahead."

"So, is this plan of yours optional, or do you already have wheels in motion?" Tim asked, already pretty sure of the answer. "You catch on fast don't you?

We... the US Government... are extremely interested in your somewhat serendipitous find. But we can't be seen to be overtly meddling in such a messy situation. Even some of our own people wouldn't like the ramifications of this. But covertly, yes we have put some options in place for you to consider." he admitted.

The car left the southern city confines and accelerated onto the open road. A short while later they entered the grounds of the airport. As they approached a checkpoint, Bob asked them to say nothing. He slowed the car as he approached the flimsy red and white striped wooden barrier. He pulled to a gentle stop some three feet from it.

A smartly uniformed man approached the car. He was from the Kenyan army. "Your papers please sir." Bob handed the soldier a dossier. The guard thumbed through it slowly, as Tim and Cathy watched nervously from behind the heavily tinted glass of the rear passenger compartment. Tim noticed the soldier open an envelope that had been buried deep within the file.

His eyes remained riveted on the contents for some time before returning the remainder of the dossier to Bob. With the envelope stuffed into his trouser pocket, he motioned to the sentry box. The boom slowly rose and the soldier waved the car through.

Some hundred yards down the road Tim broke the awkward silence. "What was in the envelope? Bribe money?" he asked, pretty sure that he was right. "Yes sir...ee!" Bob exclaimed rather gleefully. Tim nodded. "It's good to see that still works here too.

It must have cost Alex a bloody fortune in bribes to get us down here. It seems that every person we met had their hand out. Although we did recoup some of his losses when we discovered a large sum of cash in the glove compartment of the vehicle at Dawfi." Tim explained. "Money still buys entry with no questions in most places around here.

Most of these poor bastards live on a pittance. A hundred US dollars is a fortune to them." Bob explained. "For that they'd be willing to kill ten men and smuggle you around themselves." he added coldly. "Ah! There's our plane." he announced.

"So, you're coming with us, Bob?" Tim asked, as casually as he could. "Someone's got to look after you." Bob joked. "What about Charlie?" Tim added as an afterthought. Bob shrugged his shoulders. "He and his wife have been relocated. And your parents are OK, Cathy. They're still at the ranch. We have men on the ground looking out for them." he explained. "Why?" Cathy asked, unsure of the connection. "

As I said. It's in our vested interests to have this find of yours secured. We don't know exactly where it is yet, but we do know it's important, both archaeologically and technically. And we're assuming it's somewhere on the ranch." he offered.

"Ah! So you want first dibs on the technical stuff?" Tim concluded. Although such a conclusion was not rocket science. "Of course!" Bob confirmed rather enthusiastically. "That's how we've kept ahead of the rest of the world these last fifty years or so." he boasted. "Roswell?" Tim offered. "Exactly!" Bob confirmed. Tim smiled. Perhaps all Charlie's conspiracy theories weren't so crazy after all.

"Well I guess I'd rather the USA have this technology than some of the less friendly regimes. One thing though, the energy sector isn't going to like this." Tim speculated. "Why?" Bob asked, his interest piqued. "I think we've stumbled onto a fairly significant power source. And it doesn't seem to use any fuel or create any pollution. I have no idea how it works.

Charlie understands these things better than I do. I guess that'll take some serious reverse engineering. Although there are dozens of manuals that may just need interpreting.

But surely the energy companies won't like it." he suggested morosely. But Bob disagreed. "They can be pretty ambivalent. But generally, as long as they maintain their monopoly and make a profit, they'll be happy. Regardless of their energy source. Besides, if it is clean power, they can earn some brownie points from the greenies for a change."

The car came to a stop some twenty yards from a massive navy grey multi-engine jet. Obviously a very capable intercontinental transport plane. It was sitting alone on a remote apron near the southwest end of the runway. Far away from the prying eyes of the commercial administration buildings and passenger terminals.

A man in a US military flying suit stood to attention as the car glided to a smooth halt. As Bob alighted, the aviator strode purposefully toward the car. Cathy and Tim watched from the seclusion of the car's interior as a short conversation ensued. As the man left, Bob returned to the car and opened the door. "This is it. They've been waiting for us. We'll be leaving in a few minutes, so you'd better grab your things and follow me. Just remember, they think you're US citizens that I've secretly extracted. So don't say anything unless you can fake a pretty good American accent."

CHAPTER 47

The plane touched down with a series of lurching thuds, accompanied by the squealing of heavily laden tyres. Tim peered through of the small porthole, but saw nothing. It was a moonless night, black as pitch. "Where are we?" Tim asked in a near whisper. "Pine Gap... just north-west of Alice Springs. It's 2 a.m. local time, so we can get you out under the cover of darkness. Away from prying eyes. We have a plane waiting. We have a passenger too..." Bob explained.

"Who?" Tim asked suspiciously. "A journalist by the name of Adam Spencer. Heard of him?" Tim nodded. "Yes... and what about you?" Bob nodded. "I've been assigned to protect you both. And I need to see this base. It's OK. When we get to the station we've seconded your uncle and his helicopter to take us to the base. You can blindfold us if you like." he offered.

"What good is that?" Tim countered. "You've probably got a GPS tracker on you to lead your buddies straight to us." Bob shook his head. "I thought of that, but decided against it. Look you've got to trust someone some time. And it might as well be us. We need someone of your calibre to show this to the world and leave us in the background. That way you can apply for the technology patents and sell them to our preferred contractors. It's all very political. But trust me. We want you to get something out of this as well. You're our plausible deniability factor." he explained rather obliquely. "Your what?" Tim asked.

Bob smiled. "We need someone to take the focus off the involvement of the CIA in this. Call it a PR thing if you like. You become rich and famous. We covertly get our technology. We use our influence, or our military might if necessary, to pacify the religious zealots.

We replace religion with booze, sport, shopping, leisure activities, movies... intergalactic holidays. People keep consuming, companies keep earning profits and the world remains a happy place." Tim shook his head. "Hell, the politics are too scary for me. I'll just take the money and run.

But I would eventually like to turn the base into a museum. Some of the relics there are priceless." Tim tried to explain. "OK." Bob answered all too quickly. "OK?" Tim questioned. "Why the hell not? I'm not interested in relics. It's the technology we're after." Bob explained. "Oh! OK then." Tim muttered in confusion.

The lumbering aircraft slowly taxied to its designated apron, gradually slowing down before it came to a sudden, lurching stop. The massive jet engines were eventually shut down and they waited in the ensuing silence for the word to disembark.

A few minutes later, one of the flight crew poked his head through the interconnecting door. "You're OK to disembark now." They filed out of the passenger area and grabbed their baggage from the niche among the boxes of unknown cargo where they had left it. They followed the flight crew as they strolled through the cargo bay to the loading ramp at the rear of the aircraft. As they walked down the ramp Cathy reached for Tim's hand and whispered. "Are we going to be alright?"

Tim squeezed her hand as a comforting gesture. "Of course, Dear. If the wost comes to the worst, we'll spend the rest of our days in decadent luxury. Cruising the world on a massive luxury liner as Mr and Mrs Smith." Tim he jokingly reassured her. "You mean that?" she purred. "What the cruise?" Tim asked naively. "No! The Mr and Mrs Smith?" she said as she raised her eyebrows. "Of course!" Tim responded with a little smirk. Cathy reached up and gave him a gentle kiss on the lips. "I love you..." she purred.

A contingent of uniformed men appeared out of the darkness, as the small group stepped off the loading ramp. The leading man saluted the flying officer and mumbled something inaudible to the others. The flying officer stopped and waited for the others to catch up. "Your aircraft is ready. Jump into the Hummer and they'll take you over to it." Bob nodded. "Thanks for the flight." A military Humvee pulled alongside the small group and a burly marine sergeant stepped out.

He grabbed Cathy's baggage and motioned the three of them to get into the car. Luggage secured, they were driven some two thousand yards to an awaiting small, twin-engine jet aircraft. "Here you are. The pilot's on his way. He should be here in a few minutes." They were left standing in the dark for eight minutes, before a set of headlights slowly approached from the direction of some dimly lit buildings on the far eastern side of the tarmac.

They watched as a small wiry figure emerged from the vehicle. "Hi! I'm Archie, your pilot." Another figure emerged from the shadows to join them. Bob addressed the pilot as he introduced the jet-lagged trio. "Bob... Tim... and Cathy. And this I presume is Adam." Adam nodded wearily. "Hi... Adam Spencer. Pleased to meet you all." he said, as he offered his hand.

Introductions dispensed with, they set about loading their baggage and themselves into the plane. Although only a twelve-seater, the plane was well decked out for comfort. The wingtip fuel tanks and lack of visible call-sign identification indicated this plane was used for covert long distance flying. They engaged in some low-key chitchat with Adam, fending off the barrage of questions with the promise that words were of little value. Seeing would be believing. For the moment all they wanted was a shower and a good night's sleep. The sleep they could get now. The shower, unfortunately, would have to wait.

Several hours later, Tim and Cathy were woken from their sleep by the unmistakable bouncing of an aircraft landing on a dirt strip. Cathy quickly looked out the window to see the homestead sweep by, as the plane decelerated in a trailing cloud of choking red dust. It took longer than normal to pull up a jet aircraft on a dirt strip, but the pilot seemed well experienced in such things.

As the aircraft came to a stop at the end of the runway, Cathy could see several people waiting. She peered through the dust trying to recognize them. As she saw her mother waving, her heart skipped a beat. She didn't know whether it was excitement or relief. Either way, she was glad to be home.

Stepping from the aircraft into the crisp early morning air, Cathy paused and drew in a deep breathe. God that felt good! As she reached the bottom of the stairs, Dot rushed up to her with wide-open arms. The two met and embraced each other in silence for some time. Eventually Dot released her python-like grip. "Oh, Cathy... it's so good to see you. Are you OK?"

Cathy smiled reassuringly. "Of course we're OK. Why wouldn't we be?" Brett casually wandered over to give Cathy a hug. He too was excited to see her, but protocol demanded he hide his feelings. "Welcome home, Darling. What's this?" During his hug he had felt the pistol, still nestled in the holster under Cathy's left arm. He pulled back her sweater and baulked when he saw what it was.

"Jesus! What's that about?" he gasped in horror. "Don't worry, Dad." Cathy quickly assured him. "We were... Well just call it insurance. We've been travelling covertly with a Russian agent through some dangerous places. Egypt, Sudan, Ethiopia and Kenya. It's pretty exciting really. But we're OK. When we get a chance to sit down, I'll tell you all about it." Brett shook his head in disbelief.

His little girl running around Africa carrying a gun was not his idea of fun. "God, since these soldiers have turned up, your mother and I have been worried sick about you. We still don't have a clue what's going on." he confessed.

"You needn't have worried, Dad. I was in perfectly good hands. Tim has some dear friends in some strange places. Several of them helped us when it got a bit heated." Brett just shook his head in disbelief. But try as he might to suppress it, the unmistakeable smile on his face betrayed his elation. Cathy was home and she was safe. That was all that mattered.

Tim soon joined Cathy. Brett reached out his hand and shook Tim's warmly. Dot gave him an affectionate hug. Brett and Dot could not thank him enough for bringing Cathy home safely. As they walked toward the homestead Tim looked over to Brett. "I can't see Charlie. Is he here yet?" he asked, a little worried about his brother's wellbeing. "Yes." Brett assured him. "He and Becky are staying here with us. They're up at the house, keeping a low profile."

Charlie and Becky were sitting on the veranda, sipping cups of tea and looking out over the endless savannah that was the cattle station. They had been there since piccaninny light. The marines had told them of Tim and Cathy's imminent arrival the night before. They had seen the plane land and knew Tim and Cathy were on board.

They had decided to remain at the homestead to allow Brett and Dot some private time with them first. But when they saw them approaching the house, they could no longer contain their relief. They jumped up excitedly and raced towards them. As they met, Charlie embraced his brother. "G'Day Tim. How the hell are you? We've been worried shitless about you!" he confessed. "Great... and you?" Tim responded. "Bored out of my skull." Charlie informed him.

"I haven't been able to leave the homestead since we got here." Tim then turned to Rebecca. "Hi Becky, how are you? How was your trip?" She gave him a warm hug. "Great... but look at you. You look tired. And you must be Cathy. I've heard so much about you." Cathy stretched out her hand. "Hi Rebecca, so good to meet you at last. The boys have told me all about you. How's your mother?" Rebecca smiled. "She's wonderful. Upset that the boys never came to see her though." she added.

Tim looked about as he heard muffled conversations. Bob was at the gate talking with a group of heavily armed men from his SEAL team. They were dressed in black cargo pants and black T-shirts. Tim turned to Brett. "Sorry about this Brett. I had no idea this would happen." he apologised.

Brett smiled. "It's OK. I guess I'm ready to retire now anyway. I'll probably lose the station, but I hope I'll be well compensated for it." Tim leant over to whisper in his ear. "Remember, that gold bar we gave you. There's thousands more where that came from. And there's a fortune in ancient coins as well. I think compensation you'll get will be a pittance compared with that."

Brett smiled and patted Tim on the shoulder. "Let's hope it all works out OK then. Now who's this... his face seems familiar?" Cathy looked over at Adam, then back to her father. "Oh, sorry Dad, this is Adam Spencer. He's a science reporter. You've probably seen him on TV every now and then. We're going to let him release the information about the base. He's sort of our insurance policy. Sorry Adam." she added with a smile.

"That's OK." Adam admitted. "If this story's half as big as I'm led to believe, I can take all the crap you can dish out to me." Tim slapped him on the back, then turned to Charlie. "I guess they'll want us to take them to the base tomorrow, so we better get some gear together. I suppose the military ration packs will save us a lot of bother with meals."

Cathy was excited with the prospect of returning to the base. She so wanted to share the experience with her father. "Have you seen it yet?" she asked excitedly. Brett shook his head. "No. They won't let us out of their sight. They have men set up with dogs all over the place.

They've even got radar operating to detect any aircraft. They tell me it's a Federal no-fly zone, although there seems to be a lot of military aircraft activity. Helicopters and jets coming and going all hours of the day. They also reckon they have four military satellites watching every square inch of the station. Pretty scary stuff really, but they seem a great bunch of blokes.

I haven't felt threatened at all. I guess we're getting used to them. And your mother's spoiling them rotten with homemade cakes and biscuits every day. These boys seem particularly keen on the Anzac biscuits." Cathy smiled at her father. "Do you want to come with us tomorrow?" Brett looked over at the soldiers gathered around the aircraft. "You think they'll let me?" Cathy smiled. "Sure, why not?"

CHAPTER 48

The house was in total darkness as the two silhouetted figures peered through the lounge window. As they approached the front door they moved with practiced stealth, like cats stalking their prey. Upon reaching the door they disappeared, melding into the deep shadow of the house. The waning moon tried in vain to break through the low rain-laden clouds to expose the intruders, but it was not be. They had picked the perfect night for a covert operation.

It was three fifty in the morning and the street slept. They remained fixed to the spot for some time, ears cocked, listening intently for the slightest sound. There was nothing, save the faint mournful wail of a lonely dog, many miles distant. Finally the taller of the two nodded to his accomplice. It was time to move.

The shorter figure retrieved a skeleton key set from his jacket pocket and began expertly picking the lock. Within seconds it clicked. He smiled with satisfaction as he turned the door handle and gently pushed. The door swung open with the faintest of creaks and the two men slipped inside, quietly closing the door behind them.

Without uttering a word, they both retrieved small Maglite torches from their pockets and switched them on. They instinctively flashed the small but powerful beams around the entrance hall. They were alone. If anyone was home they should be in bed. That was the plan. All they had to do was find the master bedroom.

The torches probed the enshrouding darkness, searching hither and yon for a corridor that would lead to the bedroom. It was not to be. Off the entrance hall were two exiting arches. One invited guests into the spacious lounge area, the other led to the open plan kitchen.

The taller of the two took the lead and headed for the kitchen, some urgency in his gait. The other man saw his move and quickly followed in his wake. Impatiently slashing the torch beam through the darkness, the taller one soon found what he was looking for. In the left hand corner of the opposite wall was another archway. It disappeared into a dark corridor that promised to lead to the bedrooms.

The tall one flashed his torch beam in the direction of his partner in crime to grab his attention. He then pointed the beam at the corridor and strode off. Although he was a big man, his steps were practiced and silent, as he searched the corridor for exits that would mark the bedrooms. He stopped at the first door.

It was half way along the corridor on his left. It was open. He hesitated a few seconds to allow his associate to catch up. Then he placed a large hand in the middle of his chest, as reiteration for him to stay put.

Satisfied that his desire had been understood, he stepped through the doorway into the bedroom. As he sliced the torch-beam around the room, he noticed the queen-sized bed in the middle of the room. It was neatly made and decidedly empty. He probed the extremities of the room but found no other exit, indicating the absence of an ensuite. This, he concluded, was a secondary bedroom.

He rejoined his shadow and stealthily continued along the corridor. A few paces on his right was a second doorway. It too was open. Again it was empty. Again the conclusion was that it was a secondary bedroom. They moved on. At the end of the corridor a third door beckoned. It too was ajar.

This had to be the master bedroom. They shone their torch beams onto the floor to minimize the light scatter as they entered the room. They need not have bothered. Although this was obviously the target of their search, it too was empty.

As they looked around their hearts sank. They were too late. An open suitcase on the unmade bed, half filled with clothes. The draws in the chests, several still agape and spewing underclothes. The open wardrobe doors and the empty hangers scattered randomly on the bed and the floor. It was all too obvious. The occupants had left in a hurry. The frustration spilled over into verbal anger.

"Damn it! Looks like Charles has gone. I wonder who tipped him off. Better have a quick look around while we're here to see if he left any clues."

After a rudimentary but fruitless search, the intruders agreed that their quarry had escaped. They had no idea how close they had been. Charlie had left with the Americans less than an hour before.

The two men conferred in the glow of their torches before they left. "Well looks like the professor hasn't been home yet." the tall one concluded. "His house looks the same as it did a week ago. I guess he's still in Africa somewhere. Funny though. Even with all our contacts, we haven't heard a god-damned thing. It's like he disappeared off the face of the earth."

"What do we do from here?" the small man snarled. The tall man shook his head briskly. "We go to Cathy Paxton's place!"

CHAPTER 49

The next morning Tim, Cathy, Brett, Charlie, Adam and Bob prepared themselves for the trip to the base. Satisfied that all his gear was in order, Bob casually wandered over to Tim and informed him of the imminent arrival of the helicopter. "The chopper should be here in ten minutes or so." Tim smiled at Bob and gave him a sly wink. "That's OK Bob, I think we'll drive. Adam doesn't know where the hell he is and you blokes will find it two seconds after we fire up the power supply anyway. What do you reckon Brett?"

"Sounds OK to me, Tim. Like you say, we've lost control of it now anyway. We might as well just hand it over to Bob." Bob looked rather surprised, but was pleased with the unsolicited offer. "OK. Sounds good to me. I'll feel a lot better this way. We can pinpoint the base and I can get some men to guard it while we're in there. Well... I'm ready!"

Three Hummers with two armed special force marines in each were soon waiting at the gate for the group and their equipment. Dot looked over at the intimidating military vehicles, then grabbed Cathy's arm. She turned her toward her father, then looked at them both with a tear welling in the corner of her left eye. "Do you have to go?" she pleaded. "Yes Mum, but we'll be back in a couple of days. Don't worry, we're in good hands. When we get back we can all have a nice relaxing holiday." she assured her.

Dot smiled, but was unconvinced. She turned to Tim "You look after them, Tim. Won't you? Promise?" Tim nodded as he patted the concealed butt of his pistol. "Of course I will." he assured her.

The ride to the cave in the Hummer was worse than Tim had expected. Brett and Bob were in the lead car.

Tim and Cathy were in the middle car and Charlie and Adam were bringing up the rear. Each rut was amplified by the tight suspension of the military vehicles. The width of them made creek beds and ruts seem like canyons at times, though enigmatically, at other times the ride seems to be as smooth as if they were on a paved road.

After many interminable hours of bumping and grinding, they eventually reached their destination. "Well we're back, Charlie. How do you feel?" Tim asked, as they stood in front of the cave. Charlie looked around at those accompanying them. "A little nervous. I've got to be honest with you. I didn't expect this much attention."

Tim nodded. "Well Bob's assured us it'll be OK. I guess we've just got to trust him from here on." he confessed. Charlie nodded. "I guess so... but keep your eyes open anyway. We don't want anyone double-crossing us. If we die out here, no-one will ever know. Shit, no-one even knows you two are back in the country."

"Yeah, scary thought!" Tim conceded. "But I've got a good feeling about this. If we can't trust Bob, there are precious few others out there with enough clout to make a difference. Remember we're up against the bad side of organised religion. At the very least the Church of Rome and the Islamic Council. I'm not sure where Mossad sits with all this, but my guess is the Israelis aren't going to be all that happy about this stuff either. So the way I see it... it's Bob or nothing! So, let's go, eh?" he finally suggested.

Tim and Charlie took control of the equipment. They sorted out what they needed and allocated gear for each person to carry. Meanwhile the soldiers were hiding the Hummers inside the cave system, setting up communications with the base camp and setting a perimeter around the cave entrance.

Soon enough it was time to go. Tim and Charlie began lighting Tilley lamps and handing them out. When everyone had their gear and a lit lantern, Tim looked at Cathy, then Charlie and heaved a heavy sigh. "Well, here goes nothing." he offered.

He led them past the impressive cave painting, stopping for a few minutes to allow Bob to cast a cursory eye over it. Then he led them into the dank, inky blackness of the cave system. Past their old camping spot, straight to the rubble pile at the back of the cave.

Tim looked over at the debris then across to Bob. "Well, it gets a bit slow for a while here, while we clear away some of this rubble. But we're nearly there." Tim led the group over the rubble piles until they came to the final blockage. "We have to clear this away and crawl through here. It shouldn't take too long with six of us."

Everyone pitched in to remove rocks from the concealed entrance. Slowly a hole began to appear. As it grew larger, Cathy could feel a noticeable increase in her pulse rate. She looked over at Tim, resting against the wall. "Nearly there! My pulse is racing." Tim smiled. "Mine too. I'm so excited, I can hardly contain myself. I wonder how Charlie's going."

Charlie heard his name and threw the large rock he was holding onto the face of the pile behind him. "What? I heard my name mentioned." Tim smiled. "Oh, we were just saying how excited we were to be going back in. We were wondering if you were feeling the same." Charlie nodded. "Sure am. I can hardly wait to see Brett's face when he sees the base. Not to mention Bob and Adam."

Another half an hour and the way was cleared sufficiently to allow access through the broken doorway. Tim crawled up to the hole and volunteered to go first. The rest followed in mute single file.

They regrouped just inside the corridor. "Have a look at the finish on the walls, Adam. I've only ever seen this on polished granite or marble in the flashest hotels. It's so smooth it almost looks vitrified." he explained. "It's bloody incredible. Is the entire base like this?" Bob mused. "Yes... only better. Wait till you see the accommodation block of the Lord Guardian."

"The who?" Adam asked, showing keen interest. "The Lord Guardian. He was the bloke in charge of the military presence on earth. All the bases including this one." Tim explained. "You mean there are more bases?" Adam asked incredulously. "Yes... and I'll be surprised if Bob doesn't know of at least two of them." Tim suggested. Bob's ears pricked at the mention of his name. He sidled over to Tim and joined in the conversation. "And what bases would they be?" he asked a little cynically. "The Tibetan ice cave... and Lake Vostok... in Antarctica." Tim touted.

"OK. We know something's there. But we're not sure what just yet." Bob confessed. "You sure they're alien bases Tim?" he asked. Tim nodded. "Sure! I'll show you the maps, once we get the lights on."

Tim grabbed Cathy's hand and led the party down the long corridor. As they walked, the dancing flames of the kerosene lanterns reflected off the highly polished walls, giving the granite a surreal life of its own. Their strangely animated shadows obediently followed the group as they headed deep into the mountain.

Tim maintained a low key conversation about the other bases with Bob and Adam until he reached the T-intersection. Here he veered left and headed toward the power plant. "I reckon we ought to fire up the generator first. That way we can explore the base in full light." he suggested. "That's assuming it fires up again. But I bet old Bob here will be more interested in the spacecraft once he sees them." he teased. Bob stopped and raised his lamp to fully illuminate the back of Tim's head.

He stared disbelievingly at him for a few seconds. Then he rushed up to him excitedly, grabbing him on the shoulder. He spun him around to face him. For the first time since they had met, Tim noticed an air of excitement in his voice. "You never mentioned spacecraft before!" he gasped.

"You never asked!" Tim chided. "Besides, we've told no-one about them. Or anything else for that matter. Only about the map we found in an ancient book. The map that led us to Abydos and the Hall of Records.

Although rumour has it that some careless sod was caught trying to analyse some of the tools and stuff we found here." He turned in mock glare toward Charlie, who felt it necessary to defend his actions. "I'm sorry. I only wanted an independent third party to verify what we'd found. All was going well until we left that bloody specimen in the electron microscope. Besides, I didn't know Lethridge was such a bastard. By the way, what's he up to now?"

They all instinctively turned to Bob. The enigmatic, shadowy figure from the CIA. He looked back for a while, staring emotionlessly at Tim. Finally he cracked a sardonic smile. "He's on sabbatical at the moment, with his colleague Phillip. We were unsure exactly how much they knew of this, so we decided to keep them under wraps until this thing blows over. We're keeping close tabs on his brother too. The minute he tries to leave Egypt we'll grab him."

"Where are they?" Tim asked, not really expecting an answer. Bob smiled rather disturbingly. "Let's just say they're safely out of the way. Now about these spacecraft? Where are they and how many are there?" he continued, quickly changing the subject. "Well they're in the cavern beyond the power generator." Tim explained. "You'll see them once we turn on the lights. There are three large ones they used for intergalactic travel and a dozen or more little ones.

They used these for small trips around the earth or to Mars and Nibiru." he explained. Bob stopped and looked rather puzzled. "Nibiru? I thought that was just a legend." he stated. Tim smiled. "It was. Until we found out it used to be a colony of the Anunnaki, like Mars. But it was destroyed by a stray comet. We can see what's left of it as the asteroid belt between Mars and Jupiter." Bob was amazed. "I'll be damned! So you've had a look at these spacecraft then?" Tim nodded. "Of course! We had a good look inside one large one and one small one.

Interesting propulsion system, eh Charlie?" Charlie nodded. "Yeah, looks like an electro-gravidic drive of some sort." he said rather casually. "You know about these things? I thought that stuff was classified." Bob retorted. "I read the underground papers." Charlie explained. "Of course you do!" The cynical note in his voice made Charlie cringe defensively, but Bob was astute enough to recognize his error and quickly moved to defuse the situation. "Sorry for being facetious, but those god-damned newspapers make if near impossible to keep anything a secret any more. So, tell me about the spacecraft."

"They're just around the corner. After we fire up the power and get some lights turned on, we'll take you there. But once you see them, everything else on the base will just be blasé." Tim explained, chuckling to himself as they headed toward the power generator.

Although Adam had been very quiet Tim knew he was inwardly trying to come to grips with it all. He would have time enough for questions later. "Well here we are. Have a look at that will you?" Everyone stopped as one and instinctively raised their Tilley lamps to throw extra light on the large, shiny, metallic object in front of them. Tim allowed them a couple of minutes for the enormity of the golden orb to sink in. Bob was the first to speak. "Is that what I think it is?"

Charlie nodded. "Sure!" he offered in jest "It's a generator." Bob did not see the funny side. The spectacle had temporarily robbed him of his sense of humour. "No smart-arse... gold?" he insisted. Charlie laughed. "Oh, yeah. It's gold alright. Must be tons of it. Except for the legs underneath of course. They're silver I think, or maybe platinum, now I think of it. I think they've got something to do with the power flow or the fuel... or the cooling... or all three. When we reverse engineer it, we'd better start by going underneath. Something we haven't done yet."

Charlie took over the lead and drew the rest of the throng towards the flickering lamplight reflecting off the metal sphere. They all stood in silent contemplation as the dancing flames of their lamps made the golden ball twinkle in a bizarre vision of false animation. They were mesmerized as a bird is by a snake, staring silently at the mountain of gleaming precious metal. Everyone was drawn to touch the marvel. Tentatively at first with gentle strokes. It was decidedly cold.

Adam finally rapped on the generator with his knuckles, receiving a dull metallic thud in return. The shell appeared to be quite thick. Tim finally decided enough time had been consumed. He slapped Charlie on the shoulder and suggested they fire up the generator. Bob and Adam followed keenly, but Brett remained transfixed, staring at the shimmering golden mass.

Cathy sidled up and grabbed her father's arm, gently squeezing it with childish affection. "Wait till you see it in the light." she teased. Brett was already overwhelmed. "Oh Cathy... that's the most incredible thing I've ever seen. All these years it's been here and I had absolutely no idea!" he rued. Cathy smiled. "Wait till you see the rest of the base, there's some really fascinating stuff here. Come on Dad. Let's join the others. This is the interesting bit."

By the time they rejoined the others, Tim and Charlie were both seated in front of the power control console. Under the glittering light of four lanterns, Tim was re-familiarizing himself with the operator's manual. Charlie was patiently waiting to start up the generator. Finally Tim put down the book and nodded at Charlie. "Ready?" Charlie nodded. "Is the Pope a Catholic?" Tim winked. "He is for now!"

Tim had one final look across the panels, then addressed Charlie. "Alright... just follow the switching sequence as I call it." Charlie nodded once more. "OK!" The two worked quickly to follow the start-up sequence as before. Only this time they intently watched the small red indicating light, that showed the generator was working.

Finally, as the sequence ended, to their mutual relief, the small light began to glow. "Thar she blows!" Charlie exclaimed excitedly. "Great! Now to hit the lights." Tim suggested. The familiar and somehow comforting, nebulous green glow began to gather intensity in the vault of the ceiling as the small group watched in stunned silence.

As the plasma brightened, Cathy turned to Brett. "It's beautiful isn't it? Reminds me of the northern lights." Brett shook his head in disbelief. "It's unbelievable. But where does the light come from?" Cathy shrugged her shoulders. "No idea. Charlie reckons it's some sort of uncontained plasma. Like the inside of a fluoro tube, but without the tube. It just seems to be everywhere... even inside the space ships." she explained.

After a few minutes the glow reached peak intensity. Tim and Charlie returned to the console with Bob and Adam watching closely. "Now what?" Bob asked. "Now we switch on all the power circuits. The doors in here are electrically or magnetically controlled, so we need to turn the power on before we can open them." Adam turned to look at the generator again.

While he was taking photos, he could not help but marvel at the sight. "Christ it's huge! All that gold is breathtaking. And it's so quiet you wouldn't even know it's operating." he observed. Tim smiled. "I have no idea how it works. All I know is, once it's switched on, it remains silent and the lights stay on."

Tim moved past the others and grabbed Cathy's arm on the way through. "Right! Who wants to see a real live UFO?" he teased.

CHAPTER 50

Bob fell in behind Tim and Cathy, hot on their heels. The others gradually joined them in single file, as they tore themselves away from the mesmerizing golden sphere. Tim strode confidently around the generator and into the hanger area. In the distance they could see the larger spacecraft, shimmering mystically in the all-pervasive neon glow that now filled the base.

Tim ignored the nearest craft and made a beeline for the one they had previously explored. Once there, he waited patiently for the others to catch up and gather around. He then addressed them in a light-hearted fashion, as if he were the captain of the craft welcoming his passengers aboard. "Well here it is. A genuine intergalactic spaceship! Welcome aboard."

Cathy and Tim led the others up the loading ramp and into the cargo bay. They stopped near the top of the ramp to allow Adam time to take a couple of photos, then proceeded directly to the operator's console. "Well this is where it all happened. This is the control centre. Feel free to look around. You'll find accommodation, recreation areas, ablution rooms and Bob... Charlie will show you the engine room. We'll just wait here if it's alright with you. See you when you get back."

Half an hour later, three starry-eyed tourists returned with their guide. Tim carefully slid from the giant seat he was buried in and greeted them as they entered the control room. "Well... what do you think?" Bob was full of praise at the commercial and military possibilities of their find. Particularly the drive unit. Adam was thrilled to be part of the discovery and thankful for his involvement. Brett was awe-struck, finding it difficult to absorb the enormity of the find.

Satisfied they had seen enough for the moment, Tim grabbed Cathy's hand once more and headed for the ramp. "Well let's go look at the smaller ones shall we?" Everyone obediently followed them as they walked down the ramp and headed of in the direction of the smaller craft. Along the way Bob sidled up to Tim. "This is one impressive runway. How long is it?"

Tim shook his head. "I've no idea. We went to the end, but there are some massive doors there. We didn't look for the operating device. We figured the other side would be buried under rocks or something anyway. But I guess your boys could open it and try to clear it and have a look. But may I suggest you be discrete and keep it hidden from prying eyes? You know... spy satellites. The Russians at least know a bit about what's going on." Bob nodded. "Good thinking."

As they reached the first of the smaller craft, everyone stopped to look at it. Tim waited patiently for Adam to take several photos, then pointed to the one with the ramp down. "You can have a look inside that one if you like." They wandered over to the machine and stood at the bottom of the ramp, as if waiting for an invitation to board. Tim nodded at Bob. "Go ahead. I've already seen it. It's like a miniature version of the other one. I'll wait for you here."

Cathy nodded at Charlie to indicate that she too was waiting outside the craft. Charlie started off up the ramp and motioned for the others to join them. Bob and Adam rushed forward to catch up but Brett decided to remain with Tim and Cathy.

Fifteen minutes later Charlie appeared at the top of the ramp and waved at Tim as he descended. The other two men following closely on his heels. "Well, what do you reckon?" Tim asked as they joined him. Bob shook his head. "It's pretty much like the big one, but obviously way lower powered if the generator is anything to go by."

Tim nodded his concurrence then turned to Adam. "Got enough pictures of spaceships for now?" he grinned. Adam nodded. "Sure have. Now I'm keen to look at the rest of the base."

Tim led them back past the generator and into the corridor that led to the great hall. As they passed the entrance tunnel he pointed it out as the way back to the camp, just in case they were disoriented. He continued on until he reached the centre of the great hall.

Here they all gathered in a semi-circle around Tim, like a group of tourists, waiting for their guide to begin the tour. "Well this is the centre of the base." he explained. "We know there are seven levels. This one and three above... and three levels of crypt below." Bob and Adam both looked at Tim with surprise. "A crypt?" they chimed in unison.

"Yes we had a look but didn't get time to take any of the lids off. We did however go to the sarcophagus of the last Lord Guardian and place a lid on it for him." Tim explained. "What did he look like?" Adam asked. "Pretty much mummified, but dressed in full military pomp. There are lots of photos of these chaps all over the place, including one on each sarcophagus. I'll show you the one in the mess hall if you like. It's a doozy. Life-size and definitely my favourite."

Tim led them to the mess hall and pushed open the massive doors. As they entered, he steered them in the direction of the large photo that had caused all their fears to materialise on that first fateful day. How that seemed so far in the distant past. Adam stood back in awe. He looked the photo up and down discerningly before he turned to Tim. "It's awesome. Christ it's three-dimensional. So much so, that it almost looks real. I'm afraid a digital photo isn't going to do it justice." But Adam took several photos anyway. He then looked around for a few minutes then slipped off to inspect the mess hall and kitchen.

Bob meanwhile, was scrutinising the photo. Finally he wandered over to Tim and almost whispered. "Jesus! Look at the size of those bastards. I'd hate to get on the wrong side of them! It's funny though. They look like they've stepped out of some medieval battlefield. Yet they're carrying the most sophisticated weapons I've ever seen. Sort of anachronistic isn't it?" Tim agreed, then invited Bob to check out the rest of the area.

Once everyone else had gone, Tim sat down with Cathy and Charlie and heaved a sigh of relief. Things were going good, so far. They watched as the others meandered around, looking at this, poking at that and picking up all sorts of interesting things. After they had seen enough, Tim offered to show them a typical accommodation unit. They accepted and followed as he led them to the nearest corridor.

When he arrived at the first door inside the long corridor, he stopped and pointed out the hieroglyphs and translated them. "This says... *pa-aa-n-ursh qebu ua ... tcheri-t ua* ...which roughly translates to *Guardian Group 1... Room 1*." He then pushed the pad and stood back. They all watched with transfixed stares, as the door opened silently and effortlessly.

Tim motioned for them to enter and waited outside until all were in the adjoining room. Cathy and Charlie stood back and watched as Tim showed everyone around. Bob was asking questions at an alarming rate, while Adam was ceaselessly taking photos. Tim showed them everything they had found.

Before leaving, he explained to the captive audience the significance of the *hall of fame* adjacent to the entrance. Once satisfied they had seen enough, he led them outside into the corridor. "The accommodation blocks are pretty much all the same. Except for the commanding officer, the Lord Guardian. But it's getting late. Can I suggest we return to the camp and get an early start in the morning?"

CHAPTER 51

Next morning, after a restless night of endless questions and speculation, they sat down to breakfast. Tim looked over at Bob, talking quietly with one of the soldiers in the shadows behind a Humvee. He did not know whether to feel comforted or intimidated by their presence. Eventually, for ease of mind, he settled on comfort. "Well let's go gentlemen... and you too dear. We have a lot to look at today. You got some spare memory cards for that camera Adam? You're going to need them once we get to the museum."

Adam was flabbergasted. "Don't tell me they've got a museum here!" Tim smiled as he recalled the exhibits. He knew they would blow his mind, so he gave him a teaser. "Yes... and a bloody good one at that. Would you like to see what a real T-Rex looked like?" he teased. "You what!" Adam exclaimed, pretty certain that Tim was having a lend of him.

"Well they've been coming here for so long there's actually a photo of a hunting party that shot a T-Rex. The photo is accompanied by a tooth. The original enamel is still in perfect condition. Fascinating stuff. But there's way too much to explain. I'll just wait until we get there."

Adam's mind began to spin. Never in his wildest dreams did he imagine such a journalistic coup. This was award-winning stuff. He could hear the accolades of his peers from here.

By this time Bob had rejoined the group, so Tim decided to ask a favour before he took them any further. "One thing Bob. They have a repository here. A sort of storehouse. It's full of coins and other relics. We want to keep that as our reward for finding the place and..."

Bob interrupted Tim in mid sentence. "I've already told you. Gold, relics, photos, treasure... it doesn't bother me. I'm only interested in technical stuff. Things that can give the US an edge over the rest of the world. Stuff we can put to use for military and civilian applications. You can keep it all... except the generators, spacecraft and the like, of course. We want to reverse engineer them if we can. I don't even want to look in the storeroom. That way I'll never know what you took. Understand?"

Tim was amazed at Bob's response. he had expected the government to be keen on the financial rewards the base offered. "Thanks, Bob. Does that go for the library and museum too?" Bob nodded. "That was the deal!" Tim smiled cheerfully as he grabbed Cathy's hand and squeezed it gently with excitement.

Once he had settled down, he led the party toward the corridor for another foray into the base. He decided that the crypt would be interesting, as would the museum and the library. As an afterthought he decided that he would take them to see the Lord Guardian's abode as a grand finale. Just to show them how a luxury suite could be carved out of solid granite.

The group headed off to the base entrance where they were greeted by the comforting green glow of the pervasive lights. Tim took the tourists directly to the elevator and pressed the button to open the door. Once everyone was inside, he pressed the touchpad to take them to the museum level. The ride ended almost as soon as it had begun.

As the door opened, he casually stepped out and headed for the museum entrance. He stopped as he reached the doors and waited for everyone to catch up. "Look there's a lot of stuff in here, so take your time. We've got all day and there's not much more to look at. The crypt, the library and the Lord Guardian's quarters. But they won't take long."

Tim ushered them into the museum and watched with interest the expressions on their faces as their eyes focussed on the imposing statue of the two ancient warriors locked in mortal combat. He let them absorb it in all its magnificence for a time, then offered his services as an interpreter for anyone who needed to understand a photo or an exhibit.

The lightning tour of the museum still took them several hours to complete. Adam took thousands of photos and seemed to be talking ceaselessly into his small tape recorder. Bob was somewhat nonplussed by it all, as he considered it to have no military or commercial value. He was more interested in the generator and the flying craft. But he was happy to tag along, driven by curiosity and a respect he had gained for Tim's vast knowledge.

Tim eventually decided to ease them towards the elevator. "Well we'd better have a quick look at the crypts, eh?" he suggested. Charlie declined and volunteered to wait for them in the museum. Cathy on the other hand was eager to go, as she had not been before. She had always been volunteered to remain in the museum in case the power went off and the men got stuck in the elevator.

Once everyone was in, Tim leant over and pushed the pad. The elevator seemed to move every so slightly for a few seconds before coming to a sharp but gentle stop. As the door opened, Tim stepped out and beckoned the others to follow. He led them along the small corridor that opened onto the balcony above the hanger area. From here he showed them the incredible site of all the spacecraft and the generator, glowing brightly under the omnipresent base lighting. "I just thought you'd like to have a look at the hanger area from here. It gives it a more realistic perspective. It's one hell of an excavation isn't it?"

After letting them absorb the size of the hanger, Tim ushered them towards the lift. Once they were all inside, he reached over and pressed the bottom button. Again the lift pulled up seemingly as soon as it began moving. He stood back as the immense door silently slid open. "Well this is it. The third floor of the crypt. This is where the latest bodies are interred. It seems they just hollowed out another crypt below the first one once that filled up. They repeated the process once that one filled up. There's not a lot to see but you can imagine how long the men were stationed here, by the number of bodies."

He led them over to the nearest row of sarcophagi and paused while they gathered around. Once he had their attention, he pointed to the inscription on the sarcophagus and the photo of the guardian who lay therein. "I guess this is like Arlington. The place where all warriors aspire to be buried. From the snippets I've read, it seems the Guardians never returned bodies to their home planet unless they were someone extremely important or very heroic.

They also never buried anyone on earth anywhere else but here. Some here died of disease, some of old age. Many were casualties of ancient battles.

Anyway, this photo shows us what the warrior looked like in his prime. And the inscription here tells his age, the date he came to earth, when he died and how he died. Some even have a story written all over the coffins telling of their heroic deeds and exploits."

Everyone looked on as Adam took a few photographs but it was obvious they had seen enough after just a few minutes. Once again Tim herded them towards the lift. "Well let's go look at the library, eh? This has the hall of records attached, so it's where all the controversy began." The elevator pulled up obediently at the museum once more and disgorged its bemused cargo.

Tim winked at Charlie as he passed him, heading in the direction of the library. "Not far to go. Just through here." He waited for them all to gather at the door and then nodded for Cathy to press the pad. The giant door opened on command, leaving the group staring at the bejewelled walls of the Hall of Records.

Tim began to explain the writing as simply as he could, trying to explain why it was so controversial, without boring them to tears. "Well this side is the king list. It details every king of Egypt, Sumer, Atlantis and so on. See these names here? They're the kings of ancient Sumer. Only trouble is, the list is identical to the list of the descendants of Abraham in the Bible ... right back to Adam."

Everyone stared at the list as the ancient Sumerian king's namesake continued his never-ending picture taking crusade. Of course no-one could read the writing, but Tim assured them that any Egyptologist worth his salt could read the list and would come to the same conclusion.

Then, as a finale on the king list he showed them the descendants of Abraham down past Jesus the Christ to the fifth century AD. From the corner of his eye he noticed Bob's face light up into a sarcastic smile. He turned to find out what amused him so. "Nothing really. Just the irony that this proves that three of the world's largest religions are founded on some bull-shit that someone got wrong. Jesus Christ! No wonder the god-damn Catholics and Arabs are after your guts. You're right. The old Jews ain't goin' to like this stuff much either!"

Tim swallowed hard as an uncomfortable lump rose in his throat. Bob's casual remark reminded him of the deadly seriousness of the situation. It was far from over and he suddenly realised that. Regaining his composure, Tim then led the small group back to the beginning of the writing on the opposite wall.

"Well I guess this is the icing on the cake. Here in great detail is the history of the two races that called earth home for a while. The Anunnaki were the Celtic ones. The scientists, statesmen and royal family. The Zamzam'min were the warriors. The Guardians. They were the military might of the Anunnaki.

It goes on to detail exactly where their original home planet was. In the Whirlpool Galaxy M51, or rather in the companion star cluster. But even they don't know where they originally came from. They admit their home planet was a colony, but they don't know who the colonisers were or where they came from."

He stood back for a minute while Adam photographed a panoramic set of pictures, eager to get the overlapping sections included, so he could get the interpretation verified by one of his colleagues. Once finished, he stepped back and apologised, then motioned for Tim to continue.

"Well in a nut-shell, one of their two suns went supernova and melted their planet. They had lots of warning, so they evacuated and colonised several suitable planets within their shuttle range. Three of these were in our solar system. Earth, Mars and Nibiru. But Nibiru got hit by a comet and disintegrated. It's now the asteroid belt between Mars and Jupiter.

And Mars was the victim of a near miss giant asteroid that got knocked out of orbit by a comet. It apparently bounced off the surface at a very low angle. This knocked Mars into a slightly different orbit but more devastatingly, the asteroid sucked off most of the atmosphere and dragged it off into space. The survivors came to earth and settled in South America, around 3113BC. This was the start of the fabled Mayan long count." Tim looked around and noticed some blank expressions among his audience, so he decided to wrap it up before taking them to the library. "Well it seems they've been doing a bit of genetic engineering.

They've been playing with the plants and animals on earth for millions of years. Their technology is so advanced, they can create any living being they choose. They know what every single gene in the entire DNA spectrum is responsible for and they know exactly how to manipulate them. Apparently genes aren't just simply switched on and off like we thought. Each gene has a degree of variability.

Anyway, all they need is a suitably size surrogate mother and they can create anything they can imagine. By simply splicing the required genome string together and tweaking the genes. The scary thing is that they do this by computer. It's a simple matter of accessing the library, cut and paste the required genome sequence and a machine at the other end spits out the required DNA, already encased in an egg.

The records say they played with the genes of some endemic hominids they found here when they first visited. They eventually turned into the Negroid race in Africa. Apparently for all their intellectual and technical superiority, they weren't above slavery. You may have noticed some of the photos of their hominid creations in the museum. Some showing them mining gold, others showing them carrying packs like porters.

Anyway the scientists cloned a few humans from their own DNA. Eventually the Biblical Adam and Eve were cloned from the DNA of the last surviving royal in Ur. He was desperate to have his line continue. Well apparently this was a bit naughty. But the resultant humans flourished and were soon mating with the scientists. This created the Celtic race and its derivatives like the Caucasians.

You can find references to this in the Bible. But unfortunately mankind got a bit aggressive and the Anunnaki left them to it and returned home. But some of the Guardians remained for some time. Apparently because they were fond of the planet and its inhabitants.

But eventually, they too admitted that humanity was out of control, so they left. That was some time around 500AD according to my estimates. And they haven't been back since. That I know of. But I guess with all the UFO sightings, they may have been attracted back here after the nuclear tests of the 20th century. They probably picked up the radiation signatures and came to see if we'd managed to destroy ourselves yet."

Again he looked around at the faces of the group. Although they still mostly feigned interest, he could see that they were in information overload. Tim decided it best to move on. "Well let's look at the library shall we?"

He led them to the end of the corridor and walked into the middle of the room. When everyone had joined him, he invited them to turn around. Their eyes were immediately drawn to the maps and star charts that covered the wall. "Well here is our history folks. That there is the legendary continent of Atlantis. Smack in the middle of the Pacific Ocean.

Or Havi as the Polynesians knew it. See here... *the settlement of Hafi on the continent of Atlantis.*" He then went on to quickly explain the relevance of the other maps, ensuring that Bob was fully informed about the location of all the other settlements, bases and Halls of Records. A large smile indicated that Bob was most impressed. "We should be able to find all this stuff now. But it puts some urgency into freeing Tibet so the god-damn Chinese don't get hold of this technology. That's going to an interesting job."

Before leaving the library, Tim briefly expounded the depth of knowledge contained in both the written books lining the shelves of the great library and of the computer system. Charlie quickly gave a demonstration of the depth of information available on the computer cards. He proudly showed them his dexterity with the alien technology, as he flitted through one of the discs on sea monsters.

Adam was by now in information overload and for once did not even raise his camera. Charlie explained to him that they had hundreds of hours of video burnt onto DVD's that showed but an infinitesimally small amount of the computer data.

They milled around for a while as Tim explained some of the more salient tomes, but it soon became apparent that they were becoming bored. Tim thanked them for their patience and suggested they quickly look at the Lord Guardians abode on the way back to the camp. The reassurance that cold beer awaited them was enough to spur them on.

Tim quickly led them to the Lord Guardian's accommodation and stood excitedly as Charlie pressed the keypad that opened the door. Soon he was being the tour guide once more. First he showed them the spacious lounge, with its massive tables and comfortable chairs. He pointed out the entertainment screen and the Hall of Fame. The pictorial history of the thirty one Lord Guardians who had served on earth.

As he pointed to the last Lord Guardian, a lump formed in his throat. He swallowed hard to fight back the emotion. "This is the bloke who wandered down to the crypt at the end of his time. He turned out the lights and waited to die. In his message, that I showed you in the library, he asked that his sarcophagus lid be sealed. Charlie and I did this for him before we left the base last time."

Still choking back the emotion, he ushered the group towards the Lord Guardian's private museum. "You're going to love this Bob. This is the Holy Grail. He's got a collection of weapons that surpasses anything I've ever seen. You're probably not going to be interested in the ancient stuff. I'll keep that for the museum, if you don't mind. But there's a collection of their sophisticated weaponry there too. Like the stuff the Guardians in the mess hall were carrying."

"Jesus, you didn't tell me there were weapons here." Bob moaned. Tim smiled. "Again you didn't ask." he teased. "Besides, I had to determine whether we could trust you or not first. Oh, by the way, I purposely took you past it without commenting when you were looking at the spacecraft. But there's a whole arsenal down there ready to go. Charlie and I found the key to it and had a look one day.

We know a bit about weapons, but this shit is real high-tech. There's PPE type stuff that the everyday warrior would use. But there's also some interesting heavy weapons. Some of them look like Star Wars howitzers. You know, the kind of thing that could shoot a spaceship down at two parsecs.

We were too scared to try any of it out, even though we found some manuals. They had warnings in them, indicating you could do some real damage to yourself and those within a light year or two if you didn't know what you were doing. There's even a collection of things in there that look like nukes. You know... like the stuff they dropped on Sodom and Gomorrah."

Bob pushed past Tim in his keen desire to look at the weapons. The others stood back respectfully as he wandered around the hewn shelving crammed with memorabilia. This was, after all, what they figured he was really here for. Anything with a military application. He tossed a cursory glance at the stone-age weapons, then moved past the Greco-Roman collection. "You're right. This old stuff doesn't interest me. Although if you have any stuff you'd like to donate to the Smithsonian, I'm sure they'd be very grateful."

Suddenly he turned a corner and was confronted by an entire wall draped with high-tech weaponry. He could not help himself as he grabbed what was obviously some form of Guardian's PPE weapon. Similar in function perhaps to the ubiquitous sub-machine gun. "Jesus H Christ! Would you look at this!

I'm taking this little puppy with me to show the goons outside. That'll spur them on to guard this place properly." Tim nodded his approval, not that his opinion would count in Bob's decision to take a weapon. But he concluded that the more weapons Bob took, the less interest he would have in the other artefacts. They all stood back and watched as Bob went from weapon to weapon. Carefully removing it from its niche, inspecting it and almost reverently replacing it. In the end he chose another, obviously more powerful, weapon to lug back to the camp.

Tim concluded the tour by showing them the secretarial area, the Lord Guardian's bedroom and finally his private office. But as he walked into the Lord Guardian's private office he noticed that the computer screen was glowing with an unusual creamy hue. There in the centre of the large computer screen was an ominously pulsating ruby red circle.

He grabbed Charlie's arm and spun him around to look at it. As they neared the computer, Charlie looked at the red circle in the centre of the screen. He squinted in puzzlement at a tangle of black hieroglyphs flashing on and off like some ethereal heartbeat.

As he approached the screen, he instinctively reached out and touched the central circle. He was taken aback as it immediately stopped pulsing. He looked over at Tim and shrugged his shoulders in an admission of defeat. "What's it say, Tim?"

Tim leant over and began to read the text, glyph by glyph. The others watched on in silence, as he mumbled the words in their original tongue. As he neared the end of the text he stopped. Then he pierced the pregnant silence with a loud exclamation that made all but Bob jump back as one. "Oh shit!" Cathy looked at Tim's now ashen face. It had broken out in a cold sweat. The finger he was running across the computer screen suddenly started twitching involuntarily.

For the first time since their return to the base, she sensed something was wrong. Something was terribly wrong. She froze with fear, staring at the beads of sweat running down Tim's temples. She watched helplessly as the small rivulets cascaded down his neck to be soaked up by his ever-darkening collar. Finally she walked up behind him and wrapped her arms around his waist. Her first attempt to speak was stifled by emotion. She regathered her wits quickly and summoned up a confident and comforting voice. "What's wrong dear?"

Tim turned slowly and looked into Cathy's eyes. His gaze then flicked around to the others, stopping momentarily to stare into each person's eyes as he passed them. He turned back to Cathy and replied in a soft, almost inaudible whisper.

"It's them. They're coming back!"

Other Book Available from Magpie Publishing

(www.booksbymagpie.com & elsewhere)

The Queen's Prize
The Copeville Incident
Mysteries of the Bible
The Art of Reading People
Dictionary of the Gods

The 5th Witch of Zandor Series

BOOK 1 – The Staff of Destiny (Released 2010)

BOOK 2 – The Warrior Witch (Released 2010)

BOOK 3 – The Dosinian Curse (Released 2010)

BOOK 4 – The Cannibal King (Released 2011)

BOOK 5 – The Taphian Conquest (Released 2011)

BOOK 6 – The Troll Uprising (Released 2011)

CPSIA information can be obtained
at www.ICGtesting.com
Printed in the USA
BVHW041720230320
575742BV00008B/356

9 781456 566609